'AMPSHIRE BOY

'AMPSHIRE BOY

Alfred Leonard

Book Guild Publishing
Sussex, England

First published in Great Britain in 2007 by
The Book Guild Ltd
Pavilion View
19 New Road
Brighton, BN1 1UF

Typesetting in Baskerville by
SetSystems Ltd, Saffron Walden, Essex

Printed in Great Britain by
CPI Antony Rowe

A catalogue record for this book is
available from the British Library

ISBN 978 1 84624 136 9

Contents

Introduction

This is not a story of the rich and famous, or of the derring-do of high ranking military officers; neither is it a story of the basest of human actions: neither murder, excess violence nor criminal activities will be found on the following pages.

Rather it is a tale of a young farm-boy, growing up surrounded by the incredible beauty of the Hampshire countryside: his early years, teens and his move to break free of his father's wanderlust.

It is neither totally fiction nor completely true, but the basic timeline is deviated from on only a few occasions.

Characters are mostly amalgams of various friends and acquaintances, with whom the writer came into contact at some time during his life, but not necessarily within the chosen period of this tale.

Names, for the most part, are fictional, except for those in the public domain; the naval jargon, methods and procedures are mostly authentic.

BOOK 1
COUNTRY

1

Pre-estate

The small boy stood by the side of the huge pile of logs, piled up by the estate workers during the previous winter. He was clothed in somewhat ragged play clothes, hand-me-downs from his brothers before him and, no doubt worn by several other young boys before them, before his mother obtained them from various second-hand sources. His feet were shod in heavy, studded ankle boots. In his hands he carried a huge stick, cut from a hazel-nut tree. The stick was about two feet taller than Robert and looked huge in his small hands. His knuckles were white because of the strength of his grip, and his whole body shook in a combination of fear and expectation. He was six years old and this was the first time that he had been allowed on such an adventure with his two brothers: Ronald, who was eleven; and Albert, nine. In comparison, his elder brother was huge, already filling out and growing rapidly, while his younger brother, although certainly much bigger, was not that startling a comparison.

All three boys were dressed similarly and all felt the chill on this December morning, without heavy coat, scarf or glove protection against the sharp frost. All three boys wore short knee-length trousers, army-style jerkins and long socks pulled up to their knees. Ronald wore a pair of old wellington boots that had been discarded by their father, but Albert, like Robert, wore ankle-length studded boots.

They each carried a stick, cut from the nearby hazel-nut trees. Ronald's and Albert's were elaborately decorated with carvings cut into the soft bark with a penknife. Robert's decorations were much plainer than those of his two brothers, but nonetheless one could see that some effort had been made to identify the stick as his own. All three sticks tapered to a thin end of about an inch in diameter, giving an enormous flexibility. When swung with some strength, they would contact their target with amazing force.

The three boys were the sons of Alfred and Caroline Leonard. Alfred Leonard was a worker on the estate on which they lived. Their house, one of a terraced block of six, belonged to the estate. The estate was owned by the Sandsfoot family, Mr Jack and Mrs Kate, and they had two sons, Master John and Master Martin. Robert, like his two brothers, had had many a reminder of the correct titles when addressing a member of the estate owners' family.

The estate consisted of some 2,000 acres of Hampshire countryside, just outside the village of Church Wallop, a few miles west of Andover. It was a few years after the Second World War, 1945, and Alfred and Caroline found it difficult to care for their three sons on the wages paid by the estate.

The boys knew the estate well. Set in a huge valley surrounded by low hills, there was only one access road from the main road into the village of Church Wallop. This access road was very narrow and rutted from continuous use by heavy vehicles and animals. It followed the route of a small stream as it flowed through the gap in the hills. As this rutted track emerged into the huge valley, which contained the estate, a small track led off to the six cottages.

Robert lived with his family in number 3, Farm Cottages,

4

the Sandsfoots Estate. Further along the rutted track, past the turning to the cottages, was another access track to the farm buildings and the huge farmhouse. The stream continued right through the estate, disappearing through the hills at the other end of the valley, filling two large lakes in the process.

All three boys loved the estate and they regarded the whole valley as their personal play and hunting ground. They were free to roam from dawn to dusk. Playgrounds consisted of the two lakes, huge wooded areas, which the boys called copses, the farm buildings, and the surrounding hills.

Their hunting grounds were anywhere that they could find rabbits, hares, pheasant, partridge, wild ducks, geese, pigeons, etc. They brought home the flesh or the eggs from all these sources, which their mother used to supplement their food supplies.

The adventure for today, masterminded by Ronald, was designed to generate some income and, at the same time, to provide mother with some additional food. The target was rabbits, and the boys knew that rabbits used the piled-up logs as shelter when away from their burrows.

The technique was pretty simple: the boys were stationed, by Ronald, around the pile of logs; Ronald, and only Ronald, would, when ready, kick the pile of logs and rap them with his stick, making as much noise as possible, with the intention of scaring out whatever might be sheltering inside. Ronald's strict instructions were to whack anything that came out, whether it be rabbit or whatever, and it was for this purpose that the sticks had been cut.

Robert was dreading this moment. He had heard his brothers telling stories of the fierce creatures that could come out of the logs, some invented and some true, and his biggest fear was rats. These creatures could grow to quite a considerable size and, according to Ronald, would not hesitate to sink their teeth into a careless young boy, striking always for the throat.

Robert was shaking quite badly now; his soft blue-grey eyes were huge as he tried desperately not to blink. The thoughts raced around his mind; he had an extremely vivid imagination and a quick and agile brain, which never failed to assess any situation with a speed that never ceased to amaze him.

Almost instantly, he visualised huge rats leaping out of the pile of logs, not nipping gently at his heels with small teeth, but gigantic, fat creatures with enormous fangs snapping at his throat. His eyes were now glazed as his mind raced . . . *off with bum on broomstick*, his mother's version of *away with the fairies!*

The frightened young boy saw himself being carried from the copse back home, his mother bathing his wounds whilst his father dashed off on his bike to find the doctor; the terrible imagined bites from the rats were bleeding profusely and there was blood all over the floor.

A fevered imagination forced a soft groan from his throat; in fact, Robert was so distracted by his thoughts that he almost missed the thud of Ronald's boot as he kicked the pile of logs. Robert was shocked by what followed and stood, rooted to the spot, as what seemed like dozens of rabbits and hares exited the logs, dashing off in all directions.

The whooping and swish of his brothers' sticks could be heard clearly by Robert as they swung at their quarry, but he could not move. Both his brothers had taken a wild swing at a furry creature – they didn't know what it was at that stage of the hunt – and instantly raced after the other creatures as they made their escape.

They returned to the pile of logs, both carrying a dead rabbit, to find Robert still rooted to the spot and staring with his huge eyes at the pile of logs. Ronald gave Robert a shove, pushing him to the ground and shouting at him for failing to help in the hunt. Very close to tears, Robert was shaken by the violence of his brother's punishment, but at least the push had brought him back from his frozen state and he could move again.

To hide his tears he picked up his stick, turned and raced off to find his mother. All of the boys could run extremely quickly but none more quickly than Robert, especially when he adopted his unique style designed for maximum speed.

The style had been developed the previous summer when Robert had noticed that when he came to a hill it was much easier to run if his torso was bent forward at the waist, and over a period of time he had developed this method so that his hands in fact touched the ground and became part of his running stride, much like that of a monkey. He had further developed this stance by using it at all times, not just going up hills, but on the flat as well.

In later years, when he was too tall and too heavy to use this method of locomotion, he reflected that he must have been light enough and supple enough at exactly the right moment in his life to discover this technique. Using his own special method, Robert could run for as long as he wanted; he neither tired nor became breathless and, more importantly to Robert, his brothers could not catch him.

He would face weeks of teasing and a flat refusal when he asked to be taken on further hunts. Even worse, the teasing was not just from his brothers but from his father as well, who delivered his derisive comments in his characteristic pose, right hand scratching at a touch of eczema on his left elbow. The only person who understood was Robert's mother. To Robert, she was beautiful, quite short and slim, with dark hair, a kindly face, and soft voice.

The best part of each day, for the youngest in the

Leonard family, was the hour or so after tea, curling up in the armchair behind his mother, who would slide to the edge of the seat to allow him room. There he would stay, quietly listening to his parents chatting or listening to the radio; *Journey into Space* and *The Archers* were his favourites. His mind was most active whilst listening to these programmes; he would project himself into every plot and story, devising endless alternative endings to each from his own fertile imagination.

The two big armchairs that his parents used were close to the fire. They, and the huge sofa, looked the worse for wear and had certainly seen better days. One of the armchairs was reserved solely for his father's use. When their father was out of the house anyone could sit in his chair, but when he came back whomsoever was in the chair would be well advised to move, and quickly. Any delay in vacating the chair would be rewarded with a slap on the rump or the back of the legs when their father heaved the offending child from his own personal resting place. The only other furniture in the room was a wooden table and four dining chairs.

Apart from the sitting-room there were just four other rooms in the house: a small stone-floored kitchen with small windows set high in the walls; and three bedrooms, the largest of which, at the front of the house, was occupied by Robert's parents. Ronald was on his own in the largest of the two smaller rooms, with Robert and Albert sharing the smallest.

The whole house was very draughty because of the badly fitting doors and windows. There was, of course, no form of central heating or electricity, nor indoor plumbing or toilet. Water was hauled up from the well in the garden, by means of a bucket attached to a long rope, which was lowered down to the water level via a revolving spindle of wood with a handle attached to it. There was a wooden cover over the opening to the well, which everyone was always very careful to replace whenever they had finished raising water. Failure to replace this cover, by Robert or his brothers, would certainly earn the miscreant a taste of father's belt!

Warmth was provided by a fireplace in every room, however Robert's parents did not allow open fires in the bedrooms for fear of sparks igniting the carpets or bedding. Usually, fires would only be lit in the kitchen, in mother's black metal cooking range, and in the sitting room in the huge open fireplace.

Lighting was provided by candles, which were allowed to be used when, and only when, going to bed or when traipsing up the garden path to the lav; or by mother's huge oil lamp. This lamp had a bulbous brass container for the paraffin oil and a long glass tube, which magnified the light. A long, thick wick dangled down into the brass paraffin container, the other end of which, when lit, burned inside the glass tube. The heat from the top of this glass tube was surprising, considering the size of the wick producing it, and Robert had seen his father, on many an occasion, lighting his cigarette from the top of the lamp. Immediately above the lamp there was a large dark stain on the ceiling, further testament to the heat from the lamp.

The family thought nothing of the lack of inside amenities and most of the family gave little thought to using the outside toilet, but for Robert, this tiny personal space was the subject of his first nightmare.

A wooden shed with a big bucket under a wooden bench was at the very end of the long garden. If you were lucky there might be some torn up newspaper or, if not, then best to take a handful of grass or a dock leaf to clean up after a big job! It also smelled absolutely awful, but it was not the smell that bothered Robert. What did bother him was the long walk, in the dark, to the end of the garden, and sitting in that very small, dark, cold, and very frightening shed.

The noises from the surrounding wildlife and the wind sighing through the branches of the trees filled Robert with total terror. For several years he would have a recurring nightmare: he would see himself sitting in the lav, as his family referred to their lavatory, listening to the usual night noises. Suddenly he would hear scratching at the door accompanied by heavy breathing and fiendish moans. He could never predict at which moment in his nightmare these sounds would commence; they always took him by complete surprise despite knowing that they would occur; it was this waiting for the noises that was one of the worst facets of his nightmare. The scratching outside in the pitch dark would become louder and more insistent and Robert would see the soulless glint from the yellow eyes of a huge cat or mythical beast through the gaps in the flimsy wooden slats from which the door was made. Suddenly a huge clawed foot, covered in very long, shockingly white hair, would squirm under the bottom of the door; it never failed to grab Robert by the foot, even though he instinctively lifted his knees up to his chin. And then it started to drag him from the lav . . . at which point Robert would wake up screaming his head off, soaked with sweat. Following these nightmares he usually spent the remainder of that night and a couple of subsequent nights in his parents' bed.

Some years later, Robert read an article stating that an alligator could outrun a man over a distance of one hundred yards; Robert burst into laughter when he thought, *Yes, but he wouldn't catch me on the way back from the lav, because not only would I be going too fast but I would be three feet off the ground as well!* On several occasions he had asked both his father and his brothers to escort him up the garden, but was told not to be a wuss and get on with it.

Wuss, wazzock or pillock were their father's favourite terms for describing someone who was doing, had done, or might do, something a bit silly or childish. The boys had picked the expressions up very early in life, much to the disgust of the school mistress at Church Wallop, where the expressions were now in common use; Robert thought they would soon make it to the new editions of the Oxford English Dictionary.

The exterior of each of the houses in the terraced block of six was identical. The same number of windows and doors, all the same colour; the same thatched roof extending over the complete length of the block and with the same number of chimneys. The thatched roof was not much to Robert's liking either; it was infested with rats and mice; and the night noises, as these rodents burrowed their way through the thatch, could be quite frightening, especially when awoken in the dead of night.

Although the inside of each house was quite small, each had a long garden containing various fruit trees, vegetable plots, and the odd home-made greenhouse. Robert's mother had always grown a few flowers in other houses that the family had occupied before the war started, but now father had taken over the whole garden to grow vegetables.

Everything was rationed, except for whatever the family could provide for themselves, either from foraging, hunting, or from growing in the garden. Robert's father grew a variety of vegetables: new potatoes, main crop potatoes, carrots, cabbages, brussels sprouts, peas, broad beans, runner beans, swede, beetroot, parsnips, lettuce, onions, leeks, etc.

Even as young as he was, Robert was still expected to help his father in the garden. The gardening year commenced in March of each year, when his father would begin the laborious task of digging, and although all of the boys helped in this task, his father always said he liked

11

digging with Robert most of all. This was because, unlike most right-handed people (and all of the family were right-handed), Robert held the digging fork as if he were left-handed. When he and his father started digging, each from a different side of the plot, they did not get in each other's way when they met in the middle.

Obviously Robert could not keep up the heavy work of digging for very long; he tired quite quickly and would then hand the fork over to one of his brothers and would fill the empty trenches with well-rotted farmyard manure; or sometimes with not so well-rotted manure.

Through the winter his father usually brought a huge trailer load of manure from the farm and tipped it up in a huge pile in the field at the end of the garden. The boys would then wheel it into the garden, using father's old wheelbarrow, as and when it was required.

The large, metal-wheeled wheelbarrow was much too heavy for Robert, so his father, or one of his brothers, would wheel a load up to the digging area and Robert would then spread it along the dug trenches.

This communal gardening activity was something that the boys were quite used to; their father had insisted on their helping out from an early age. None of the boys would make any attempt to avoid this work and Robert actually loved it because it was one of the few things that the whole family could do together. Their mother would help out with fetching and spreading the manure, seeding, hoeing, and watering.

In April most of the seeds would be sown and from then on, until each crop was harvested, it was just a matter of keeping the weeds under control and some watering during the really dry periods. Wishing to keep the work in the garden to a bare minimum, their father did not make too much of an effort weeding, unlike most of the neighbours, who seemed to spend endless hours in the evenings and at weekends hoeing in the garden.

His gardening philosophy was much more simple: *shove the seeds into the ground and let them get on with it.* Just the occasional walk around the plots, pulling out the larger weeds. His method certainly produced results, because every year there would be enormous crops of every vegetable, sufficient to see the family through the winter until the next season.

Main crop potatoes were dug and left to dry in the sun, then bagged up for storage in the garden shed. Carrots were pulled and stored in large boxes of sand. Beetroot and onions were pickled in vinegar. Cabbage, brussels sprouts, leeks, parsnips, and swede remained in the ground and survived most of the winter, to be harvested for the table as and when required.

Despite food rationing, the family certainly did not go hungry. The garden and the estate provided most of their needs. The many woods and copses provided an endless source of timber for fuel, which the estate workers cut into manageable logs during the days when the weather was too bad to get outside.

Some of these logs would be up to 3 feet long but they would easily fit into the huge living-room fireplace. Other logs would be cut into smaller logs for the cooking ranges, and yet others would be split into kindling for fire lighting, another job for the boys.

When the supply of pre-cut logs was used up, as happened most winters about the middle of January, it was up to each family to supply their own. Neighbours would band together, take one of the carts with a couple of the huge cart-horses into the woods, and return with a huge load of branches, which had fallen from the trees or had been previously felled and stacked during planned forestry work.

Cutting these large branches into manageable lengths and then into fire-sized lengths was a task in which Robert was able to help his father or his brothers. Sawing cradles, created from pieces of rough timber from the estate, were made by their father; they were somewhat shoddily built and did not last long, but served the purpose.

The log to be cut sat on this cradle and, with a boy on each end of their father's handsaw, they would pull and push until sufficient logs were cut to last for a few days. Later, using his father's small axe, Robert or one of his brothers would chop some of the smaller logs into kindling using an enormous log as a chopping block.

Although their mother did not deliberately let the range fire go out, it sometimes did during the night or whilst she was out shopping, so a ready supply of kindling was essential. Chopping kindling was a job that required great care and concentration, since the axe was extremely sharp and would easily slice through fingers or hands, or, if the axe did not actually hit the log, it would continue downwards and might sink deeply into a leg or thigh. Most of the estate workers and their families carried some evidence of injury caused by cutting fuel for fires, although Robert did not know of anyone who had actually lost a finger or suffered any major injury.

Already Robert carried several scars on various parts of his small body and was rarely seen without a selection of cuts and bruises, inflicted whilst involved in the games in the trees and generally playing around the estate. His left arm had been badly burned when he was a baby; crawling around in the kitchen he had stumbled into his father's shaving water which had, for some reason, been placed temporarily on the floor. The whole underside of his left arm was deeply scarred, but not the hand. Fortunately Robert had no memory of this incident. In fact he had very few memories from his early years.

One of his earliest memories was when a younger sibling was born, his brother Michael, who lived for just a few short weeks. The cause of the new baby's death was to remain a mystery to Robert; he was not told why his tiny brother had died. His mother would not speak of the lost baby, but Robert never forgot the joy of holding him in his arms. He was always to wish in later years that Michael had lived because he would not then be the youngest in the family. Some years later his mother took him to see Michael's grave, in a small churchyard in the village of Old Alresford. His parents had been living on a nearby farm when Michael was born and thus most of Robert's early memories were from this period.

A more recent and much more painful incident had left a large scar on his right hand. This injury, still slightly red and in the healing stages, would, eventually, leave a large half-moon shaped scar. Experimenting with the small axe, Robert had been sent by his mother to chop kindling for the fires. Having noticed that he did everything with his right hand, Robert had wondered if he could use his left hand as efficiently as he could his right.

Luckily, Robert was very biased towards his right side and the feeble chopping movement with his left hand had merely dropped the axe onto his right. Years later, following a routine medical examination, Robert was to discover that the whole of his right side was much more developed than his left. His right eye was keener than the left; hearing on his right side was clearer than that on his left; and his right arm and leg were much stronger than their opposite numbers.

Even so, the experiment had caused quite a deep injury. A very practical woman, his mother had not fussed around very much; she simply bandaged up the injury after wiping some iodine on it. That had hurt, but at least he knew what to expect!

The first time he had experienced the initial effects of this remarkable medicine was about a year or so ago when, at about four years of age, he had grazed his shin sliding down a tree. Every inch the fallen hero, Robert had sat wide-eyed, his leg trembling in anticipation, as his mother reached for the bottle of dark brown liquid. Prone to exaggeration, his brothers had told him, in graphic detail, about how much the application of iodine hurt and he had watched his mother shake the bottle, smear a little over the bandage, and wipe it across the graze. Nothing happened for a few seconds, and Robert thought that his brothers had once again exaggerated their story. Then it hit! His mother had sat him on the edge of the table to administer the iodine, and his leg shot out in front of him, hitting his mother in the stomach. She cried out in shock and pain but made no other complaint, just gave him a hug and called him a wuss. In many ways the experience had been an unfortunate one, because it proved the veracity of some of his brothers' stories; Robert would find it much more difficult in the years to come to decide which of their tales were fact or fiction.

Young children are enormously susceptible to tales of the supernatural and Robert had a very clear recollection of his brother Albert's experience with a ghost. At the time he had been badly frightened, as had Albert, by the whole experience. The house they lived in, at that time, was at the end of a very long grassed track, well off the beaten track and completely surrounded by woods. The overhanging thatched roof dominated the house, extending far out over the windows, leaving the rooms dark and forbidding.

The interior always seemed dingy; the air felt somehow heavy and seemed to cling to Robert's body, and the whole atmosphere had an *unfriendly* feel to it. Also, unusually, the house had two staircases leading up to the first floor landing, and there was a connecting door between the two bedrooms that the boys shared.

Their father told them that the old house had at some time been two separate dwellings, hence the two staircases. At about three years of age, Robert had heard countless stories of ghosts, ghouls, and other supernatural phenomena from his brothers, but his greatest fear at that time was the two staircases. His fear was very real to him; he did not know why and could never, in the future, explain this fear; it was just there.

It had been a particularly hot day, in the middle of the summer months, and Albert had been sent to bed early for some minor misdeed. Against his father's instructions, Robert had sneaked up to the bedroom to play with his brother.

The two small boys had played with their few toys, and after a short while, heard thuds and scraping noises on one of the staircases. It was dusk and the already dark and dismal room had got noticeably darker; neither had brought a candle to the bedroom. The two boys looked at each other, instinctively knowing the source of the strange noises. Albert screamed one word at the top of his voice – *ghosts!*

Whether it had been Albert's intention to frighten Robert, he would later not admit, but the word had an electrifying effect on the smaller boy, who shot through the connecting door and down the other set of stairs to his refuge behind his mother's back. Almost immediately the family heard the sounds of Albert screaming, but not from upstairs, from out in the garden.

Later, Robert overheard his brother explaining to his father that, after they had heard the noises on the stairs, he had noticed the door to his bedroom start to open and he had seen a ghostly figure start to come through the door.

17

Not wishing to be confronted by what was making an entrance, Albert hadn't waited to find out more; he had opened the window and jumped – straight down into a bed of tall stinging-nettles. He was not injured in any way, except for the stings all over his arms, legs and face. If you have ever been stung by nettles you can imagine how much pain he must have been in. Whether the incident had been somehow staged by his two brothers, Robert could not be sure, but the small boy watched with a certain amount of perverse pleasure as his mother applied the iodine to Albert's stings!

One thing Robert did know for certain: it was not his father playing a joke on his sons, because he was downstairs with mother when he had leapt into his refuge at the back of her chair. It could have been Ronald playing the ghostly role – he was forever making up gruesome stories of the supernatural – but whenever he was asked he always denied any part in the proceedings. As far as Albert was concerned, he was adamant and always insisted that what he saw was real; the figure had not been a figment of his imagination, and it could not have been one of the family. Although Robert had heard the strange sounds on the stairs, he had not seen the figure forcing its way into the bedroom, but his own fertile imagination, together with the memories of that evening, plagued him for many years to come.

A short time after the ghostly incident, towards the end of 1943, when Robert was just over four years old, he had watched his father take a pot-shot at a German aircraft flying over their house. In common with all other agricultural workers, Robert's father was exempt from military service during the war. However, he had joined up with the local Home Guard and would, on a couple of evenings each week, put on his khaki uniform, take his .303 rifle from the padlocked cupboard and set off on his bike for training.

On this particular evening the family had been out in the garden when an aircraft was heard flying overhead. The whole family searched the cloudy skies, hoping for a sight of the aircraft. Robert's father spotted it first and identified it as a German bomber. Quite how he managed to identify its country of origin, Robert could not understand; it was flying so high it was almost out of sight.

Determined to do his bit for King and Country, his father raced off indoors to get his rifle, and, fingers fumbling with bolt and bullet, managed, eventually, to blast off a round at the fast departing aircraft. It was doubtful that the bullet went within a few miles of the aircraft at such an extreme range! A notoriously bad shot, his father was never allowed a gun on the estate shoots. It was said of him, by the other estate workers, that he couldn't even shoot himself in the foot! The incident provided Robert with an endearing memory of his father: having deterred the German pilot from his bombing mission, Robert's father swaggered back towards the house, rifle over his shoulder and with a huge grin on his face.

The last of Robert's early memories was his first day at school. Approaching the end of 1944, the family was living in a house right opposite the school house in the middle of the village of Old Alresford. It was strange, and was not very much liked as a place to live for a farm-working family, because it meant that their father had to cycle several miles to and from work each day, and he could not get home for dinner (as the family called the midday meal).

A few days after his fifth birthday, Robert was taken across the road by his mother to the school. Robert had no memory of this initial journey across the road; what he did remember was the first playtime at about 10.15 in the morning. Every child was given a small bottle of milk to drink and then let out into the playground. Having drunk the small bottle of icy milk, Robert thought that was it, school finished for the day, not too bad really, just an hour or so sitting still and listening to the teacher. He left the playground – there was no such thing as school security – opened the small latched iron gate, looked both ways as his mother had taught him, and went home.

Even at that early age it always puzzled Robert why his mother should continually drum into him the rules for crossing the roads, since there was so little traffic. A few bicycles, horses, and carts, and very occasionally, a bus, car, or delivery vehicle. Sitting in her comfortable old armchair, his mother was a little surprised to see him; she made no fuss, just gave him an apple and carried him back across to the school, much to Robert's chagrin.

As with all such childhood events, the incident becomes funnier with each telling, and his parents and brothers didn't overlook a single opportunity to recount Robert's mistake to everyone they met; Robert was the butt of the joke for some time to come. His teacher, whom Robert remembered as a wizened old lady of about 35, sporting tiny metal-rimmed pince-nez perched on the end of her nose, would also remind Robert, for many weeks to come, that it was *playtime* and not *going home* time.

Unlike his two siblings, Robert actually came to like school. With a fairly long attention span, he usually found something of interest in the lessons and was generally regarded as a bright and attentive student. At times his mind seemed to leap ahead and form its own conclusions, as if driven by some form of *déjà vu*, and he could almost anticipate what the teacher was about to write on the blackboard.

Maths, reading, English language, physical education (PE), and games were his personal favourites. He had little interest or time for geography or history. His reaction to religious studies was mixed, he did not really know whether to believe or not. He would certainly say his prayers, silently

20

to himself, when he went to bed each night, but only because his mother asked him to. Even at such a young age he found it difficult to understand why such an all-powerful being would allow the world to be at war, but he was careful not to voice this opinion. Deep in his mind was the nagging doubt that such thoughts might be considered to be treason, and he had heard many a story, from his father, about the punishments meted out to traitors.

During his first year of infant school, he attended three different schools. Agricultural jobs were easy to come by: the war had created a shortage of manpower and skilled workers were few and far between. For reasons unknown to Robert, his father quickly became dissatisfied with his employers and wasted no time in moving on when this happened. In the weeks leading up to each move, Robert would have no indication that his father was losing interest in his current job; his parents must have discussed it after the boys had gone to bed.

The first indication of a move would be on a Saturday morning, when some form of transport, a horse and cart, an open flat-bed lorry, or a cattle truck would arrive and the whole contents of the house would be thrown into it. This did not take very long, the family had little furniture, and Robert suspected that the continual moving was one of the reasons for keeping so few items. The bedding was rolled up inside the mattresses, tied with lengths of baling wire or string and thrown straight onto the cart. The iron bedsteads were bolted together; father always kept the special spanner for these bolts hanging from a piece of string beneath his own big double bed. The remainder of the smaller items were tossed into large tea chests, which when turned upside down with a cloth thrown over the top, doubled as bedside tables or chairs. Well worn from constant use, these tea chests were never discarded and were therefore always ready for the next move. Curiosity eventually got the better of him, but when Robert asked his mother why the family kept moving from place to place, he was told that his father had *itchy feet* and could not stay in any one place for too long. 'One day,' she would often tell him, her soft blue eyes dreamily gazing off into the distance, 'father will find somewhere that he likes, and we will stay there forever.'

The arrival at a new house was always an exciting time, especially for the youngest in the family, except, of course, for the traumatic processes of joining a new school. Dashing around the house from room to room arguing with his brothers about which room they might have as their bedroom, their father yelling after them to 'give us a hand to unload the lorry'. No matter how many times the family moved, Robert always checked first where the toilet was. He was usually disappointed since it was invariably at the end of the garden. It was to be many years before they experienced the luxury of indoor plumbing.

Sometimes the cottage would be so remote that the lorry was unable to get up to the house. Their possessions were then unloaded at the side of the road, their father would trudge off to the farm, returning with a horse and cart, or a tractor and trailer, and the whole lot had then to be reloaded and taken to the family's new house.

The continual moving did not bother Robert too much. He did find it difficult during the first few weeks at each new school; but he made new friends quickly and easily so he soon settled in. One of the most enjoyable events of a school day, for Robert, was the first playtime. Each child was given a small bottle of milk issued by a 'milk monitor', one of the class nominated each week for this task. As for most young children, Robert hated being last in the queue for anything and he therefore disliked carrying out the duties of milk monitor, simply because he had to wait until everyone else had received their bottle before starting on his own. However, he was always careful to put a bottle aside, in the corner of the crate, to ensure that he got one!

On most farms there was no shortage of milk, and Robert had consumed gallons of it from a very early age, sometimes straight from the udder. School milk was different, and the reason Robert liked it so much was not just because it was milk – he could have any amount of that at home and it was probably much fresher than the school version. What Robert liked about the school milk was the novelty of it being served in a sealed bottle, with a shiny top, and that the milk, particularly in winter, was usually very cold, sometimes with a thick layer of frozen milk at the top. At home, father brought the milk from the farm, in a large half-gallon container that was used for no other purpose.

During the hottest part of the summer, this container spent its days in a deep hole outside the back door. Digging this early refrigerator was one of the first things Robert's father did when arriving at a new house. To Robert, drinking directly from the small milk bottle was a novelty; at home the boys used whatever came to hand as a drinking vessel: cups, mugs, jugs, jam-jars, or empty tin cans; but there was no such thing as a milk bottle in their house. The only time that the family used matching drinking vessels was when mother made the tea, and on these occasions the strong, almost black liquid was poured from the big brown earthenware teapot into large, unbreakable, yet mostly chipped, enamel mugs.

School dinners, another novelty to Robert, cooked in the school's own kitchens, were also enjoyed by all three boys. Mostly the schools that the boys attended were too far from the farm cottages to allow them to return home for a midday meal, and Robert took his shilling to the teacher each Monday morning and at midday each day he would queue with the other children for his hot dinner.

On the whole, the dinners were, to Robert, freshly

cooked, very tasty and he rarely found much to complain about. As a country boy, he was used to a varied diet, full of vegetables of all shapes, sizes, and colours, and, unlike most of the other young children, he would eat just about everything and anything. At one of his schools there was a particular sauce, served with apple crumble, that Robert spent years, later in life, trying to identify, never successfully.

It was during this first year that one of Robert's best friends had a nasty accident. Another ragamuffin from a farming background, Ben Johnson was born just three days before him and the pair were often mistaken for twins; they were inseparable during school hours. Recently built, the school had a very large gymnasium, which had a flat roof with domed plastic roof lights.

During a kick around in the playground, their football, kicked high into the air, floated on the wind onto the gymnasium roof. After some discussion, Robert and Ben were elected to climb onto the roof to recover the ball, a very risky exercise since it was out of bounds to all pupils and a caning was inevitable if they were caught.

Getting onto the roof was no problem to the boys, as simple as climbing a tree; they simply shinned up the black metal drainpipe, ran across the roof and kicked the ball down to their friends. Amidst the cheers from the boys on the ground, Robert and Ben were jumping around and throwing their arms in the air in celebration of their achievement. Clearly enjoying the acclaim from the crowded playground, Ben got a little more carried away and jumped onto one of the domed roof lights, crashing straight through onto the gymnasium floor. Luckily he landed on his feet and got away with a broken leg and a few scratches.

However, the gymnasium did not fare so well! Shortly after Ben fell through the roof, there was the most horrendous thunderstorm. The rain fell into the gymnasium, flooding the beautiful wooden tiled floor, lifting and distorting most of the tiles. Safely ensconced in the ambulance, Ben escaped any punishment; he was taken off to hospital for treatment on his broken leg and did not return to school for some weeks. Most unfairly, in his own opinion, however, Robert received the full punishment that he was expecting.

Ordered to report to the Headmaster's study, he trudged off, knowing full well what was going to happen. There were no seats outside the Headmaster's study, the unfortunates ordered to attend there had to stand, and Robert could not control the trembling in his legs because, once again, he had suffered badly from the descriptions of this experience from his brothers. He walked up and down awaiting the call to enter the room. Some minutes later he heard a very quiet 'come in'. He knocked, opened the door and entered the room.

In front of him, sitting behind his huge desk, was the headmaster, the most feared person in the school. On his desk, pointing at Robert in a most accusatory way, was the cane. It looked very much like the stick that Robert used to hunt rabbits, but much shorter, only about 18 inches long. His mind was trying to assess the difference in pain levels from receiving the punishment on the hand or on the bottom, and for a few moments he forgot about his predicament. In his considered opinion, he thought that the blows on the bottom might be the easiest because at least there would be a layer of cloth between cane and skin, and one would not actually see the blow being delivered. However, he was to be bitterly disappointed.

Rising slowly to his feet, the headmaster towered above him, leaned forward, and rested his hand on the cane, tempting Robert to hope that he was, at the last moment, reconsidering his punishment. At last, with the young boy's eyes following every tiny move, the stern-faced Headmaster picked up his cane. No explanation was asked of Robert and neither was he given any chance to make excuses. In a very deep and very quiet voice, he asked Robert if he understood all the rules of the school, emphasising the word *all*. Tempted, for just a fraction of a second, to disclaim knowledge of *all* the rules, in the hope of diverting the weapon presently swishing through the air as the Headmaster waved it threateningly at him, Robert finally said, 'yes, sir.'

'Hold out your left hand!' Three whacks, each heralded by a loud whoosh before making contact with his hand. 'Hold out your right hand!' Four whacks from the cane with the same whooshing sound preceding each. Wishing fervently that he had at least been told how many strokes to expect, Robert might have borne himself up a little, knowing how long the punishment would last. The additional fourth stroke on his right hand was the worst because he was not expecting it, having assumed that he would receive the same amount on each hand. The very chastened little boy left the Head's study with smarting hands; but still the hero of his classmates.

Strangely, the strokes left no mark on his hands, a hint of numbness and just a slight redness lingered for a few hours. They tingled for a while but such slight discomfort was considered by Robert to be a small price to pay for the newly acquired fame and deference he was afforded by his school chums. When Robert returned home that evening he told his mother of the caning; she asked what had happened, called him a wazzock and told him that he had deserved all that he had got.

2

After the Move to the Sandsfoot Estate

It was not until the end of his first full year in infant school that the family moved to the estate and, thankfully from Robert's point of view, to a period of stability. However, the walk to school was much longer, about three miles. He would set off each morning with his brothers, no matter what the weather, only deep snow keeping them at home. The walk to school was very hard, three miles seemed such a long way to the small boy; his brothers made no exception for his shorter legs, always expecting him to keep up.

Occasionally Ronald would be allowed to take their father's bicycle to school, and he would let Robert climb up onto the handlebars, Albert on the crossbar, and they would wobble their way along the narrow roads to school. Accidents were commonplace and Robert's short trousers were patched and mended in several places where they had been ripped, catching on the bracket for the front light when he fell off the handlebars.

It was extremely fortunate that there was very little traffic about, because the bike was in poor condition. The brakes especially needed some attention but the boys cared little about this as they sped down the hills whooping with glee. Sometimes, when a reduction in speed was required, Ronald would tell Robert to put his foot on the front wheel and allow it to drag along the rubber tyre, and it was this that usually precipitated Robert into the nearest ditch or hedgerow.

If the boys were really lucky the postman sometimes picked them up in his red van and gave them a lift to or from school. At other times they were offered lifts from passing trades vehicles setting off or returning from their country customers: coalman, grocer, the smelly butcher's van, or even Mr Sandsfoot in his beautiful Wolseley car.

Each day, whenever they left home for school, the Leonard boys took their decorated sticks with them and walked along the country lanes, with high, sloping grassed edges and even higher hedges, swishing at whatever took their fancy. If they were lucky enough to be offered a lift they would quickly slide their sticks into the hedgerows for collection at some later date.

In the summer months there grew a wild plant (cow parsley), which grew profusely on the banks of the road. It was the plant that the boys fed to their tame rabbits, and had large, heavily veined leaves. The plant, as it grew older and taller, eventually produced lofty, spindly trunks, which in turn produced a large, white-headed, delicate head of flowers. These tall trunks were hollow and the boys used them to make small peashooters, using the berries they found in the hedgerows as ammunition.

A small, readily available weapon, peashooter battles were common at school, and sometimes the battles were carried over into the classrooms. Sitting quietly in class, a sudden *ping* indicated that someone had fired his peashooter at an opponent or, if feeling particularly brave, the teacher! Rose-hips, the fruit of the dog-rose, which grew profusely along the hedgerows, provided further ammunition for pranks. Their contents, when unobtrusively slipped down the neck of an unsuspecting victim, almost immediately resulted in the recipient frantically scratching whilst trying to stop the incredible itching.

In springtime, whenever the wild birds were nesting, the boys took great delight in finding a nest. Already with a large collection, Albert took one or two eggs from each discovered nest, going to extreme lengths and making sometimes dangerous climbs to claim his prize.

The boys risked life and limb, climbing to the jackdaws' nests, high up in the tallest of trees, and removed a chick or two once they had hatched. The baby jackdaws were placed in a small cardboard shoebox by their mother's kitchen range and were fed on bread soaked in milk. The birds, with the characteristic grey hood clearly visible against their otherwise black plumage, became remarkably tame, and after some considerable patient training, responded to a call and fly onto one of the boys' shoulders. The feathered pets were not allowed to remain in the house for long; as soon as they were fully feathered their mother insisted that they were moved to an outside cage. Every inch a country woman, their mother tolerated her sons' pets in the house for short periods, at least until one of them pooped over the furniture!

In fact, the countryside provided the boys with quite a menagerie of pets: baby rabbits found stranded after a hunt; baby ducks and moorhens found along the river banks; baby chickens hatched by their mother or found wandering around the farm; the jackdaws; and a huge Alsation dog called Tuscan. Whether their mother always believed the boys' accounts of the circumstances surrounding so many lost baby birds and animals, the boys never knew. She usually made no comment and accepted the additional task of providing the necessary long-term care once her sons had lost interest.

One particular animal was banned from the house. Their father would not, under any circumstances, allow the boys to have a cat; in fact he had been heard on many occasions, praying for the animal's extinction. He detested them and thought nothing of blasting off with his 12 bore shotgun or yelling at his sons to let fly with their catapults and chase off the pests. The cats – their father preferred to call them 'pests' except when instigating Tuscan to kill – dug up his precious garden and he hated their habit of never damaging their own gardens, only those of their neighbours. Almost apoplectic with rage if a cat dug up his vegetable garden just after it had been seeded he would jump up and down, waving his arms, throwing stones, and yelling for mother to bring the dog and his gun.

Cats lurked around their garden, hunting their pets, and it is not surprising, therefore, that not one of the boys ever favoured cats and persecuted them at every given opportunity for the rest of their lives. At the merest glimpse of a cat out of the kitchen window, the whole family erupted into attack mode, dashing out of the house in a screaming mob, throwing whatever came to hand in the general direction of the cats, to chase the pests away. There was always a pat on the head and a few sweets from their father if they managed to hit one with their catapults, whether or not it was in their own garden!

The boys did not dally on the way to school; the older siblings had both experienced the wrath of the Head for such a misdeed. Returning home at the end of the day was a different matter; their route passed a field in which there was a deep, steeply sided chalk pit. Whether the chalk pit had been created by early chalk mining, or from bombs falling during the war, the boys did not know; but they did know that it was the site of a great deal of fun.

Armed with a piece of cardboard, or an old sack, or, if nothing else was available, the seat of their pants, they would climb to the top of the chalk pit and launch themselves over the edge, careering down the steep slope to the bottom. It was during one of these chalk pit playtimes that Robert had a most painful encounter with a bumble-bee.

One of the largest drains on the family's income was that of keeping the boys in footwear. Ever mindful of their mother's constant reminders to avoid damage, the boys removed socks and shoes when messing around in the chalk pit. Sliding down the steep slope caused considerable damage and their mother had issued an unequivocally severe warning that she would speak to their father if they ruined any more shoes in that way. Already having enjoyed several runs down the slope, Robert was running up the hill, bent over in his unique method of running, when he trod on a bumble-bee that had been quietly feeding amongst the clover blossoms.

Instantly defending itself, the bumble-bee lashed out in the only way possible, sinking its long, barbed sting into Robert's foot. The almost instant effect of the sting alarmed all three boys; Robert's foot ballooned with swelling and became very painful to any touch. Being both biggest and eldest, Ronald decided that Robert needed urgent attention and, assisted by Albert, carried their youngest brother the mile or so back to their home, leaving Robert's shoes and socks at the foot of the chalk pit!

After the excruciating pain associated with the application of iodine Robert did not know what his mother was more upset about, the fact that he had been injured in yet another accident, or that he had come home without his shoes. Complaining bitterly about always attracting the dirty jobs, Ronald was sent back later that evening, on his father's old bicycle, to collect the shoes.

Memories of his first encounter with Tuscan were to remain with Robert for the rest of his life, and the experience was to form the basis of a prolonged fear of very large dogs.

Shortly after the family moved to the estate, Robert and his brothers had been exploring their new surroundings and had found, tucked away at the rear of the farm buildings, a small cottage. It was an idyllic spot, perched on the side of a hill, which sloped down to the river's edge. The house, previously used as a gamekeeper's cottage, was quite small and beautifully built with dormer windows at front and rear of the roof.

The boys did not see Tuscan that day, but a few days later Robert was asked by his father to run an errand to the house with a message from Mr Sandsfoot. Only too pleased to run this errand, Robert was hoping for an opportunity to have a closer look inside the house and meet whoever lived there. As soon as he opened the front gate he heard the deep, menacing barking of a large dog, but he had no fear for he was quite used to animals of all shapes and sizes.

Shutting gates, on any farm or estate, is an absolute must as part of the country code, and remembering his father's instructions, Robert carefully closed the gate, and as he turned to start walking up the path he was bowled off his feet by a very large, hairy animal. Lying on his back, the frightened young boy stared up into the snarling face of a big Alsation dog. The large dog was straddling Robert's body, and as he looked up he could see drops of saliva beginning to form on the side of the floppy mouth; he also felt something wet and warm running down the right side of his face and thought, at first, that it was saliva from the dog.

Almost immediately Robert heard a man shouting at the dog, but he could not make out what the man was saying, it was a foreign language. The huge dog pricked up its ears, barked once more, turned and bounded back up the garden path towards its master. Instinctively Robert wiped at his face. When he looked at his hand he found that it was covered in blood and he had an unsettling vision of his mother applying more iodine.

The man looked down at Robert and asked him, in very broken English, if he was OK. Apart from the injury to his head, Robert had suffered no other injury and, for some unknown reason he imitated the broken English mode of speech when replying: 'Yes, OK, but where all blood come from?' The stranger knelt at his side and, picking Robert up, carried him into the house and sat him on a table.

Whilst he was cleaning the blood from Robert's face, the stranger was mumbling, 'That Tuscan, he one nasty son bitch, but he good friend.' The English pronunciation of Tuscan is not exactly how the man pronounced the dog's name, but it was the closest that Robert, or eventually his family, could come up with. At the time, Robert was simply relieved that the stranger did not appear to have any iodine.

Throughout the short time that the man spent cleaning Robert's face, before taking him back to the farm buildings, there was a delicious aroma of cooking in the background, which made Robert feel ravenous. He asked the man what the tasty smell was and was told that it was macaroni and he was frying it up for his dinner. The man asked if he would like to try some and Robert jumped at the chance – he was always ready to eat! It was fantastic, the strange lumps of what looked to Robert to be small rolls of bread, sprinkled with a fine grated cheese, were absolutely delicious.

A deep gash very close to his right eye had caused the heavy bleeding, and much later, his father said that he was lucky he had not lost the eye. The dog was lucky too that his father did not reach for his shotgun, accepting that Tuscan had not made an attack but had accidentally crashed into Robert, with his mouth open and teeth exposed; it was just unlucky that Robert's eye and the dog's mouth were about the same height.

The stranger was, his father later told him, an Italian prisoner of war who was hoping to remain in England rather than return to his own home. This small, isolated incident, left Robert with three lifelong consequences: the small scar on his face just above his right eye; a general mistrust of large dogs; and the memory of a smell that he would never experience again. Just a few short months later, the Italian disappeared and the family obtained Tuscan as a family pet.

In response to his youngest son's question, father explained that the Italian – Robert never knew his name except that it was something that sounded a little like Seppi – had learnt that he was going to be refused permission to remain in England and, rather than be forced to return to Italy, had *done a bunk*. Before leaving, Seppi had asked Robert's father to provide a good home for Tuscan, because he did not know quite where he was heading and he would not be able to care properly for the dog. What became of the Italian, Robert did not know, for that was the last he, or his family, ever heard of him.

The summer months on the estate were magical to Robert. Throughout the long summer school holidays, every opportunity was taken to make a little pocket money. The owner of the estate, Mr Sandsfoot allowed the boys to work in the fields with the men, particularly during harvest time, and he always paid the boys a fair wage, even to a boy as young as seven!

One particular job that no one else seemed willing to do was allocated to Robert, probably because in completing the task, size did not matter. The river that ran through the estate was filled with all sorts of wildlife; moorhens, ducks, geese, and swans built their nests in the reed patches at the side of the river. During the nesting season, clearly visible at the bottom of the crystal clear water of the river were a number of duck eggs.

How they got there Robert did not know; maybe they were dragged out of the nests by predators, or laid by the ducks as they swam along the surface, or perhaps ducks are just a little bit on the wazzock side and do not know when an egg is due! Whatever, Robert knew that Mr Sandsfoot liked these eggs and would pay well for them. Helping himself to one of his mother's large serving spoons, Robert tied it on to the end of a long, stout pole and retrieved the eggs from the river. The going rate at the time was a penny for each egg, a useful source of income for Robert and in a good season he managed to make a few extra shillings.

Helping in the fields was not expected of him, but it was another opportunity to do something with his father, and Robert spent much of his time struggling to keep up with the grown men. This, his seventh year, would be the last year in which the cart-horses were the main source of power on the estate. Mr Sandsfoot already had one tractor, a bright and shiny new machine with 'Fordson' emblazoned across the front, which, at first, no one except the estate foreman was allowed to drive.

The enormous cart-horses were father's pride and joy and the young boy just loved being around the immensely powerful yet docile and intelligent creatures. Their smell was an incredible mixture of earthy manure, not unpleasant, mixed with that of the polished tack. Every conceivable task on the estate was tackled by Robert's father with his team, Samson and Delilah, maybe not the most original of names but perfect for a mixed working team. The two horses were about ten years old and had been together since they were foals. The stallion, Samson, of course, took the lead, occasionally twisting his head back along his flanks to give Delilah a corrective nip with his teeth, especially when she allowed her concentration to falter. For the most part, however, the mare was content to follow the stallion's lead without the slightest hesitation. From heavy ploughing, harrowing and rolling to seeding, harvesting or grass-cutting – the list of jobs was virtually endless – the team had the strength for them all.

Agricultural work involves a very long working day. Out of bed at six o'clock, Robert's father would come into the kitchen to a hot, cooked breakfast, which Robert's mother had already prepared, washed down by two huge enamel mugs of tea. Half an hour later he would leave the house, throwing his satchel, an ex-army khaki bag, over his shoulder. This contained his sandwiches for the ten o'clock tea break and an empty Tizer bottle full of cold tea. In his pockets he carried his tin of cigarette tobacco – Old Holborn or Shag were his favourites – a packet of Rizla cigarette papers in which to roll up the tobacco, and a box of matches. Disdainful of the modern filter-tips or ready rolled cigarettes, father liked to roll his own because he said he liked the peaceful few moments it took, standing against a tree or one of the horses, anticipating his smoke.

One essential item of farming equipment that Robert's father was never without was his trusty penknife, a large multi-bladed, multi-implemented tool that was used for anything from slicing an apple to cleaning the hoofs of the horses or digging out the cattle grubs that were deeply embedded in the skin of the farm animals. All it ever got, in terms of cleaning, between each different use, was a casual wipe across his father's sometimes less than clean trouser leg.

Getting through the day without his other item of essential equipment would have been impossible for Robert's father. His large-faced pocket watch, tucked into the top pocket of his waistcoat hung on a long brass chain and was with him everywhere he went. He always dressed in his working clothes: sturdy trousers kept up by a wide leather belt with a huge buckle; heavy studded boots; waistcoat and jacket over a collarless shirt; and his trusty old cap on his head.

He was about 5 feet 6 inches tall, about average height for the period just after the Second World War. Very stocky and immensely strong, he could throw sacks of corn or bales of hay or straw around as if they were weightless. Or he could hurl Robert high into the air, catching him on the way down.

Having left the house, he walked slowly across the fields to the farm buildings, puffing at his second roll-up of the day and savouring the early morning freshness of the countryside, arriving in plenty of time for the seven o'clock start of the working day. Most of the other estate workers also arrived early, all enjoyed the chance of a chat and the passing along of various items of news, anticipating the arrival of Mr Sandsfoot and his orders for the day.

Although Mr Sandsfoot employed both manager and foreman, it was always he who came out to give the initial orders for the day. At precisely 7 a.m. he stepped out of the imposing farmhouse, flanked by his two sons, Master John and Master Martin, followed by both manager and foreman, and walked down the cobbled steps to the small barn in which the men were waiting. It was something of a daily ritual and it would be a very rare day when any of the five-strong management team would be missing for early morning orders. The giving of the orders was never hurried, in fact very little of life on the estate was ever hurried. The pace of the estate was always very sedate, redolent of the days when everything happened at the pace of a horse, and there always seemed to be plenty of time to get the work done.

The estate owner insisted on speaking to each man personally, banding them together into whatever group sizes he needed to accomplish the daily workload. Throughout the rest of the day the men took their orders from the foreman who seemed to spend his days whizzing around on the new tractor, issuing new or changing existing orders. What the manager actually did was something of a mystery to Robert! Each day he was seen beavering away in his office, at the rear of the farmhouse, working at his desk; *paper-pusher* was what Robert's father called him, and on the very rare occasions that he came into the fields to help, he was always the 'useless wazzock'.

The first rest period in a farm worker's day occurred at ten o'clock; it consisted of a short 15 minute tea break. In the summer months Robert's father took his sandwiches and tea cold, sitting on the ground wherever the horses stopped, the concept of washing hands before eating unheard of.

Robert's father always carried an old tarpaulin, rolled up and slung over the back of Samson, to put on the ground if it was damp, or throw over the horses like a tent if it was wet. This afforded him a temporary shelter and he stood between the horses, sheltered from the rain, to eat his food. The horses nosed contently into a small bag of corn. During the winter months a fire was built; some newspaper and a bundle of dry kindling from his khaki bag soon got the nearby broken branches from the hedgerows burning brightly. A forked twig, cut from a nearby hedgerow, made a fine toasting fork, enabling his sandwiches to be gently browned over the dying embers of the fire. He held them horizontally so that the butter did not drip out, whilst his enamel mug of tea warmed up. Hot toasted sandwiches, prepared in the fresh air, tasted absolutely gorgeous, and Robert liked nothing better in those days than sitting on the back of Samson and enjoying the picnics with his father at tea break.

Work continued until midday, which signalled the start of the dinner hour. Most days Robert's father made an effort to return home for his midday meal, which usually comprised a full cooked spread. If he was working some distance from the house, and this was always possible on the 2,000-acre estate, he would quickly collect his old bike in the morning and push it alongside the horses as he led them to work. At dinner time he pedalled vigorously back to the house for his cooked meal, which Robert's mother arranged to have waiting for him when he came through the door.

Although Mr Sandsfoot made no complaint if the men were a few minutes late back to their allocated work site for that day, they all felt obliged to return within the allotted hour. In later years, as the tractors replaced the horses, the machines made it so much easier to make this journey and the additional fuel used was, apparently, regarded as a legitimate expense by the estate owner. If the boys were working with the men then they too shared this midday meal. If, however, the boys were not actually working, then they were rarely at home at that time of day, and, if they were, they took pot luck with whatever food might be available. The food that their mother prepared was sufficient only for their father and she did not partake of this large midday meal, preferring to make do with a small snack.

A full day's work was usually completed at about 5.30 p.m. and father's return to the house was usually sometime between 5.30 and 6 p.m., at which time the family sat down together for their main meal. The boys, of course, were not always present, still out on the estate, sometimes until dark. Invariably, in their absence, their mother served up the boys' meals and set them to one side ready to be warmed up in the oven of the big, black kitchen range, one by one if necessary, as the boys returned home.

This late afternoon meal was a much more substantial affair. A main course of meat and vegetable with a pudding to follow. A couple of their mother's home-made loaves would be in the centre of the table, not yet cut into slices; if you wanted bread then you hopped up and cut it yourself; *kangaroo bread* as mother would have it! A large bowl of home-made butter was next to the bread and the boys, like their father, preferred more butter than bread.

Bread and jam had a whole new meaning when prepared

by the boys, two thick slices of bread with a generous spreading of butter topped with a tablespoonful of jam. Although main course portions were large for the male members of the family, puddings were never refused and their mother's rice pudding was everyone's favourite. Everyone watched very carefully when mother shared out the pudding because no one wanted to have less than their perceived share, and many an argument took place between the boys if their share was less than expected.

When such disagreements took place, Robert's mother took no part whatsoever in disciplining the boys; she had no need really, just the mention of *talking to their father*, whether or not he was present, was sufficient to end any disagreement: this usually ended in a sulky silence, but it ended! The boys knew very well what their father's punishment was, if and when it was applied.

On the rare occasions that such punishment was deemed necessary, the boys' father stood up from his chair, very slowly, and even more slowly removed his leather belt, folded it into a loop so that the buckle was enclosed within his hand, and smacked a few practice strokes on the edge of his armchair. Whichever of the boys was the unfortunate recipient of this punishment would be told, in a very stern voice reserved only for such occasions, to bend over the armchair and subsequently received two or three strokes of the belt.

The whole family were assembled to witness this punishment, whenever it was applied, so that all would know what to expect. Over the years the boys had developed an instinctive awareness of precisely how far they could encroach into their mother's seemingly bottomless tolerance towards them. When the boundaries were exceeded her reaction was to walk up to whichever of the boys needed dissuading, put her face very close to his, and in a very deep voice, which she also reserved for such occasions, would simply say very slowly, 'Do you want me to speak to your father?' Ronald and Robert learned to hold their tongues and calm down when their mother spoke those meaningful words, but Albert was the headstrong boy and it was to take a few more painful sessions of 'kissing father's armchair' before he too learned his lesson. Although having witnessed such punishment, on several occasions, Robert had not yet had that pleasure, but it was an inevitable event just waiting to happen.

After the evening meal, if overtime was required to be worked, by Mr Sandsfoot, their father sometimes returned to work, particularly during the busy planting and harvesting seasons. If such evening work was required, he finally returned home shortly after dark, walking from the fields with his trusty work horses plodding behind him, rubbing them down, watering, feeding and stabling them for the night.

He spoke to them continuously, as if they were humans, and Robert felt sure that they understood every word, pricking their ears and making soft sniggering noises in response to his voice. On his return to the house, particularly during wet weather, he firstly removed his muddy boots and placed them next to the kitchen range, then peeled off his shirt in preparation for a good wash down, using a large flannel and an enamel bowl kept for that purpose in the kitchen.

Hot water, for whatever purpose, was heated on the range using a huge black urn, much like a witch's kettle. Baths were taken in the old tin tub that doubled as a boiling pot for large items of clothing or bedding; each member of the family bathed, whether needed or not, once a week in front of the range. It was not a very large bath and although there was room for Robert to almost lie flat, everyone else had to sit upright. In the vigorous motions of bathing, most of the water spilled out of the bath,

41

particularly when one of the boys was feeling a little playful, and their mother used the spillage to clean the kitchen floor.

After his wash, a large mug of tea, and a home-rolled cigarette, Robert's father sat down to his supper whilst his mother cleaned up the water that he had splashed all over the kitchen. Of course it wasn't until Robert was many years older that he was up late enough to witness his father partaking of his favourite stomach-churning supper.

The estate provided much of their needs, keeping all manner of livestock, some of which was butchered for home use. A huge herd of pigs provided all sorts of delicious meals, amongst which was Robert's father's bed-time gourmet meal.

The pigs selected for estate consumption were rounded up and shot in the head using the special gun kept by the foreman. The still warm carcasses were then hung by their rear legs on large butcher's meat hooks and their throats cut with a single swipe from a very sharp long-bladed knife. The initial jet of blood, as the knife sank deeply into the pig's throat, shot clear across the slaughter room that had specially installed drainage channels running through the middle of the floor; the blood from the slaughtered pig's throat eventually slowed to a drip.

After smoking, the meat was salted and stored away in the special storage rooms at the rear of the farmhouse. The outer layer of fat on a fully grown, well-fed pig, can be anything up to 3 or 4 inches thick. When cooked, it has a milky white, cheese-like consistency and is usually left with its hairy outer skin attached. It was this delicacy that Robert's father enjoyed so much; Robert's mother sliced it into thin slabs, about 2 inches wide, much like a carefully prepared slice of melon, and father would sit with his penknife, carving off chunks, dipping them into a saucer of mustard, chewing for what seemed minutes on end, before swallowing.

Despite Robert's best efforts, he was never able to stomach his father's preferred supper; he could not rid his mind of the use his father made of the penknife, and it was this that mainly turned his stomach.

It was during a pig slaughtering that Robert witnessed his first remembered sign of Albert's stubbornness. The two younger boys had pestered their father to be allowed to witness and help with the slaughtering process. They had happily helped round up the selected animals, indicated for slaughter by a large splodge of red paint on their backs, and had stood to one side whilst the killing shots had been fired; the actual killing did not upset the boys – they were completely in tune with country ways.

A short time later, the two boys were standing in front of the pig, wanting to see all that occurred, as their father raised the knife in preparation for the bleeding stroke. Hesitating for a second, he had noticed his sons standing in front of him, and told them to move around to the side. When their father spoke the boys usually obeyed instantly, but Albert was determined to be that day's wazzock and stood his ground. Seeing that his second son was determined not to move, and deciding that the boy had to learn one day, he cut the pig's throat, drenching Albert from head to foot in blood.

Every small boy likes to see his peers taught a lesson, and Robert, who had instantly obeyed his father's call to move, now jumped up and down in glee at his brother's misfortune. Despite his obvious joy, Robert had a niggling doubt at the back of his mind; perhaps he had been a tad hasty at demonstrating such elation at Albert's discomfort; he suspected that he would receive a few painful punches later that day from his brother, but it would be worth it!

For their father, there was no such thing as a normal working week; he worked every day except Sunday, unless of course there was even more overtime available on

Sunday, in which case he was always willing to make a few extra shillings. On Saturdays the working day started at seven as normal but finished at midday, giving the estate workers an occasional short weekend of rest. Once a month, on a strict rota basis, each worker was allowed to take a long weekend off work, from Friday evening until Monday morning. If, however, they chose not to take this extra time off, they were paid for the Saturday morning as if it were overtime.

These generous arrangements were unheard of on any other estate that the family had known. Naturally, all the estate workers were very pleased with the arrangement, and, of course, the practice instilled a considerable amount of loyalty towards their employer. In fact, although the work was extremely heavy, the estate workers were very well cared for. Milk, and therefore all its by-products – meat processed by the estate together with whatever game they could catch; eggs both estate produced and from hens kept by each worker; potatoes, turnips, and a host of other vegetables, produced in bulk for the estate owners – were made available to the estate workers, free of charge. Fuel for the cottage fires, in the form of timber products, was also freely available, however, coal, which was delivered from the nearby town of Andover, was very expensive and therefore had to be paid for by each individual family.

Every Friday evening the estate workers were paid their wages. The men managed their return to the main farm buildings by five o'clock to stand around, smoking and chatting, awaiting the arrival of their pay. Mr Sandsfoot, once again accompanied by the whole of the estate management, began the weekly ritual by walking along the cobbled path linking house to farm buildings. The manager, meekly following his employer, and for once with a useful task to complete, carried a small drawer removed from his desk, which contained the tiny brown pay packets for each worker. Each man walked forward in answer to his name and stood in front of Mr Sandsfoot with his hand out; employer looked employee straight in the eye and, without a word, handed over the packet of money.

Most of the estate workers immediately tore open the packet of money to count out the contents, but Robert's father took very little notice of his, shoving it into his pocket without even bothering to open it. After the Friday evening meal, the ritual of handing over the week's wages was standard, Robert's father patting each of his pockets, pretending to have lost the precious envelope, Robert rooting through his father's jacket pockets until, at last, the packet was found. Whoever discovered the packet handed it, unopened, to their mother who, at some more peaceful time, checked its contents.

On Saturday afternoons, if their father was not busy, the family worked in the garden (if work needed doing), or walked down to the village store with their mother to purchase whatever was needed for the coming week; and to settle up their bill. The shop was a general store and sold almost everything a house and family might need, including food, both fresh and tinned, clothing, hardware, paraffin for the oil lamps, tobacco, beer and spirits, and even small items of furniture. Most farming families employed a semi-bartering system in their dealings with the village shop, and the boys' mother employed the same system. Her purchases were added to a running account, and credits, in the form of cash or produce were deducted as and when they became available. The shopkeeper was always willing to accept eggs, pheasant, rabbits, or garden produce to sell on to the village residents.

This system allowed Robert's mother to pay for more expensive items, like furniture or household goods, over an extended period of time and was known as 'tick'. Whenever the boys' mother sent one of them down to the shop, usually Robert as soon as he was old enough, they were told to put it on tick. On Saturdays their mother's normal practice was to pay for whatever everyday supplies they had purchased during the preceding week, plus a little off the main amount owed. She always had to be very careful how she managed this account because she had very little advance notice of her husband's growing dissatisfaction and his inevitable wish to move on.

In the year or so that the family had been with the Sandsfoot estate, however, Robert's father had seemed to settle in and was much happier than she had ever known him. She felt more willing to start buying a little more on tick for the house; furniture, new curtains, and who knows, maybe some *new* clothes for the family. She was careful, however, to buy one single item at a time and made a special effort to not only pay as much as possible each week, but also to put a few odd pennies in an old biscuit tin for a rainy day, just in case her husband's itchy foot became active again. Money was in short supply in the Leonard household and saving these few extra pence was usually only possibe when Robert's father was able to work a few extra hours overtime.

The shortage of money was not due to any vices on the part of Robert's parents, nor to mismanagement of the wages that his father earned; it was more to do with the low wages paid to agricultural workers. Alcohol was not to his father's liking, he very rarely drank beer and abstained completely from wines or spirits, in striking comparison to the other estate workers who Robert regularly heard staggering home from the village pub every Friday night. A bottle of cider was acceptable to father, brought out to the fields by Mrs Sandsfoot on very hot harvesting days, or maybe a small glass of beer at some family celebration, but other than that he was teetotal.

A deeply religious man, Robert's father was a member of

the Salvation Army band, or as Robert's mother called them, the Soldiers of Jesus. His chosen instrument was the cornet. This shiny instrument, in its black box with bright red lining, fascinated Robert, who had tried, on many occasion, to blow the instrument sufficiently hard to make any sound. On Sundays, except on those days when Robert's father was working overtime, his custom was to pedal off on his bicycle into Andover, shortly after the midday meal, wearing his Salvation Army uniform and with the box containing his cornet strapped beneath the saddle.

The work of this fine religious organisation is well known and, for Robert's father it was time consuming; he would not return home until quite late in the evening having marched around Andover, or one of the surrounding villages, playing stirring marching tunes, as he described them. Dreary noises was how Robert remembered them after hearing his father practising in the evenings. 'More likely annoying the neighbours' his mother often muttered under her breath. One obvious benefit of his father's band practice was that it certainly kept the cats out of the garden!

Apart from smoking and practising on his 'infernal instrument,' an expression Robert heard many times over the garden fence, his father's only other vice was that of daydreaming. On rainy evenings the whole family remained absolutely silent as they listened avidly while he spoke of winning the football pools, the exciting things that he would buy, and the wonderful places that the family would go on holiday; the expensive new dresses he would buy for Robert's mother, and the whole family beginning a new life when they emigrated to Canada.

In common with most other men, he had a dream; he had heard that land was very cheap in Canada and that it was readily available and wonderfully productive: 'The fields are so big you can drive a tractor and plough for a week before turning around to come back again.' Little did he know that his wife was totally against the idea; she would not dream of dragging her Hampshire boys to the other side of the world, particularly where wild grizzly bears roamed free and actively hunted humans. Occasionally Robert would walk quietly into the house and surprise his mother as she stood over her washing-up bowl, gazing out into the garden and singing softly to herself; Robert knew she was happy with her life just as it was; emigrating to Canada would have to be over her dead body!

To fund this dream father needed to win the football pools and, to this end, like thousands of others in the country, he had his own system that he was sure would win the jackpot one of these Saturdays. The system that father had devised and which he thought unique did not involve picking his football pool entry by predicting the likely result of the various matches; he simply completed the same numbers each week based on various birthdays and special family occasions. It being most likely that the vast majority of Littlewoods customers did the same did not occur to him.

Totally in accordance with his father's expectations, the impossible happened, and the whole family was ecstatic the week that father's numbers came up, all eight of them; he was a jackpot winner and was about to be £15,000 richer! A fortune by anyone's standards in the late 1940s. The only problem was that mother had misplaced the copy coupon and without that father could not claim. The whole house was turned upside down, father stormed from room to room, ranting and raving at his misfortune, but the winning coupon was forever lost. He could never tell his father, but Robert had a sneaking suspicion that mother had *disposed* of it because she didn't want to go to Canada, but he kept this suspicion to himself, not wanting to enrage his father any further!

For the God-fearing members of the estate and of the

local village, Sunday was a day of rest, that is unless they were required to work overtime! Similarly most of the children of these same God-fearing folk attended Sunday school; not one single child, however, attended from their own choice, but were washed, dressed, and sent off to comply with their parents' wishes. Flanked by his two brothers, Robert attended Church Wallop Sunday school every Sunday morning in the village hall, but since his parents were not regular churchgoers, the boys did not attend other Sunday services.

Robert found the weekly religious activity nothing more than an additional chore, an intrusion into his rest period from schooling, especially during the long summer school holidays: apparently God never rested and children therefore were not entitled to a rest from their education about His Works.

The most difficult part of Sunday school was that Robert, unlike his father and brothers, was tone deaf and could neither sing nor whistle in tune. Strangely though, he knew precisely when his father, or any other person singing or playing an instrument, was out of tune. The Sunday school teacher often conducted regular individual singing tests within her flock, obviously with the church choir and the good graces of the bishop in mind.

Such tests were extremely embarrassing to Robert, no matter how hard he tried; although it did not sound too bad within Robert's own head, the sound that everyone else heard was lamentable. Throughout the rest of his life, whenever Robert was involved in community singing, he would silently mouth the words whilst trying desperately to appear as if he was actually enjoying the process. However, if he was feeling particularly naughty, he might, during early morning school assembly, sing as loudly as he could, completely out of tune, and watch for the glares from the

Headmaster as he searched the room for the culprit; he would drop his eyes and concentrate hard on the hymn sheet whenever the Headmaster searched in his direction.

Despite feeling somewhat hard done by, Robert listened carefully, quietly and politely to the religious stories told by the Sunday school teacher. He neither totally believed nor totally disbelieved these stories; he accepted many based solely on the fact that the Sunday school teacher was very pretty and had a wonderful way of consoling upset young boys by dragging their heads to her ample breasts, moaning softly as she stroked the back of their necks. She must have thought Robert a strange lad; he always seemed to be upset about something or other.

The trouble was that Robert was a very practical country boy and he very much doubted that anyone or anything could actually write in stone, at least not without a hammer and chisel; and as for making a walkway through the middle of the sea, well it was all a bit doubtful. His biggest doubt surrounded the death of Jesus. How could someone with such powers and with the all-powerful God as his own father, allow himself to be treated in such a way? Surely such an intelligent Being, who had made heaven and earth and all things in it and on it, could have devised some other way to instruct His mere mortals to understand, without any shadow of doubt, that both He and His son had existed. Perhaps he could have reserved a small part of the brain, which would be pre-programmed to know, believe, and understand what His teachings meant and how to behave during their temporary stay on earth.

In some long-forgotten conversation, Robert had heard it mentioned that most wars were designed to control the population of the world, and again he thought that if He decided when each person should die, then all He had to do to control the population was to recall a few earlier than scheduled; it all sounded so illogical to the questioning mind of the young boy. However, Robert kept these doubts to himself, he refrained from mentioning them to his mother, who consistently asked about the new stories he had heard at Sunday school. As soon as he rushed into the kitchen, hand reaching for an apple, she asked the same question: 'What did you learn today, Robert?'

As consistent as his mother, Robert always replied, 'Nothing, Mother!'

Sunday afternoons were regarded as the time of the week for everyone to do their own thing; if the weather was nice, Robert's mother liked to take a stroll around the estate. Invariably Robert accompanied her, with Tuscan running along behind, dashing from one interesting smell to another, seemingly permanently out of breath, with his long tongue lolloping from the side of his mouth, spittle flying in all directions. Tuscan was willing to go anywhere with the boys, either individually or collectively, but if he was in the house, even if apparently in a deep sleep, when mother went out he would spring to his feet and follow her. Even it was just out to the garden to hang up the washing, Tuscan followed her, always staying close and on guard.

The dog had a quirky way of holding his mouth just slightly open, with all teeth just in view, almost a menacing grimace that intimidated human and animal alike. Tuscan adopted this grimace whenever a stranger or another dog approached, always accompanied by a threatening raising of the hairs along the length of his spine. Robert's mother sometimes felt it necessary to explain the dog's grimace: whenever passers-by asked if the dog was dangerous, she smiled sweetly at them and said the dog was *just smiling!* None seemed too reassured and all kept a good distance between themselves and the smile.

The Sunday afternoon walks with mother usually covered several miles but they seldom left the confines of the estate;

51

that being said, the estate covered quite a large area and there were many different footpaths that could be taken. The most regularly used walks were either along the river and around the lakes, or up into the coolness of the surrounding hills. If it was really hot, Robert stripped off his clothes and both he and Tuscan would jump into the river and thrash around in the shallow water, the boy totally naked. Drying off after these soakings was not a problem, mother routinely carried a stick in one hand and a shopping bag or father's old khaki lunch bag in the other. The bag contained a couple of apples, a bottle of cold tea, a few cow cakes for Tuscan, and an old towel, plus whatever they had managed to forage during their walk.

Their eyes were constantly on the look out for anything useful or edible, including birds' eggs if Robert could shin up the tree to reach the nest, which were always way out on the flimsiest of branches. Or nuts from the hazel, walnut, and chestnut trees. Flowers picked from the hundreds of different species around the estate from the simple primrose, violet and bluebells to exotic wild orchids, although mother insisted that the boys did not, under any circumstances, dig up the roots of these plants. Buried deep in Robert's memory was a particular Sunday, when father, deciding not to attend that afternoon's Salvation Army band practice, had accompanied them on their walk and they had decided to go down to the stand of hazel-nut trees alongside the river.

It was September and the trees were heavy with nuts, their shucks just browning slightly, indicating that they were ready for picking. Most of the nuts were out of reach and whilst Robert and his mother stood under the trees, father climbed up into the largest and shook one of the thicker branches as hard as he could. It literally rained nuts, and Robert and his mother had to put their hands over their heads and run out of the trees to avoid possible injury. Every tree alongside the river in that particular stretch of hazel trees was just as heavily loaded with nuts.

It had been an exceptional year for tree fruits, the family was not to know the like again, and for several weeks afterwards they returned to collect the fallen bounty. Most were eaten over the following days, some were shared with their neighbours, yet others bartered at the local store, and some stored away for later in the winter. There is a special art to storing hazel-nuts and only mother knew the secret. Robert knew part of the secret, selecting those nuts still in their shucks and filling a couple of large tin buckets sealed with just a layer of folded newspaper, finally burying them in the garden. In later years, when he used the system for himself, the nuts usually turned mouldy and rotted. What the missing part of the secret was he was never to discover.

When the time came to eat the stored hazel-nuts, and this occurred most years just before Christmas, they did not taste quite as nice as when first picked and eaten straight from the tree, however, the whole family loved them and never tired of eating them. The hazel-nut tree, apart from its delicious fruit, provided the boys with their trusty sticks and also strong flexible lengths of wood suitable for making bows, together with the thin, straight lengths for making arrows. The pole for the bow needed to be about 4 feet long, notched at each end so that a suitable length of twine, baling string, or linked shoe laces could be connected to it. Arrows were notched at one end, pointed at the other, with a piece of cardboard cut into shape and slotted into the notched end as a flight. These bows and arrows were the source of endless fun for the boys, chasing after game and firing off the arrows; but they were completely useless because not once, in the many years in which the boys used them, did either one of them manage to hit anything. Occasionally during their war games one or other of them would be hit by an arrow but no serious injury was ever done, except maybe for the odd bruise.

Prior to the move to the estate, the Leonard family had moved from house to house quite often and Robert was to live in some strange places during the early years of his life. During Robert's fifth to thirteenth year the family enjoyed a period of stability, living on the Sandsfoot estate and were exceptionally happy. They lacked for little except possibly for some of the more expensive trappings of life, such as nice furniture and holidays away from home. In fact, Robert was not to have a single holiday away from home during his school life. He did not feel any disappointment about this fact, rather it did not really occur to him that he might be missing out on something. Other boys from his school were full of boastful stories when they returned to school for the autumn term, telling of the wonderful holidays they had enjoyed at Blackpool, the Lake District, Wales, Scotland, or some other homeland resort; very few had travelled abroad.

Listening to these tales, Robert felt not the slightest envy, looking back on memories of his own long summer on the estate; spending so much time with his father, he felt content. During the long summer school holidays, if they were not involved in the work of the estate, the boys would be up by about seven-thirty and, having had a quick breakfast, be out of the house by eight. For Robert, the choice of spending the day with his brothers or walking into the village to spend the day with one of his school pals became increasingly difficult as he grew older.

Ronald was now 14 and approaching the end of his school years. This was to be the last summer that the brothers were to play as a group; by next year Ronald was expected to find full-time employment, either on the estate or elsewhere. Most of their games involved climbing trees.

Across the road from their cottage was a large copse and the boys had recently discussed whether or not it would be possible to traverse the copse without touching the ground. After much planning and establishment of the rules, each rule decided by the two older boys, the attempt was made on a beautiful summer day. The boys, dressed in their usual short trousers, shirts, and plimsolls, left the house shortly after eight.

They climbed the first tree, a large oak, slithering out along its extending branches and leaping across to the adjacent tree. All three boys were exceptionally fit and agile, and, in truth, were more like monkeys when in the treetops. Balance and judgement was almost a second sense, even to Robert, now eight, because they had spent so much time chasing after birds and their nests.

They were fearless in the treetops and felt intense exhilaration. Lost in a world of their own they stretched out for each successive branch, swinging high above the ground. It was enormous fun and after about two hours they had managed to reach the centre of the copse. Here, to one side of a large clearing, they found a tree completely covered from top to bottom with old man's beard. This vigorous plant was a vine that grew very quickly, climbing until it reached the very top of its host tree and then falling back to the ground, growing profusely and branching off in all directions as it went. In the course of the vine's journey to the top of its chosen tree and back to the ground, it produced a closely knitted, dense mat of vegetation that undulated downwards to the ground. To Robert it looked like a snow-covered hill, but green. The boys knew this tree well, it had provided hours of fun over the past two or three summers. They climbed to the very top of the huge tree and then launched themselves into the air, landing on the sloping greenery and sliding towards the ground, a green chalkpit. Occasionally their feet might catch in the vine and they then tumbled over and over until they could either regain their seated sliding position, or hit the ground.

Old man's beard was the source of another activity enjoyed by the boys: as its branches aged they dried up and left long thin lengths of what looked like thin cord, which when cut into the correct length provided an excellent smoke. All three boys had experimented with these cigarettes during the preceding summers; one of the trio usually had a box of matches in his pocket.

The game at the 'sliding tree', as the boys referred to it, lasted for well over an hour. Actually touching the ground during this time was not counted as a failure in their main goal of traversing the copse in the trees. They simply re-climbed the tree and continued tree hopping.

Abundant wildlife provided much to see and investigate as they swung from tree to tree: the flimsy nest of a pigeon consisting of just a few twigs lodged precariously on a few cross branches; the huge nest of a squirrel made from closely woven twigs, with a soft inner lining; the tiny nests of other birds, too numerous to mention, from blue tit to blackbird. Ever the opportunist, Albert took a sample or two for his growing collection, climbing down until just off the ground and carefully dropping the eggs for later retrieval.

Squirrel nests, wherever they were found, were carefully noted by the boys, for these were another source of income. Grey squirrels were regarded as a national pest and their tails, when handed in at the village shop, fetched a shilling each. The boys hunted the squirrels with catapult, airgun or bow. The preferred method was father's airgun, if he could be talked into letting them borrow it and provide a few pence for pellets. The tiny, acrobatic animals were extremely difficult to hit when up in the trees, however this didn't stop the boys from trying, blasting away with whatever weapon and ammunition became available.

Their best chance of catching a few squirrels was when they came down from the trees to feed, and if the boys made an early start and sat very quietly under a bush there might come a chance of a clear shot whilst the animals were in the open.

The three Hampshire boys felt no remorse when hunting and killing the wildlife; they had been doing it for many years and it was very much a part of their lives. One of Robert's favoured hunts was with his father, late at night, armed with torch and airgun, seeking out their target, the very tasty pheasant. Everyone knew that a rabbit, when lit by a car's headlights, will freeze. A pheasant will do the same and it was Robert's job to light up the pheasant while his father did the shooting. A brace of pheasant would provide a very nice meal for the family; a second brace would provide additional bartering opportunities at the local store.

The boys reached their goal of traversing the copse late in the afternoon and returned home for the evening meal. Elated at having conquered the copse, they fell into the house. Their movements, always rambunctious when together, involved a lot of pushing and shoving; they were tired but happy and, of course, absolutely ravenous. Their mother, trying hard to listen to all three of her sons describing their adventure, was not so pleased; all three were covered in scrapes and bruises and their clothes were ripped to shreds. Worst of all, and to Robert's extreme disappointment, she insisted on an unscheduled bath before their meal and put the big kettle on to heat some water.

If forced to name his list of most hated activities, Robert would undoubtedly include the weekly bath at the top of his list, and his mother was intent on his having an additional dip! It was not the process of getting undressed in the kitchen, on view to any visitors, nor the actual bathing procedure that bothered Robert, he hated baths because he was always the last to use the water and it was more than a little discoloured when his turn came around. He often reflected at bath times that being the youngest, in a family of three boys, is the hardest thing to deal with when you are growing up. Only his mother called him by name; his father usually called him *boy* and his brothers had a whole range of names for him, *mush, kiddo, titch, nipper, flower* being some of the less profane.

It was definitely a hard life being the youngest: Robert *always* came off worst in the rough and tumbles that the boys loved to indulge in; his clothes were *always* hand-me-downs from his brothers; he *always* missed out on the last biscuit or cake; he *always* went to bed first; and he would, in the future, be the *only* one to go to school on his own, conveniently forgetting that Ronald must have done that as the oldest! He was also the *only boy* that father still insisted upon kissing before he went to bed!

The family had its own collective name, taken from one of father's quaint expressions that he would use when the estate men were having a communal tea break, or standing around chatting casually at the start of the day awaiting their orders. He would make some preposterous statement like, 'Do you know that the Chinese people tie their daughters' legs together until they are five years old to make sure they don't go bandy legged!' The short statements usually 'drew the long bow' as tight as possible! Someone would always make some comment about father's worldly knowledge and he would say, 'Arh, us 'ampshire boys knows all about that.' When chatting to friends or extended family, mother used it occasionally to describe her family, and *'ampshire boys* became a collective name for father and the

58

three boys. Eventually the expression was taken up by the rest of the estate workers and even extended to the nearby villages, and it was used frequently in the local pub, often associated with deeds of derring-do to impress townie visitors.

During the winter of Robert's tenth year, 1949, there was a period of heavy snowfall. The estate was covered in a layer of snow some 20 feet deep and almost all normal activity came to a stop. All schools were closed and most roads were impassable since the road was completely obliterated from sight; the whole landscape changed to a wilderness of white instead of the normal vista of winter's brown and green.

Huge snowdrifts built up around most windbreaks that would remain for weeks after the main snow had finally disappeared. The estate workers who lived in the six attached cottages banded together and dug a route to the main farm buildings, and from there Mr Sandsfoot organised the daily chore of feeding the livestock; all other work was suspended. After a few days of hard frosts, the snow had a thick upper coating which supported the weight of a full-grown man, making walking through it much easier; but a few soft spots sometimes dropped the unwary up to their knees in snow.

After some months of painstaking search, Ronald had, by this time, left home to live and work on another farm, and the two younger boys saw very little of their elder sibling. In comparison with his younger brother, Albert, now 13, had grown considerably and was now almost as big as their father. During the period of this deep snow, Robert and his brother Albert had enormous fun; with all schools closed their lives became almost a holiday and they would be out of the house on most days from morning to evening.

They spent their time in a number of ways: building snowmen; sliding down the slopes, sitting or lying on flattened cardboard boxes; having snowball fights; and, when the snow was soft enough, rolling huge shapes, like great concrete pillars that would remain for weeks after the rest of the snow had disappeared. It was during this period that Robert and Albert left the house one afternoon under snow-laden skies to make an attempt at reaching one of the lakes on the estate, hoping that the water might be frozen hard enough to support their weight, allowing them to skate, or rather slide, since neither of the boys possessed skates.

Most of the snow had, by this time, been blown off the open fields by the strong winds into the valleys and woods. They had with them, as they would have on any other day, an apple and the usual stick, catapult and matches. It took a couple of hours to reach the lake, after many diversions off route investigating various signs left by the wildlife, and they arrived at the lake about two in the afternoon. It had been snowing quite heavily again throughout their journey. The lake was beautiful and, Robert thought, might have been even more so had the sun been shining on it. It was completely covered in snow, but this snow was only a few inches thick and could be swished away with their sticks. Under the snow was a thick layer of ice, so thick that the boys could not smash through with their sticks, and even with both boys jumping up and down together on the same spot there was no sign of cracking. There was a huge pile of whiteness in the centre of the lake, the island, where the boys had spent many an afternoon playing all sorts of adventure games from pirates to invading armies, during the previous summers.

Out of sight, somewhere along the side of the lake, there was a rowing boat that the boys normally made use of to get to the island, but there was no sign of it on this day; it must have been removed by the estate workers or was buried under a snowdrift. They ventured out on to the ice with the intention of reaching the island, but after about

30 yards the ice started to flex; it did not crack or make any ominous noises, just an unstable feeling of almost imperceptible movement under foot. The movement created an unusual, unsettling feeling in the pit of Robert's stomach and he felt his shoulders lift in an unconscious effort to lighten his body. Having made a plan, the boys did not like to be deterred from completing it, but Albert thought it unwise to go any further and both agreed that their chances of survival, if they fell through into the freezing water, would be remote. Instead they swished the snow away from a length of ice, about 20 yards long, running parallel with the shore, and used this as a slide.

It was enormous fun and the boys played happily for some time, never tiring of sliding from one end to the other, all thoughts of reaching the island completely discarded. They were extremely pleased with themselves when, reluctantly at about four o'clock, they trudged back towards home, already anticipating their evening meal. They realised that they had misjudged things a little, because they would not now reach home until a little after dark, but returning home in darkness was nothing unusual for them.

Forever casting their eyes from side to side, seeking fresh items of interest, they passed a small copse of huge fir trees, and Robert saw a couple of dead pigeons on the ground, with a scattering of feathers in a wide circle. A few drops of bright red blood could be seen on the whiteness of the snow, and Robert shouted to Albert, who was leading, of course, that he wanted to stop to investigate what had happened. Albert shouted for him to 'pull his finger out,' and continued across the fields towards home.

At first Robert assumed it was the work of a fox, but the birds were virtually undamaged and would certainly be fit for the table. The birds were lying under the huge electricity cables that had been erected across the estate a few months previously, and Robert then understood what had happened. The birds must have flown into the wires, the impact killing them and causing the spread of feathers on the ground. Looking around for evidence of any other birds, Robert saw some marks leading away into the copse. He was hoping that the marks might lead him to further dead pigeons and he followed the tracks towards the trees; mother never failed to appreciate anything the boys brought home for the table.

The tracks took a twisting, haphazard route and Robert followed in the now heavily falling snow, venturing some way towards the copse, which was in a deep ravine. The snow from the surrounding fields had been blown into the depression and virtually buried the huge fir trees. Hesitating for just a moment, Robert looked around to locate Albert but could not see him. He stopped and debated whether to venture across the deep snow over the ravine; visibility was now very poor and he called out a few times but there was no response.

There was no sign of the fallen pigeon, no tracks, not even his own in the frozen ground. It was frightening how quickly the blanket of new snow had covered every sign of life. The boys took every chance to play pranks on one another and Robert, thinking that Albert was at that moment engaged in plotting some misfortune for him, saw this situation as a golden opportunity to trick his brother. Gingerly, he edged into the ravine, prodding at the deep snow and trying to gauge its depth. His intention was to ambush his brother when he returned to find him. Although the stick sank several feet into the snow, it appeared firm enough to support his weight and Robert decided to take the bull by the horns and edged forward deeper into the ravine.

It was a strange feeling, almost as if he were sleepwalking, crossing the ravine at treetop height, with just the tips of the trees peeping through the snow. After about 50 yards he stopped, losing his nerve a little, and looked around for Albert who, once again, was nowhere in sight; it would be a waiting game to see who forfeited his own prank to seek out the other. Beneath his feet Robert spied the top of a fir tree, emerging from the deep snow, and as he looked down he could see the dark shadow of a gap between the tree and the snow. Leaning forward slightly, Robert poked his stick at the tree to see if the branches moved, when suddenly he just dropped; the earth just seemed to open up beneath him and he felt himself falling and the darkness enveloped him.

When Robert regained consciousness he was lying at the bottom of the huge fir tree. It was dark, except for a faint glow of moonlight filtering weakly down from above, and for a few seconds he was unsure of his location. He could not see the stars or anything around him but he could feel open space around his body, at least for as far as he could reach. He tried to reach the matches in his pocket but his left arm was extremely painful and he could not move it; the arm felt dead and Robert panicked when he realised he could not move his fingers.

It took him some time to calm himself, his brain having switched to panic mode, but eventually he managed to reach across with his right arm and retrieve the matches from his left pocket. Trying to strike a match was almost as difficult, using only one hand, but he eventually managed it. In the brief period of light he saw that he was lying under the branches of the tree. A few feet away was the thick trunk with long side branches bent over a few feet above his head, forming a small cave.

Slowly and painfully, Robert shuffled his body over to the trunk and sat up, leaning against it. The struggle to sit up and move had caused extreme pain in his left arm, which continued until he had amassed sufficient courage to lift the damaged arm into a temporary sling formed by the V of his jacket. As far as he could tell he had no other injuries; he was quite dry and not *too* cold, probably, he surmised, because he was completely sheltered from the wind.

In his attempt to assess his situation, Robert forced himself to remain as calm as possible; he was hungry and very thirsty and he wished that he had not eaten his apple earlier in the day. A reviving drink was what he needed first and Robert reached out with his good arm and picked up a small amount of snow, he put it into his mouth and immediately felt better as it melted down his throat.

From somewhere in the deep recesses of his mind, Robert instinctively felt that too much would not do him any good. He thought perhaps that too much lying in his stomach might lower his body temperature, and he was cold enough already. For some time Robert lay still under the tree, curled into a ball, trying desperately to keep his damaged arm still, thinking about how he might clamber out of the cave-like hole into which he had fallen.

In the brief light of the match, he had seen that the branches above him, as with all fir trees, were very close together and left very little room to climb up. With two good arms he might well have made it, but with a single usable arm there was clearly no point in making an attempt; he might even injure himself further in the process. It might help if he knew what time it was and he tried to work out a possible timeline. He must have fallen at about 4.30, give or take 15 minutes, but he had no knowledge of how long he had been unconscious. *If I assume I was out for about an hour,* Robert continued to assess his situation, *it must now be about 5.30.*

At some point Albert must have come back to look for him; Robert knew that his parents would be furious if his brother had not made some attempt to find him, at least until it got quite dark. The light had been fading quickly when Robert left his brother; maybe Albert assumed that his younger brother's prank included evasion and continued his journey home. Whatever the truth of the matter, Robert had heard nothing, no calls or whistles or any other indication of anyone searching for him.

Quite what his mother's reaction might be, Robert did not know. He guessed that she would await the return of father, by which time Robert, if he was just playing some prank, should have returned home. Some time had elapsed whilst different scenarios and possible explanations teased his mind, and he estimated that the time might well be anywhere from about 6 to 7 p.m.

Of one thing he was quite sure, it was past his evening meal time, because he was now feeling very hungry and his stomach was complaining noisily. The jet-black darkness was beginning to bother him and he desperately wanted to light another match but thought better of it; better to keep them for when he heard rescuers above, he could then light up the matches in the hope that they might see the light.

The injured boy lay under the fir tree, his imagination drifting towards the future. His mind seemed to be suspended in the air, and as he looked down, he could see a macabre scene, his own body lying in an open coffin around which his family stood, dressed in black. Try as he might, Robert could not see his mother's face; she was wearing a black veil, and his inability to see through the veil upset him greatly. Forcing back his own tears and becoming angry at the deep emotions evoked by his own fertile imagination, Robert managed a glimpse of his mother as she lifted the veil slightly to dab at her eyes, sobbing and choking occasionally. Standing just behind his mother, father looked very grave; strangely he seemed to have acquired a new suit, but his two brothers were fidgeting much as if they really wanted to be somewhere else. *Blow that for a game of soldiers,* thought Robert and chuckled softly because that was another of his father's favourite sayings. *I'll not think of that,* he said to himself, and he forced his mind back into the past. Concentrating hard, he forced his mind to drift back in time to previous moments in his life, searching carefully for the happy events, with no apparent logic or sequence.

A picture of a large, dark-green tractor flashed into his mind, and he remembered the day his father had been delegated as the driver of the latest mechanical addition to the estate. The pristine machine, with not a drop of mud on it, was called a Field Marshall and it was particularly unusual in that it had an exhaust pipe, poking vertically through the engine cover, shaped like a woman; narrow at the top like a neck, widening as for a bust line, narrowing again like a waist, widening again for a hip line, and finally narrowing again as it entered the engine space. It was also unusual in the method employed when starting the engine. His father came home from work on the first day that he had driven it and explained this strange starting procedure. At the time Robert had thought it was another of father's wind-ups. He was grinning widely, which also usually preceded one of his pearls of wisdom. The list of tools required to start the engine included a shotgun cartridge and Paddy's screwdriver.

Some years previously, father had had a really good friend as a neighbour, an Irishman called Percy, who was totally inept at the simplest of DIY tasks or of anything mechanical. It was father's opinion that Percy even found it difficult to hammer a nail into the wall and would use a hammer for every job, whatever it might be; even to the extent of hammering in a screw rather than use a screwdriver. From that moment onwards father had always referred to a hammer as Paddy's screwdriver. A slight giggle at the memory distracted Robert for a few seconds. He lay very still for a few moments, trying to regain his chain of thought; he could not remember what he had been thinking about before Paddy's screwdriver.

Then it came to him. *Of course, father's tractor!* Apparently the procedure involved placing the shotgun cartridge into a special container, striking the firing pin with the hammer, and the explosion turned the engine over! This all sounded a bit far-fetched to Robert and he just did not believe it. Most likely father just practising a tall tale for the morning muster, Robert had thought at the time. However, a few days later Robert had been with his father when the time came to start the engine, and that is exactly what had happened, the bang frightening the life out of him in the process.

Sometimes it took two or three cartridges to get the engine going and Robert knew that in the morning during the muster his father took great delight in firing off a cartridge just as one of the other workers entered the barn. The look on the newcomer's face as he jumped out of his skin delighted everyone. Even Mr Sandsfoot had fallen victim to this prank.

The tractor's engine had a most unusual sound as well, Robert remembered, it did not purr like any other engine, but had a very loud pop-pop-popping sound, and he found himself mouthing *pop pop pop*. While his mind struggled for coherent thought, Robert lost all track of time and, periodically, drifted in and out of consciousness. Each time he awoke he had forgotten about his damaged arm and would remember only when the pain jolted up into his shoulder.

At one time he thought he heard voices, far off and very faint. Unsure of the reality of his hearing, he thought to shout or light a match, but when he tried to shout nothing but a croak came from his throat; and when he felt for his matches they were no longer in his pocket. Searching for some recollection of what he had done with the matches, Robert remembered that he had kept the box in his hand, as a reassurance that they would be readily available when next he needed them, but he must have dropped the box when drifting in and out of sleep. Despite a careful feel around his body with his good arm he did not manage to find them. Thinking to revive himself a little, Robert had another small mouthful of snow and, once again, felt much better. He could even manage a small shout; but he could no longer hear whatever it was he had thought was voices.

Darkness and shock seemed to have a wearying effect upon his mind and he started to drift, once again, into the past. This time, despite concentrating hard, he could not avoid his disobedient memory returning to an extremely frightening experience, the lav! At the end of the garden! In the darkness! Dropping the torch, or the candle blowing out. Sitting there, feet firmly clamped against the door to prevent it being pushed inwards, the evil-looking claw, the strange noises, whether real or imagined. Bolstering his courage before finally being able to pull open the door, and the mad dash back down the long garden path, which seemed endless. Finally, leaping into mother's armchair and cuddling up behind her, only to be told to go and shut the back door.

With a superhuman effort he forced his mind away from the lav and focussed on another, particularly unpleasant chore that his father delegated to the boys. Emptying the lav! The huge metal bucket, with a sloping rim much like the fluted wine glasses that Robert had seen in Mr Sands-foot's office, and a big fold-down handle, resided under the wooden seat. At the rear of the wooden shed there was a hinged rear access and the boys had to manhandle the bucket out on to the grass path, trying not to spill any of the contents over themselves. Dragging the bucket out was the easy part because father insisted that the bucket be emptied at the far end of the garden, away from the house, and not on his vegetable plots. Partly carrying and partly dragging the very heavy and evil-smelling bucket to the end of the garden, the boys dug a deep hole and emptied the contents into it, returning the bucket to the lav on completion.

A very clear memory of the first time he was told to help Ronald with this chore remained with Robert. Everything had gone quite well really since Ronald was quite used to it and knew the process well. They had dug the big hole the day before, pulled the bucket out and started carrying it up the garden, only occasionally slopping the contents over their legs. Someone had then released the dog and Tuscan came bounding up the garden after the two boys. The big dog came silently up the garden, intent on joining in with whatever game the boys were involved in, and took a playful nip at Robert's ankles. The playful attack had happened so unexpectedly that Robert yelped and dropped his side of the bucket, and the lumpy contents splashed all over Ronald's boots and long school trousers (which both younger brothers envied greatly).

Oh halcyon days! A quick glance at his older brother's face convinced Robert to leg it. Ronald was furious; he knew all the most expressive profanities and treated anyone within earshot to a fine selection. Father was none too pleased either, because the slops were soaking into his seed bed, and he insisted on the mess being picked up and disposed of in the correct place.

Time and again mother washed Ronald's long trousers; he had only a single pair and she scrubbed them vigorously on the corrugated washboard. Regardless of her best efforts, Ronald's shoes and trousers smelled quite awful for some time after this event, but finally accepting the humour of the event, Ronald said that at least he always got a seat on the school bus! The underlying cause of the smelly episode did not escape scot-free; Tuscan had also received a dose of the slops, and he, poor chap, was banned from the house for several days until the boys took him down to the lake and kept him jumping in, chasing after thrown sticks, until he smelled a bit fresher.

A weak smile crossed Robert's face at the memory of Ronald's trousers and he attempted to sit up, but he felt deeply weary and was not able to move. His mind still drifting into the past, he recollected a time when the estate workers had been demolishing an old gamekeeper's cottage, which had fallen into disrepair and was no longer required by the estate. They had found the remains of some small animal in the foundation walls. At the time the find did not create much interest, but the next day at morning muster father reopened the subject, adding that Betty, as he referred to Robert's mother (her middle name was Elizabeth), had delved into her knowledge of the travellers, handed down through the ages from mother to daughter, and had declared that it was an old Gypsy custom to brick up a pair of cats in the foundations of a new house as a good luck gesture, effectively burying them alive.

Obviously proud of her heritage, mother spoke often of her family's connection with the Romany Gypsy clan, far back in the mists of time. Other workers at the morning muster waited for father to complete the preparation of a hand-rolled cigarette; they all knew there was a punch-line yet to come, and father added that as far as he was concerned, particularly in light of the huge post-war rebuilding schemes around the country, it was a custom that should be reintroduced immediately! Robert vividly remembered the glint in father's strange-coloured eyes, neither blue nor grey but somewhere in between, as he added the sinister coda to this tale, turning the knife for the two unfortunates who had found the skeletons. 'Bad luck will hound the footsteps of those who disturb the remains!'

Returning to full awareness, Robert felt quite cold and attempted, as best he could, to scrape the thick carpet of fir tree detritus around him. As his body warmed slightly, he returned to his time-consuming thoughts of the past. Harvest time, when he was very small, following father's team of horses pulling the harvester, with its large revolving paddle forcing the corn onto the blades and the corn tied into neat sheaves before being ejected on to the ground.

To him the corn sheaves were enormous and he struggled to help stack them vertically to await transport to a nearby threshing machine. The stacked sheaves made wonderful hiding places from where he might jump on to an unsuspecting rabbit or brother, or doze for a few moments. The boys followed the corn-cutting machine, which cut the corn and left a stubble of about 8 inches of stalk standing in the ground, carrying knobbly sticks ready to pounce on any rabbits that survived the passing of the machine. As time passed, Robert was struggling to stay awake and keep his memories flowing, but he was now feeling groggy and drifted once more into a deep and dreamless sleep.

The next time Robert awoke it was daylight. He could see patches of sunlight as it shined down the hole into which he had fallen. His heart soared as he also heard Tuscan's unmistakable bark and assumed, correctly, that it had been the barking that had awoken him.

Recalling his inability to cry out the previous evening, Robert quickly took a small handful of snow and sucked on it vigorously. He wanted to be able to shout at the first attempt and made a few test calls. Shouting as loudly as he could, Robert called up to Tuscan who barked again, signalling that he had found something of interest. Soon Robert heard the unmistakable sound of people approaching, shouting his name. Once again he yelled as loudly as he could until he heard his father ask if he was injured in any way.

Relief was palpable. Robert replied very simply that his arm hurt, he could not say any more. Somehow all the fight had gone out of him and he just wanted to curl up in his bed and go to sleep for a long, long time. Later Robert thought that it must have been his will to survive, having done its job and not being needed any more, which suddenly left him feeling so deflated and completely devoid of energy.

From what seemed a long way off he heard his father shout down that they were going to dig him out. Robert mumbled some reply that no one above heard and drifted back into unconsciousness.

The next time he awoke he was lying on the old settee at home, his head on his mother's lap. She was stroking his face very gently, in a way that she used to do when he was a small child; small circular motions with just the tips of her fingernails all over his face and neck. It was very soothing, and the feel of his mother's warm body next to him made him feel very safe and secure once again. However, there was pain from his damaged arm. His father was lifting it as gently as he could to try and find out how badly it was damaged. He heard his father say that the boy needed to go to the doctor and he then heard the voice of Mrs Sandsfoot say that she would get the car. *What's she doing in our house?* Robert wondered. He was later told that the whole estate had turned out to search for him, throughout the night, including Mrs Sandsfoot.

The search for the missing boy brought to a satisfactory conclusion, Robert heard Mr Sandsfoot tell the estate workers, including his father, to return to work whilst Mrs Sandsfoot and Robert's mother took him down to the local doctor. Often, in the past, Robert had seen Mrs Sandsfoot's car speeding around the estate, but this was to be the first time he had been allowed to travel in it and he found it very exciting, despite the dull pain from his arm. Fully awake and satiated from a hearty fry-up, Robert sat in the front seat of the car carefully watching Mrs Sandsfoot as she skilfully manoeuvred the car along the narrow roads. It was a large dark-green machine, a Facel Vega, and the smell inside was of leather and newness.

The purpose of the array of shiny dials, switches, and buttons was beyond the small boy's comprehension and he giggled as he imagined, for some strange reason, Mrs Sandsfoot swinging a huge hammer to start the engine! Strangely tongue-tied in the presence of the 'lady of the estate', he occupied his mind in an attempt to guess at the purpose of each button and switch, but in the end he gave up. Mrs Sandsfoot gave him no clue as to the intended use of the switches, she did not touch any of them, other than the gear lever, the pedals under her feet and the steering wheel.

The impressive machine came to a screeching halt in a shower of gravel outside the doctor's surgery and Robert, hand firmly held by Mrs Sandsfoot, was swept imperiously straight in to the doctor's surgery.

Bit rude, thought the young boy, *she didn't even knock!* Seeing the doctor was another of Robert's more fearful experiences; he had never actually been *ill* in his life, apart from the odd sniffle and routine minor complications like measles, mumps and chicken pox, and of course his many minor injuries. The nurse next door in the treatment room had lanced a particularly large and painful boil on the back of his neck a few months previously. He clearly recalled the pretty nurse holding the long, thick needle in front of his face in one hand, whilst her other hand squeezed the boil ready for the strike. That had really got his attention!

Apparently he had been in hospital as a baby, for treatment on his burned arm, but he had no memory of that.

At this point he became quite agitated, he knew that the doctor would want to move his arm to assess the damage and he was not looking forward to that. In the background he heard Mrs Sandsfoot and his mother talking to the doctor, and Robert felt quite embarrassed because the first thing the doctor said was that the boy could do with a bath. *I've already had one this week*, Robert was about to object, but at the last minute he decided to keep his objections to himself.

After some painful poking around, the doctor diagnosed 'just a fracture' and Robert hoped that either his mum or Mrs Sandsfoot might ask what that meant, because he didn't know, but of course no one did and he was much too shy to ask himself. Taken out to the nurse, his arm was bandaged tightly, placed in a bandage sling and he was sent off home to take a bath.

For the next few weeks he had a grand time, no chores, no school, and no pushing around from his brothers. Most days he spent the majority of his time with his father, sitting with him on the tractor as it plied its way around the estate on whatever task it was scheduled to do. Akin with all other small boys, Robert loved being with his father; he never tired of sitting on the tractor, watching the enormous range of wildlife, enjoying a chat at tea break, the only time it was possible to chat because of the noise from the tractor.

If the weather was inclement he covered himself with one of his father's old rubber rain capes, with an overly large rubber trilby-style hat on his head. Occasionally his father allowed him to steer the tractor, however it sometimes took considerable effort to turn the wheel and usually his father had to complete the manoeuvre. At every given opportunity father liked to reminisce about his beloved horses, Samson and Delilah, and Robert noticed that his father's face softened as he spoke about the horses.

The tractor had not made his life any easier, his father reflected, just more lonely. He, perhaps, did not have to walk so far each day whilst about his work, but despite several attempts, he had not found it possible to chat to the tractor. 'Makes me feel a bit daft, talking to this damn thing,' father turned his head towards his youngest son and shouted.

Even though father enjoyed an easy and relaxed relationship with his team of cart-horses, Robert had not really felt totally comfortable with the giant quadrupeds. Even with his father close to hand, they towered over him, and he had more than one nasty experience with them as a very young boy. One such an event had been when out with the estate workers one summer during harvesting, shortly after the family's arrival at the estate when about five years old. Knowing his son wanted to earn his three-penny bit, father encouraged him to lead the horse and cart from one stack of corn sheaves to the next. His father speared the sheaves with a long-handled fork, threw them effortlessly up to another worker who stacked them neatly on the cart; he then shouted 'Go on, boy' to Robert.

Awaiting the call to move, Robert then tugged on the reins, looking way above his head to the horses' eyes, which always seemed so fathomless and unfriendly, trying to encourage the team to move on. Many, many times Robert had stifled his fear of the huge hooves trampling him into the earth, but he could not bring himself to mention his fear to his father or his mother. He somehow knew that if he did he would not be allowed into the fields again.

However, on this occasion one of the other estate workers asked his father if he thought Robert could lead a loaded team, a much larger cart loaded with corn sheaves and pulled by a team of four cart-horses, to the threshing machine at the bottom of the hill. 'What do you think, boy?'

his father asked. Not wishing to be seen as a wuss, Robert said that he thought he could do it and tugged on the reins to get the team moving.

The horses tossed their heads and snorted, disdainful of the tiny imp leading them away, prancing before their eyes and tugging on the reins. The team's handler, Jim, seizing an opportunity to take a break, remained on top of the cart full of sheaves, intending to have a short snooze whilst the load was taken down to the thresher. 'Come on, boy, get 'em moving,' shouted Jim, and Robert pulled harder on the reins, swinging his legs clear of the ground. What caused the team to react so violently, Robert never really knew, maybe he pulled too hard on the reins, irritating the mouth of one of the horses, but, suddenly the team shot away.

As the team bolted, Robert desperately tried to hang onto the long lead reins, as the horses gradually picked up speed down the hill towards the threshing machine. Normally the safest route, which Robert knew very well, was across the slope using the gentlest gradient. But the team were panicked and just bolted. Letting go of the reins, Robert jumped to one side; if he had hung on he might well have been dragged under the wheels of the cart, and, as it was, he was acutely aware of how closely they passed him by. As the team and cart picked up speed, going straight down the hill, the cart became too heavy for the horses to hold. The only thing they could do was to attempt to turn along the slope, but the cart was going so fast that it just turned onto its side, spilling the load all over the place.

Huge eyes wide open in shock and fear, Robert stared after the galloping team. He saw Jim struggling to jump clear but his only hope of escape was to jump downhill. It was Jim's misfortune that the load followed him and he ended up covered in a deep pile of corn sheaves! Luckily,

Jim was not badly injured, just a few scrapes and bruises and he got up and came back up the hill where Robert stood trembling, expecting to be given a good telling off.

To Robert's great surprise and relief, Jim just picked him up. 'Are you all right, boy?' he said. Shaken by the recent events and with a tear in his eye, Robert said that he was fine but wanted to go home to his mother and he didn't want to lead the horses any more today.

Later that day, at the evening meal, father explained that the horses bolting was nothing to do with anything Robert had done. 'They are like people, boy, they can be real wazzocks at times, especially when they are very hot and very tired.' Although this reassured Robert and made him feel a bit better, the memory of the crazed flight of those heavy horses returned to haunt him whenever he found himself in the company of horses of any shape or size.

It was 1950 and the family had now lived on the estate for a little over five years and Robert, now eleven, was about to move up to the secondary school in Andover. His older brother, Albert, was now 14 and in his last year at secondary school, and Ronald, a strapping 16-year-old, was still happily ensconced in lodgings and earning his own living. With the move up to the secondary school, Robert accompanied Albert on their daily walk into the village of Church Wallop to catch a bus to the school in Andover.

The school bus was regarded by the local children as an extension of their school; to the brothers it was another place to get up to mischief, and, although it was usually Albert who instigated the mischief, it was usually Robert who took the blame!

Although catapults and penknives were banned at school, both the boys still left the house each day armed with their weapons. The catapults, however, were much smaller and designed for flicking small, tightly rolled balls of paper. Endless fun could be had with this weapon, particularly from firing down the length of the bus towards the driver.

The old-fashioned school coach had a sliding door on the side and all the boys wanted to sit by this door, in charge of its opening and closing as children got on and off. Of all the boys on the coach, Robert and Albert were the only two that did not vie for this seat; they were much happier sitting further back, hopefully unnoticed.

One of the bus drivers was elderly, at least 50 years old, and possessing a very volatile character. He became extremely angry at the slightest provocation. Of course, everyone on the bus knew this and always went that extra mile to be noisy and troublesome: standing on the seats (which really infuriated the driver); throwing things at one another; or, in winter, breathing on the windows and drawing pictures. Surreptitiously using his catapult, Albert's favourite trick was to fire a few paper balls towards the front of the bus, hoping to hit and annoy the driver.

The driver's angry response pleased every child on the bus and instigated an epidemic of giggling and spluttering that rippled through the coach from front to rear, much like a Mexican wave. On a really good day the driver stopped the bus, screeching to the side of the road, and stormed up the centre aisle demanding to be told who had thrown the paper balls at him. As far as Robert was ever aware, the driver never suspected that both he and his brother had catapults, and none of the other children on the bus ever grassed them up. This was not surprising really, given that every child on the bus knew that Ronald was the boys' big brother and that both Albert and Robert were also formidable fighters.

The schoolboy method of combat was wrestling and it was this activity that settled most playground arguments. Both Albert and Robert, although not as big as some of the other boys, were extremely quick, supple, and strong, and they both had enormous reserves of stamina, built up over many years of running around the estate, climbing trees and working in the fields. Although not very tall, Robert could tackle any of the boys of about his own age and was almost always victorious.

An argument, invariably escalating into a wrestling match, could occur at almost every playtime and the teachers had to be ever watchful, responding immediately to the cry 'fight, fight.' These wrestling matches were always hard fought and the victor was the boy who managed to wrestle his opponent to the floor; 'I'll get you down' was a common threat.

Only once had Robert been involved in a more serious encounter, which occurred about two years ago when, on returning to school after the long summer holidays, he had been taunted for some weeks by a particular gang of boys. The taunting was in response to his new school clothes, which his mother had managed to obtain from a Salvation Army jumble sale in Andover. Modelled on an army uniform, Robert's new clothes were a combination suit, short trousers and a waist-length blouson with large breast pockets.

The suit was a very nice shade of blue, or at least that is what Robert thought of it and indeed how his mother had convinced him to wear it! However, the boys at school decided he looked like a bluebottle and started to tease Robert unmercifully, ganging up and taunting him. The teasing went on for several weeks, and despite Robert's efforts to remain aloof (his mother's words) he was rapidly losing his patience.

Inevitably there came a day when Robert just snapped, losing his temper and at the same time all self-control. He launched himself at the largest of the boys in the taunting group, fists and feet flying in all directions. After some minutes of flaying arms and feet, the fight ended when Robert managed to land a solid punch to the boy's mouth, knocking his two front teeth out and depositing him on his backside, his head whipping backwards to contact the ground with a meaty thump. For some minutes Robert was worried – the other boy had gone down so hard, almost as if he had been felled by an axe. He was lying prone but he was alive, for Robert saw his chest moving from shallow breathing. Both boys were covered in blood, Robert from a long split around his central knuckle on his right hand that had taken the full impact with the other boy's teeth. The solid impact had jarred Robert's arm, and, looking down on his injury, he saw the bone of his knuckle. At the sight he felt the gorge rise in his throat and he swallowed hard to stop himself from being sick.

The injury to his hand instantly dampened his animosity towards the other boy, and he was extremely fortunate that the other boy, sitting up and spitting blood and teeth down his shirt, had also lost the will to fight, because he could not have continued. On playground duty, a very rotund teacher, Miss Owen, waddled across to the battlefield, obviously in response to the usual cries of fight, fight, fight, heard all around the school.

She barged her way through the throng of onlookers. Bodies seemed to bounce off her in all directions and, although the boys were no longer fighting, she grabbed Robert by his shoulder and, lifting him clear of the ground, threw him bodily to one side. Concentrating on his damaged hand, Robert tried to protect it as he fell, but he was taken unawares and landed awkwardly with all his weight on the bleeding cut.

When Robert managed to sit up, he looked at the cut and found it full of grit from the playground. He immediately thought, *That's going to hurt when someone puts iodine on it.* Both boys were dragged into the office of the school nurse who washed the blood from the other boy's face and sent him back to his class; he would, for as long as Robert knew him, speak with a pronounced lisp, which pleased Robert enormously every time he heard it. Both boys had numerous cuts around the face with grazes on hands and legs, but Robert seemed to have come off worse, again!

Turning her attention to his damaged hand, the nurse started to clean the pieces of grit from the cut and Robert, determined not to make a sound, clamped his teeth together and looked over the nurse's head out of the window. No matter how deeply the nurse dug to remove small stones and grit, Robert uttered not one sound and eventually the nurse's touch softened and she completed the cleaning of the cut in a more gentle fashion. The familiar brown bottle of iodine was produced and the nurse even made sympathetic mewing sounds as she dabbed a liberal application over the deep cut, but the anticipated shocking pain that followed did not drag more than a soft groan from the boy's mouth.

The wound was not stitched, to Robert's intense relief, it was just heavily bandaged and the arm placed in a sling; after which he was ordered back to his class. The injury did not heal properly and for the rest of his life Robert was incapable of straightening his middle finger, which for ever sported an impressively large knuckle and a curving moon-shaped scar.

Every boy in the school knew the punishment for fighting and, as expected later that day, Robert was ordered to report to the Headmaster's study. He knew what that meant. Another chance to feel the strength of the Head's arm wielding his cane!

Walking along the long corridor to the Head's study, Robert saw his opponent leaving the room, tears streaming down his still bloody and bruised face; he had paid the required penalty for daring to break school rules. The elder boy tried desperately to stop sniffling as he sighted Robert and sobbed 'sorry,' whilst holding out his hand to be shaken. 'Headmaster says I must apologise for teasing you,' Robert's antagonist grizzled, attempting to wipe eyes and nose with the same hand.

Flagging spirits lifted immediately; perhaps Robert was not going to get a taste of the cane today. The Headmaster had clearly been informed that the continuous teasing had instigated the altercation, but deep in his heart Robert knew that he had made the opening attack.

'Enter,' the softly spoken command was heard from the Headmaster, and Robert entered the study, more hopeful than confident. However, his hopes were soon dashed. The Headmaster picked up his cane and without another word told him to hold out his left hand: six of the best!

For the rest of the day Robert could do very little since one hand was sore from the cane and the other throbbed viciously from the iodine! As if by magic the teasing stopped immediately: the bluebottle joke was never mentioned again. The two antagonists did not exactly become best friends but they maintained a healthy, wary distance from that moment on. A slightly hangdog expression did not extract much sympathy from his mother later that afternoon when he arrived home with his arm in a sling. She took her usual unworried stance and checked that she had enough iodine to change the dressings.

Apart from being occasionally dangerous and aggressive places, school playgrounds can also yield much enjoyment. Many games were invented, but two of the most commonplace and enjoyable, at least for the boys and possibly for some of the more butch girls, were flicking cards, and marbles. Every boy in the school had a store of cigarette cards tied up with elastic bands and small drawstring bags, specially made by doting mothers, full of marbles. The cards were included in packets of cigarettes as a sales gimmick; the pictures on the cards covered a variety of subjects including famous footballers, boxers, runners, animals, countries, etc.

Each participant in the game stood a pre-decided number of cards against the wall of the school, retreated back behind the firing line (a chalk line drawn about 10 yards away from the wall), and flicked their remaining cards at the standing line. Whoever knocked down the last standing card was the winner and picked up all the cards thrown by the boys. If you were unfortunate enough to have used up all your cards then the boys' other time-consuming activity came into play: that of swapping. Almost anything had a value and was available for swapping, from sandwiches and fruit to toys and coins and, of course, cigarette cards, a very valuable form of currency. Until he damaged his flicking hand, Robert had hundreds of cards, but since the fight he had seen his stash slowly disappear. The injury left him with a weakened grip and a slight loss of sensation in his middle finger and from then on he could not grip the card well enough to flick it properly and his prowess at the game dropped to that of the 'less able'.

Shortly after commencing his secondary education, still about eleven years of age, Robert suffered another injury that was to plague him for the rest of his life. The school bus had arrived at Robert's stop, the door monitor sitting in the seat by the door had leapt to his feet and slid the door open just before the bus stopped, displaying his efficiency at his task. Moving extremely slowly, which never failed to rile the drivers, Robert waited until the bus stopped before rising from his seat. Taking as much time as possible, he stepped down into the road. In his desire to be as obnoxious to the driver as he possibly could, hoping of course for some response, he had forgotten to pick up his school bag. As the helpful door monitor pushed the door shut, Robert put his left hand into the opening with the intention of getting back on to the bus.

The door slammed on to Robert's fingers but, fortunately, did not latch. The injuries did not seem too bad at first, lots of blood, some localised bruising, but no broken fingers; however, the nail on the middle finger refused to grow properly again and was always slightly misshapen and continually cracked. Forever reminded of the incident, every afternoon each driver took great delight in trilling in a niminy-piminy way, 'Mind your fingers boy!'

It was this same school bus, with the volatile driver, that was to see the end of dear old Tuscan as well. Shortly after the incident with Robert's hand, mother had decided to meet the boys at the bus stop in the afternoon, probably to check up on whether Albert had actually gone to school. However, she had Tuscan with her, on his lead as normal because of his bitter hatred of cats and his tendency to attack them on sight; he had been trained and encouraged by the whole family, from a very young age, to attack a cat as soon as it came into view. Afterwards mother said that it all happened so suddenly that there was nothing she could do. She had been standing chatting to a group of mothers when Tuscan just bolted, dragging the lead from her hand. The dog had seen a cat on the other side of the road and dashed out under the wheels of the school bus.

That wonderful animal had been a most loving, loyal, and protective member of the family and would be sorely missed for many years. The body was too heavy for Robert and his mother to carry home so they left it there for later collection by their father. After a great deal of discussion and argument between the two brothers, Tuscan was buried up in the hills of the estate, where he had played with and protected the boys on so many happy days. The scar on the side of Robert's face, inflicted unintentionally by the dog, was to Robert a sign of a special relationship and he often wondered if Tuscan's death was his payback, from whoever might be controlling such things, for his behaviour on the school bus.

At the time of this tragedy, searching for someone on whom to apportion responsibility, Robert secretly blamed his brother Albert for Tuscan's death. Only recently, Robert had become aware that his brother Albert had, for several years, been bunking off from school, not for any long consecutive periods, but a day here and a day there. At least, his brother *claimed* that he had been playing truant for several years. Robert only knew that on some days, since he had been travelling on the school bus, Albert had not actually got on to the bus, and, if he had, he had not always gone into the school.

Apparently their mother had become suspicious, again quite recently, when Albert had declared that he no longer wanted to have school dinners but would prefer to take sandwiches. She knew that both the boys enjoyed the school dinners and, at first, could not understand Albert's change of preference. As it happened, on that fateful day of Tuscan's death, Albert had not been on the bus and Robert had, later that evening, explained briefly to his mother that he thought Albert had remained in town after school. Not long after Tuscan's death, the school authorities discovered that Albert was playing truant and visited the family home on many occasions.

By this time Albert had decided that, at 14, he had obtained enough education and no one was going to make him go back. He aroused so much anger in the education authorities that he was taken off to a remand home for wayward boys at one time, halfway through his fourteenth year, but he escaped and returned home so many times that the authorities eventually gave up and returned him to his family.

During his first escape from the remand home, Albert had taken refuge in a ruined country house at the far end of the estate. These old ruins were the site of many of the boys' adventures and they had spent many happy hours there. Most of the remaining walls had been reduced, over time, to a few feet of rubble, but a few were almost complete with grand arches and with the gaping openings for windows and doors still to be seen. There was always an eerie silence about the place, with very little wildlife noise, and Robert refused to accompany Albert to the house after dark. The house must have been impressively large and very grand in its heyday, and Robert often dreamed that one day his acquired wealth would allow him to return and rebuild the house for his own family.

The boys had discovered an opening down into one of the cellars. The entrance was hidden at the base of a fully grown oak tree and the boys had left the opening quite small so that any estate staff would, at a glance and without a closer look, mistake it for a fox's den or large rabbit hole. As far as the boys knew, none of the estate workers visited the ruins, but the gamekeeper roamed far and wide and he was so quiet that you didn't know he was watching you until he shouted or showed himself.

Signs of other human visitors, alongside their own footprints, were completely absent. It seemed that the boys, apart from the odd passer-by, were the only regular visitors to the ruins. They had further hidden the entrance by dragging a large fallen branch over it. The cellar was quite large, oblong in shape, and had, at the end furthest away from the boys' entrance, a row of small cells, each with very thick iron grilles set deeply into the floor and ceiling. Beyond the iron grilles, the roof had collapsed and the cells were half full of earth and other debris. Into each of these cells there was a solid wooden door with massive metal hinges. The boys had been unable to open any of these doors, the metal being seized solid after many years of inactivity.

These cells were the subject of endless speculation for the boys: perhaps the estate had been owned by a pirate captain and were used to store the chests of treasure trove; or maybe there had existed a slave trade in England and these were the cells in which they were housed; or, perhaps, in those long ago times there were no police forces or authorities and the lord of the manor had to impose his own laws and the cells were for incarcerating the law-breakers. More bloodthirsty suggestions were usually favoured by Robert's young imagination, and he deduced that the large cellar was a torture chamber, and the cells were where convicted traitors were detained. The floor of the main cellar sloped from each wall to the centre of the room where the boys could see the remains of a drain, obviously where the blood and bits of bodies were washed away.

Whatever its previous usage, the boys regarded it as their own and had enthusiastically cleaned and tidied the main area of the cellar, which, provided it did not rain too heavily, remained quite dry. The first time they had entered the cellar, it had smelled awful, musty and rank from the smell of dying animals that had fallen in and been unable to escape.

A length of stout rope was tied to the fallen branch that they used to partially hide the entrance; when they left after each visit they removed the rope from the branch and looped it over a large iron protrusion just below the entrance. The cellar was their own special secret, never to be divulged to anyone, not even mother.

They had, since they discovered the cellar, taken lots of useful things that they found on the village refuse tip back to the cellar to make it more homely. An old mattress, an old oil lamp (they had removed the wick from mother's now redundant lamp, which she kept as an ornament), a can of paraffin, boxes of matches, lots of firewood, and a supply of apples. They also wanted to include a couple of old chairs that they found on the tip, but that would have involved making the entrance bigger, and they both wanted to avoid a bigger entrance in case it attracted other people's attention.

On the day of Albert's first escape from the remand home, Robert had just returned home from school to find a strange man and woman sitting around the kitchen table with mother. Still out in the fields, father was not due to return for some time. The man said that he was from the education authorities and wanted to know if Robert knew where his brother might hide if he ran away from the remand home. There could only be one place. Robert instantly knew where Albert was, in the cellar, but he shook his head in denial. There was no way he was going to tell this strange man anything until his father returned home.

In an effort to dissuade the officials from further questioning, Robert did mention that there were hundreds of places, not only on the Sandsfoot estate but also on the other estates where Albert's friends lived, that he might be hiding. When his father returned from work, mother asked the two visitors to go into the living-room whilst father ate his meal. Throughout the meal mother outlined the reason for the officials' visit and what had been said so far. Father did not say anything until he had finished his meal. He just sat at the big kitchen table, staring at Robert in an almost intimidating way, eating, it seemed to Robert, in a much noisier way than he would normally.

The house was totally silent except for the noise of father chewing and the occasional spitting of firewood from mother's range. No longer able to tolerate his father's intense stare, Robert gazed at the fire, counting the number of vertical grilles at the front of the fire against which they often toasted their generous chunks of sliced bread from one of mother's loaves. He thought how carefully cleaned and polished it was and had often sat and watched his mother lovingly wipe a cloth over it when she was cooking.

Finally father finished his meal and drained his mug of tea and, whilst mother refilled his mug, he asked Robert, in the very quiet, deep voice that meant *you have gone far enough*, if he knew where his brother was. Throughout his father's meal Robert had been in a quandary as to what to tell his father; he knew that his father would ask him and he also knew that as brothers he and Albert had sworn to each other that neither would divulge the whereabouts of the cellar.

However, long before father had finished his mug of tea, Robert had made his decision; he knew that Albert was in no danger for Albert was, like any member of the family, extremely hardy and could look after himself, but . . . Robert knew that he could not defy his father. He knew, from somewhere deep within himself, that if he was not now honest with his father then their special relationship would forever be tarnished. There is only one love stronger than a father's love for his son, and that is a son's love for his father, and Robert loved his father in a very special way and saw parts of him in the comic book heroes that he read about and the story heroes that he heard on the radio.

The treacherous words spilled from his mouth: Robert told his father that he thought he might know where Albert was hiding and, in a desperate effort to gain some time, added that it was getting dark and it might be better to wait for morning. An opportunity might arise whereby Robert could sneak out of the house during the night and warn Albert so that he could make his escape. As expected, Robert's hope was a forlorn one, and any other excuses dissuaded, when his father decided 'no, we go tonight,' opened up the door to the sitting-room, and told the waiting strangers to get ready to leave.

Told to take the lead, Robert set off towards the ruin. All except mother traipsed along behind him as he led them across the estate. Persuading mother to remain at the house took father a few minutes, but he asked her to start preparing a hot meal, just in case Albert was found, and mother saw the sense of that.

There were many different routes to the ruins and Robert could have led the way along the winding farm track that passed within a few hundred yards of their destination. This track, although not surfaced with Tarmac, had been resurfaced with gravel, stones, and sand each winter for many years, and the passing of the heavy farm vehicles had compacted it into a hard surface. However, he had noticed that both the education officials were wearing lightweight shoes and Robert decided, with a wry sadistic smile, that they *would at least get their shoes dirty.*

Leading the group at a fast pace, he knew that father would find no difficulty in keeping up but he was hoping that the officials might suffer from the exertion. Robert took a wide overlapping route, twisting and turning as much as he could and finally led them to the ruins, but instead of approaching using the easy route from the track, he led them around the big lake and through the most dense undergrowth.

Certain that he could never disguise the location of the ruins from his father, no matter how much he twisted and turned, Robert felt that at least the other two would not have a clue. As they approached the entrance, Robert shone his torch along the branch and saw that the rope was attached, indicating that someone was down in the cellar. There was only one conclusion: it could be none other than his brother feeling relatively safe in their hide-away. There was no light shining up from below, nor any other indication of occupation. Albert would have heard their approach and immediately doused any light. 'Better come up, son,' father shouted, 'we know you are there.'

Nothing was heard for a few minutes until, quite suddenly, Albert's head and shoulders appeared out of the entrance to the cellar. Overwhelmed by his deceit, Robert's heart sank, for he knew that in that moment he had truly betrayed his brother.

For months afterwards he would lie in bed and berate himself for his actions; his usual sunny disposition deserted him, he lost his appetite, did not sleep well, and started playing truant himself. Rebuking himself time and again, Robert could find no way to forgive his action.

Officialdom had won the day and departed immediately to return Albert to the remand home after his discovery in the ruins. Before they left, they poured oil on to the fires of Robert's emotions by thanking him for his help. At home, mother had been furious because the authorities had not allowed Albert to eat the hot meal that she had prepared, but had insisted on leaving immediately for the remand home. Robert had not had a chance to speak to his brother, to explain exactly why he had broken their pact. No one, not even his mother, seemed to understand what he was suffering; his existence, once so carefree and happy, now seemed meaningless and dull.

He no longer sat, nor would ever again sit, in his favourite place behind his mother in her big old armchair. He spoke little, not to family, or friends, or teachers, except for the odd please, thank you, or grunt. He no longer cared to accompany his father about the estate, nor read, nor copied the drawings from the comics, which had been one of his most enjoyable evening activities. Robert seemed to have become a different person, not just to his parents but to himself. He could not, no matter what he tried, shake off his terrible, all-consuming guilt.

By Christmas, several months later, Robert had lost weight and looked gaunt. His body had always been slim, muscular and free of fat, never overweight, but his physical appearance had deteriorated considerably and he was now painfully thin. In an effort to cheer him up, Robert's mother had asked him if he wanted to attend the Christmas children's party that Mrs Sandsfoot provided each year for the village children.

This event was held each year on Christmas Eve at about 5.30 p.m. It was held in the huge ballroom in the main house. The furniture was removed, and tables covered in Christmas decorations were lined up down the centre of the room. About 50 or so children usually attended, and Robert and his brothers had enjoyed several such happy Christmas parties. Each child arrived with a handmade Christmas card for Mrs Sandsfoot. She greeted each child personally and by name, and in exchange for the card, she gave each child a present. Each present was carefully wrapped and had a small tag attached to it on which was written the child's name and a small note congratulating that child on some small achievement during the preceding year. Over the past few years, Robert had tried to fathom out how Mrs Sandsfoot managed to avail herself of so much information and, at first, assumed that she called on every mother in the village to get the information she needed.

It wasn't until the previous year, when Robert was standing in the local grocery shop with his mother, waiting to be served, that he had overheard the grocer's wife chattering away to the person she was serving. Clearly the village gossip, she seemed to know everyone's business, down to the last detail, and thought nothing of passing it on to anyone who came into the shop. This then was the source of Mrs Sandsfoot's information, Robert thought, feeling quite pleased with himself and rather smug, but he kept this to himself and refrained from telling the other children.

The tables down the centre of the room were laden with enormous, colourful serving plates decorated with scenes of Christmas and loaded high with fairy cakes, marshmallows, slices of fruit cake (which strangely most of the children left), sandwiches, jam rolls, doughnuts, and bowls filled with cream, fruit, and nuts. Each child had a large bottle of Tizer or lemonade, collected from crates under the tables. Around the outside of the room were other tables laden with finely sliced ham, beef, and turkey, with bowls of salad, fresh homemade butter, and huge piles of sliced chunky bread. This was for the mothers who accompanied the children.

In his depressed mood following his traitorous action towards his brother, Robert had said that he did not want to go to the Christmas party, but his mother had said that if he didn't then he might upset Mrs Sandsfoot. Remembering the numerous small kindnesses of this lovely lady over the preceding years, Robert reluctantly agreed to go.

As he entered the big ballroom he noticed that almost all the other children had already arrived and that Mrs Sandsfoot was not in her usual place greeting each arrival. This year the greeting was being done by Mrs Sandsfoot's daughter-in-law, the wife of Master John. It was clearly going to be a different format for this year, Robert decided, thinking it a bit odd because when he handed over a Christmas card he was not given a present in return. *Probably having an economy drive*, thought Robert. His mother was always on about such things. Without the presence of Mrs Sandsfoot, Robert returned to his house of recrimination; he really wasn't interested in any of the lovely food on display, he felt ill and light headed and, just as he was about to walk over to take his seat at the long line of tables, Mrs Sandsfoot appeared in the room.

She walked straight over to Robert and took him by the hand. 'Come with me, Robert, I want to have a little talk to you,' she said, and led him back through the door from which she had emerged. She led Robert, still holding his hand, for what seemed ages, up long flights of stairs and along corridors until they reached a small, brightly lit sitting-room. It was exquisitely furnished and, Robert noticed, had the most enormous sets of curtains that he had ever seen, at each of the windows. It must have been a corner room, Robert later thought, because it had windows along two walls. There was a small cast-iron, free-standing fireplace set back into the wall, the doors of which seemed to have glass in them, and Robert thought, *I wonder why they don't explode!* In front of the fire were two quite small armchairs, and Mrs Sandsfoot sat Robert in one of them and, still holding on to his hand, sat in the other.

She had always been very kind to him, and it seemed to Robert, more so to him than any of the other boys on the estate or in the village. She never failed to reach into her pocket, searching for something to give him, whenever they had met, whether it be an apple or a sweet or sometimes the odd sixpenny piece. The pair remained silent for sometime, enjoying the cosy atmosphere and soaking up the heat from the fire, Mrs Sandsfoot looking into Robert's eyes and gently stroking his hand; the softness of her touch reminded Robert of his mother stroking his face when he was a child, and he felt the tears spring into his eyes.

Very softly Mrs Sandsfoot started to speak. 'So you found the ruins of my family's original house.' It flashed into Robert's mind that she therefore knew about his betrayal and almost giggled when he thought, *I wonder if that gossip in the grocer's shop told her that.* Her eyes lifted to an ornately

94

framed picture above the fireplace. 'Those are my ancestors,' she continued, 'they lived in that house for two hundred years.'

Another thought flew through Robert's mind, *I wonder if she knows what the cells were used for in our cellar,* and flitted quickly to another tack, *I expect she wants me to stay away from the ruins,* but he was completely wrong in this assumption. Mrs Sandsfoot, still speaking in a very soft voice, told Robert that she knew what had happened with his brother and that she understood what he was going through because she had endured a similar experience when she had been a little girl. She told of how, when only about his age, she had been living in this very house when this very room had been her bedroom.

Her older brother, who was eventually killed in the war, was about five years older than she and would, had he not been killed, have become Master of the Sandsfoot estate. Her father routinely kept a battered old biscuit tin with a small amount of cash in it. Mrs Sandsfoot called it 'petty cash' and Robert made a mental note to check up on that later on. Several people used this supply of cash, her parents, the manager, and sometimes the estate foreman, but there existed a standing rule that if any money was removed it must always be supported by a receipt. Neither Mrs Sandsfoot nor her brother were yet old enough to be allowed to touch the petty cash. However, it had become apparent, over a period of months, that money was being taken from the tin without such supporting receipts.

Her father had, for some time, laughed it off and suggested that it was his wife's 'dotty brain,' forgetting how the system worked; she was after all the most frequent user of this reserve of cash for various household expenses. The situation became more sinister as time passed and the thieving, as her father now considered it, continued. He no longer thought that it was the fault of his wife but suspected that it was either the manager or foreman stealing from him. The petty cash system could not be discarded, it was needed in order for the estate to run efficiently and it would have been impossible for her parents to deal with everything.

Robert was becoming increasingly interested in Mrs Sandsfoot's story but his quick mind had just noticed an anomaly. Why did Mrs Sandsfoot still have the family name? She was a girl and would clearly have married someone with a different name. Mrs Sandsfoot welcomed Robert's question, which interrupted her story, he was showing some interest in something, at last!

She asked what Robert would like to hear first, the completion of the story about who was stealing the money or an explanation about her married name. 'Your name,' said Robert, and Mrs Sandsfoot explained that she had asked her husband, before they were married, if he would agree to change his name to Sandsfoot.

'His love for me was great enough to do it,' she said, quite simply.

'And the money?' Mrs Sandsfoot said that she had been passing the manager's office one day, where the petty cash tin was kept, and had seen her own dear brother remove some money from the tin. She now faced the same quandary that Robert had faced: should she tell her father or mother about what she had seen? She, of course, loved her brother as Robert loved his, and had wrestled with her conscience for several weeks before deciding that she must inform her parents about what she had seen. It would have been most unfair to both the manager and foreman to have left them under suspicion for any longer, and, of course, she may well have been a suspect herself.

Her father had thrashed her brother and, within a few weeks, had packed him off to boarding school. She had seen little of her brother since. He progressed from boarding school to university and then transferred immediately from university to the military, finally meeting his fate in the war. The confession had clearly opened old wounds and Mrs Sandsfoot was now quietly crying and dabbing at her eyes with a fine lace handkerchief. Robert's heart went out to her, clearly reliving her harrowing experience had upset her greatly. She told him how she had felt after betraying her brother and her thoughts and feelings so closely mirrored Robert's that he was amazed. She said that even after all the years that had passed since the event, the memories still caused her great pain, and, she supposed, she would never ever really forgive herself.

However, she added, as she grew older she realised that her actions were, in fact, quite correct; she had done what she considered to be the right thing at the time. She now looked deeply into Robert's eyes and asked, 'Do you think that what you did for your brother was the right thing to do?' The directness of the question caused some consternation and Robert thought hard for a few seconds. He was feeling distinctly better and quite hungry; it was amazing just how quickly his spirits had risen, just knowing that someone as important and grand as Mrs Sandsfoot could have had the same sort of experience as he filled him with wonder.

Yes he had acted correctly, he knew that now. Albert could not have lasted for long in that cellar; the cold and hunger would have eventually become unbearable and he had been duty-bound to obey his father; it was a simple matter of loyalty to one or the other and he had made his choice. Mrs Sandsfoot reached down the side of her chair and handed Robert a most beautiful air rifle, with a delicately engraved stock together with three tins of pellets. 'This was my brother's,' Mrs Sandsfoot told him as she handed over the gift, 'I want you to have it with my love.' The surprise and generosity of the gift launched Robert into tears and he lay sobbing in the arms of Mrs Sandsfoot, she too sobbing gently; the grand lady and the farm-boy remained thus linked in mutual understanding and support for some minutes.

She eventually asked Robert if he was ready to join in the Christmas party. Robert said that he was and they both stood up and left the room to return to the ballroom, again holding hands. As they left the room Robert knew that although he now accepted that he had done the right thing, he very much doubted, like Mrs Sandsfoot, that he would be able to fully forgive himself for his actions. But he could now live with himself and looked forward to taking his rifle out into the estate for some practice. He wanted to go back to school, be with his father especially, and to be happy again.

From that day on, his feelings for Mrs Sandsfoot deepened and he could not refuse any request from her to run whatever errand she wished. Overjoyed at his sudden return to normality, Robert's mother did not seem too surprised at the appearance of the air rifle, and Robert suspected some collusion between his mother and Mrs Sandsfoot. The night after the party, he lay in his bed reviewing the day's events, as he did most days before falling asleep. He could not get Mrs Sandsfoot out of his mind and eventually fell into a very deep, very long, and very peaceful sleep, the first he had managed for a long time. The last thing he remembered, before the healing oblivion of sleep, was Mrs Sandsfoot saying, as they left her small private sitting-room, 'And, Robert, you must remember to take me to the cellar, for I have never seen it.'

Robert did not know what unsettled his father, whether it was the incident over Albert's running away from the remand home, Robert's decline in health and demeanour, the death of Tuscan, or the perceived break up of his family. Approaching national service, Ronald, who they saw very little of these days, was still living in digs on another estate some miles away. He was courting a young lass, the daughter of his employer's gamekeeper, and had little time for visiting his family. At the time, Albert was still in the remand home, and all of this, combined with Robert's period of severe depression, must have taken a toll on father. Whatever the reason, father had become dissatisfied, and the family left the estate and moved to a small farm some 40 miles away, on the edge of the small market town of Alton.

Robert had no inkling of the impending move, the subject was not discussed with him or at any time when he might overhear. The removal lorry, really just an old horsebox cleaned out for the move, arrived outside the cottage, as it had on so many previous occasions when he was a small boy. Their possessions, such as they were, were quickly carried out to the lorry, and Robert, now a robust 12-year-old was expected to do his bit. His father and the driver of the lorry carried the heavier items out of the house, and Robert and his mother teamed up to carry the smaller pieces. When they picked up the large base of his parents' bed, Robert noticed that his father's bed-spanner was still tied onto one of the large metal springs, still on the same piece of string, and Robert made himself a promise: *if we ever return to this estate, I will cut that piece of string and throw the spanner into the lake.*

He was very quiet whilst helping his mother load the lorry and was feeling extremely depressed; his life on the estate had been an extremely happy one, except for the betrayal of his brother, about which he still punished himself by identifying the incident as a *betrayal* rather than calling it something less upsetting. His mind drifted and he considered how his life might change after leaving all his friends in the village and also, most especially, leaving Mrs Sandsfoot.

He had seen her often, after that Christmas Eve party. He had taken to calling at the big farmhouse most evenings, under the pretence of taking one of the farm's dogs for a walk. They had grown very close and on many an occasion Mrs Sandsfoot had accompanied him on his walks. They chatted easily in one another's company, or sat by one of the lakes quietly watching the wildlife.

He remembered the day, during the February after *that* Christmas party, when Mrs Sandsfoot asked Robert to show her the cellar. It was a bright, sunny, cold day, not a cloud in the sky, and there had been a hard frost. Robert had called at the back door to the farmhouse and asked Mrs Sandsfoot if he could take one of the dogs out. She replied, as always, that yes, he was quite welcome to take one of the dogs but added that she had also planned for a trip to see the cellar in the ruins.

Robert was not in the least perturbed by this suggestion, he had been contemplating it for several weeks and had come to terms with the fact that it was inevitable. He had not answered Mrs Sandsfoot as they left her sitting-room at Christmas, but the unspoken agreement had been made, Robert would show her the cellar. They left the farmhouse, the golden retrievers running off in front, and headed off along the lane towards the ruins.

The dogs, Bosun and Kitchy, were not on leads and ran freely as they walked. Again Robert did not take the easiest route along the track; not this time for any malicious reason, but because he wanted to prolong the expedition. As they approached the ruins, the dogs put up a brace of pheasant, and Mrs Sandsfoot imitated the action of raising a shotgun and said, very loudly, 'Bang bang, got you!'

Robert stood by the entrance down into the cellar waiting for Mrs Sandsfoot to catch up, she had stopped and was standing in the midst of the ruins, with one of the remaining arched walls behind her. The sun, low in the winter sky, was shining through the arched outline of a window in a beautiful, brightly golden sunbeam, and the sight of her calmed Robert's tormented thoughts, reliving the events of that fateful night. He would forever picture her thus, standing in that sunbeam, whenever he thought of her in the future, and her silently mouthed 'steady, Robert' would calm his fears about whatever might be troubling him, just as it did at that moment.

As time passed, the memory faded slightly and he could no longer see her face, just the outline of her body. It was to become his bedrock in life and it was to this memory that his mind inevitably returned whenever any major decision needed to be made; his mind's eye saw himself standing by the entrance to the cellar, dressed still in his old short trousers and wellies, with one hand on the fallen branch and one of the Labradors standing next to him, as he silently discussed any vexing problem or situation with the vision standing in front of him.

Access down into the cellars was not possible: the rope had been removed and Robert doubted whether he or Mrs Sandsfoot were capable of climbing back out without it. She lay on the ground and shone a powerful torch into the opening but made no comment. They discussed the possible use of the cells but Mrs Sandsfoot was unable to offer any definite usage for them, apart from suggesting that they were probably where the family had kept their store of wines, spices, and other treasured supplies.

Rudely returned to the preparations for the move, Robert heard his mother tell him to 'stir his stumps' and his mind quickly returned to his present activity, now almost complete, that of loading the lorry for the family's move to Alton. He was somewhat overwhelmed by his thoughts of Mrs Sandsfoot and asked his mother if he might go for a last look around the estate. His mother readily agreed, for she could see how upset Robert was and feared a return of his terrible depression.

Seeking only solitude, Robert did not go far, about a mile into the estate to the edge of one of the lakes. He lay there on his back, looking up into a mackerel sky, watching the clouds changing formation; after a while it seemed as if it were he rushing through space rather than the clouds being blown by the wind. It was a most unusual sensation and he had to force his mind to discount what he was imagining. His thoughts turned to the six happy years that he had spent on the estate. He remembered the winter estate tasks on which he had accompanied his father: ploughing the fields, cutting back the hedgerows, digging out the ditches, road repairs, painting, cleaning, repairing buildings and machinery, forestry, log-cutting, re-thatching, etc.

The fast moving clouds lulled his senses into a state of peace and tranquillity and he recalled the first time he had been allowed to accompany the rest of the estate workers on the annual shoot. He would earn two shillings and sixpence as a beater, the locally recruited helpers who spanned out in extended lines and noisily swept the fields and copses of game towards the waiting guns. These shoots were confined to the winter months, usually from about November until Christmas, and Robert was about seven when he was first allowed to take part. He worried all day about the fact that they were beating *toward* the guns and could not work out, in his mind, how the beaters would avoid being shot. It all became clear later in the day, when he saw that all the guns were shooting into the sky, at game on the wing, so there was little danger of the beaters being hit.

With a small smile he remembered how excited and thrilled he had been when he had staggered into his mother's waiting arms that evening, clutching the brace of pheasant and half a crown that Mrs Standsfoot had given him. He had insisted that his mother take the half crown and felt quite grown up as it occurred to him that he was now earning his keep. He was soaked to the skin from the neck down: the last sweep of the day had been through a field of kale, grown for cattle food and which grew taller than Robert. It had rained during the day, and the leaves of the kale were still full of water, which splashed in all directions when moved, drenching him as he struggled through the field. He could not see where he was going and had to jump up and down to keep in line.

As he lay, deep in thought, one of the clouds above him suddenly took the shape of a cup and Robert thought of the story his father had told him about his grandparents. The elderly couple had lost their teeth, a common event amongst the elderly in those days, and each had a set of false ones. The false sets of teeth were removed each night, carefully cleaned and put into a cup for overnight soaking. Father said that it had been so cold one winter that the water had frozen and his grandparents had each awoken to a frozen, toothy lollipop. Before he had been told this story, Robert had not noticed that his own parents had also both had their teeth removed and each wore a set of 'falsies,' as his mother called them. For some time, after his father had told him this story, Robert would dash into the kitchen, on the days when he awoke before his parents, to see if the two glasses containing the falsies on the windowsill over the sink, had frozen. One of Robert's biggest fears was that of having his teeth removed, like his parents, and he therefore diligently cleaned his teeth morning and evening.

The clouds seemed to be feeding his memory, their shapes continually changing and nourishing his brain with other memories. He saw clearly the shape of a ferret and his memory banks spilled out the well-loved outings with his father and brothers to catch rabbits. Father kept two ferrets called '*it*' and '*im*'. An unfortunate choice of names because the conversations got quite confusing with so many 'its' and 'ims'. *It* was brown and white whilst *im* was black and white. Both ferrets were ferocious, vicious creatures, in Robert's eyes, and he distrusted them completely. As often as possible, father encouraged the boys to pick up and hold the ferrets so that the animals would, eventually, become accustomed to human handling; but he was careful to explain to them the importance of being gentle. If the ferrets felt in any way threatened, by even the slightest of squeezes, their short, sharp teeth snapped together into the nearest flesh. And, father added, when a ferret bites it hangs on and is reluctant to let go.

Robert was never bitten: his distrust and wariness around these fierce creatures, together with his father's warning and the sight of his brother Ronald dancing around with a ferret hanging from his thumb, ensured that Robert developed the softest of hands when picking them up. He avoided touching the ferrets whenever possible; he carefully refrained from looking directly into the animals' eyes, which were the deepest, coldest eyes that Robert had ever seen, with not the slightest hint of softness, recognition or emotion.

Unlike his son, father seemed quite at home with the pair of ferrets, taking them out of their incredibly smelly cages, kept in the old garden shed, and bringing them into the house. That odd sounding *tch tch* sound that mother made with her tongue usually gave warning of the ferrets'

104

arrival indoors, a sound that indicated her deepest displeasure and opposition to the ferrets sharing the house. Their smell was offensive, even to humans, and it lingered *so*. Much like the smell of father's obnoxious roll-up cigarettes, their smell seemed to permeate every fibre of furniture and clothing. The ferrets busily climbed all over father, sitting in his old armchair, they snuggled into any opening, inside his waistcoat and shirt, in his trouser pockets and up his trouser leg.

Whenever father brought them into the house, the boys would watch for only a short while and then, miraculously, find something that urgently needed their attention elsewhere; father was a very kindly and generous man and could be relied upon to share his pets with anyone else in the room, assuming, of course, that they were silly enough to hang around that long!

There was an abundance of rabbits on the estate, far too many from the landowner's point of view, for they were regarded as pests and feasted heavily on the lush green corn seedlings as they sprouted above ground. The family used rabbits as both a food source and a method of generating a little extra income; the local butcher gladly accepted a dozen or so rabbits, hanging the carcasses on large metal hooks outside his shop, at a much inflated price of course.

Skinning the rabbits was mother's job, as was boning them and cutting the meat into chunky pieces for cooking. Served in a vegetable stew with chunks of home-made, butter-laden dunking bread – absolutely delicious. The only preparation of the rabbit that mother did not have to do was the removal of the gut; father or the boys accomplished this with their trusty pocket knives; and the only preparation that mother refused to do was beheading, a task usually delegated to the lowest ranking member of the family (namely Robert), which he completed using the small axe that was normally used for chopping kindling for the fires. Such was his skill at this task that it usually required a single sharp chop to sever the head.

The boys, Robert in particular, were always keen to accompany their father on a rabbiting expedition. The *'ampshire boys* following their father to the cages at the end of the garden, each hoping not to be selected to remove *it* and *im* from their cages and transfer them into two individual small hessian sacks, especially made for this purpose by mother from disused and damaged potato sacks. The openings of the sacks were firmly tied with a piece of string to prevent the ferrets escaping. The small, permanently agitated animals, were well used to this treatment and seemed to calm down as soon as they were placed into the darkness of the sacks.

Although the rabbit population was legion, father had explained to his sons the importance of rotation when harvesting the fruits of the many rabbit warrens, usually leaving a return visit for about a year or so. As they walked through the estate there was no shortage of rabbit warrens; they were usually built on rising ground in the hedgerows or copses where normal farming activity and flooding would not disturb them.

Evidence of current usage was all around their chosen warren, numerous entrances, fresh diggings and droppings. In father's large khaki ex-army kitbag he carried the other necessary tools for this activity, string nets about 2 foot square, wooden pegs, a couple of Paddy's screwdrivers and some old pieces of canvas to sit upon. It was a time-consuming task, stretching and pegging the nets covering all the entrances to the warren, which sometimes reached as many as 20, and, when this was completed, the team of *'ampshire boys* usually stretched out for a short rest and a swig of lukewarm tea. If the number of holes exceeded the number of nets available, the remaining holes would be filled in with a mixture of stones and soil firmly tramped deep into the holes.

When the time came for the ferrets to be taken from their sacks to be inserted into the nearest hole, the boys took up their well-spaced positions around the warren. Knowing what was expected of them, from many such previous outings, the ferrets would instantly disappear out of sight into the darkness of the hole. An expectant atmosphere then fell over the hunters, kneeling over their assigned netted hole, heavy sticks raised in preparation for the strike.

It was very much a waiting game and little happened for several minutes, except that the frenzied noise of many running feet could be heard, very faintly, if an ear was placed close to the ground. Total surprise was Robert's usual reaction to the sudden explosive emergence of the rabbits seeking escape from the unseen menace of the ferrets, their smell spreading rapidly around the burrow; as he often drifted away, *bum on broomstick* during the wait. Their intended prey burst from their holes and became entangled in the nets; it was then just a case of grabbing the rabbit, either by the ears or the back legs, despatching it and resetting the net. Despatching their prey was not a gory bloodbath of shooting guns or pounding sticks. The rabbits, stunned by a single blow from the heavy sticks, were held by the rear legs with one hand, the other hand around its throat; a quick stretch and turn and the job was done.

It required considerable arm and shoulder strength to complete this killing manoeuvre and Robert was not strong enough to complete this task himself until he was about eleven years old. Even grabbing and holding some of the bigger rabbits was too much for a small boy; he usually hopped around replacing the nets and popping the dead rabbits, discarded quickly by his father and brothers so that they could deal more quickly with another, into the now empty kitbag. Two dozen rabbits was not an unusual bag

107

from these expeditions, which provided a dozen for the table and a dozen for the butcher.

Still lying on the ground, gazing up at the clouds, Robert gathered his wits and dragged his mind back to the present: *Well, I've got to go sometime so it might as well be now.* He jumped up and strode purposefully back towards the waiting, loaded lorry. He angled his return slightly so that he might call in at the big house and say his farewells to Mrs Sandsfoot. Knocking at the back door, he was, eventually, greeted by the estate manager who said that unfortunately the whole family was out in the car. Politely Robert left his farewells to the estate and the Sandsfoot family with the estate manager and walked back to their cottage.

The ancient lorry was now fully loaded and mother was scrubbing the kitchen floor for the last time; she said she did not want the next family to think she was untidy. The effort seemed a waste of time to Robert, since the incoming family would make quite a mess going to and fro with their possessions. Getting a tad ratty, father eventually chivvied mother out of the house and into the lorry. A huge cloud of black smoke broiled out of the lorry's exhaust-pipe, there was a grinding of the gears, and they were gone.

Handkerchief in hand, mother was in tears and it took a huge effort from Robert not to succumb to a terrible urge to join in, but he was now 12 and regarded himself as fully grown, and men, his father had said to him on numerous occasions, do not shed tears.

The lorry meandered through the country lanes, striving to exceed its maximum speed of about 25 miles an hour, encouraged by the agitated stamping on the throttle (Robert thought of it as a foot throttle, as in the tractor, rather than an accelerator), and the swaying and pushing on the steering wheel by the driver in his efforts to make the lorry go faster. *Probably trying to push the bleeding thing,* thought Robert.

3

Alton

It took almost three hours to travel the 40 miles or so from the estate near Andover to their new home at Alton. When they arrived Robert was astounded to see that the house was not deep in the country, as he had been expecting, but on the very edge of the town, in a row of terraced cottages opposite a large, lush, green park. The house itself looked quite old, but to both his and his mother's delight it had an indoor toilet, proper bathroom with a big bath at one end, and indoor plumbing with both hot and cold water at the taps. There were three bedrooms, one for his parents, one for Robert, and one for Albert who, father said, might be coming home from the remand home quite soon. At one end of the row of cottages was a small grocers and general store, and Robert's first thought was that he would, at least, not have to walk quite so far for father's tobacco supplies.

Their cottage was in the middle of the block and their immediate neighbours, on both sides, were elderly people, reclusive and rarely seen. As far as Robert could ever discover, none of the occupants of the row of cottages were country folk. At the other end of the cottages, opposite the park, there was a small lane, which sloped downhill, under the railway line, past an old mill, and up a very long, twisting lane to the farm where father was to work. Opposite the old mill, to Robert's delight, was the town's refuse tip and this was to be the scene of many happy days in the future.

The family settled into the cottage as best they could. It was a strange first few weeks; not even father, whom Robert assumed had instigated the move from the estate, seemed very happy. It was obvious to Robert that his mother certainly wasn't, although she tried very hard to hide the fact from both him and his father. She seemed to have lost her contentment. She did not express this discontent to Robert or father, but Robert was aware of it. Her normally bright and sunny disposition seemed to have disappeared the moment she had first seen the new house.

She had always seemed so happy with her life and her *'ampshire boys*, despite the hard work and hardships of country life, but, Robert thought, in a moment of sudden realisation, she had undergone a particularly trying period. A period most mothers probably face at one time or another, the family growing up, striving towards their own independence, making and solving their own problems. Her team of *'ampshire boys* were no more, at least not in terms of collectivity, for Albert was still in the remand home and Ronald was now over 40 miles away. She had been uprooted – a good description Robert thought – as into his mind leapt the memory of an enormous oak tree that had been blown down during a gale, back on the estate.

This once mighty tree was lying on its side in the middle of a large 20 acre field and had once been a favourite climbing tree for the brothers, its foliage still green and, it appeared, still alive. However, on closer inspection, the thick roots, with thin jagged strips at the breaks, bearing evidence of the tree's efforts to survive, were ripped from the ground and poking through an enormous bowl of earth. The tree had remained where it fell, the estate

110

workers had, over time, trimmed away most of the branches, but the large trunk had been left as a jump for the winter hunt meetings. If trees have feelings, and Robert was never quite sure, then that tree must surely have felt as mother was feeling now; once so strong and confident, standing tall in the sunlight, now looking towards an unknown and uncertain future.

Seeking to delay the inevitable, Robert had asked his father if he might delay his first day at his new school. He was extremely apprehensive about this forthcoming event: it would not be like his move from junior to secondary school when he had his brother and all his friends doing the same thing, laughing, joking and skylarking on the bus, and generally supporting one another. It was easy, Robert reflected, to be confident and brave in a group, but not so simple on your own. Rather surprisingly, father allowed him a week before starting, during which time he would accompany father to the farm each day, to stay out of sight.

During the evenings of that first week, Robert walked all around the town and surrounding area, getting his bearings. He found the secondary school to which he would walk each day; it was only about a mile away from the cottage, a mere hop, skip and jump to a country boy. He did notice, however, that all of the boys his age were wearing long trousers and thought, self-consciously of those that might see him, *hope they think I'm just big for my age.* Knowing that if he turned up at school the following Monday morning in short trousers he would be in for some serious teasing, he resolved to ask his parents to fork out for a pair of long trousers.

As expected, Robert's initial request, made to his father, fell on deaf ears! However, this did not deter Robert; he knew that, despite his father's dire warning 'not to ask your mother,' that she would be his next target. In the usual

111

scheme of parent responses, his mother asked, when faced with the same request for long trousers, 'What did your father say?'

Why do *they*, and they in this case were the enemy, the opposition, always do that? Robert wondered. They must have discussed the matter otherwise how could mother have known that he had already asked his father? *Not fair.* The accusation flew into Robert's mind; *they're ganging up on me!* He mulled the problem over in his mind for a while until he decided, craftily, *Two can play at that game, mother,* and replied, 'He told me to speak to you, mother,' lying through his teeth.

Later when mother produced the longed-for pair of long-legged, grey trousers, Robert was overjoyed and silently summed up the entire rigmarole: *Well that will help a little next Monday morning, but why all the fuss and games? Why not, if they had intended all along to let him have the trousers, just agree straight away!* Surprises are fine, but not at the cost of so much heartache.

The trousers, his first pair of grown-up trousers, the item of clothing he had longed for since he had gone up to the secondary school at Andover, were awful. Probably two sizes too big for him, made of heavy grey flannel with huge turn-ups, he needed one of father's old leather belts to stop them from falling around his ankles. But with his long, sleeveless pullover pulled well down, they didn't look too bad, if you ignored the lumps and bumps around the waistline. He stood there, the first time he tried them on, in front of the full-length mirror in the door of mother's wardrobe, looking at his reflection. He saw a very small boy in a very large pair of trousers, but they *were* long, very long. *I look like a right wazzock*, Robert decided. In an attempt to assuage her son's disappointment, mother said she would try to turn up the legs for him; that way they would last him a bit longer, which would make a huge difference. Thinking it unlikely that the trousers would last until he was 30, Robert realised that it would most certainly take him that long to grow into them!

Nevertheless, on the following Monday morning Robert left the house at about 8.15. He could no more eat breakfast than he could sleep the night before and left the house in plenty of time to walk to the school. When he arrived at the school he walked up to the front entrance, a large imposing door, opened it and entered into the highly polished hallway; only to be greeted by an irate member of staff shouting at him to go around the side. His attempts to explain that he was a new boy were totally ignored. The person seemed to be in an all-consuming rage, shouting once again for Robert to go around to the side entrance 'with all the other yobs,' all the time waving his briefcase in the air. 'Yobs!' The derogatory outburst coursed through Robert's head. *That's a new one on me, obviously not an 'ampshire boy but definitely a proper wazzock.*

The teacher had spoken in a very posh but threatening voice, which unsettled him badly and totally removed whatever little confidence he had been able to muster whilst walking to school. The voice, however, reminded Robert of Mrs Sandsfoot who also spoke in a soft posh voice, a bit like the Queen. Immediately the vision of her standing in the sunbeam came to him and he saw, once again, the silently mouthed words, 'Steady, Robert.' Confidence restored, Robert looked the teacher straight in the eye, lifted himself to his full 5 foot 1 inch, said very politely and in an almost faultless imitation of Mrs Sandsfoot, 'I'm very sorry, sir,' emphasising the 'sir', turned and went back out of the door. He was no longer afraid, not even when he found himself standing outside the Headmaster's study a few minutes later, waiting to be assigned his class.

He seemed to have found an inner strength and discovered that if he kept *the vision* in his mind and spoke slowly and carefully then everything seemed to go so much more smoothly. He did not see the Headmaster. Instead a young lady, who said she was the school secretary, took him along to her office. After many questions and much filling in of forms, Robert was taken to his class, 3D. They both entered the classroom, and the school secretary handed a form to the class teacher, said quite simply, 'This is Leonard,' and left. Glancing quickly at the blackboard, Robert saw that the class had been doing mathematics prior to his arrival. Long division, noticed Robert, *piece of cake!*

The teacher, a Mr Roberts, seemed to be a kindly person, softly spoken and friendly; he pointed to a vacant desk and told Robert to sit down. Given a few moments of silence, allowing Robert time to reach his desk, Mr Roberts said, 'Class!' his voice imbued with a little more authority, and returned to the lesson. He was to be the only teacher that day and for several days to come, who did not embarrass Robert, sometimes to the point of tears, by insisting that he stand in front of the class and 'tell the class about yourself!'

The rest of the day went quite well, despite the fact that Mr Roberts seemed to think that Robert's Christian name was Leonard. The teacher had instructed one of the other boys to ensure that Robert got to the right places at the right times, and the boy, Jimmy Warrington, dutifully led him around. From classroom to classroom, Robert traipsed behind Jimmy until dinner time, then to the dining-hall for dinner, and again, in the afternoon, around the classrooms until it was time *at last* to go home.

Since their homes were located at the same end of the town, Robert and Jimmy walked part of the way home together. Jimmy lived on the council estate at the far end of the park opposite Robert's home. They agreed that Robert would call for Jimmy in the morning and complete the walk to school together. Alton Secondary School was much the same as any other, Robert realised, later that

114

evening when he went early to bed. He was feeling very tired: the emotional strain of his first day at a new school and his sleepless night had left him feeling drained.

The school was very similar to Andover: the lessons were the same, in fact they seemed to be continually going over previously covered subjects that he had tackled during his first year of secondary school. Long division, for example. Robert had been through the lesson on several different occasions, both in his latter junior days and last year at Andover, and he could almost quote the lesson word for word! The only changes were the other pupils and the teachers, but with Mrs Sandsfoot silently supporting him he knew that any unforeseen problems would not overwhelm him. However, he was, deep down, extremely relieved that the school work wasn't so different; life would have been so much more difficult had it been so.

All things considered, Robert settled into his new school quite quickly, helped not inconsiderably by Jimmy, who quickly became Robert's willing companion in all escapades and adventures that were to befall them over the next two years. The school itself was spread over a large area with very large, high-ceilinged, well-lit classrooms. It had a well-equipped gymnasium and large playgrounds and sports fields. Large corridors linked the classrooms within the buildings, which would become a hive of boisterous activity when pupils changed from one classroom to the next.

Unlike junior school and, to a large extent, Andover Secondary, pupils were not confined to a single classroom for the whole day, but went to the classroom where the appropriate subject was usually taught. Thus, maths, English, geography, history, etc. would be carried out in different classrooms, which meant a lot of chopping and changing around, which, for Robert, would have been completely unmanageable without his good friend Jimmy.

During the summer months it would become intolerably

hot in the classrooms, the tall glass windows no longer a boon, and on some days, particularly during Robert's less interesting subjects like religious education, he would gaze up into the cloudless sky and drift off, *bum on broomstick*; only to be brought back to earth by a piece of chalk whizzing by his ear or a hand descending on his shoulder!

Despite his occasional lapses in concentration, Robert considered himself to be a model student; he rarely took part in classroom pranks, sat still most of the time, was always willing to put up his hand and attempt an answer to any teacher's questions, and generally behaved himself.

He did get into some problems in his RE class; any blossoming belief in the Almighty had been shattered by his being forced, in Robert's opinion by *Him*, to leave the estate. Robert continually badgered the RE teacher about the events of his life that had been adversely affected by *Him* and, thinking back, he could identify nothing in his parents' actions that had precipitated their move, so it must have been *Him* up to his old tricks. The stories of Jesus feeding the multitude with a couple of slices of bread and a few fishes, and of parting the seas, were, to the practical farm-boy, quite preposterous. In truth, Robert had some difficulty in grasping exactly what the sea was anyway; he had seen the maps of the world etc. and knew that they were great expanses of water, but he had never been to the seaside so had no first-hand experience. How deep were they? What was on the bottom of them? How big did the waves get? How did a person find their way across them? Exactly how many fish were in them? And the mind boggling question of just how did they remain salty, if fresh, clean, drinkable rain fell on the land surfaces and eventually fed back into the seas to replenish them? How the hell could they still be salty after all these millions of years? His mind was full of such questions but all the teachers mentioned were their names, the Atlantic, the Pacific, the

Mediterranean etc., deferring Robert's questions with the usual, 'We won't go into that today, thank you, Leonard.'

No child can possibly avoid all trouble and somehow during that first summer at his new school Robert did manage to get into a few troublesome spots. The very first day, when he had walked into Mr Roberts' classroom, he had been seated at the desk behind a pretty little girl called Patricia. She was always very nicely dressed, clean and was the cleverest person in the class. Unfortunately for her, she also sat in front of Robert in RE! She had very long dark hair, which was at times twisted into two pigtails and at other times twisted into one big, fat one. At the end of the pigtail, or tails, were dainty, meticulously tied, colourful ribbons.

It was Patricia's misfortune one hot summer afternoon to be sitting in front of Robert during a particularly boring RE lesson. As was his custom when totally disinterested in his surroundings, Robert had been off, *bum on broomstick*, and had returned to awareness just in time to catch the end of a question, thrown at the class by the RE teacher. Everyone waited expectantly (and some no doubt fearfully) to see who would be chosen to provide the answer. Fearful that he might be required to provide an answer to the unheard question, Robert was greatly relieved when some other, hopefully more alert student, was chosen to display his understanding of the lesson, and his mind started to wander once again. He started to fiddle with the ink-well on his desk. A hole had been strategically placed in the centre of the desk, near the front edge, and Robert began to wonder just why it had been placed in the centre and not adjacent to his right hand, in which he normally held his pen. 'Ah ha,' said Robert, without realising he had said it aloud.

'And what, Master Robert, does the ah ha indicate, have you come to some meaningful conclusion that you might wish to share with the class?' the teacher asked. Caught completely unawares, he cleared his throat which had suddenly become constricted, and, thinking rapidly, mumbled something about the moral of the story having just become clear to him.

A time-consuming punishment was awarded: Robert was invited to write the meaning of the word 'moral' 100 times and present it the following day. *You idiot*, Robert chastised himself, *I bet that wazzock has been just waiting for a chance to give you a few lines!* He was so miffed with himself that he returned to fiddling with the ink-well, and, as he did so, Patricia turned her head to one side, which pushed the one big, fat pigtail across Robert's hand. It was then that Robert realised he could, if he stretched forward, reach the pigtail. He also found that, if he was very careful, he could pick up the pigtail and could pull it towards him, not only that but, joy of joys, it would also reach the ink-well!

After the class snitch had told the RE teacher what Robert had done he was told to report to the Headmaster's office, his mind immediately leaping back to the cane in previous years, and he had to once again call upon his *vision* whilst trudging disconsolately along the cavernous corridors.

He was quite calm when he walked into the Headmaster's office and was somewhat surprised to see that there was no evidence of a cane. *Keeping that as a nice surprise*, Robert guessed at the Headmaster's duplicity. In answer to the Head's request for an explanation, for dunking the fat pigtail into the ink-well, Robert decided to risk telling the truth! He explained his doubts about *Him* and how he struggled to believe in most of the RE lessons and of his thoughts about the ink-well. He said that, since Patricia had dark hair, no one would notice the ink (and indeed they wouldn't have had it not been for the sparkling white blouse she had been wearing at the time!). Robert would have much preferred a few strokes of the cane, it would have been nothing compared with writing an apology to both the RE teacher and Patricia, writing an essay on the subject matter of the earlier RE lesson together with the moral of the story, in addition to the 100 lines he had already won; all to be completed by midday the following day.

It was fortuitous that Jimmy, who to Robert's extreme surprise enjoyed the RE lessons and fully supported all *His* teachings, had not only heard the lesson but understood it fully and had taken copious notes. Robert had not the slightest inkling of what to prattle on about in his punishment essay, but luckily Jimmy produced ample evidence of their strengthening friendship by dictating an excellent appreciation of the lesson subject and completing half the lines, both boys disguising their writing as best they could. Neither Patricia nor her family made any formal complaint about the incident, but it would be a few more years before Robert discovered the reason why.

A few weeks after the family moved to Alton, Robert and Jimmy visited the town refuse tip, which they referred to as the 'dump'. This was to become their own special adventure site; everything they needed for whatever adventure or project they could devise came from this site. There were no access controls on the site, work only occurred when a loaded lorry arrived to be dumped onto the already mountainous and steaming piles of refuse. It was simply a large field, about 10 acres, fenced on all sides, with a wide metal gate, drooping on its hinges, which the boys were to find permanently open.

Gently flowing parallel with the dump ran the river Wey, about 20 feet across and up to a foot deep, with deeper pools in the lee of the roots of the large trees that grew along its banks. The river provided endless fun for the boys. Whenever they could find an empty 40-gallon oil drum, complete with its screw-in stopper, they partly rolled and partly carried it down to the river. The oil drums were used as the vehicles for their own unique and self-devised competition, which they dubbed *wey rolling*, the basis of which was to discover who could stand on the drum for the longest period and who could roll it furthest down the river. Removing the stopper allowed some water to enter the drum and ensured that, when combined with the weight of the boys, the drum rolled along the bottom of the river. A long stick helped provide balance and forward motion but it was a very delicate balancing act and required many hours of practice to travel any distance.

The trick was, of course, to avoid a full body ducking in the river, and as their skill at the competition grew, the frequency of their total immersions decreased. The boys removed their shoes and socks, the better to grip the slippery curvature of the barrels, and rolled their trousers up to the knees, but both Robert and Jimmy, before they became adept at the required balancing skills, received regular soakings. The greatest fun was when they were able to find a drum each because the competition then evolved into a mock battle in which a certain amount of pushing and shoving was quite acceptable.

Their early battles inevitably resulted in one or the other receiving an early bath in the river, following which they would run back up the lane to Robert's house to dry off. The back door to the house was kept unlocked and they were able to gain access even on those occasions when Robert's mother was out.

Strangely, the drums seemed to disappear almost as quickly as the boys found them; quite who was responsible for removing them, or to what use they put the drums, the boys did not ever discover. The two boys had built a den in a corner of the dump, made from old sheets of tin, cardboard boxes, and old carpets, and for a few weeks managed to keep a drum hidden there, but even that was eventually discovered and taken.

Old Dinky toys: cars, lorries, tractors, etc. were collected over a period of time and they built a large miniature road system on the slopes of a pile of soil that they had scraped into a cone shape. They constructed miniature bridges, garages, tunnels, lakes, rivers, and trees from the human detritus available and sometimes, during the long, warm summer holidays, spent a whole day at their dump. Most of these discarded Dinky toys were in poor condition, paint and doors broken off, and with some or all of the wheels missing; the duo was not deterred however, their imaginations filling in the missing parts.

Many prizes were unearthed at the dump, and Robert took great delight in taking things home: an old table lamp; a brush head; an old shovel or spade; all manner of bits and pieces for bicycles; spanners and tools; anything that he thought might be useful. The boys had found an old perambulator in which they piled their treasures to transport them to their homes. Both sets of parents eventually lost their patience with the ever-increasing pile of rubbish in their respective back yards, and insisted that the boys return it to the dump. Indignant at discovering that their treasures were seen as nothing but rubbish by their parents, the two friends continued to add to their ever-growing collection but stacked it in and around their den at the dump, where it remained for as long as Robert lived in the area.

The pram, now redundant as a treasure transporter, had its wheels removed and provided the basis of a trolley on which the two friends dragged each other around. Occasionally, when negotiating deep ruts, the thin section of boarding, linking the two axles and onto which the boys clung tightly, would snap, dragging their fingers along the ground and causing quite severe scrapes. Such minor injuries became a part of their lives and caused them little discomfort.

Towards the end of that first summer in Alton, Robert and Jimmy were at their favourite place, down at the dump. They had found a long piece of very thick rope and had decided to build a swing down by the river. There were several very large trees on the river banks that the boys had always wanted to climb; however, the lowest branches were too high to reach and the girth of the trunk too great to provide purchase, so they had given up all hope of ever being able to climb them.

On one particular tree the branches were so long that they virtually straddled the river, drooping back to about 15 feet above the ground on the opposite bank. The possibility of reaching one of these, if one of them stood on an upturned oil drum and threw one end of the rope over the lowest branch, was discussed for some time. The rope might then provide access to the tree.

Electing to take the first attempt, Robert grabbed one end of the thick rope; it had been agreed that if he failed then Jimmy would have his chance. Holding firmly to the other end of the rope in case Robert missed, Jimmy waited for Robert to take his turn; the last thing they wanted was to lose the rope in the river.

Honed from years of hard chores, Robert's strong right arm flexed, and he twirled the rope over his head a few times and let fly. His aim was true and the rope sailed over the branch and fell at the boys' feet. Clambering up the rope was easy for the two nimble boys and they took a few moments to sit together in joyous contemplation of their feat, finally pulling the rope up behind and isolating them in a new world of their own. Sliding along the branch on their bottoms, their feet dangling high above the water, they crossed over the river and finally made it to the trunk of the tree. Intensely excited by their achievement, the boys retied the rope to the branch, a few feet from the main trunk and shinned back down to earth on the opposite side of the river.

Although the rope was attached to the branch some thirty odd feet above them, the rope was still much too long and they had plenty of spare rope to tie knots and provide foot holds, which made climbing the rope and access to the tree that much easier. Higher in the tree they started to build a new den using, of course, whatever materials they could find from the dump. It was a long, laborious task, but eventually they had a wonderful, private retreat, which no one else, once they had pulled the rope up after them, could reach.

The labour of building their new den completed, the boys searched for other schemes involving the length of rope. After much deliberation they decided to see if they could use the rope as a pendulum to swing across the river. There was a steep slope behind their den-tree and they thought it might be possible to climb up this slope, clutching the rope, and launch oneself into space hoping to let go of the rope and land on the other side of the river.

On this occasion Robert deferred to Jimmy's decision to take the lead, and he supported the weight of the rope as his friend climbed up the slope, Robert's last-minute instructions ringing in his ears: 'Keep your feet up, don't let go too soon.' Jimmy decided to add his own last minute instruction: 'Make sure you come up the slope as high as me,' he shouted breathlessly before launching himself into space, hanging on grimly to the rope.

The system worked faultlessly, except that Jimmy landed on one of their temporarily forgotten oil drums, which they had left on the opposite bank. Above the tinkling sound of the river, Robert heard the crack, as Jimmy's leg broke, just a split second before Jimmy screamed. Stunned at the ear-splitting scream, Robert's mind, having been temporarily relieved of its decision-making properties, whirred once again into activity, as he thought how best to get help for Jimmy.

The boys were equal in size and weight and Robert knew with absolute certainty that carrying Jimmy any distance was out of the question, and he did not know what additional damage he might do to Jimmy's leg if he tried to move him. On the opposite side of the river to Jimmy, he decided that the quickest route to reach his friend was to wade across the river. The rope was dangling in the water just out of Robert's reach and, although he considered recovering the rope and going up and across the branch to drop down the other side, he considered it risky. The drop was a good 15 feet and he could easily twist an ankle or break a leg himself. Also unwilling to turn up at someone's house soaking wet and asking for assistance, he eventually settled upon a course of action, to run parallel with the river and call in at the large farmhouse about a half-mile away for help.

This decision was arrived at in seconds and he shouted to Jimmy that he was going for help before careering off through the copse toward his goal. When he arrived at the imposing front door of the farmhouse, Robert hesitated before knocking: *better go round the back, don't want a repeat of what happened at the school!* He raced around the side of the house, opened the arched side gate, and promptly tripped over a fat old cat, sitting in the middle of the path, sunning itself.

Robert was severely tempted to give the mangy-looking cat a good kicking or take out his catapult and give the wretched creature a good pelting, but he decided he did not have the time and *best not upset these people or they might not want to help Jimmy!* He knocked hard at the side door several times before it was finally opened, with an ominous squeal, by a very large man.

Robert, disconcerted for a moment at the size of the

man, gathered his wits and gabbled out his story about Jimmy; the man told him to follow him inside the house, indicating in a very deep, hoarse voice, that he was going to make a phone call to the emergency services. Robert's reluctance to follow the man into the house stemmed from his mother's warnings not to trust strangers and, in particular, not to enter into strange houses. On this occasion Robert had no choice other than to ignore his mother's instructions, relying on his own strong instinct that the man was only trying to help, and forced himself over the threshold into the house. After his phone call summoning help, the large man told Robert to wait with him until the ambulance arrived; they would need someone to guide the crew to Jimmy.

It took almost an hour before the ambulance arrived at the farmhouse, during which time Robert was subjected to a barrage of questions from the farmer whilst being refreshed with a glass of lemonade and biscuits. Reluctant to give this stranger too much personal information, Robert refused to speak about anything other than the circumstances surrounding Jimmy's accident. Clearly offended, the stranger left Robert sitting at the kitchen table. *Great,* Robert decided, *you have served your purpose.* Throughout this enforced waiting period, Robert was acutely aware that Jimmy was on his own and in pain, but he knew he must wait for help before returning to his friend.

The siren heralding the arrival of the ambulance was clearly audible long before the vehicle finally arrived at the farmhouse. Hastily tumbled into the ambulance, Robert directed the crew to the dump and then down the slope to find Jimmy, sobbing in pain, at the water's edge. After the ambulance had taken Jimmy away to hospital, Robert promised that he would call at Jimmy's house to tell his parents what had happened and secured the rope to its usual stowage.

A frosty reception awaited him at Jimmy's home; the Warringtons clearly regarded Robert as being wholly responsible for the accident to their son and they even refused Robert the courtesy of thanking him for the information. *Wazzocks!* Robert awarded them his seal of disapproval, and a darn good job it was that Jimmy did not resemble his parents too closely!

Missing his friend, Robert was at a loss as to how to entertain himself without his compatriot. Jimmy remained in hospital for a few days before being allowed home, his left leg encased in plaster from ankle to knee, struggling manfully to manipulate the crutches, which he needed to hobble around. The Warringtons were reluctant to let Jimmy out with Robert for a few more days but eventually succumbed to his constant nagging; and another old pram was forced into service to transport Jimmy down to the dump. The boys cared not one jot for the sneers and jibes from the other children, as they passed through the park on their way to the dump, they were just happy in their own company.

Tree games were out of the question, however, they still had their old den and mostly messed around with the Dinky toys, or rummaged through the loads of new refuse brought in each day. It was quite odd that no one else, particularly youngsters of their own age, made use of the dump. The boys rarely saw anyone except for feral cats and dogs, snarling at one another over the morsels of food, or a passing flock of gannets winging their way inland seeking food. It was almost as if the area was their own private adventure playground. As far as they could tell no one used the rope either although there must have been people who walked along the river's edge. They were very careful, after each visit, to pull the rope close into the trunk of the tree and keep it out of sight as much as possible.

One of the unfortunate consequences of the oil drum

games was that it reawakened another of Robert's nightmares. As a very small six-year-old, shortly after the family moved to the estate at Church Wallop, Robert had been out with his father on the farm when a seemingly inconsequential accident took place. Father had been rolling a full 40-gallon oil drum from one of the upper barns, where it had been delivered, down a fairly steep slope to the lower barns where it was normally stored for everyday use on various pieces of machinery. Moving the oil drum was a simple, effortless task: father simply toppled the drum on to its side and, keeping downhill of the drum to prevent it from rolling too quickly, allowed it to roll of its own volition down the slope.

In his customary place, Robert had been by his father's side, his hands on the drum and pushing with all his might, pretending that he, alone, was preventing the drum from rolling over him. A loose stone under father's foot caused him to lose his footing and without his weight the drum toppled over both of them. Fortunately for Robert his father took most of the weight of the drum and he was unhurt, if a little shaken. Sitting up almost immediately, Robert turned to watch the oil drum smash through the double doors into the lower barn!

The estate manager, hearing the resounding crash as the drum smashed its way into the barn, came dashing out of his office to see what had happened and to make sure they were both all right. Apologetically, father assured him that they were both uninjured and the manager returned to his hideaway, totally ignoring the damaged door!

Putting the event to the back of his mind, Robert thought no more of the incident after he had returned home and related the whole story to his mother. Several months later, just after his seventh birthday, Robert had his first oil drum nightmare. He saw himself, a tiny little person laughing happily whilst assisting his father, attempting to

127

hold a huge oil drum against the slope. As if by magic, father disappears; Robert is left alone and the slope gets progressively steeper and the footing more and more slippery until the inevitable occurs. The tiny body, arms and legs slowly draining of strength, can no longer hold the drum, and he collapses whilst the drum, achingly slowly, starts to roll down towards him until, quite suddenly, his vision blacks out as if he had indeed died. It is at that moment that he wakes up screaming, soaking wet with sweat.

This particular nightmare continued, about once a month, until he was about ten and then, to his absolute joy, quite suddenly stopped. By some trick of the mind, Jimmy's accident had once again invoked the nightmare, possibly because Robert blamed himself for his friend's pain; it really should have been him who made the first attempt at swinging across the river. Very little of the content of the nightmare had changed, the sequence of events remained as in the original, the only noticeable difference was that the two main subjects, himself and the oil drum, were larger. The nightmare was back with a vengeance and would remain with him, with no set periodicity, for some years. Having reached the age when he was old enough to count his blessings, Robert was happy that his *first* nightmare was not invoked again!

While Jimmy recovered from his accident, the boys did not see as much of one another as they might normally, and Robert spent a little more time with his father. The new job, on a dairy farm within about a mile of the dump, along a winding dirt track, which led to the isolated house and farm buildings, was vastly different to his father's work on the estate. At first Robert was keen to accompany his father, but very quickly tired of it; there was little variety in the day's work and his father's description sounded boring and repetitive.

Each day was the same for his father: get the cows into the pens; feed them a small amount of cattle cake; wash them; attach the automatic milking machine; release them back into the fields; take the full churns to the end of the winding lane; and stack them onto a raised platform for collection by a large milk lorry. Clean out the cattle shed; feed the cattle bales of hay from the store, which was stacked in one of the barns; and repeat the whole process again in the afternoon.

The most frustrating part of father's day, not only to Robert, but also, the boy suspected, to his father, was that the majority of the work was *indoors*. They were Hampshire men, they worked outside on the land in all weathers; working indoors was for poofs, pen-pushers and estate managers. Only one of the day's activities pleased the boy: he did enjoy driving the old Fordson tractor, with its very wide wheel arches, on which he perched comfortably when his father drove across the fields, sliding around in the deep mud churned up by the continual passage of the cattle. If he was forced to admit another concession, he agreed that he also enjoyed the taste of the creamy fresh milk, taken directly from the base of the rippled cooler, much like a vertical washing board, just before it dropped into the waiting churn.

The work was so different to the work on the estate where there was a huge variety of tasks requiring different skills, tools, and machinery. Robert could not understand how his father, who was so used to working on the large estate and who possessed all the necessary skills, could continue with such a monotonous existence. Privately he thought that father would not stand too much of this! It wouldn't be long before the lorry turned up one fine Saturday morning, and more new schools!

Despite his father's description of the work on the dairy farm, Robert had not actually witnessed the events, so, quite soon after Jimmy's accident, he decided that he would get up early the following morning and accompany his father on the early morning milking session. Up at five o'clock, a quick cup of tea and a bowl of porridge, and they were off, father puffing at his cigarette as they walked the mile or so up to the farm.

Robert helped as best he could, slapping the somewhat slow-witted cows across the rump with his stick when they failed to go the way in which he intended. He chained the beasts into their stalls and fed them some cattle cake, but refused to wash the muck, which could have been anything, off the engorged udders, and generally watched as his father went about his business. Before attaching the automatic milking equipment, father would grasp a fat teat in each hand and give it a squeeze. 'Gets the milk flowing,' said father! Robert tried to do the same but got little more than a quick turn of the head and a soulful gaze from the cows, sometimes accompanied by a vicious kick. Father told him to squeeze a bit harder, but he could not bring himself to do it; he was afraid of hurting the animals!

At about nine o'clock that morning the local vet turned up at the farm to do some artificial insemination. Not too sure what that meant at the time, Robert got not a little confused when his father, in answer to his question, said, 'Vet does the bull's job, boy!' Especially when the vet's arm disappeared up to the elbow in the cow's rear end! *Well,* thought Robert, *whatever happens to me, I am most definitely not going to become a vet!* A couple of years later when Robert was asked to complete a form listing his choice of professions when he left school, the teacher was mystified by Robert's answer: *not a vet!*

As that first summer in Alton came to an end and autumn followed on in its usual way, the boys were planning ahead for bonfire night. Whilst the family had lived on the estate, very little fuss was made on November 5th other than building a large bonfire in the back garden onto which, at the end of the evening, father would stack his old garden refuse for burning. A few bangs and flashes could be seen and sometimes heard from the nearby village of Church Wallop, but neither the family, nor their neighbours, ever bothered to buy fireworks. Around thatched roofs, father said that he considered them a fire hazard and refused, point blank, to allow the boys to purchase fireworks.

However, Jimmy had told Robert of a different 'big city' attitude towards Guy Fawkes night. Most families invested a few shillings on a few bangers, rockets, and sparklers for use in their back gardens together with a small bonfire. Many of the larger organisations, like the local football or rugby clubs, spent hundreds of pounds producing a public display on one of the town parks, lighting a huge bonfire, topped with its characteristic dummy and exploding an impressive display of fireworks.

The plaster had been removed from Jimmy's leg a few weeks before November 5th, bringing joy to both boys; Jimmy had been a bit unsteady for a few days after the removal but had gradually regained full use of the leg. The Warringtons had expressly forbidden Jimmy to play at the dump or the river, or to have any further association with 'that farm-boy.' Ignoring the Warringtons' strict instructions, the two friends had immediately returned to their den in the tree, swinging across the river on the long rope, always ensuring that the landing area was free of obstacles! An honorary '*ampshire boy*, it was doubtful if anything could separate the two friends.

Making their plans for fireworks night, Jimmy recalled how one of his older brothers had described how he and his friends, on a previous bonfire night, had bought a supply of bangers and had gone around the houses putting the bangers through the letter-boxes. Money was tight for the daring duo, but Jimmy had saved some money over the preceding month or so whilst he had been in plaster, and this together with the few odd shillings that Robert had begged from his mother, enabled them to buy a selection of about 20 bangers.

In mentioning his share of the firework fund, Jimmy said that he had saved his share from his pocket money, which made Robert feel quite envious because he knew there was not the slightest chance that his own parents could afford to give him any sort of regular allowance. In fact Robert was only too aware of his household's finances since his mother had encouraged him to practise his maths by adding up the weekly costs. Where the cottage on the estate had been rent free, his father was now expected to pay a weekly rent for their present home. Coal, gas, electricity, food, school dinner money, father's tobacco, and the odd item of clothing left little from father's small income, and there was very little opportunity for Robert to generate his own. Living in the town provided few opportunities to hunt rabbits, and helping with the harvest was impossible, since father now worked on a dairy farm.

The shopkeeper gladly sold the two young boys their selection of fireworks; there were no restrictions and they could be purchased in almost every corner shop. The bangers were stashed away in an old biscuit tin under Robert's bed until November 5th finally arrived.

The boys met at about 7 p.m., both armed with a box of matches and an equal share of the small, cigarette-shaped bangers, and made their way to the nearest council estate. It was quite dark except for a few well-spaced street lights, and the boys flitted from shadow to shadow, turning the approach to their quarry into another game, trying to stay out of sight as much as possible. They came to a block of two semi-detached houses; each silently crept up the path to the front door, looked over the separating fence at each other to coordinate the lighting of the fireworks, lit the short, blue touch-paper and popped the bangers through the letter boxes. Coordinated in flight, they each turned and sprinted back through the gates and up the road to a red telephone box, from behind which they peered at the houses awaiting the bangs.

A few short seconds later their efforts were rewarded when they heard two loud bangs, separated by little more than a few seconds, and were overjoyed at the amount of noise the fireworks had made. For a few seconds there was no reaction from their targets, until suddenly both the front doors opened in unison and a woman appeared at each waving their arms and shouting at each other. The boys were too far away to make out any of the words but it appeared as if the two women were accusing each other of being responsible for the bangs. Out of sight behind the telephone box, the two boys waited until the women returned inside, slamming their doors heavily behind them in anger and frustration. They were well pleased with the results of their first attack; the bangs had been impressively loud and they gave not a moment's thought to the feelings of the occupants.

During the next hour or so they made nine other attacks, always on semi-detached properties so that they could both participate in the adventure. They fully expected to get away without recognition or punishment for their evening's activities but the old adage of crime doesn't pay finally caught up with them. On the very last pair of houses, just as Jimmy was about to push the already lit banger into the house, the door opened and Jimmy was confronted by the tenant.

Mouth agape in shock at being caught *in flagrante delicto*, Jimmy dropped the banger, turned and ran, their combined hopes of not being recognised dashed as they both clearly heard the man say, 'I know you, Jimmy Warrington, I'll be round to see your father about this,' followed instantly by 'bugger!' as the banger exploded at the man's feet!

Both boys, exhilarated at their night's work but apprehensive at being caught, agreed that their money had been well spent. The fireworks had produced enough fun for one night and the scourge of the council estates returned to their homes.

The next day, after both had spent a sleepless night worrying about the consequences of their evening of fun, Jimmy told Robert that the man had called round the previous evening and spoken to his father. Furious at his youngest son's escapade, especially since he had already gone through the same experience with his older sons, Jimmy's father had been almost apoplectic, and, despite Jimmy's refusal to identify the other boy, had made the connection and had given the man Robert's identity. The tenant of their final target had also declared his intention of reporting the incident to the police, and it was thus that a few days later, just as Robert thought they had got away with it, a knock on the front door heralded the arrival of Robert's first brush with the law.

Expecting to escape unpunished and assuming that he had not been implicated with Jimmy, Robert had not told his parents of the firework adventure; it was as an adventure that the boys saw it, not something intended to cause harm or damage, just another prank! The policeman explained everything to Robert's parents, reading from a well-thumbed notebook and adding laborious notes as Robert or his parents answered the countless questions. Taken aback by this unexpected brush with authority, Robert stood, shaking at the knees, whilst the extremely fat bobby lectured him about the dangers of fireworks and how such behaviour might well, in the future, result in Robert being dragged away to remand home or prison.

After the policeman's departure, Robert fully expected to spend a few minutes reacquainting himself with the arm of his father's armchair while his father removed the big belt for punishment. However, his father must have been in a particularly lenient mood because he simply said 'you big wuss' and sent him off early to bed. Punishment for Jimmy was a little more severe and hit him where it hurt most, in his pocket, for Jimmy had his pocket money withheld for several weeks!

Christmas in the town was also very different from those that Robert had enjoyed on the estate. The town was lit with lights dangled across the High Street; every house seemed to be decorated with its own Christmas decorations and tree. Most people did not draw their curtains at this time of the year and Robert and Jimmy spent several pleasant evenings just wandering around the estates looking through windows. Not a very adventurous or exciting way for two young boys to spend an evening, but the colourful decorations, holly and mistletoe somehow captivated them and filled them with a wonderful feeling of expectation.

Since it was the festive season, Jimmy, still under withdrawal of pocket money punishment, suggested that they might try to make a few extra shillings by carol singing, and for several evenings, during the week before Christmas, the boys stood outside numerous front doors singing their hearts out. They knew only a few lines of each carol and they sang whatever came into either boy's head. Since Robert was totally tone-deaf, and Jimmy was little better, it must have sounded pretty awful, and Robert often thought that they were being paid to move on rather than in gratitude for their musical efforts! The choristers found that if they shivered violently, stamped their feet, and rubbed their hands together as the door was opened, they were sometimes given a hot drink and a crusty mince pie, in addition to a tanner or two.

Robert, reconsidering his own definition of tone-deaf, thought that it was the wrong way to explain his inability to sing, whistle or make any other noise in tune. There was nothing wrong with his ability to *hear* others, whether singing in or out of tune, it was just that he could not *make* any tuneful sound himself. Perhaps a better definition might be tone-tongued, or tone-throated!

They did, however, manage to amass a few shillings and Robert used his share to buy his father an ounce of Shag and his mother a nail-file. *Not very imaginative Christmas presents*, Robert thought as he attempted to wrap them in the colourful paper the boys had found at the dump, but as everyone kept telling him, *it's the thought that counts!*

In the Leonard household that Christmas, it was not a very joyous affair. Little spare money was available to spend on decorations; mother had picked some holly and mistletoe and put up some chain-link paper chains made from old newspapers cut into strips. His was to be the only sock hanging from the mantelpiece this year: both his brothers were unable to get home, the elder from lack of interest, and the younger, due to being detained at the education authority's pleasure. Not much point in getting up early on Christmas morning to check for exciting new toys; he already knew what Santa had struggled down his chimney to deliver – a few items of fruit for his stocking and a new pair of shoes for school.

The highlight of the day, Christmas dinner, was served at about one. Mother had subscribed to a Christmas savers account at one of the local grocery shops and they shared the usual fare. The empty chairs at the table were noticeable and seemed to further dampen mother's enthusiasm for the day, and father had to return to work shortly for the afternoon milking session. During the meal, mother made her customary Christmas Day salute, 'happy birthday, Jesus,' to which Robert responded with a doubtful grunt.

Town life was not to Robert's liking: the winter months passed slowly in a mind-numbing round of school and boredom; he saw very little of his father, and mother seemed to have lost her zest for life and had taken on a haggard look that upset the impressionable young boy.

He knew there was a problem, but the remedy, a return to their old close-knit family life, was not his to give.

During his second summer living in Alton, Robert had his second, and final brush with the law. Almost directly opposite their dump was an old mill, surrounded by high wooden fencing, and it was this fence that roused intense curiosity in the boys' minds.

The fence, in addition to its height, had a second line of defence, pieces of broken glass pushed into the wood along the top edge. The fence was much too high to allow a visual inspection of the garden beyond; there was a big brick-arched gateway into which was fitted a heavy, chained and locked gate.

However, a little way up the road, towards the railway line, there was a large oak tree and the boys discovered that, if they climbed high enough into this tree, they could see down into the protected garden. There was not much to see really, some very tidily laid out vegetable plots, a few fruit trees and bushes and a couple of free-standing small greenhouses. Along two sides there was a high brick wall and against these walls were long, lean-to greenhouses, the glass painted white to protect the fruit within from the summer sun.

The boys could not see what was in the greenhouses and both later agreed that if the owner had not painted the glass white they would not have had the overwhelming desire to find out just what was in the greenhouses, and, therefore, would not have got into any trouble. However, the heavily defended wooden fence and the painted-out glass became too much of a challenge to them and they just had to find a way of getting in and having a look.

From their vantage point in the oak tree Robert carefully inspected the rear wall of the hidden garden and, almost instantly, found what he was looking for, a tree with branches that extended quite close to the wall. Armed with the knowledge of a possible access point into the garden, the boys left the big oak tree, climbed the gate into a large field and headed off towards the tree they had selected as their entry system into the hidden garden.

As they walked across the field discussing whether or not both should make the entry or whether one should remain as a lookout, a Farnham to Alton train passed along the line behind them and emitted a *whoop-whoop* as it passed. Both boys nearly jumped out of their boots because both knew that their intentions were not strictly legal, and they turned and waved angrily at the train driver.

Arriving at the selected tree, they saw that it was not quite as big as they had at first thought. It was much higher than the wall but the branches that reached out towards the wall looked a little on the flimsy side. Nothing ventured, they climbed the tree and Robert carefully edged out on a branch that they thought would bend down to the top of the wall. The branch, they had decided, was certainly not strong enough to bear the weight of both of them.

Robert removed his old pullover and dropped it over the embedded glass as he slowly edged further out along the branch. The branch slowly dipped towards the wall and, as it came level with the top of the wall, Robert simply stepped off the branch. Elated at his success so far, Robert whispered loudly for Jimmy to do the same and sat on the top of the wall waiting for his pal to join him. Still a bit nervous about moving around in the trees, Jimmy was much slower than Robert. Actually climbing them and staying close to the main trunk was, of course, easy, but Robert, it seemed to Jimmy, always wanted to be leaping through or swinging on the branches, and his confidence had not yet returned fully to him.

Very slowly, Jimmy forced himself along the branch and eventually made it to the wall. As the branch returned upwards to its normal position, both boys realised their first error: they could not return via the tree since the branch was now out of reach! They looked down into the garden and saw that the ground level inside the garden was much lower than that on the field side, and the drop into the garden was about 8 foot. They were stranded on the wall, both undecided about whether to continue into the garden or give up. Between the devil and the deep blue sea, they were in clear view to any passers-by and in danger of discovery.

Finally, after several minutes of heated discussion, they both agreed that since they had come this far they might as well see if they could drop safely off the wall into the garden. Deciding not to risk Jimmy in any further lead attempts, Robert swung his body off the wall, holding onto the top with his fingers, and, when he was at full stretch, asked Jimmy the distance between his feet and the ground. Looking down at his friend hanging full length from the wall, Jimmy giggled and carefully estimated the drop at about 3 foot, which Robert thought was manageable.

Not without effort, Robert pushed himself away from the wall and dropped into the garden, landing nimbly on his feet, no problem! Copying Robert's demonstrated method, Jimmy launched himself from the wall and also landed safely in the garden, but when they looked back to the top of the wall it seemed enormous, much too high to jump up and grab the top, dangerous too since they would not have the protection of their pullovers covering the glass; they would have to find some other method of escaping.

There was no one in the garden, and surrounded by its high perimeter walls and fences, it seemed unusually quiet, somehow menacing in its silence; even the birds had stopped their twittering. It was in just these circumstances that Robert's mind became so fickle and troublesome and he had to force his thoughts away from the 'lav' nightmare! He shook himself, and grabbing Jimmy by the arm, dragged him off towards the nearest of the painted-out lean-to greenhouses. As they approached, Robert could see that the wall supporting the lean-to greenhouses was much higher than he had at first thought, more like 20 foot.

Everything inside the greenhouse was immaculate. The floor was beautifully paved in marble tiles, set out in intricate patterns, and at the far end there was a single wicker chair and a small, marble-topped table. *That chair must have cost a bit!* Robert fancied himself as a good judge of quality; it had a high back, large rounded arms and there were two comfortable-looking cushions on the seat.

Running along the base of the wall was a strip of soil, only about 3 foot wide, and growing out of this, neatly trained up the height and length of the entire wall, were the roots of several trees bearing the most delicious looking peaches. The boys could not resist the temptation: they would have to try the fruit, but there was none in reach, except for a couple of peaches that might be accessible if Jimmy stood on Robert's shoulders.

At that moment it was their only option and Robert leaned against the wall to steady his body as Jimmy climbed up onto his shoulders, but he still could not reach the fruit. Moving to the second lean-to greenhouse in the hope of more success, the boys were frustrated to discover that the

140

peaches were also out of reach. Feeling somewhat disconsolate, they started to explore the rest of the garden.

Tucked away in one corner of the garden was a small shed, almost out of sight since it was virtually covered in a vigorous ivy. The door was not locked and inside they found a myriad of garden implements: forks, spades, hoes, rakes, a huge wheelbarrow with a fat inflatable wheel, and *whoopee*, a ladder!

Anticipating their tasty reward, they carried the ladder back to the lean-to greenhouse, leaned it against the wall and helped themselves to three peaches each, one in each trouser pocket and one to eat straight away. No point in being greedy: by taking too many they risked discovery; that was enough for one day, they could always come back another day and the ladder would also enable them to make their escape.

They reached the top of the wall and sat there, once again using their pullovers as cushions, in the warm sunshine, wondering whether to leave the ladder against the wall or drop it back to the ground. They hoped that maybe the owner, or his gardener, might think that he had not returned it to the shed when last he had used it. Having decided not to leave it leaning against the wall, a dead giveaway, each holding one end of the ladder, the boys pushed it away from the wall, counted one, two, three, and dropped it into the garden below. Looking down they could see that it had landed exactly as they had planned, lying neatly parallel with the wall.

Dropping into the field on the return journey was no problem and they raced back to their den in the dump, elated at their escapade. The peaches certainly justified their efforts: they were delicious, sweet and juicy, with a very fine, almost hairy covering, and like nothing Robert had ever tasted before.

In the euphoria of their success, the boys sat in their den, their stomachs full of peaches. There was still a couple of hours left of the afternoon and they planned to spend a little time just lying in the den and having a little snooze, before going down to the river. Feeling strangely weary, Robert's tiredness overwhelmed him. The peaches had reminded him of a baby's soft bottom and, already planning a return to the secret garden, he smiled contentedly as he drifted off to sleep.

The boys were rudely awoken by a stick whacking on the tin roof of their den and a deep voice, which Robert identified instantly, shouting, 'Come on you tykes, out of there!' It was the same constable that had called to speak to his father after the firework escapade, and Robert's heart sank.

Climbing sleepily out of the den, Robert, ever the quick thinker, said in his most polite voice, 'Hello, constable, how are you?' Also having dozed off and awakened so suddenly, Jimmy followed Robert from the den and, without waiting for the constable to explain his interfering with their siesta, immediately launched himself into a gabbling apology for their scrumping escapade.

The tall and very fat policeman – he actually looked much larger than Robert remembered – stood in front of them patiently listening to Jimmy incriminating himself, all the time barring their way to the narrow path that led through the piles of rubbish to the road. The law enforcer stood quietly for a few seconds, quietly ruminating over Jimmy's unforced statement, before finally saying in his finest booming *you're nicked* voice, 'Well I didn't know you tykes had been scrumping, I just come over here to ask if you had seen any strangers about! But since you've been good enough to tell me about it, I suppose I had better take you back to the station and do something about it. Can't have tykes like you breaking into people's property and stealing things, can we!' The large mouth exhaled a satisfied chuckle with the final two words.

The happy bobby, having made his collar for the day, turned and led the boys back to his parked police car and opened one of the rear doors for them to get in. Arriving at the police station, a few minutes later, the two lawbreakers were shown into a small room furnished only with a large table and a few wooden, straight-backed chairs. Interview Room. The sign on the door clearly indicated its use.

The boys remained silent, sitting on the uncomfortable chairs for well over an hour, both afraid that anything they might say would be overheard by some devious listening device before the constable returned, accompanied by another man. *Making us wait, prolonging the agony* thought Robert as he sat, trying to conjure up some story that might counteract Jimmy's thoughtless outburst.

The other man was a small, plumpish, elderly man, with just a circle of snow-white hair around the top of his bald head. He wore glasses and reminded Robert of how he imagined the face of the narrator of *Journey into Space*, the radio programme he listened to as a small boy. The voice, when he spoke, actually sounded a little like the narrator, slightly foreign but soft and kindly.

'This is Mr Julienne,' the constable introduced his companion, 'he owns the gardens that you stole the peaches from this morning.'

Remaining silent, Robert was relieved to find that Jimmy had learned his lesson well, and was keeping his mouth tightly shut. The old gentleman asked why they had decided to enter his garden and how they had got in. Unsure of who was expected to answer, Robert glanced at Jimmy and the unspoken agreement was that Robert would do the explanations.

There was no point in denying their actions; Jimmy had already removed that option and Robert slowly, carefully, and calmly told the old man exactly how they had seen inside his gardens and how they had managed to get in and how many peaches they had eaten. He remained quite controlled during the telling; he had already called upon the support of Mrs Sandsfoot whilst sitting quietly with Jimmy, and his bedrock had not deserted him.

The kindly-sounding old gentleman then glanced at the constable and nodded. The latter took the opportunity to lecture them for some time on their 'appalling behaviour' and added that he would be calling round to see their parents within the next week or so. *Blimey*, Robert thought, *that means I will have to wait a week before I get the belt!* Actual punishment, reflected Robert, is not nearly as bad as the time spent waiting and anticipating that punishment and that was most probably why the constable was waiting so long before speaking to their parents.

For the whole of the next week Robert wolfed down his evening meal and shot out of the house as soon as he had finished and went to call for Jimmy; the boys had agreed that they would prefer not to be present when the constable called! After a few days of dashing out after his meal he heard his father ask mother, as Robert dashed headlong out of the house once again, 'What's the boy been up to, he's got a bee up his backside about something?'

Each night Robert had great difficulty in getting off to sleep, despite feeling very drowsy before climbing the stairs. By the time he got into his bed he was wide awake and worrying about whether the constable would call the next day. When he did manage to drift off into oblivion it was only for a few short minutes before he awoke and tossed and turned for what seemed like hours. The constable never did call on father, but Mr Julienne did!

About ten days after their scrumping expedition there came the dreaded knock at the front door to Robert's house, just before father came home from work, and there, standing on the front doorstep, was Mr Julienne. Recognising the voice, as his mother answered the door, Robert was speechless when his mother brought him into the small, sparsely furnished living-room. The consequences of their scrumping expedition had taken an unexpected turn and he adopted a chastened expression, just in case!

His mother looked puzzled as Mr Julienne introduced himself and asked, in his soft and friendly voice, if he might wait 'for the master of the house' before saying anything further about his reason for calling. Whilst mother made a cup of tea, and Robert could hear her frantically searching through the cupboards for a cup and saucer rather than their usual mugs, the old gentleman just sat and looked at Robert.

Shortly after Mr Julienne had finished his tea, father came home, his boots still spattered with cow dung and smelling pretty grim. Standing up as his father entered the room, Mr Julienne told father of the boys' scrumping. Robert thought, *now I'm in for it*, but the old gentleman said that he did not want the boys punished, adding that he had enjoyed a few scrumping expeditions of his own when he was a boy! Instead, Mr Julienne offered the boys a job: he would give them five shillings a week if they would work each Saturday morning in his gardens. 'That way they won't have to risk life and limb to get at my peaches,' he added.

Scrumpers United were overjoyed and relieved, more so Robert than Jimmy because he had been anticipating his father's wrath; surely he was not to escape the belt a second time. Notwithstanding Mr Julienne's plea for clemency, father delivered a tongue-lashing to his youngest son, completing his tirade with the words, 'That's it now, boy, I've had the police around twice now and I don't want them here any more.' Robert knew he had reached the very limit of his father's leniency and made a pact with himself that he would, in future, be more careful about keeping his activities within the law, at least as best he could.

The two inseparable friends were destined to spend many a happy Saturday morning during the rest of that summer and autumn working in the peaceful gardens of Mr Julienne. The boys agreed that Mr Julienne had been so reasonable about their stealing from him that they would give good value for their five shillings; and they did, sometimes working the whole day to finish a task that Mr Julienne had asked to be completed. The garden was a pleasant place to work and Robert, used to helping his father, was quite capable of completing most gardening tasks. At first Jimmy was a completely useless wazzock, but after a little training he too became quite adept at their tasks.

The only disadvantage of their Saturday job was that the boys could no longer attend the Saturday morning matinee at the local flea pit. Everyone wanted to be near the front of the queue to ensure getting a front row seat and both Robert and Jimmy had always got to the cinema early. The rows of young people sat in the darkened cinema, all heads tilted backwards, looking up at the big screen, screaming advice at the actors or howling with glee when the consistently victorious hero triumphed again. *Hopalong Cassidy, Roy Rogers and Trigger, Lost in Space* were serialised, and the boys would eagerly await each week's episode. It cost a whole shilling admittance each week and, when they could no longer attend each week, they consoled themselves with the fact that they were gaining six bob a week rather than losing one at the cinema.

Towards the end of November on a very wet Saturday

morning a lorry turned up and parked on the road outside Robert's front door. As soon as Robert saw it he knew what it meant. *'Ere we go again,* he thought, and was immediately overwhelmed with grief at losing both his best friend and his job with Mr Julienne. It was not totally unexpected by Robert; he had foreseen this day many months previously, instinctively knowing that his father would not endure the continuous monotony and routine of dairy farming for long.

Once again, as had happened so many times before, father had become increasingly dissatisfied with his job. The pay was very low, even by farming standards, and Robert knew that his mother was fighting a weekly battle to make ends meet. Using the small general store at the end of their terraced block, mother had incurred quite a large bill over the previous months and Robert worried about how that might be settled. Not privy to the actual means employed to settle this debt, Robert did notice that father had lost his pocket watch, and some of mother's brass ornaments seemed to have disappeared.

During the loading of the lorry, Jimmy called at the house to accompany Robert to their Saturday job. Lost did not do justice to Jimmy's crestfallen look when Robert told his friend of their impending move. He asked his father if he might go down to see Mr Julienne before leaving, but his father refused, adding, 'I'll need some help loading up.' Playing hookey from his Saturday job for the first time, Jimmy decided to stay and help with the loading of the family's meagre possessions and waved as Robert left in the lorry; he promised Robert that he would explain to Mr Julienne and say his farewells.

Neither boy made a fuss, not at that time; they considered themselves much too grown up to indulge in hugs and tearful farewells. Later that evening, however, Robert had a tearful moment when he realised that he might never see Jimmy again. He felt a little better when he promised himself that one day he would make an effort to go back and find his friend.

Before leaving Alton in the lorry, Robert had asked his parents several times where they would be living and what new school he would be going to. He was already feeling that awful unsettled fluttering in his stomach as he thought of going through the whole process of new teachers, new school bullies, possible new and harder lessons, etc. 'Wait and see!' His father flatly refused to elaborate further, despite Robert's repeated attempts to encourage him to divulge their destination.

After about an hour or so Robert began to recognise their surroundings and realised that they were heading back towards the estate and was jumping up and down in sheer exhilaration when the lorry entered Church Wallop and then turned up the long drive to the Sandsfoot estate. The lorry turned up towards the row of familiar cottages and stopped in front of the same house that they had previously occupied. Mr Sandsfoot, the neighbours later told Robert, had decided not to find a replacement for father when he left and the cottage had remained empty for the whole time that the family lived in Alton.

4

The Return

Almost unbelievably, sitting outside the cottage on a battered old suitcase, was his brother Albert. The authorities had decided that Albert was, at almost 16 years of age, way past the age at which he should be supporting himself and had simply turned him loose. That, at least, was Albert's story and as far as Robert ever knew, the authorities made no further attempts to remove Albert from the family home.

Speechless with joy and with tears running down her face, mother knelt down and hugged and kissed Albert, much to his extreme embarrassment. The whole family knew that Albert had always been mother's favourite son, the other two siblings accepted the *status quo* with equanimity, and, as far as Robert was concerned, felt no rivalry for mother's affections.

The oldest son Ronald, although greatly missed by his parents, had been independent for several years; he was now 18 and had been called up to serve his country under the National Service Act. Throughout his life, Ronald had not needed much in the way of parental guidance, or so it had appeared to Robert; he just seemed to get on with his life in his own way. His latest letter revealed that he was now in the Royal Artillery Regiment and was undergoing initial training somewhere in the Midlands. With a mind on his future, Ronald had discovered that if he elected to join up for three years instead of two he would earn a lot more money and leave the army as a trained motor engineer.

The family quickly settled in to their well-remembered cottage, jobs, and surroundings. Immediately the lorry had been unloaded, Robert took the familiar walk across to the large farmhouse to see Mrs Sandsfoot. He was very much looking forward to seeing her again and telling her how much her imagined support had helped him. He walked up the cobbled path that was so firmly implanted in his memory and knocked on the back door, trembling with anticipation of this longed for moment. The door was answered by Master John who greeted Robert with, 'Good to see you back, boy.' Smiling broadly, Robert asked if he might see Mrs Sandsfoot, and Master John's eyes saddened and he quickly looked over Robert's head in to the distance. 'I'm sorry, boy, there's been a lot of changes around here since you left. Mother died about a year ago, father has retired to a golf course in Spain, and I am now *Mr* Sandsfoot.' Vocal cords seized solid with shock, Robert had no words; he struggled to maintain his composure and groped for some words of condolence, but nothing came out no matter how hard he tried, he just turned away and ran.

It wasn't until he arrived at the old ruins that he *returned from his ride on the broomstick*; his mind had blotted out everything and he had no recollection of the familiar journey along the river, over the fields, and through the copse. He had no idea of the time or what day it was, nor in fact what he was doing at the ruins. He found himself standing by the entrance to the cellar: it remained almost exactly as he had last seen it and the branch hiding it from any casual passer-by was in its customary place.

He turned, somehow hoping that he might see the same sunbeam streaming down through the windowless opening, but it was a bleak, wet November day and he saw nothing

150

but dark clouds filling the skies. The sight of the rain-threatening clouds darkened his mood even further and as his eyes turned back towards the entrance to the cellar he saw a pile of rocks and stones where none had been before. Bending down, Robert saw that it was obviously a small grave. It was almost buried under a pile of wind-blown fallen leaves and there was a small engraved cross at one end, into which were inscribed the following words:

Here lies the body of a dear friend, Bosun,
If a friend of that friend should return one day,
Remind him, I pray, of their last sojourn,
And know him, that I will linger here, along my way.

Suddenly weakened legs collapsed beneath him, Robert fell to his knees at the side of the grave, and as his mind whirled in the depths of grief he looked back towards the place that he had seen the vision of Mrs Sandsfoot. As he stared at the opening in the ruined wall he saw a small hole appear in the clouds and the deep fathomless blue of the sky beyond. He clearly heard the words, spoken in that so familiar voice, *Steady, Robert!* It was another mystical and magical moment and Robert cared not whether the events were induced by his own deeply emotional state, or whether in fact, as he so firmly believed, the soul of Mrs Sandsfoot had waited, in some place unknown to the living, to say her farewells to him.

He knew that he need not concern himself about what others might think of his two experiences at this beautiful and peaceful place; he would not relate the events to another person as long as he lived. He would not allow others to share, analyse and rationalise the two deeply moving, and yes, Robert finally admitted it, heavenly experiences. His mood lightened slightly as he accepted this religious thought, perhaps there *is* something or somewhere to which we all go when our earthly time is complete. Maybe not an all-knowing, controlling influence on our earthly lives or the way that we lead them, but a place to rest, be rewarded or punished, before being sent back in some other living form. Heaven? Yes he could accept that!

It was almost dark before Robert regained his feet and left the ruins. He knew that his parents would not be worried about him; he had, after all, been wandering around this estate since he was about six years old, and he would be home when he got hungry.

When he arrived at the cottage, the family had settled in, each piece of furniture had been replaced at its previous spot. The beds had been made and mother had a hot stew simmering in a large earthenware dish, ready for serving, together with thick slices of bread and some home-made butter kindly donated by their neighbours. Sitting in front of the open grille of the range, mother was toasting bread and roasting chestnuts as an additional treat. The smell was lovely, and Robert was suddenly very happy, too happy to ask his father why he had not been forewarned of the death of Mrs Sandsfoot; clearly father had not felt able to tell his son the bad news.

Attempting to repeat his unscheduled break from school when the family first arrived in Alton, Robert had asked his father if he might defer going back to school until the beginning of the new term. There were only a few more weeks before the school term ended anyway! This time, of course, father refused and said that he might as well get that nasty experience out of the way as soon as possible. The very next morning, when his parents were in the garden chatting over the fence to their old neighbours, Robert went into his parents' bedroom, found the bed spanner tied with the same piece of string, and cut it. That

152

afternoon Robert threw the spanner far out into the big lake. The disappearance of the bed spanner was not discovered by his father until the family's next move.

Despite his father's insistence on his immediate return to Andover Secondary Modern, Robert did not go. He made all the necessary preparations for going to school each day, telling his mother that he preferred to take sandwiches for the rest of the school term, but in fact walked down the lane towards the bus stop and just veered away into the copse and spent the days staying out of sight. Strangely, no one seemed to notice his absence, not the teachers when he finally restarted school after Christmas, nor any of the village children that came to the Sandsfoot estate Christmas party, nor was he spotted by any of the estate workers. Whether his mother suspected his truancy, since he used the same excuse about school dinners as had his brother before him, Robert did not know; if she did have any suspicions she kept them to herself. The change in his mother was dramatic: she looked young again and full of health and vitality, and her obvious happiness at having most of her *'ampshire boys* back together made up, in a small way, for Robert's grief at parting from Jimmy.

The interior of the cottage had changed considerably in their absence. The windows and doors had all been replaced, ceilings and walls stripped and replastered, a smart new kitchen with interior plumbing had been installed, and, best of all, a proper bathroom with an inside lav. The smart new kitchen had been installed into a new extension at the rear of the cottage, which Robert had not spotted when the lorry had first arrived. This kitchen boasted an electric cooker, which mother refused to use for several months. The old black range had been left in what was the old kitchen. It was in a bit of a mess since it had obviously been used by the builders, but mother shined it up to its former glory and used that for cooking. 'Got to

153

light it to keep warm, so might as well cook on it!' It wasn't until the following summer, when she realised how easy it was to get up and turn a switch, rather than rekindle the range, that she finally started using the electric version. 'And I don't have to get up so early,' she said.

Education complete, Albert was given a job on the estate and, for a time, seemed very content. They had both grown considerably, but Albert had changed in additional ways: his personality was different and the brotherly closeness had gone; he seemed strangely distant to Robert. In truth Robert saw very little of him over the next year or so. After the evening meal each day, Albert would borrow father's old bike and pedal off to who knows where and would not return until everyone else was in bed. At weekends he would disappear Friday evenings, after his weekly bath, togged up in his best clothes, and would not be seen again until early Monday morning. After a few weeks of this behaviour, father said 'he must be courting some wench' and teased Albert unmercifully. 'For goodness sake hurry up and marry the girl, much more of this and you'll wear the tyres out on my bike!'

Just over a year later, a little after his seventeenth birthday, Albert broke the news to the family that his girlfriend was pregnant. It was the first admission that the family had heard of a girlfriend, although they had all believed father's reasoned explanation of Albert's many absences. The young girl's name was Fiona Cartwright. She was 16 years old, an only child and lived with her parents in a very large house in a small town called Whitchurch, a few miles south east of Andover. The couple intended a hastily arranged marriage towards the end of January and Albert was expected to move in with his in-laws, at least until he was able to obtain another job with accommodation of their own.

This was a turning point for Robert; he could see his

brother's life stretching in front of him, moving from farm to farm, never really settling down anywhere for very long, following in his father's well-trodden footsteps. From an early age, Albert had demonstrated his disdain for authority in all its shapes and forms, and he had already got himself into several disagreements with Master John; he did not want to start at the bottom and could not seem to grasp that he must learn the skills required for estate working before he could be paid as a skilled man.

Attended only by the two sets of parents, the wedding was a very quiet affair in a register office in Andover. The wedding was on a school day, and Robert did not attend; his father gave this as the reason for his not going, but Robert knew, deep down, that his brother did not want him there. Knowing full well the disgrace still associated with illegitimate birth, Robert, now 14, could quite understand that Fiona's parents, obviously a well-to-do family, would want to keep both the quickly arranged marriage and the impending birth as quiet as possible. In spite of his discontent at not attending the wedding he welcomed the knowledge that he had a new sister-in-law; he had always wanted a sister, but since he had not as yet met the girl, he would not be able to recognise her if she walked by him in the street.

After his self-approved holiday playing truant, Robert had returned to his old secondary school in Andover early in the previous January. On his first day he walked down to the bus stop, got on the bus, and went into the school with virtually zero comment from anyone; it was almost as if he had not been away.

Not a word was said about his truancy during the few weeks leading up to Christmas. He settled into school life, did all his homework on time, passed all his exams, finishing in the top five for every subject with a number one spot for maths, and was the only pupil for that year who achieved a hundred per cent attendance record. He was not actually shunned by his old cronies, but inwardly he felt much more mature than them; he no longer wanted to join in the proposed pranks and misbehaviour and became, as his form teacher wrote on his final report, *a bit of a loner.* However, apart from the loss of his friend, he was very content with his lot and had a marvellous summer helping on the estate.

Now old enough and big enough to earn a proper wage, Robert left the house each morning with his father during the long summer school break to attend the morning work muster on the estate. Master John usually teamed him up with his father. Despite Master John being the current master of Sandsfoot, and although everyone else on the estate called him Mr Sandsfoot, Robert still thought of him as Master John and continued to address him as such. A few attempts to correct him were made by Master John and his own father, who on several occasions got a trifle hot under the collar about it, but eventually they both gave up.

Knowing of his own mother's fondness for this boy, Master John knew that one day, when Robert eventually left the estate, he would have to fulfil one of her final wishes. It became very noticeable, not only to Robert, but to everyone else on the estate, that Mr Sandsfoot was always very tolerant towards Robert, and most guessed at the reason. Life on the estate had changed. 'Master John', Robert's own father would say, 'is not his father's son.' Unlike the old Mr Sandsfoot, who Robert occasionally imagined wandering aimlessly around some far distant golf course, Master John was very intolerant towards every other person, including his own wife. 'Don't interrupt me when I'm dealing with the men,' he barked rudely at her when the new Mrs Sandsfoot came out with a telephone message during a morning muster. Discontinuing many of the perks that the estate workers had enjoyed under his father, cash payment was now demanded for milk and meat products and rent for the cottages was deducted from pay.

A few weeks after the family returned to the estate, Robert had gone over to the big house and asked Master John if he might take the surviving Labrador, Kitchy, out for a run. Robert had taken the opportunity to ask Master John how Mrs Sandsfoot had died and Master John's face, which had been distorted in rage when he opened the door, softened and he asked Robert inside. They went into the estate manager's office (a post now vacant and never to be reassigned) and Robert sat in one of the worn leather armchairs. 'Do you know what cancer is, Robert?' asked Mr Sandsfoot. Robert nodded his affirmative and Master John whispered quietly, 'It was cancer of the breast.'

Equally quietly Robert whispered, 'Thank you, Master John,' took the long lead from the hook on the wall, slapped his leg for the Labrador to follow him, and left the room.

During that summer and the next there was much speculation amongst the estate community concerning Master John's hardened attitude towards his workers. Perhaps the profits from the estate had fallen, maybe the huge investments in machinery over the last few years, from new tractors to the frighteningly expensive combine harvesters, had drained his reserves; or maybe it was simply that, despite having been married for several years, the young Mrs Sandsfoot had not yet produced an heir. Once considered a bit of a chatterbox, Robert had slowly developed into an excellent listener and would usually express an opinion only when asked directly. Although he listened to all the estate gossip he at no time expressed his own private opinion that it was the lack of an heir that was the root of Master John's attitude. He knew Master John: he was, after all, the son of Mrs Sandsfoot and could, therefore, not be all bad, and he was consistently kindly in his dealings with Robert.

As school broke up for the summer break in the second year of the family's return to the estate, Robert decided that there would be no point in returning to school for the last few weeks before his fifteenth birthday. He spoke with his father and they both decided that it was time for Robert to start full-time employment and it was thus that Robert, at the age of 14 years and 9 months, started his first full-time job. There was no question about where he would work – on the estate – and this had already been agreed by Master John some time ago.

The change from schoolboy to estate worker created very little difference in Robert's life: he got up a little earlier and went off to work with his father exactly as he had been doing during the school holidays. His mother prepared his meals just as she did father's; he had an identical old khaki army bag to carry his sandwiches and a metal flask for hot tea.

Familiar with the many agricultural pranks and tricks that the more experienced estate workers routinely set to embarrass any new apprentices, Robert averted all attempts to trap him. One such commonly used prank was to wait until the team were working at the other end of the estate, pretend to find a section of broken fencing, and send the boy all the way back to the farm to ask for a new post hole! The unfortunate young man usually spent the rest of the day being sent from person to person in search of the elusive post hole until finally, returning to the team with a message from the foreman to try and make do with the old one! Some of the more Neanderthal young men spent anything up to a week running around in circles.

Continuing the same kind of work on the estate that he

had been doing for many years, Robert quickly enlarged his range of skills. He rarely required more than one demonstration of a particular task, for he was a quick learner, and as the months passed he was given more demanding tasks to perform. By the time he was 16 he was capable of completing almost any task on the estate, except maybe operate the cumbersome combine harvester; no doubt Master John judged him too young to be placed in charge of such an expensive piece of equipment.

Allocated his own tractor, a little grey Ferguson, which was a delight to drive and enormous fun, Robert whizzed around the rough tracks between jobs. He knew how to attach and use all the tools that came with the tractor, from a plough at the rear to the forward mounted pick up attachment. Life was very good indeed for Robert during this period; many times he would be working near to the ruins, and if he was on his own would walk over and take his morning tea break sitting by the small grave, often lighting a small fire to toast his sandwiches.

Now that he was earning a regular wage packet, Robert agreed the amount of his pay that he would give to his mother for housekeeping. Encouraged by his mother, he also tried to save a few shillings each week though not too successfully. On Sundays, which was usually his only full day's rest, he sometimes, if he was not working overtime, caught the bus into Andover to wander aimlessly around the shops, dreaming of what he would buy when he was rich.

It was shortly after his sixteenth birthday, late in October 1955, when he met Dave Skinner. As was his custom when unable to fill his free time, Robert had gone into Andover after dinner one Saturday and was walking up the high street when he decided to take a rest on one of the wooden benches, set into small islands in the centre of the road.

159

Many other people had, in spite of the blustery, cold autumn weather, decided to do the same thing, and there were very few spare seats.

Normally Robert would have turned away from the crowded seats, but spotted a young sailor, in full uniform, sitting alone on one of the benches. He sat down next to the sailor and sat quietly for some minutes. Glancing in Robert's direction, the sailor then reached down inside his jacket and removed a packet of cigarettes and a lighter. 'Want a fag,' said the sailor, and Robert took one from the box and sucked away at it whilst the lighter did its work. Though not unused to smoking (very few of the young people of his age did not smoke), Robert did not, at that time, smoke a great deal and could just as well do without them.

The two lads introduced themselves. Dave was 19 and said he was a stoker on the *Thesius*. 'What's a stoker and what's the *Thesius*,' asked Robert, and Dave explained that he worked in the engine room of an aircraft carrier. The lads talked for some time. Robert told Dave about his life on the estate and Dave told Robert about his family and life in the Royal Navy. Unhappy at home and not wishing to be conscripted, Dave had joined the Navy, and his stories fuelled the expectations of a better life for the young farm-boy.

The conversation lasted for some considerable time, both unaware of the crowds passing by, probably Christmas shopping. Time had passed quickly and Robert noticed that it was a little after 7 p.m. when Dave asked if he fancied a pint. Explaining that he was not yet old enough to go into the pubs, Robert added that he had, following in his father's footsteps, drunk nothing stronger than the odd half glass of cider during summer harvesting. 'Don't worry about that,' said Dave, 'we'll go into my local and I'll tell the landlord you are a pal of mine. You'll be OK.'

Breezing confidently through the entrance Dave walked into the pub, followed somewhat self-consciously by his newly found pal. The public bar, which was situated on the crossroads in the centre of Andover, was a dark and dingy room in an old building with very small windows. A noisy round of hellos and much slapping on backs welcomed Dave, whose parents were also in the pub and to whom Robert was introduced. 'Have a proper pint,' said Dave in astonishment, when Robert asked for a small shandygaff. 'I'm on black and tan, I'll get you a pint of that!'

As slowly as possible, Robert drank the pint, having asked and been told that it was half Guinness and half bitter. It tasted very bitter to Robert; he would much rather have had the shandygaff as ginger beer was more akin to his taste, but he finished the pint and insisted on buying another round himself. Halfway through the second pint Robert was feeling a little light-headed; he kept wishing that his palate might more readily accept the beer with each new mouthful. Enjoying himself immensely, Dave had already finished his second pint and was looking rather pointedly at his empty glass, which worried Robert; he was sure that he had already bought a round of drinks but his brain was becoming fuzzy and he was no longer certain. It was a very unsettling sensation, incomprehensible to Robert; he knew the whole room was spinning around his head but he could not think why! His last memory for that night was Dave's parents carrying over another tray full of pints, for even Dave's mother had a pint!

Returning to his senses, early the following morning, Robert awoke in a strange room in a strange house. It was still dark, his head ached, and he needed the lav, but he didn't know where it was. Stumbling awkwardly from wall to wall he managed to creep out into the garden and relieved himself against the wall, returned into the house, and sat waiting for the remainder of the household to

161

come to life. There was a strong smell of stale beer and vomit in the room, which made Robert feel quite queasy once again and he had to dash for the back door and stood outside breathing deeply of the fresh air. Despite his churning stomach and several heaving sensations in his throat, he was not sick, and after a while he went back inside and resumed his wait for the household to appear. He realised, whilst outside in the fresh morning air, that the smell of vomit must have been all over his body, because it was still strongly evident.

Sitting quietly, not wishing to disturb the sleeping household, it seemed like hours before he heard the sound of movement upstairs. Light had begun filtering through the thick curtains and Robert stood up and opened them to allow more light into the room. Now able to see more of the room, he noticed a door on the far side. It was partially open and he could see a stairway disappearing out of sight.

Quite suddenly he heard the toilet being flushed and a pretty young girl, about Robert's own age, appeared into view. She had not noticed Robert and was dressed in little other that a very short, flimsy man's shirt. As the girl stepped down the stairs the shirt bounced off her thighs, revealing all beneath! Instantly Robert could feel the blood rushing to his face, blushing bright red at what he saw, and he reluctantly dragged his eyes away before the girl should see him staring at her.

She was not very tall and a little on the bulky side, much like a slightly smaller version of Mrs Skinner, Robert thought. The girl started when she saw Robert but did not seem to find the presence of a stranger in her living-room too much of a surprise. 'What's that smell?' she said, and at that precise moment in time Robert realised exactly who had caused it.

The pleasures of kissing and holding a girl had not, as

162

yet, been discovered by Robert. There had been very few opportunities, apart from the furtive groping with the village lasses under the mistletoe at Mrs Sandsfoot's Christmas parties. He was totally devoid of any previous experience to call upon and whilst at school he had, like all the other boys, looked upon girls with total disdain. Realising that his attitude towards the female species had changed radically, he now felt awkward, embarrassed and unable to decide what to do. He was also quite mortified, knowing that he had to admit that it must have been he who had caused the vile smell of beer and vomit.

Tongue-tied, he was totally at a loss as to how to behave towards this girl. He could think of nothing to say and found himself wishing that she would go back upstairs and get properly dressed before her parents caught them together. At the same time he wished for her to stay so that he could secretly peek a little more! She seemed totally unconcerned about the way she was dressed and walked closely by Robert to the window, and opened it. As she passed Robert smelt that delicious odour of a young woman's body mingling with the fading odour of last night's perfume.

With not another word being spoken the girl went into the kitchen, returning a little later with a steaming mug of black coffee, which she handed to Robert and went back up the stairs. Grateful that the girl's back was to him, Robert could not drag his eyes away as more and more of the girl came into view as she went up the stairs!

Eventually Dave's mother came down. She sniffed the air, rather angrily Robert thought, looked at the empty cup and asked who had made the coffee. Briefly Robert explained and apologised profusely for his behaviour. Seemingly unaffected by her Saturday night on the beer, Mrs Skinner confirmed Robert's conclusion that the girl was her daughter, Maureen. She added that he should not worry too much about being sick, he wasn't the first and would not be the last to be sick on her carpet. Her son was always bringing home his Navy friends and the whole family enjoyed a Saturday night out. There was a sting in the tail though, for before she turned away to commence cooking him a delicious fry-up she said 'never seen anyone that pissed on two and a half pints though!'

Sitting on the top deck of the bus returning to Andover, where he would change busses to Church Wallop, Robert reflected on his night out. Before taking his leave of Mrs Skinner he had discovered that the house was on a council estate in a village called Upper Clatford. Neither Dave, Mr Skinner nor Maureen appeared again before he left, but Mrs Skinner said that Dave had asked if he would like to meet up again the following Saturday.

Apologising for his behaviour once again, Robert quickly agreed. He had started to feel much better whilst wolfing down the cooked breakfast, but he had suddenly developed a very unsettled feeling in his stomach. He was afraid he might be sick again and was anxious to leave the house.

Arriving at his own home, Robert's parents said that they were not overly worried by his overnight absence. They had gone to bed before the last bus arrived in the village and had not realised he was still out until half way through the morning. Observing the tell-tale dark rings around his mother's eyes, Robert knew that she was lying, obviously to protect his feelings. He suspected that she had lain awake most of the night waiting for Robert's return.

His parents had commented on the unmistakable smell of sour alcohol and vomit on him; it seemed to radiate from every pore and he could hardly stand it himself. A second bath – he had taken his usual Saturday bath just yesterday – was required, a most unusual event in the household. Firstly, he apologised to his mother for staying out without prior warning, told her everything that had

164

happened, except of course about Maureen, and blushed deeply again at the memory. Closely monitoring her son's face during his description of his night out, mother must have noticed his blushes but she made no comment. Not one of the six cottages had a telephone and, except for sending a telegram, there was no way of telling her where he was earlier in the day. Sitting in the hot bath, relaxed, clean, and no longer smelly, his mind drifted back over his meeting with Maureen and he wondered if he might get to know her better; he promised himself firmly, however, that in future he would stick to drinking shandygaff!

Over the next few weeks Dave and Robert became good friends and spent most Saturday evenings in the pub, riding to Dave's home on the bus at closing time and spending the night there. Just as Dave had promised, the pub's landlord made no comment about Robert's age.

Over the following few weeks Robert refrained from joining in with Dave's binging sessions. He avoided the potent brew that Dave had introduced him to and stuck doggedly to his promise of drinking only shandygaff. Sitting in the smoky atmosphere of the pub – every occupant puffed at one source of nicotine or another – Dave outlined his Navy life, telling Robert stories about the exotic foreign countries he had already visited; despite being only 19 he had been in the Navy for 4 years, joining when he was just 15. The stories had captivated Robert's imagination and Robert enormously enjoyed the pleasant Saturday evenings in the pub with his new friend. A week or so before the yuletide festivities of 1955 commenced, Dave, who had been on extended foreign service leave, lasting several weeks, returned to his ship.

The meeting had a lasting effect on Robert: he had been given a vision of a different path that his life might take and resolved to follow Dave's example, join the Royal Navy. According to Dave, Robert was, at 16, still young enough to join as a boy entrant but he would need his father's permission. Instinctively Robert knew that getting his father's permission would be a problem, brother Albert had made sure of that!

Following in his elder sibling's footsteps, Albert had now reached the age at which he was required to donate his time in the service of his country, and had, like thousands before him, entered into an unwilling contract to complete two years of national service. Within weeks of his conscription into the Army for his national service, Albert decided that army life was not for him and began to challenge the Army authorities by playing truant: French leave, or as the army preferred it, 'absent without leave.'

Each time Albert rebelled and walked out of the army establishment, where he was still under initial training, he made no effort to hide. On the rare occasions that the brothers had discussed these unapproved absences, Albert's version of his escapes was that 'the gate was open so I just walked out!' It was easy for the military police to find him, he simply returned to his wife and baby son; he did not come to the estate to visit his parents, an omission for which Robert would be forever grateful. The last thing he wanted was a re-enactment of his previous experience when Albert absented himself from the remand home.

However, father's health began to suffer, he complained of severe stomach pains, had lost a lot of weight, and, at only 50 years of age, looked quite old. For several days after he had made his decision to join the Navy, Robert considered the best way to approach his father for the required permission. It would upset father, of that he was certain, and he was loath to broach the subject while his father was so ill. However, time was of the essence and he must make his bid to join soon or he would be too old to join as a boy seaman. Finally deciding to defer speaking to his father until after Christmas, which would also give father a little time to recover his health, Robert continued to ponder his immediate future. Getting quite excited and anticipating a favourable response from his father, Robert began planning his next moves.

Information was the key: he must get the address of the nearest recruiting office; obtain information about specialisations open to him; make a choice from the list of available jobs; and perhaps a reference from Master John might be helpful. He would use the next week or so to gather as much information as he could and each time a new requirement occurred to him he added it to his growing list, hoping to impress his father with the amount of thought and effort already expended.

Early in January, Robert could wait no longer and he made the decision to speak to father. Lying awake in his bed the night before he planned to broach the subject, Robert had a premonition; he knew what his father's answer would be before the question was asked: he would refuse. Despite Ronald's successful and trouble free three years in the Army, his father's most recent memories were of Albert rebelling, once again, against authority, and Robert knew that his father's judgement would be influenced greatly by that knowledge.

The first time Robert spoke to his father the answer was just as he had expected and feared: father refused his permission, adding that he did not want to hear of the matter again. Refusing to give up at the first hurdle and hoping still that father might, over the next few days, think about his son's hopes for the future and reconsider his decision, Robert nonetheless wrote to the local recruiting office and received the appropriate forms. The anger on his father's face was clear when Robert pushed the forms across the table, following their evening meal, and once again he flatly refused to sign. After failing to persuade mother to speak to father on his behalf, Robert gave up any hope of joining the Navy as a boy; he must wait until he was seventeen and a half, at which time he would be entitled to make his own decisions, and join as an adult entry.

Robert was of course deeply disappointed at not being able to go straight into the Navy, but he was happy working on the estate and settled down, once again, to wait until he was old enough to make his own decisions.

By now Ronald had left the Army and had got a job with the post office as a vehicle technician. He was settled into digs in Portsmouth and was courting a girl called Marjorie from the nearby Hayling Island. Now like a distant memory, jagged around the edges and difficult to bring into focus, Robert had seen very little of his eldest brother from the moment he had left the family home to find work. The gamekeeper's daughter, who Ronald had been courting so seriously at that time had died two years previously. It had been about the time that the family had moved back to the estate and Robert had enough grief of his own at that time, and had paid little attention to the death of the girl who he hardly knew. The sensitive Robert did feel very guilty about not having written to Ronald at the time but it was now too late; time and the *'ampshire boy* brothers had moved on. She had died of tuberculosis.

After Dave returned to his ship Robert saw very little of the Skinner family. He did call into the pub a few weeks later and Dave's mother told him that her son was expected home in about two months' time, just for a weekend before his ship departed for some other exotic cruise. Warm memories of a short shirt and a brief sight of the 'temptress's tool,' prompted Robert to compose some opening words that might divert his conversation with Mrs Skinner to her daughter. He wanted to ask about Maureen, how old she was, what she liked to do, whether she had a boyfriend, but he just could not pluck up the courage; he would just have to wait and ask Dave.

It is amazing how slowly time can pass when waiting for something special to happen, and the two months leading up to Dave's weekend leave seemed to last forever. The Saturday that Dave was due home Robert told his parents that he probably wouldn't be home that night, and left the house to catch the four o'clock bus into Andover. As the bus bounced along the country roads into Andover, Robert's fevered mind rehearsed the questions to which he so desperately wanted answers. At six o'clock he was waiting at the door of the pub for it to open. 'Blimey, you're a bit keen,' said the landlord, recognising Robert.

'Yes,' said Robert, 'Dave is coming home for the weekend and I have something rather special that I want to ask him.'

Not wishing to befuddle his mind with drink, Robert asked the bartender for a shandy, and sat quietly in the pub while he waited, his heart beginning to thump unusually heavily as he anticipated the hoped for meeting with Maureen. A little after seven o'clock Dave sauntered through the door, followed by his parents and then by Maureen, and just for a second Robert's heart flipped; but then holding on to Maureen's hand there was a fifth person, another sailor in full uniform, cap pushed cockily onto the back of his head. *Oh well,* Robert mused philosophically, *that answers all my questions.*

Strangely, he did not feel too upset, he had not actually formed any relationship with the girl, but he had assumed that a relationship might happen given further social meetings. Feeling his pride a little dampened, Robert remained at the pub, pointedly ignoring Maureen, for the next couple of hours. He made sure that he bought them all a round of drinks and excused himself by saying that he had to work overtime the following day.

Gazing out of the window of the Church Wallop bus, Robert caught sight of his reflection in the darkness of the glass. 'You wazzock,' he quietly whispered to his reflected image, chastising himself for getting his hopes up too soon. The house was silent when he finally walked into the new kitchen. His parents had already gone to bed and he just sat at the small table mulling over his life, questioning again whether he really wanted to join the Navy. Perhaps father had sensed that he was unsure, or too young to decide his own future. He reviewed the events of the last few months since meeting Dave and, in the easy way of the young, wiped all remaining thoughts of Maureen from his mind with his own withering silent comment, *Oh well, she was a bit on the porky side for my taste,* and went to bed. He was never to see Dave or any of the Skinner family again, but it had served as a road sign, pointing to as yet unknown feminine pleasures in his future.

Earlier that summer, Robert was given a stark reminder of just how dangerous agricultural work could be and the event further stiffened his intention to find another way of earning his living. The incident occurred when the estate was busy haymaking. Robert had been teamed up with another young man of about his own age who worked on the estate.

His name was Bill Simmonds. He did not live on the estate but turned up each day on a shiny new BSA motorbike, which Robert envied greatly. The two agricultural apprentices drove identical Ferguson tractors and they were currently both engaged in picking up the freshly mown grass and taking it to a previously dug silage pit. There was a special attachment to the rear of the tractor, operated by oil pressure, which looked like a small trailer but instead of a floor it had long metal poles that slid under the mown grass. A large and very heavy load of grass could be man-oeuvred onto this contraption by reversing along the lines of mown grass, lifted by pneumatic pressure and carried away to wherever it was needed.

The two lads had been dashing to and from the pit all day; they had filled it completely and were busily extending the height above ground. The width of this pile of grass was little more than the width of the tractors and it was getting ever higher. Great care was required when driving up onto the top of the pile: approach too quickly and the weight of the grass would tip the tractor back onto its rear wheels, or if the tractor got too close to the edge it would tip alarmingly sideways.

Occasionally the two lads took it in turns to pump molasses from nearby 40-gallon drums over the grass. It was the molasses, together with the self-generated heat of enclosed organic matter and the fermentation process, that created the abominable smell when it was dug out as feed for the cattle during the winter.

The two drivers had been trying to out-do each other all day, pulling on the short, stubby throttle as hard as they could in their efforts to obtain more speed. A couple more loads and they would be finished for the day and they could have their customary race along the mile or two of twisting, bumpy, rutted tracks to the farm buildings.

The pile of fresh grass was now about 10 foot above ground and had recently been dampened by a quick shower and a coating of molasses. Sitting on his silent tractor, Robert watched as Bill brought the final load of grass up to the pile, drove his tractor up to the top, and pulled the lever to dump it. No one could really explain what happened next: the tractor seemed to slide to the edge of the pile and toppled over to the ground below, trapping Bill beneath it. The crushing weight of the tractor killed Bill outright. The incident did not stop Robert from

171

tearing around on his tractor, whenever he got the opportunity, but he was more mindful of the possibility of an accident and was much more careful.

One of the big changes that Robert noticed on the family's return to the estate, was the virtual non-existence of rabbits. Where they had once been so numerous as to be regarded a pest, they were now virtually wiped out. The huge warrens, previously surrounded by droppings and foot marks, were now almost completely devoid of any signs of usage; and if a rabbit was spotted it was usually an infected specimen, the lethargic swollen-headed symptoms of the killer disease myxomatosis clearly visible.

Some years previously, Mrs Sandsfoot had told Robert that the wild rabbit, the creatures that the boys preyed upon so heavily, had been introduced into the English countryside many years before from some foreign sounding country, and yes, their zealous breeding habits and subsequent numbers had turned them into a pest to farmers; but to deliberately introduce a man-made virus to so drastically control their numbers, once again confirmed his doubts about the existence of an all-powerful celestial being. He found the countryside a lesser place for their absence and his resolve to join the Navy stiffened further.

Although his mother very often purchased a rabbit or two from the estate's gamekeeper and made her delicious stews, Robert's imagination always conjured up the sight of the infected animal and he was never again able to eat rabbit. As long as he lived, he was always to associate the meat with the symptoms of the horrible killing disease.

The months passed slowly, the work of the estate dictated by the changing seasons. Another summer passed and, just before his seventeenth birthday, his mother told him that the family would be moving again. This was a bolt from the blue for Robert, who was very content with his life at that time. He knew there would be no point in asking his father if he might remain on the estate, taking lodgings somewhere locally; his father seemed determined to treat his youngest son differently than he had his two oldest boys.

The health of his father had deteriorated quite alarmingly and he found it difficult to work a full day; there were no other options, they would have to leave the estate. Undoubtedly there must have been an underlying expectation that Robert would provide some income for the family during his father's incapacity, which must have also influenced father's decisions about both the Navy and his remaining alone on the estate. It was left to mother to outline the family's plans: she explained that the family intended moving in with father's sister, who, Robert was told, lived in Alton!

A sister – this was news indeed to Robert – he had no idea that his father had a sister; as far as he could recall his parents had never mentioned brothers and sisters. His father quietly explained to Robert that when he had met and fallen in love with mother, his own parents, Robert's paternal grandparents, had not approved of his choice of partner. These grandparents had been a middle-class, business family, running a small coaching firm at a place called Tadley, near Basingstoke. They apparently thought that father was marrying below his station and cut him out of their lives, severing any inheritance. To cut off all contact with a child seemed an extremely drastic and unkind action to Robert. He felt no loss at missing out on the joys that grandparents brought to the lives of his friends and acquaintances or of not knowing these bigoted people. If they didn't want to know his beautiful mother then he wanted nothing to do with them, *shower of wazzocks.*

On his last Friday at the estate, Robert, with all the other estate workers, lined up to be paid outside the big house. The same timeless ritual followed: Master John came out carrying the old wooden tray with the familiar brown envelopes and started calling the men's names to collect their pay. Normally this was done in alphabetical order and Robert was somewhat surprised when his name was not called immediately after his father's. In fact all the envelopes had been issued and there was nothing left on the tray, which of course seemed very odd to Robert, and he looked at Master John, who just winked and said, 'Follow me, Robert.' It was the first time that Master John had called him by anything other than boy! Heading toward the imposing farmhouse, Robert dutifully followed Master John into the warm office, which Robert still thought of as the estate manager's office, and sat in the same leather armchair that he had occupied on several previous occasions.

'Firstly,' said Master John, 'here is your pay, and I have put in a little bonus for you and a written reference.' With a sincere look on his face, he told Robert that he had been very pleased with his work over the past few years and if he ever needed a job, a home, or anything else, he should ask firstly at the estate. Without pause, Master John went on to say that just before she had died his mother, Mrs Sandsfoot, had written a letter to Robert and said that when the boy finally left the estate, to make his own way in the world, as she knew he one day would, he was to be given £100 and the letter. Almost in tears at his bedrock's final kindness and generosity, Robert was handed two more envelopes and Master John stood up and offered his hand. 'Goodbye, Robert, I wish you well' were his final words.

There was only one place that Robert wished to be when he opened up the letter from Mrs Sandsfoot, the clearing at the site of the old ruins. At this place he felt close to her again and, sitting on Bosun's grave in the gathering dusk, he read her final words.

Sandsfoot
21 July, 1952

Dearest Robert,
　I know that when you read this letter you will be preparing to make a new life for yourself, away from our beloved Sandsfoot. I saw in you something of the good in my own dear brother and for that I loved you.
　Walk a straight and true path, always in the knowledge that I walk beside you, and remember always, steady, Robert!
　Your loving friend
　Kate

Hastily removing the letter from beneath his streaming tears, Robert reread the letter several times before carefully folding the sheet of paper and returning it to its envelope. Bracing himself, he stood erect and shouted into the surrounding darkness, 'Steady, Robert!' The shout quenched his tears and cleared his mind.

Later that evening, having read the letter again, Robert moved in front of the dying embers of the living-room fire and let the heavily embossed sheet of paper slip from his fingers. A brief flash of flames greedily engulfed the letter and he poked the remains into oblivion amongst the ashes of the fire. Robert did not need the written words to remind him of the contents of her letter, the words were forever engraved on his heart.

The following morning the familiar scene was re-enacted: the lorry turned up to take their sparse possessions to their new home. There were to be no last minute, wistful visits down memory lane this time, Robert was quite ready to leave, his mind was totally focused forwards to the time when he would join the Navy. The impending move and

175

his growing dissatisfaction with country life, together with the awful sight of Bill dying under his tractor, had reinforced his decision to join. Where he lived for the next few months made little difference. And he was looking forward to seeing Jimmy again.

Much to Robert's disgust, father hardly seemed to notice that the bed spanner was missing when he came to dismantle the old iron bedstead; he merely tutted when he found it missing and went off to find an old wrench. Not wishing to upset his father, who was finding it difficult to help with the heavy lifting into the lorry, Robert did not tell his father about throwing the spanner into the lake. His symbolic act had clearly not had the desired effect, and he decided to keep that information to himself.

The lorry chugged away down the lane and into Church Wallop, a brief stop to allow mother to settle the family account at the village store and off, once again, towards Alton. When they arrived at Tan House Lane, in Alton, where Robert's newly acquired aunt lived, the majority of their belongings were unloaded into the back garden and covered with tarpaulins. There was not much room in the small cottage: there were only two bedrooms; Robert would sleep either on the floor in the sitting-room or on the large settee. As soon as the lorry had departed and all the work of moving was completed, Robert left his parents and went off to find his old friend Jimmy.

5

Back to Alton

When Robert knocked on Jimmy's front door, the old friends were overjoyed to see one another again and they hugged each other; a strange experience for Robert since he had rarely hugged his own brothers and then only when he was very small. The two felt no embarrassment however, it was a completely spontaneous action and felt completely natural.

The same pleasure at seeing Robert was not forthcoming from Jimmy's parents: they did not seem too happy to see him again! *They probably think I'm going to drag Jimmy into all sorts of trouble,* thought Robert; he instinctively knew the reason for the Warringtons' coldness. Left alone to chat in the Warrington kitchen, Robert asked after Mr Julienne and was saddened to hear that he, too, had died, about a year previously. 'Cancer,' Jimmy said, in answer to Robert's question.

Almost exactly the same age, Jimmy had left school at the same time as Robert and had been working in a foundry in the nearby village of Farringdon. Already having outlined his plans for the future, Robert continued the conversation. 'I shall be putting in my application to join the Royal Navy very shortly now,' said Robert, 'but I could do with a temporary job until about next Easter.'

It was difficult to talk with Jimmy's parents continuously coming into or passing through their kitchen, so the boys left the house and walked aimlessly towards the nearby park. They were chatting away, catching up with all that had happened to them over the past four years, and quite naturally, it seemed, ended up at the dump. It was now completely sealed with a formidable exterior fence and a high, metal, firmly locked front gate. Large signs proclaimed it as private property, warning trespassers of dire consequences.

It was Jimmy who suggested a visit to Mr Julienne's garden, but Robert thought that it might not be a very wise move. Had Mr Julienne still been alive they could have, if caught going over the wall, claimed that they were simply visiting the owner; but it was more than likely that the place had been sold and Robert wanted no complications before he made his RN application. They did climb the old oak tree, by the railway bridge, but there was no activity inside the garden.

Suggesting a visit to the pictures that evening, Robert was surprised to see Jimmy blush deeply. *Oh dear*, thought Robert, *he's courting!* Six months previously Jimmy had started going out with his current girlfriend. Her name was Joy and she worked at the local egg-packing station. She was, said Jimmy, an egg-candler, and there were lots of the local girls and boys working there.

Without the slightest conception of what an egg-candler was, Robert asked for an explanation and was told that it was a person who tested eggs by holding them against a bright light and looking for deformities or abnormalities. Imagining himself sitting inside a building all day testing eggs filled Robert with distaste. 'No thanks, I'm an outdoor person,' he heard himself saying, assuming that Jimmy was suggesting it as temporary employment for him.

Slightly miffed at Jimmy's experience with the opposite sex, Robert had been impressed by the easy and confident manner that Jimmy used when speaking about girls. The very thought of them filled Robert with awe and he very much doubted that he would ever be able to talk to one!

Eventually they agreed to meet that evening outside the cinema. Jimmy would try to get Joy to bring one of her friends with her, just to balance the group. A suggestion that filled Robert with dread, but he could not, of course, object.

That evening as Robert approached the queue waiting outside the cinema, he saw Jimmy standing in line with two girls. He was introduced to Joy and then to Pat. Robert recognised Pat instantly: she was the girl whose pigtails he had pushed into the ink-well at school! She had obviously changed considerably and her hair, now much shorter, had been permed into soft waves and curls, which tumbled around her face. She was, to Robert, very pretty, tall and, despite a heavy winter coat, obviously very slim. When she held out her hand in greeting, Robert very gently took it in his own and was amazed how small and graceful it was; he didn't want to let it go.

Remembering their eagerness as boys to get good seats, Robert noted that Jimmy and the girls had got to the cinema early and Robert thought, *good old Jimmy, going for the front seats again!* He couldn't have been more wrong; as soon as they had purchased their tickets Jimmy seemed anxious to go straight in to their seats, but the girls wanted to buy sweets and go to the toilet etc. As they waited in the foyer for the girls to complete their ablutions, or whatever else females seemed to spend endless time in the toilet doing, Jimmy became quite agitated. Robert could not understand, at that time, exactly why. 'We'll miss our seats,' cried Jimmy. Eventually the girls came out of the toilet and the group went through into the already darkened interior of the cinema, where they were met by the torch-wielding usherette. Taken by surprise, Robert was astonished when Jimmy said to her, 'Any seats going in the back row?'

Back row, thought Robert, *we won't be able to see a bleeding thing from back there!*

All became clear as the film progressed when Robert glanced along the row towards Pat who was sitting furthest away from him next to Joy. The two young lovers, to Robert's embarrassment were glued together in an endless, and somewhat noisy, snogging session, which lasted throughout the B film, the news, and the A film. *Won't be any point in discussing the film with you tomorrow*, Robert chuckled to himself, *you won't have a clue!*

Much later, jostled by the crowds dashing off in all directions as they exited the cinema at the end of the evening's screenings, Jimmy said he would have to walk Joy home; she lived at the Butts end of the town. Feeling somewhat obliged to make the offer, Robert asked Pat if he might escort her home and she readily agreed. They walked through the short-cut alleyways towards the council estate where Pat lived, chatting idly about the film. Mentioning that Joy was her best friend, Pat added that they did everything together and told each other every scrap of news. *Better watch my tongue*, Robert warned himself.

Arriving at the gate outside Pat's house, Robert refused to go any further and they stood for a few minutes continuing their conversation. Robert looked at the window to the house and saw the curtains twitch and the quick glimpse of a bespectacled face, before the curtains were replaced. *I'm off*, he thought, remembering suddenly that this was one of the houses, through the mailbox of which he and Jimmy had shoved the already-lit bangers!

Fearful of a confrontation with the owner of the bespectacled face, Robert quickly asked Pat if he could meet her again the following week. She immediately agreed, seeing his sudden agitation and eagerness to be gone!

Taking his time, Robert returned to his aunt's house. He knew that everyone was in bed but the back door had been left unlocked for him. He had been carefully briefed about his behaviour whilst staying with his aunt, and his father had emphasised the importance of locking the doors and windows if he was the last to retire at night. It occurred to Robert that it was a very strange suggestion from his father because the family had not bothered to lock the doors before, except for the front door when they had lived in Alton a few short years before, and only then because it opened immediately on to the pavement. 'Times have changed,' his father added thoughtfully, 'best not to trust anyone these days!' It was a sure indication of his father's diminishing confidence, but Robert remembered his father's instructions and ensured that all the doors were locked, the windows were secured, and the lights switched off.

Undressing quickly in the chill of his aunt's house, Robert curled up on the settee feeling very content and somehow different. He quickly previewed the events of the following morning when the household came to life, and decided that he had better get up very early and get washed and dressed before anyone else. *Might get a bit embarrassing if I have to crawl out of bed with auntie looking on!* He eventually drifted off to sleep with the memory of Pat's delicate perfume all around him.

The following evening, after an almost fruitless trip to the Employment Exchange, Robert went off to call for Jimmy again. The trip to the Employment Exchange was fruitless in that he could not find any temporary employment, but worthwhile in that he did manage to obtain the address of the nearest RN recruiting office and some information leaflets on joining the RN.

Frittering away time, Robert spent most of the afternoon sitting in the park reading the leaflets, which described the types of jobs available, filling in a form, and checking on the train times to Southampton, where the nearest recruiting office was located. On his way to meet Jimmy he posted his application form.

Later that evening, sitting in Jimmy's kitchen chatting away about everything and everybody, Robert noticed that Jimmy's parents seemed much more relaxed, even friendly towards him. He later mentioned it to Jimmy who said that he had told his parents about Robert's refusal to enter the garden again. Over the next few months he would come to feel completely relaxed at Jimmy's home, almost a member of the family, and was always made welcome from that moment onwards.

Their conversation that evening eventually got around to that of employment. Jimmy said that he had spoken to his employer earlier about the possibility of some part-time work for Robert, at the foundry. The foundry owner had said that in a week's time he might have need of some extra help because he was expecting to win a big new order. None too keen at the prospect of working indoors, Robert was unsure about accepting the offer. Was he capable of actually doing an indoor job? But on the positive side, it was working with Jimmy and the money would be very useful.

He told Jimmy that he would like the work if it became available, but he did not know how he would get to Farringdon each day. 'Don't worry,' said Jimmy, 'you can come on the back of my motorbike.' Towards the end of the evening, after Robert had given Jimmy a detailed account of his Navy application, Jimmy mentioned something that Robert had not, until this moment, considered: national service.

Like all young men of his age, Robert knew of the requirement for national service. Both his brothers had been called, but he had assumed that the system had been discontinued! After some minutes of stony silence, during which both lads were *off with their bums on a broom*, Jimmy said that he had recently made some enquiries of his own; he would be in the last group of young men to be called up. Since the two lads were almost the exact same age, they would both reach 18 in a few short months, and Robert knew that he too would be conscripted. They both sat quietly for a while, deep in thought, Robert wondering how it might affect his application to join the RN, and he made a mental note to talk to the recruiting office when he went for his initial interview.

Passing through the small kitchen, Jimmy's father had overheard this part of their conversation. 'Make a bleeding man of you,' he growled and stomped off back into the living-room. *Didn't help my brother Albert*, the retort leapt into Robert's brain, but he was careful to keep this thought to himself.

Early the next morning, unable to sleep on the uncomfortable settee, Robert lay in the darkness daydreaming of his future. It now occurred to him as odd that Jimmy had not questioned him about Pat, and, almost in the same instant, realised that Joy had obviously told Jimmy whatever he needed to know. As Pat re-entered his thoughts, he started to think about the coming date with her and, as in most forthcoming pre-planned events, began to preview the evening in his mind.

He suddenly realised, with a shock, that they had parted without making any arrangements for meeting. Pat had simply agreed to meet him the following weekend. After some consideration, he decided that the best thing to do would be to wait outside the egg-packing station one evening and speak to her as she left work. It was for this reason that he waited at the end of the long alleyway that led up to the double doors of the packing station the following Friday evening at about five o'clock.

Knowing that he had not yet been spotted, Robert watched carefully as Pat and Joy, the first of the workers to leave, walked towards him chirpily, chattering away at one another. They were never, whilst together in his company, lost for words! The girls had spotted him, however, and as they came level with him he heard Joy say, 'I'm going straight off home, Pat, see you Monday.'

Finding himself suddenly left alone with Pat, he would forever be grateful to Joy for that little intuitive knowledge of his nervousness that had prompted her to leave them be. Walking home together, Robert was unsure whether he should attempt to hold Pat's hand. How early in a relationship should one attempt such intimacies? It was all a mystery to him! The touch of her soft hand when they had first met outside the cinema lingered hauntingly in his memory, but he thought better of making an attempt for fear of rejection. They made arrangements to meet by the telephone box near her home. Robert added that he would prefer not to call at her house. Pat, who knew of the firework incident, walked along the pavement towards her home, turning at the last moment to give him a little wave as she went through the door.

The following evening they went to the pictures again. Robert did not have the nerve to insist on being seated in the back row, although he really wanted to; the advantages of the increased privacy were only to clear to him! Throughout the film he desperately wanted to put his arm around her shoulders, as he could see the other courting couples doing, but did not have the courage. Faint heart may not win fair maiden, but fools also rush in . . . !

After the film, once again taking the short cuts through the alleyways leading towards Pat's home, she, probably fed up with his reticence, took his hand and they walked the remainder of the way home so entwined. That first touch as their hands met was like an electric shock and Robert loved the feel of Pat's hand in his. It was so small and smooth, with long, slender fingers and beautifully manicured nails.

He became agitated and very nervous at the gate. Pat asked him in for a cup of tea, but Robert refused. He was not yet ready to meet Pat's parents. He had enough problems dealing with his present emotions, and he had now to decide whether or not to try for a goodnight kiss! Whilst he was struggling to make a decision, Pat decided the issue herself: reaching up only slightly, for she was almost as tall as Robert, she planted a gentle kiss on his lips. Before he had time to respond or put his arms around her waist, she was gone, through the gate and up to the front door. She turned, blew him another kiss, and went inside. They had not made any arrangements to meet again, but both knew that Robert would be waiting outside the packing-station very soon.

The next week Robert started his temporary job at the foundry at Farringdon. Fulfilling his promise, Jimmy's old motorbike, an Excelsior with a small 2-stroke engine, carried them to and from work each day. Running with the hare and hunting with the hounds, Jimmy had neither licence, tax, nor insurance. After their first trip to work, Robert decided that Jimmy also did not have much experience in piloting the machine. It wobbled alarmingly and in the early mornings when there was a hard frost, the bike would slide around all over the road.

The machine was incapable of any great speed, however, and on the occasions that the bike slid into the verges, they simply picked themselves up, dusted themselves off, and continued with their journey. A few more dents and scratches made little difference to the appearance of the bike! For the next few months Robert found the work hard, muscle straining, repetitive, uninteresting, uncomfortable – it was always extremely hot in the foundry – and worst of all, indoors! Nevertheless, he needed to earn some money each week. He still had to give his aunt a weekly housekeeping allowance and he was seeing a lot of Pat which, although she paid her way, still meant that his weekly expenditure was much greater than had been the case on the estate when his only outing had been an occasional Saturday night. Fortunately his share of the home to work expense for petrol amounted to very little; the bike seemed to go forever on a few pints of fuel.

About a week after he had sent off his Navy application, Robert received a letter from the recruiting office in Southampton. The letter asked him to attend for an interview in a week's time, about the beginning of December. Robert was thrilled, and best of all, there was a naval travel warrant included, so he would not have to pay the train fare. On the day of the interview, Robert left his aunt's house and caught the train to Winchester, changed trains, and continued to Southampton. The recruiting office was only about half a mile from the docks railway station so he did not have far to walk and quickly found the office.

Sitting in the waiting-room, glancing at the impressive display of naval posters depicting famous battles and famous leaders, Robert pondered the fact that there had been only two other candidates waiting when he arrived. Was this a good omen or bad? Robert decided that the low numbers must be in his favour: the fewer the candidates, the better his chances. They all sat quietly, not wishing to get involved in conversation. *Probably reconsidering, worried, like me, about doing the right thing*, Robert finally decided.

Passing time reading various brochures that were left casually lying around on the small tables, Robert was eventually called into an adjacent office. As he entered the office he saw a man, much older in years than he had been expecting, dressed in full naval uniform. At the time Robert did not know his rank but he subsequently discovered, on reading yet more brochures, that the man was a chief petty officer, with three buttons just above the cuff of each sleeve identifying his rank. Feeling more and more at ease, Robert gradually relaxed while answering the numerous questions about his life, where he had lived, his family, his interests, etc. and by the time that the crucial question of 'What sort of naval job are you interested in?' came around, Robert was ready. He explained that he had lived his life in the country, doing outside jobs, and that was what he wanted to do in the Navy. He most certainly did not want to be a stoker. Dave had explained that depressing job to Robert; *nor a vet*, Robert whispered to himself, not wishing to explain that remark to the CPO.

The recruiting office had, in response to his initial letter requesting joining information, sent him a number of pamphlets describing the roles available, and Robert had decided that the most suitable for him was that of signalman. The description of the job seemed to fit Robert perfectly, on the signal deck in all weathers, signalling with flags, fresh air – perfect. Throughout the long session of questions, the recruiting CPO had been carefully looking through the various forms that Robert had completed before his arrival; unbeknownst to Robert he had been checking for legible handwriting and spelling ability.

Looking up from the pile of forms in front of him, the CPO came to a decision and severely dented Robert's hard won confidence by saying, 'In that case we will have to set you an aptitude test,' and promptly left the room for a few minutes. When he returned he turned to a specific page in the book that he had fetched, and pointed to a page with the morse code printed on it. Robert, of course, knew *of* the morse code; it could be picked up quite easily when twirling the tuning knob on the family's old radio at home. He could not think what the morse code had to do with flags, which Robert assumed were the only tools available to a visual signaller, but he had warned himself to expect *anything* and to go along with *anything* at this interview. He was told to read the page in the book and then to memorise, in the next ten minutes, the six morse code characters that were underlined.

Trying desperately hard to concentrate because the CPO was fiddling around in the corner of the room, setting up some sort of apparatus, which distracted him a little, Robert stared down at the morse characters, trying to identify some sort of pattern or clue to aid his memory. Writing a list of the characters he rewrote the list over and over, much like a child writing punishment lines at school, in his bid to commit them to memory. Handing Robert a pair of headphones, the CPO told Robert to sit down at the desk next to the strange apparatus and listen carefully, adding that he would hear through the headphones the six morse symbols that he had been learning. Robert sat, slowly relaxing as the man played a tape, which transmitted the morse symbols to the headphones.

Over the next minute or so the tape repeated the morse symbols and Robert realised that he recognised them; he was still looking at his written list and he mentally ticked off each character in turn. The naval man explained that he would now play a different tape, once only, on which the six morse symbols were randomly mixed together in groups of three. Robert was to write down as many as he could recognise.

Sitting in the brightly lit room, headphones firmly clamped over his ears, Robert read the morse transmission. Fortunately it was very slow and he had ample time at the completion of each individual symbol to make his decisions. In his peripheral vision Robert noticed another person enter the room during the test and, when the transmission ended, his written efforts were passed to the new arrival; presumably for marking, Robert decided, as the new arrival left the room with his test in his hand.

The recruiting officer asked Robert if, while they were waiting for the results of the test, he would like to hear how the morse sounded at normal speed and Robert was completely lost when he heard it; he was not able to identify a single symbol. It was just a complete blur of sound without identifiable gaps between symbols and Robert doubted his ability to ever achieve sufficient skill to read it.

When the results were returned, the recruiting officer told Robert that he had some good news and some bad news. Apparently he had passed the morse aptitude test with flying colours, almost 100 per cent accuracy, which was the good news; the bad news was that there were no vacancies for visual signallers for the foreseeable future. However, it appeared there were other vacancies in the Communications Branch for telegraphists, and the recruiting officer added that he was confident that Robert would be accepted for such a post based upon his morse test. Handing over yet another pamphlet, explaining the role of a naval telegraphist, the CPO told him to sit outside in the waiting-room, read the pamphlet, and make up his mind.

Feeling deeply disappointed, to say the least, he had not at any time considered that he would not be offered the job for which he was volunteering and did not understand, at that time, that the recruiting officer was trying to steer him into the most suitable career path. After the last applicant had left the building, the recruiting officer came back to see Robert, who had been sitting alone for about half an hour trying to come to a decision.

'Well, Mr Leonard, what have you decided?' he asked.

Mentally tossing a double-headed coin, Robert made up his mind almost instantly; despite his doubts about his eventual ability to master the fast morse transmissions he knew that he must accept, there seemed no other option for him. If father recovered his health and started moving from job to job there was no telling where he might end up. At least this way he would have a secure home, secure income, and secure future. If the price of security was having to work in an office, then so be it!

Almost out of the door, Robert recalled that he had not asked the recruiting officer about national service. 'Don't worry about that,' the recruiting officer replied, 'we will take care of that and you will not hear any more about it, unless of course you fail to complete your training or are discharged for any reason.' It was to be another spur to Robert: he dare not fail and he must be ready to accept whatever hardships that may be waiting for him in the future.

Before leaving the recruiting office, Robert was told that the next process in his recruitment would be to return to Southampton in a couple of weeks time for a medical examination, after which, subject to a favourable result, his joining instructions would follow. He would have to wait until about the end of April, when he was seventeen and a half, unless he could get his father's permission. Knowing that to pursue that line again was futile, Robert reluctantly decided to wait. The delay might be put to good use, however, and he collected many of the informative brochures and pamphlets from the waiting-room, intending to gain as much advance information as possible. At least he had something to tell Pat and his parents, all of whom he knew would question him closely about the day's events.

It was clear to both Robert and Pat, who were now seeing each other on a regular basis, that there existed some deep feelings between them, despite their tender years. They were so comfortable in each other's company; their conversations probed into their probable future and they spoke, quite freely and naturally, of marriage and children and where they would live, making all sorts of extravagant plans and had so many hopes and expectations. Both came from happy marriages and saw their own mirroring that of their parents.

With a soft and mostly forgiving and submissive nature, Pat seemed quite content about Robert's decision to join the Navy. He had told her of his fears if he did not settle into some sort of permanent and reliable means of earning a living. Accepting that Robert must make his own decision, and realising that he might soon be gone for long periods, she agreed to accompany him on a visit to meet his parents at his aunt's house. She made not the slightest fuss about the meeting and seemed totally at ease with whoever she met.

She was still only 16 and Robert's father, now thankfully in improving health, could not resist pointing out that Albert's wife had been the same age when she fell for a baby. Of course they did not tell his parents, but the young couple had spoken about this possibility and both had agreed that, when the time came for their relationship to move to the inevitable level of such intimacy, they would make completely sure of there not being any accidents. Having visited Robert's parents, Pat repeatedly asked him to attend an afternoon tea with her parents, but Robert always made up some weak excuse. Still doubtful of his reception from the Wilson family, Robert was wary of meeting them.

Exasperated by her boyfriend's continual refusal to meet her parents, Pat finally admitted that her parents knew all about the pigtails and the fireworks and, in fact, had now told so many of their friends and family that it had become a standing family joke. She told Robert that, after the pigtail episode, her mother had been furious because of the ruined white blouse and was intent on going to the school to berate the Headmaster and claim some form of compensation. Surprising her mother, Pat had forestalled her intentions by declaring that she would one day marry Robert, and did not want him punished in any way; she had been twelve at the time! This declaration astounded Robert and he felt a wonderful calming feeling of security as he realised the completeness of her love for him. He knew that she would always be true to him and also that he would always be true to her; the knowledge hit him and for several minutes he could not speak, he had truly found his soulmate.

No longer with any valid excuse for refusing, the following weekend Robert spent a most uncomfortable Sunday afternoon with Pat's parents. He wished that he had thought the visit through a little more thoroughly. He had agreed to an initial short visit, maybe for a cup of tea and he sat with Pat in the Wilson family kitchen, agitated and nervous beyond belief. The Wilsons were not in the house when he arrived, they were in their garden, a favoured activity for them both. The further delay in meeting them was agony to Robert, who was now very anxious indeed.

Thankfully, Mr Wilson was a kindly man. Mild mannered and softly spoken, he reminded Robert a little of Mr Julienne, and Robert took an immediate liking to him. The face behind the twitching curtains, however, that of Mrs Wilson, Pat's mother, was an entirely different proposition. She was fearsome! Always very abrupt, no matter to whom she was speaking, she did all things in a most belligerent manner, or at least that's how it seemed to Robert. *Blimey*, he thought, *I'm glad Pat takes after her father! What a mother-in-law she's going to be!* The poor lad took a moment for reflection when he remembered the old adage: he who would the daughter win, must with the mother first begin. *Bloody hell!*

The railway system provided work for many of the people from Alton, and Pat's father had been with the railway company for the whole of his working life, currently as a train driver. He almost continually smoked a pipe, which Mrs Wilson detested, shouting at him, in her very loud, fierce voice, 'Take that smelly thing out of my house.' Mr Wilson, Robert decided, was a very brave man, because he took not the slightest notice of her and continued doing exactly as he pleased. It was, however, many weeks before Robert would dare light up a cigarette in their house.

Also living at home with the Wilson family was Pat's older sister Ann, aged 19, and already married to George, who had also found employment with the railway as a porter at Alton station. Currently large with child, Ann was an older version of her younger sister and was expecting to give birth to her first child at about the same time that Robert expected to join the Navy. The older couple were hoping to rent a house of their own in the near future. In the meantime they occupied the second of the three bedrooms in the Wilson home, with Pat in a small box room.

After this initial visit, and encouraged by the warmth of Mr Wilson's reception, Robert felt more and more at ease in the Wilson household. He was always made welcome, fed and watered, and spent more and more of his time there. Mrs Wilson seemed to think that it was up to her to feed everyone that came through the front door, no matter what time of day or night.

The Wilson family had a television. Robert had, of course, watched it before but his own family had not, as yet, caught up with the times. After a few weeks, Mr and Mrs Wilson would, increasingly, spend their evenings in the large dining-room at the rear of the house and leave Robert and Pat to cuddle up on the settee and watch television. In time, Robert came to enjoy the never ending food and the cosy evenings with his sweetheart, and it certainly helped him to manage his meagre wages a little more easily.

Continually having to harden his heart against these new found homely comforts, Robert still went through moments of indecision about his future. Doubts were increasingly invading his mind; had he made the right decision? Perhaps the Navy was not the only option. Millions of other people seemed to have made a life without joining the military, perhaps he could do the same. Indecision attacking his brain from every angle, Robert considered approaching the railway management for a possible career, or maybe the busses, or apprenticing himself to one of the larger retail outlets; but his mind rejected every suggestion, returning always to the wonderful stories that Dave Skinner had related to him about the Navy.

With such grave doubts nagging at his mind, he found that, as the day for his medical examination drew ever nearer, he began to dread the thought of leaving both Pat and his family, possibly for weeks or months at a time. His final waking thought, before eventually drifting off to sleep each night, was the security that he somehow knew a life in the Royal Navy would provide for him and for his own family. An alternative argument, which reinforced his decision to join up, was that his own friend Jimmy had to work in that noisy, dirty, hot and smelly factory all day and every day for the rest of his working life. Just the thought was anathema to Robert; living such a life would be no life at all, he could not face it, he wanted something better.

Whenever the two young lovers were alone together, the conversation usually included plans for their marriage. They discussed the possibility of one day buying their own house, being independent of everything and everybody; this was almost an undreamed of concept for a small house could cost anything up to £1,000. They knew about mortgages, interest rates, inflation, the consequences of falling

194

behind with repayments, and they also knew that once committed to 25 years of mortgage repayments, it would be better to have some form of guaranteed income. Each night the decision to join the Navy was reconfirmed in his mind, only for the doubts to start all over again the following morning.

At last the day of his medical examination arrived. Robert was greatly relieved and was anxious to get this next milestone, on his journey into the RN, out of the way. Thankfully the recruiting office had sent another RN travel warrant, again saving Robert's hard-earned and dwindling funds, and he set off once again to Southampton. Feeling none of the uncertainty he had felt on his first trip, this time he knew the train times, which platform to use for the change at Winchester, which station to get off at in Southampton, the exact location of the recruiting office; he had done this before – no problem.

The first to arrive, Robert sat in the same waiting-room and the same recruiting officer greeted him as he passed through the waiting-room to his office. 'Come for your medical have you? Good lad,' he responded to Robert's cheerful 'Good morning, Chief!' Reading his many pamphlets and brochures had confirmed Robert's first assessment that the three buttons on the end of each sleeve did indeed denote a chief petty officer, and that such persons were normally addressed as Chief. Immaculate in his navy blue uniform, decorated with a long row of medal ribbons, the Chief smiled and continued on his way.

As the waiting-room filled up, the lads started chatting amongst themselves. There was a different atmosphere this morning, no anxious faces and fiddling fingers, but excited expressions and confident expectations of the coming medical. Hoping to glean whatever information he might, Robert overheard several stories bandied around the room about older brothers' experiences during these assessments, some reassuring and some instilling a degree of fear into each and every one of the candidates.

The room fell silent as the Chief came back into the room. 'Right lads, follow me,' and they were led into an adjoining locker room. 'Everyone bollocky-buff, the MO will be here very shortly!' *Bollocky-buff! What's that?* Robert waited to see what the other lads did and eventually got the message when a lad, who they later discovered had returned for a second medical, started to strip off his clothes. At school Robert had, of course, to undress for PE in front of the other boys and had been totally unselfconscious about doing so, however, this was different, these were all strangers and his old Y-fronts were not as new as they could be!

In not anticipating a group medical he now found himself considerably embarrassed. He had previewed it in his mind as a private consultation with a kindly old doctor and he strove to regain his composure and, above all, to stop blushing! All of the lads in the room, including the young man having his second attempt, stripped down to their underwear, and whilst awaiting further instructions, stood quietly, gazing at *anything* rather than at another person. Now that crunch time had finally arrived, all the cocky, confident tales had ceased. There was absolute silence in the room and not a few very worried faces. Robert jumped when he heard the Chief shout, 'I said bollocky-buff, that means everything, get 'em off, through that door and line up in the next room.' The Chief's friendly nature seemed to have deserted him!

Self-consciously, the would-be sailors slipped off their remaining underwear and shuffled through into the next room, hands hiding their private parts from view. Electric lighting was not necessary in this room, the line of lily-white young men, with their glowing red faces, would have lit up the whole of Southampton! One of the last to enter the room, Robert's eyes flew wide in astonishment when he saw the reason. There, seated at a small table, was a female doctor, dressed in a brilliant white coat and wearing huge, horn-rimmed glasses. Chief yelled, 'Keep silent, hands at your sides, you ain't got nothing Ma'am hasn't seen before!'

Standing up, she called each lad forward, eyed him up and down from the front, then, placing a hand on each shoulder, turned him around and did the same from the back. All the time she asked questions, the answers being recorded on a form by the completely unconcerned Chief, now sitting at the small table.

Soft hands reached up to rest lightly on Robert's shoulder. She was standing in front of him, much shorter, possibly in her late twenties and, he quickly assessed, quite attractive for an older woman. It was also quite obvious that under the fitted white coat was a very curvy figure. Responding to the gentle pressure on his shoulders, Robert turned and presented his backside for examination. Over the rear of his shoulders and down the rib of his backbone, the soft hands continued their search for defects, stopping just above the waistline. That wasn't too bad. Robert had quite enjoyed the touch of those soft hands and he was beginning to wonder why he had got so anxious about the whole business, allowing his previously rigid muscles to relax, looking forward to getting dressed and starting off home.

They were standing in line. The other lads to Robert's left were out of his sight, and he heard the Chief say, 'Keep your eyes to the front.' He heard a cough, several seconds later another cough, a slight delay, and another cough. Wondering what was causing the sudden coughing epidemic, Robert could resist the temptation no longer: he had to see what was going on. Leaning forward slightly he looked to his left along the line of waiting young men. To his horror he saw the female doctor grasp the scrotum of one of the lads and say, 'Cough!' *Bloody hell, this was not going to be easy!*

A little later he heard a slap and the female doctor say, in a stern voice, 'None of that!' Knowing exactly what had happened, Robert tried desperately to think of something that would prevent the same response in him. He need not have worried though, by the time she got to him Robert was totally incapable of any such response and was mortified when his cough was not considered strong enough and the warm hand remained in place for a second attempt! He would later joke to Jimmy that 'it was so nice I wanted a second go!'

During the ensuing frantic race to reclothe, the Chief told them that they had all passed the medical examination and would receive their joining instructions very shortly. The cheer that went up from the Navy's latest batch of recruits was deafening, which drew another smile from the Chief as he waved them goodbye.

Some few days later, after a gruelling day at the foundry, Robert received a letter with his joining instructions, again with a naval travel warrant. He was to report to HMS *Victory*, RN Barracks, Portsmouth, before midday on 30th April, 1957.

The night before his departure he had said a heart-wrenching and tearful goodbye to Pat. Having said farewell to his father earlier, Robert left his aunt's house on a wet and windy April evening to spend the evening with his sweetheart. A return to better health had enabled his father to obtain a part-time job helping out at the local bus station and he would be up early the next morning to go to work. The evening with Pat was a sombre affair, neither quite knowing what to say nor wishing the evening to end. Time, as ever, was relentless and unforgiving and at about eleven o'clock Robert kissed his love goodbye, dashed out into the rain lest his tears betray him, and walked disconsolately to his aunt's house.

A little after midnight, the night before his departure, he retrieved his blankets and pillows from behind the settee and tried to sleep. Tossing and turning for most of the night, he had finally woken, bathed in sweat, having had his oil drum nightmare once again. He lay on the settee for a while, at first not really sure where he was. His mind was in a turmoil. Today was his last chance to change his mind: he knew that once he had signed the forms in the naval barracks, he was committed to at least nine years' service.

Over the preceding week Robert had been checking train departures for his trip to Portsmouth, a city that he had not visited before, and, following his nightmare, he tried to calm himself in his own proven way, by previewing the day's coming events. But the knowledge had disappeared, his mind was a blank, in his present state he could no more get to Portsmouth than get to the moon. Once again, without any known self-induction, the vision of Mrs Sandsfoot magically appeared. *Steady, Robert!* Once again it was as if an electrical switch had been made in his brain. Suddenly calm, he remembered the exact route to Portsmouth and the sequence of events that would get him there.

Robert listened to the noises of his father getting up, washing and shaving, and for probably the first time in his life, making his own breakfast, mother having refused to prolong the agony of saying goodbye to her youngest son by getting up early. Feigning sleep, he waited until he heard his father leave the house. He wanted to get up and say a last farewell, but he knew that he could not face that again; he still had to say goodbye to his mother.

As quietly as he could, Robert got out of his settee-bed,

199

folded the sheets and blankets, and placed the whole pile of bedding at the rear of the settee, as he did every morning. There were no suitcases to pack. He was permitted to take with him only toilet necessities and these would make the journey to Portsmouth in a small polythene bag. Having tiptoed up to the bathroom, he washed quickly, cleaned his teeth, and waited until a little before eight o'clock when he heard his mother in the tiny bathroom. Robert made a fresh pot of tea. He would not be able to eat anything but a cup of warm, very sweet tea might bolster his flagging spirit. Upstairs Robert heard his mother return to her bedroom and he clearly heard the sound of her quiet sobs.

He was due to leave the house at 8.30 to catch the nine o'clock train to Winchester, but the sobbing was upsetting him badly and he left the house for a last walk along Flood Meadows to try and regain some composure. He was all ready to go, he told himself, just grab the polythene bag, kiss his mother and go. Don't prolong the goodbye, for both their sakes. At the last moment his courage failed him, he could not face seeing his mother. He returned to the house at about 8.15, shouted up the stairs to his mother that he was leaving, grabbed his plastic bag containing his toiletries, birth certificate, medical card, joining instructions, and naval travel warrant, and rushed out of the house into the April rain.

Having left his aunt's house and chickened out of a tearful farewell to his mother, Robert was beginning to feel more his old self, but still very upset. In the inside pocket of his jacket there was an envelope containing the £100 in new £5 notes, bequeathed to him by Mrs Sandsfoot, and an additional £20 that he had managed to save from his recent earnings. Luckily, he had managed to deny all temptation to spend any of his savings over the past few months. A little nest egg, he was sure, would always come in handy.

As he walked up the hill towards the secondary school, he was in an extremely agitated and emotional state. Today was his coming of age. Also this was to be his first day of fending for himself, having relinquished the support of his parents and, except for the night under the snow and a couple of nights with Dave Skinner's family, the first day on which he would not return to his home.

The steep hill narrowed considerably towards the apex of the hill, leaving very little room for the large double-decker busses that regularly used this route ferrying children to Amery Hill Secondary School. He was desperately trying to choke back the tears and it was not until he stepped off the pavement to cross the road that he heard the bus, trundling up the hill to the school.

Robert nearly died that day.

BOOK 2
KRANJI

6

RN Barracks, Portsmouth

The two young men walked out of Portsmouth railway station and stepped down onto the cobbled forecourt. They looked up at the clearing April sky, there had been a huge thunderstorm on their journey from Eastleigh. One of the young men, a handsome man about 5 foot 8 inches tall, with black, wavy hair and dressed in black blazer and grey flannel trousers, glanced up at the overhead electrical and telephone cables spreading like a spider's web over the forecourt. He could see the pigeons sitting in lines on the cables, and there was already ample evidence of their presence on the taxis waiting below. The two young men looked around; they were not sure how to get to their destination, RN Naval Barracks, Portsmouth. To the left could be seen a tunnel under the railway line. In front, the road was jammed solid with traffic in both directions; one thing they did know, they were not about to waste money on a taxi!

The two had met on the train just after it departed Eastleigh Station. The handsome young man had been sitting alone in a carriage containing at least 50 seats, and the newcomer looked around as he entered the carriage through the connecting door. The newcomer, seeing the other young man, walked the length of the carriage and sat down opposite him. They sat in silence, looking at one another. They were dressed similarly, each wearing collar and tie and shiny shoes.

The newcomer was a bubbly extrovert, full of life and the exuberant happiness of the young. 'Hello,' he said, in a broad Scottish accent, 'I'm James, call me Jock, Muir, and I'm off to Pompey to join the Navy.'

The other young man seemed to brighten from his depressed mood, and thinking very quickly, he said, 'Hello, I'm Robert, call me Bob, Leonard, and I'm off to Pompey to join the Navy as well!' During the remaining 40 minutes or so of the journey to Portsmouth, the two young men exchanged details of their respective families and lives and discovered they both had the same orders to report to the naval barracks by midday.

The broad Scottish accent, to Robert's unaccustomed ears, was extremely difficult to understand, almost a foreign language and, initially, he had to ask Jock to repeat much of their conversation. The friendly introduction from Mr James Muir had dragged Robert from his depressing thoughts, and he, instantly knowing that a similar response was required of him, had to think very quickly for something suitable. The only diminutive or nickname that he could come up with for himself was Bob. *So be it,* he thought, *from now on I shall be Bob.* Robert had been his mother's name for him and he felt the tears start to well up inside him again. No more of that, he told himself firmly, a new name will help with the break from home and the start of his new life.

He had been extremely fortunate whilst walking up the hill from his aunt's house – he could not think of it as home – but as soon as he heard the bus he knew that he had made a very dangerous mistake and a flashback of Tuscan going under the wheels of the school bus flitted across his mind. Suddenly he had been whisked off his feet and bounced against the houses that crowded the pavement. He turned sideways and found himself looking at the beaming face of a huge black man. 'You want to watch where you're going, man,' Bob's black saviour said, his wide mouth and sparkling white teeth beaming in a wide smile, and without another word strode off up the hill.

Bob, as he now thought of himself, shouted his thanks after the departing black giant. There was no response and the man disappeared into the churchyard and was gone. For several years Bob would keep an eye out for the huge man, hoping to express his thanks, but was never to see or hear of him again.

Standing outside Portsmouth Central, Bob and Jock had about 30 minutes left to beat the midday deadline for reporting at the barracks. They decided to risk walking and asked a very smart-looking elderly lady, standing at the steps to the station, if she knew how to get to the barracks. She gave them some directions: 'Turn left, under the bridge and follow the footpath at the side of the Guildhall, through the park and the barracks are right in front of you.' She added that it would take them about ten minutes.

They started off and as soon as they emerged from the far end of the tunnel under the railway line, it started to rain heavily. Emerging from the far end of the park at a crossroads, they could see on the other side of the road a high wall, enclosing numerous large brick buildings within. This was obviously their destination, but they hesitated, not sure whether to follow the wall to the left or right, since they could not see any entrance into the barracks. After a few moments of indecision Jock asked a passer-by where the entrance was. The poor chap must have struggled for comprehension over the Scottish accent just as Bob had done, for he looked blankly at Jock and said, 'Pardon?' Quickly appreciating the problem, Bob repeated the question. The passer-by looked to his left and pointed along the wall and said 'about a hundred yards' as he turned away.

The two young men stood outside the imposing gates to the barracks. The gates were wide open and they did not know whether to walk through this gaping entrance or through the small door they could see to the right. On this occasion there was no need to ask; someone barged past them, opened the side door and disappeared within.

Having pushed his last moment of doubt out of his mind, Bob led his new acquaintance through the small side door. The reception was none too friendly. 'What do you two want?' asked a burly sailor, dressed in full blue uniform but also wearing white anklets and a white belt. 'We're joining up,' said Jock and they each handed over their letters containing their joining instructions. The burly sailor hesitated and glared at the two young men standing in front of him soaking wet and dripping over the shiny floor, searching to identify some imagined insolence in Jock's voice – 'Not more wet-behind-the-ear PJs!' A huge rubber stamp, raised theatrically into the air by the angry sailor, was slammed down onto an ink pad and then, with yet another flourish, smashed down on their joining instructions, leaving an imprint that recorded their arrival – *Main Gate, HMS Victory, 30 April, 1957*. Beneath this stamp the white-belted sailor had written *1150A*.

Neither of the two young men knew what PJs were – surely the chap could not have been talking about pyjamas – nor why the letter 'A' followed the time, but they both thought that their present location was not the place to ponder, and perish the thought of asking their receptionist! 'Wait there,' they were told, and after a few minutes a much younger sailor arrived, dressed in what looked like blue denim shirt and trousers. He was a very tall and very skinny young man; his arms looked like twigs protruding from the rolled-up ends of his shirt sleeves. A curt 'follow me' and they were led, dripping wet – in more ways than one – into the barracks to a large classroom with desks and chairs laid out in precisely placed rows as in a schoolroom.

Inside the room sat about 50 other young men, dressed still in civilian clothing, with a petty officer standing at the front. 'Good morning PO,' said Bob in his most polite voice.

'You're bloody late and don't call me PO,' was the unfriendly response. 'Sit down at the back and shut up!' Bob felt deflated: he had spent hours studying the brochures from the recruiting office and knew that PO was the correct address for this person; the crossed anchors atop three stripes on his left arm left no room for doubt. *Go with the flow,* Bob reminded himself of his own promise, and concentrated whilst the PO told them that the 53 young men were to be a basic training class, and he was to be their class instructor.

No mention was made of the fact that both Bob and Jock were soaking wet and no opportunity to dry out was offered. The PO had a strange accent and Bob discovered later that he was a Geordie, from the Midlands. The class would address him, at all times, as sir; in fact, they were warned, it would be better if they called *everyone* sir for the next twelve weeks of their basic training.

They were each given their serial numbers and informed of their rating 'rank, for those of you who don't know nothing,' the PO added. The PO seemed to be in a particularly foul mood and shouted that Bob and Jock's rating would be 'Ordinary Telegraphist,' to be written as O/Tel, as would be eleven others in the group. 'I'm a gunnery instructor and I don't much care for bloody sparkers, so watch yourselves,' he added for Bob and Jock's benefit.

The entire group was signing up for nine years' service, which would not commence until they were eighteen years old; when they had completed the first nine years they would have an opportunity to sign on for a further five, and after completion of fourteen years', signing on to complete the full twenty-two years service that qualified for a naval pension. If all those in authority were the same as this agitated and angry PO, then perhaps a slight change in plans might be wise, but just in time Bob remembered to go with the flow.

To Bob's dismay there were 14 ordinary signalmen, the specialisation that he had first chosen, and he finally realised that the recruiting officer in Southampton had obviously guided him towards what the Navy needed rather than what the recruit wanted. He smiled inwardly, thought of national service, and, wisely, kept his mouth shut; he was certain that any request he might now make would mark him as a troublemaker and that was the last thing he wanted.

Most of the branches of the Royal Navy had their own in-house nicknames; sparkers, Bob later discovered, was the in-house nickname for telegraphists. Bunting tossers were the visual signallers; dab-toes, the seamen branch; 'airy-fairies, the naval air branch; pussers, the supply branch (in fact the word pusser also indicated *anything* naval); stokers for the engine room branch; greenies, the electrical branch; and crushers were the Navy police force or regulating branch. The other arms of the military services were known as pongos (Army); Brylcreem boys (RAF); and bootnecks (Royal Marines). Obviously the other arms of the military services returned the compliment: the Royal Navy was, apparently, known as sandscratchers.

All of this information tumbled out of their instructor's mouth as the class, for the next hour or so, completed what seemed to Bob and Jock an endless pile of forms, each one requiring the basic information of Name, Rating, Official Number, Next of Kin (NOK), NOK Address, Ship, Date, and whatever additional details each particular form required. Bob's official number was PJ971623 and Jock's, PJ971624. They were told to memorise their official numbers by the following morning. Bob did not know what to include under the *Ship* heading, but he wasn't about to ask any questions today. He could feel the instructor's eyes boring into the top of his head as he concentrated on completing the forms. *I'll wait and see what happens.* Sure enough, a few minutes later, the instructor roared, 'What do you mean you don't know what ship you're on, this is HMS bloody *Victory* and don't you forget it,' in answer to a very polite question from some unfortunate, puzzled young man. The gunnery instructors of the Royal Navy, Bob was later told, had to have their brains and balls removed and replaced with additional lungs so that they could shout louder!

Whilst laboriously filling in the multitude of forms, Bob wondered why the instructor had to shout all the time, even inside this classroom. They were all young men with perfectly good hearing but the instructor seemed incapable of lowering his voice. *What will the neighbours think?* thought Bob and giggled, which he instantly regretted when he heard, 'what do you find so funny, you expletive deleted!'

Their instructor was never heard to actually swear, other than the odd, mild *bloody* or *sod*; instead he used the expression *expletive deleted* whenever he really wanted to swear. The class eventually christened him Echo Delta, the phonetic equivalent of the first letter of the two words, and they quickly came to recognise exactly when the phrase would be used. Whenever Echo Delta felt really exasperated with some failure by the class or by some individual, he would slowly raise his arms, extended straight out in front of him until they were parallel with the ground, point both digit fingers at whoever or whatever had incurred his displeasure, and say, for example, 'Expletive deleted, I have told you a dozen times how to press these expletive deleted trousers, did your mother not teach you how to use an iron you expletive deleted excuse for a (psst) sparker!' He also had a quaint way of indicating his extreme dislike of certain things and would imitate a spitting action, without actually spitting, before mentioning the offending subject, indicated in the above example by (*psst*).

The form-filling marathon completed, the class was led to an adjacent building to collect their kit. No attempt was made to organise them into a squad, they just followed Echo Delta wherever he went. Jock and Bob, about the same size, were almost glued together; they were an alliance of two, which gave them a slight advantage because the rest of the class, at that stage, were still mere individuals.

The process of issuing all their kit took at least two hours and it was after 4.30 by the time they left the naval stores building, staggering under the weight of their kitbags. Each member of the class had been issued with an enormous amount of kit, including a gas mask and something called anti-flash gear – long elbow-length white cotton gloves and a white cotton balaclava for protection from the flash that accompanied the firing of a warship's main guns. *Gas mask?* thought Bob; having lived with two brothers he was used to a certain amount of flatulence, *but will there be that much farting!*

They were given blue serge uniforms with wide bell-bottomed trousers that had a flap at the front instead of buttons or a zip; the denim outfits that they had seen the other sailors wearing when they first entered the barracks; two pairs of boots – one pair rubber-soled and another pair, leather-soled; shoes; blue sailors' collars; lanyards; blue seaman's jerseys; and white fronts – the collarless, short-sleeved cotton tops with blue piping around the neck. These were also belts, gaiters, shoe cleaning equipment, and a housewife, which was a sailor's repair kit containing needles, thread, wool, scissors, etc. in a small roll-up canvas container. Plus caps, cap-tallies, and, to everyone's total disbelief, coarse underwear that should have been white but was, in fact, a very off-white, yellowish colour! When Bob later opened up a pair of folded underpants they were impressively large with plenty of room for both himself and Jock plus three other members of the class to have climbed inside!

When they thought the issue complete, they were told to go back along the counter to collect their tropical kit, gigantic blue and white shorts, sandals, white shoes, white suits, more white fronts, and white socks. They were not, at this stage, issued with any badges to sew onto their uniforms to denote their branch; they would have to earn those at their respective specialisation training establishments.

Echo Delta led his charges – each laden with kit – the long way around the perimeter of the parade ground, a large open area in the centre of the various buildings, explaining that if they ever had cause to cross the parade ground it must be done at the double (running). He doubted their ability to run under the weight of their kitbags and other bits and pieces tucked under arms, draped around necks, and shoved into pockets. They had been allowed to leave their hammocks, a large sausage-like parcel, neatly strapped with rope, and their suitcases, both large and small (Echo Delta called them a 'Pusser's green' and a 'Pusser's brown'!) in the issue room for collection later that evening.

Echo Delta's latest challenge were led, eventually, to a large barracks block containing living accommodation on five floors, each of the floors above ground level being reached via two sets of stairs. Their mess deck was, of course, on the top floor, and the effort to carry their kitbags up the eight flights of steps left them all gasping for breath. Some of their number had to dash back along their route to recover items they had dropped; at the time they had been so fearful of losing sight of Echo Delta that they had left the items where they had fallen.

The room into which they were led was open plan and cavernous, with wide, round, metal poles supporting the roof and communal toilets ('heads' in Navy speak), and bathrooms at the far end. Each floor was subdivided into three sections by the metal supporting poles, and Bob later worked out that there were beds for about 450 people on each floor. The beds were metal framed, stacked three high, and were placed down the sides of each section; each tier of bunks had a stack of three metal lockers to one side and there was a large table with about a dozen chairs in the centre of each living area, or mess deck.

The accommodation for the class had already been allocated, but not the individual beds. By pure chance, Bob and Jock managed to reserve the stack of three at the furthest end of their mess deck, and, as each young man took his pick, were pleasantly surprised to find that the top bunk was left spare. There were 53 in the class.

Echo Delta gave them no time to recover. As soon as the stragglers had recovered their kit he told them to grab the tin mugs, knife, fork and spoon that they had been issued with and led them down to the ground floor dining-hall for supper. *Nothing is the same*, Bob thought wryly, *not even the expletive deleted dining-room!*

Bob was now ravenously hungry and desperately thirsty after the long, stressful and strenuous day. He had been too upset to eat any breakfast, and had not been offered an opportunity to obtain any lunch. The class had been listening to the public announcements all afternoon, over the loudspeakers, which seemed to be fitted absolutely everywhere. One of the many announcements had been, '*Stand-easy!*'

Echo Delta had explained that stand-easy usually signalled a short rest period of about 20 minutes, during which time 'proper sailors' could get a cup of tea, have a smoke or whatever. 'And they're not public announcements, you expletive deleted, they're pipes!' At the time, Bob silently wondered if he was joining a foreign country. The Navy seemed to have a language of its own, however, he could not have expressed this thought because he was, at the time, like all the other young men, up to his armpits in kit!

The dining-hall covered the whole of the ground floor, with long lines of large dining-tables, each capable of sitting ten sailors. The kitchens ('galleys' in Navy speak) were enclosed within a long, single-storey extension to the main building, with the serving hatch, the width of the block, separating galleys from dining-hall. Each man took a metal food tray, partitioned into areas for main course and two receptacles for separate metal soup and pudding bowls.

The noise in the dining-hall when they arrived was ear-shattering, with about 200 young men talking to one another added to the general noise of chairs scraping and boots tramping around the room. Waiting as patiently as possible in the long queue of hungry sailors, Bob and Jock awaited their turn, all the time watching how those in front dealt with the mountains of food. When their turn came they filled a bowl with soup, grabbed a pile of sliced bread, and held out their trays to the serving staff, who dropped huge portions into the main course receptacle.

There was no question of choice or any attempt to display the food in an appetising layout; a portion from each of the steaming trays of meat, potatoes, vegetables, etc. was deposited, one on top of the other, onto each tray, whether the food was wanted or not. A huge wedge of pudding ('duff' in Navy speak) was deposited into the remaining metal bowl, followed by a ladle of runny custard, after which they carried their meals in search of the nearest vacant table. At some stage during the meal the metal mugs could be filled with tea from a line of large urns in the centre of the dining-hall.

Both Bob and Jock got stuck in, in truth they could have eaten a raw cow or even Echo Delta himself if necessary. Brought up on meals containing lashings of vegetables, Bob watched the pile grow on his tray. There were few vegetables that he did not like; the same for meat except that he did not much care for offal dishes. As he looked at the other men, sitting at the same table, he could see that some were used to more selective fare! One or two were gazing down at the metal trays in total astonishment, or picking over the pile of food, wondering which pieces were actually edible! They were still in their civilian clothing, Bob and Jock still a little damp, and it seemed to Bob that some of the other, *real sailors*, were keeping a sharp eye on them.

At the time he could think of no reason why the new group should attract so much attention, but did not discover the answer until they returned to their mess deck. A very boyish-looking member of their group was overheard asking, in a very frightened voice, 'Were we supposed to wash-up our mugs, knives and forks and bring them with us?' obviously having only recently noticed that most of the class had done just that! Several of the class, including the boyish lad, had scraped the remaining food off their trays into the big waste bins and tossed the soiled tray, together with their personal mug and utensils, into the waiting washing-up sinks. And that, Bob suddenly realised, is what the more experienced sailors were waiting for, the chance to obtain some of the mugs and utensils inadvertently discarded by the newcomers, either to barter or retain as spares. To have lost items of kit, on the very first day, would be regarded by Echo Delta as a serious crime, which no doubt would attract some terrible punishment for those involved. *That's good.* Bob felt no sympathy; at such an early

216

stage it was every man for himself. *Perhaps it will give old Echo Delta someone else to keep his beady eyes upon!*

Echo Delta had already explained, earlier that afternoon, that all of the issued kit was now the responsibility of each individual, adding that included in pay was a small allowance for kit upkeep. However, with 53 men struggling to keep track of each piece of kit and the general noise and mélée, it was not always possible to hear every pearl of wisdom that Echo Delta dropped. Back in the mess deck, Bob and Jock now feeling much better after their meal, all was total chaos. Echo Delta's vocal capabilities now came into their own as he roared for silence, told everyone to gather round while he demonstrated how to fold each item of kit so that it would fit inside the small locker.

Striding up to the end of the mess deck, in his tick-tock fashion, he opened Bob's locker and proceeded to fold the pile of kit and fit it neatly inside the metal container. Bob was inwardly elated at his good fortune. He was not to escape though. Echo Delta pulled the whole lot out again and threw it on the floor. 'I hate expletive deleted (psst) sparkers,' he mumbled and strode off shouting for the bunch of 'expletive deleted morons who have already lost some of their expletive deleted Pusser's kit!'

A short half an hour later Echo Delta was screaming for everyone to get a move on. 'We have yet to collect hammocks and cases from the slop room and then I will have to teach you mother's rejects how to make your beds, but,' he continued quickly, 'I am not tucking you in or giving you a good expletive deleted night's kiss!'

Echo Delta must have been desperate for a pint because he invited the class to 'pick up the double' back to the kit-issue room and the class ran, through the sudden rainstorm, around the perimeter road once again. When the class finally struggled back up the eight flights of steps, soaking wet, each trying to balance the long sausage of hammock and the two suitcases, they had just about reached the end of their tethers. All they wanted to do was climb into bed; it was eight o'clock. On top of each of the bunks was a thin rolled-up mattress, two course cream-coloured blankets, a pale-blue bed cover with a naval motif embroidered into it, and a pillow. 'No sheets or pillow-cases,' Bob heard one of the men groan as he attempted to follow Echo Delta's demonstration of making up a bed.

Their instructor, the two legged shouting machine, left them to their own devices, with his parting orders ringing in their ears. 'I'll be back at 0530 in the morning and I want to see those beds as you found them, all of you washed, shaved and dressed in number eights.' He knew they were tired and he also must have known that they had no idea what number eights were and would have to go begging an explanation from one of the other classes who had been in the RN for more than a day.

Until this time the class had been allowed precious little time to get to know one another, except for the short period when eating supper, and they now collapsed onto their bunks and gazed around at each other. The room was a shambles: most had not managed to complete the storage of their kit; suitcases and hammocks littered every available floor space. They were leaderless, most totally disorientated and baffled by the enormous amount of information that had been hurled, carelessly, and at maximum volume, in their direction. They were so tired that they could hardly move.

Desperate for the toilet and a shower, Bob jumped from his bed and went bounding off to the end of the dormitory. When he got there he met a young sailor coming out, dressed in his smart, neatly pressed serge uniform. 'Excuse me, sir,' Bob kept his voice as polite as possible, 'can you please tell me what number eights are?' The smartly dressed sailor explained that it was the blue denim-like clothing, added that it included boots, belt, and gaiters, and left with a departing 'oh and remember to use the mess deck clock for everything' and 'you don't have to call me sir.'

After a refreshing shower, Bob repeated the information gleaned from his chance encounter to Jock who immediately passed the information to the class in a fine imitation of Echo Delta. Unfortunately another class member had also spoken to a passing sailor and been told that it was the blue serge uniform, with plimsoles. Both lads suspected that if each of the 53 members of their class were to ask the question, they would each return with a different answer.

Some time later, after a considerable amount of trial and error, Bob and Jock had managed to store all their kit into their lockers, had made up their beds, and stowed their hammocks and suitcases on top of the spare top bunk. Tired as they were they had tried to preview the following day and had already sorted out the kit for the following morning. They decided to react to the information that Bob had been told; the young man had seemed very genuine, he told Jock, and they both curled up into the rough blankets.

On this, his first night, sleep would not come easily to Bob. The noise from the surrounding mess decks was very loud and some of his own class had not yet managed to sort themselves out. The blankets were itchy and the cover of the pillow was rough and coarse to the touch, with annoying little feathers poking through the outer covering. The whole class had reacted as one in respect of the gigantic pairs of issued striped pyjamas, unanimously rejecting them, preferring to sleep in their civilian underwear or naked.

Hours later, with his thoughts turning to Pat, Bob fell into a deep, dreamless sleep. Almost immediately, it seemed to Bob, he was awoken by a clattering of dustbin lids being banged against the supporting poles, accompanied by young men screaming 'wakey wakey, rise and shine, you've had your sleep now I want mine!'

There was an awful smell in the room. Some of the class had not been used to eating that much cabbage, guessed Bob, a thought which restored his usual good humour. Well used to getting up early, the *'ampshire boy*, closely followed by Jock, sprinted through the other mess decks in a bid to obtain a vacant sink before the queues built up. Bob had discussed this tactic with Jock the previous evening when they had noticed that there most certainly were not enough sinks to cater for the 450 young men at the same time. Their tactics worked beautifully and they were the first two back into the mess deck, feeling refreshed and ready for the new day.

Some of the class had remained in bed, arguing that the mess deck clock was fast. Most of the 53 new arrivals folded their bedding and replaced it as near as possible in the way in which they had found it, and waited for Echo Delta to arrive.

About 15 minutes later Echo Delta arrived, heavily studded boots ringing on the stone floors. Bob looked up at the mess deck clock, which read 0525. '*So Echo Delta works by the mess deck clock*,' Bob whispered to Jock and they felt more comfortable about their decision to believe Bob's discovered definition of number eights. As they looked around, the whole mess deck, apart from their own little space, was again in chaos, as were most of the other members of the class.

One or two lingered still in bed, some were queuing in the bathrooms or toilets, some dressed in the blue serge uniforms and plimsoles, others dressed in similar outfits to Jock and Bob. One chap, for some unknown reason, had untied his hammock, perhaps in the hope of a more comfortable night's sleep, and it lay in an untidy heap on

220

the floor when the chap had been unable to retie it. A small group of about six had decided to risk the wrath of Echo Delta by not dressing, waiting in their civilian underwear to see how he reacted to the appearance of the class.

The whole class had decided that the service underwear and pyjamas would never be used; they were, without exception, much too big and much too rough. With a sardonic smile on his face, Echo Delta stood silently in the midst of this chaos for a few minutes, then grabbed one of the class dressed exactly as Bob and Jock and said, 'I'll be back in fifteen minutes and when I get back you will all look like this sorry expletive deleted specimen.' He then turned and marched noisily from the mess deck. He was back almost instantly, and pointing at the group in their civilian underwear, said, 'except for those, you expletive deleted lot stay exactly as you are.' Fifteen minutes later he was back again and smiled, or grimaced, since it was difficult to tell the difference, at the order that had been restored to the mess deck. He strode up to the small group still in their underwear, ordered them to strip off and put on the service underwear and then parade up and down the mess deck. It was hilarious: the underwear was more like pyjamas than pants and vests, and the small incident served as a much needed release of tension, if only for a few minutes in what was to be another extremely tiring and trying day.

And so to breakfast, another huge affair consisting of porridge or cereals ('wheaties' in Navy speak), a full English fry-up, toast, fruit, and tea. This morning as an extra treat the chefs were serving their own, uniquely tasting dish consisting of devilled kidneys in a dark brown, runny sauce served on fried bread, which the Navy called, in its own inimitable way, 'shit on a raft!' Although very hungry, Bob refused to try the disgusting-looking concoction; it was, after all, offal. Much later, on Jock's recommendation, he tried the dish and was pleasantly surprised at how delicious it tasted, and for many years afterwards would relish the distinctive smell as he entered various dining-halls.

After breakfast they returned to their mess deck to commence the day's activities. Their first job was to mark their kit with their names and to this end the class was escorted back to the kit-issue room (the 'slops' in Navy speak) to make up their name tallies. These were made from individual lengths of wood, about 3 inches long and a half inch square, with a letter carved into the end. Each person chose the letters that made up his initials and surname and inserted them into a special frame. This name tally was then pushed into a tray of black or white paint, depending on the colour of the garment to be marked, and, if you were very careful for it was a very messy business, left a neat outline of your name. This name tally then became a part of your kit and every item of kit had to be marked. Any item of kit found without your name on it, or without a name at all, was not considered yours and was instantly confiscated and put into special storage, overseen by the regulating branch, called the 'scran-bag.'

The scran-bag was the first port of call when anyone lost an item of kit. Even if you did not recover the exact item you had lost, there might be a similar item that you could purchase, at a nominal cost, that the 'crushers' transferred to the 'ship's fund.' Echo Delta later warned them to be very careful if they ever purchased any kit from the scran-bag. If the item of kit that they needed already had a name stamped upon it, they should ensure that they asked the crushers to put a DC stamp over the original name. The crushers were not averse to letting someone trot happily away with a piece of kit with someone else's name on it, knowing full well that it would soon be confiscated and returned to the scran-bag, bolstering the ship's fund.

The marking of their kit had been carried out on the mess deck, and the scene when they had all finished looked as if there had been a paint throwing contest. Most of the class had stripped off their clothes, and were doing the job in underwear and bare feet, better the paint on skin than on kit. However, there would always be a few, amongst the 53 of them, that got something wrong in whatever endeavour the class was currently engaged upon, and several had dripped paint over items of their kit.

Echo Delta had no mercy. Anything with paint on, other than the name, was confiscated, and the perpetrators sent back to slops to buy replacements, the costs being set against forthcoming pay if necessary. The only items of kit not name-stamped in this way were socks, footwear and the gas mask. Each man had to sew into each sock a small white label with his name handwritten in black ink upon it. Having watched his mother on many occasions sewing, darning, and knitting, Bob had no difficulty with this chore; but he had to chuckle when he saw some of the other efforts! One man had sewn all of the white labels using black cotton and was seen, late that evening, trying to re-sew them before the lights went out at ten o'clock. Names were stamped onto footwear and on to the small, brown disc attached to the gas mask, using metal dyes; and whilst they were in the special stamping room they used the hammers to stud their leather-soled boots.

Growing more and more exasperated with the many mistakes made by his new class, Echo Delta told them that they would have to remove the studs when they joined their first ship, because they could cause sparks and start fires. On the way to the slop room to make up their name tallies, Echo Delta had arranged them into a marching group and they had made their first uncoordinated effort at walking as one.

Working himself into a fine old rage at their pathetic efforts, their instructor shouted at the top of his voice; 'Left, right, left, right,' as he pranced around the group, snapping at their heels, *like a good sheep dog*, thought Bob. Late in the afternoon Echo Delta took his revenge for their depressing efforts and, as each man sat in the barber's chair, took great delight in ensuring that each head was virtually shaved of all hair. It was a somewhat brutal experience: the barber was none too gentle and his sneering 'something for the weekend, sir?' when he finished each man did not raise even the slightest chuckle from the class. Strangely, they all looked remarkably similar after the haircut, and when Bob looked into the mirror that evening he thought *Pat's not going to like that!*

The 'Awkward Squad' would not be allowed out of the barracks for the first month, and during that time they learned a whole new way of life. In addition to the new language, a huge and complicated feat in itself, they had to learn how to dress themselves, wash, iron, sew, and darn their clothes. They had to press the bell-bottom trousers with the seven horizontal creases, in each leg, exactly the same distance apart as the width of the naval pay book (about 4 inches wide and eventually superseded by the naval identity card); fold and press their seaman's collars; tie the silk; and fit the lanyard correctly. Not to mention fold their bedding and tie their cap-tallies so that the bow was directly over the left ear and of the correct size whilst ensuring that the centre letter of HMS *Victory* was directly in line with one's nose. For many years Bob would chuckle when he remembered some of those cap-tallies, it had taken several attempts for him to get his own bows correct!

They learned how to scrub the floors, clean the windows, clean out the bathrooms and heads, dish out the food, wash the enormous piles of metal food trays, and fill the hundreds of condiment sets on the dining-hall tables. How to salute, learn the marching commands, march and manoeuvre individually and as a group. They were taught rifle and guard commands; how to shine their boots and shoes; to recite the monosyllabic responses at church services; basic seamanship such as tying knots (Bob's weak subject!), firing rifles, pistols, and machine-guns, fire-fighting, and ABCD (Atomic Biological and Chemical Defence), which included hours of dreary lessons about totally incomprehensible things like roentgens, at which Bob would drift off, *bum on broomstick!*

They would learn to recognise the different badges of branch and rating and the various ranks of the officers, how to find one's way around a warship made up of many small compartments, how to behave when ashore, the various leave and travel warrant allowances, their pay structure and promotion (the Navy uses the term 'advancement' for the lower deck), how to contact their naval surgeon (a GP was available in most large towns to fulfil this role) when on leave, and differentiate between the various numbered generic activities. Almost everything was done by numbers, for example, 'number nines' was both a punishment and a dress code!

Some needed more help than others. There were those in the class who had obviously been mollycoddled and seemed incapable of the most basic tasks; some even did not know how to shave! Even more had not actually had any experience of working for their living before joining up, relying on their parents to keep body and soul together. The practical life on the estate had served Bob well, for he was confident in problem solving, making do, interpreting orders, doing as he was told, and looking after himself.

Contrasting starkly with Bob, Jock's almost unbelievable upbringing in the tough Gorbals area of Glasgow made him a formidable fighter; even his fierce Scottish accent turned away most challenges and it was no surprise when, several years later, Jock became the Navy's middleweight boxing champion. On the several occasions that the pair had to defend their extra mess space it was usually Jock that influenced their challengers to back down! Not that Bob was any slouch: his body was covered in hardened muscle from the manual work on the estate and he, too, could hold his own with most.

The duo were a solid, dependable team; what one did not know the other usually did and they stuck closely together. Even when marching they were able to stay together, because they were almost the same size, and Echo Delta's plea of 'shortest in the centre, tallest on the flanks' did not separate them.

Throughout the second evening of their twelve week stay at *Victory*, Jock was suffering a little. He wanted a pint and Bob remembered the smell of beer on him when they had sat opposite one another on the train. But they were not allowed into the beer canteen until they were 18, and although they were allowed to move around the barracks in their free time, they had to carry their station cards at all times, which identified them as both under age and trainees, which effectively barred their access to most of the recreational areas.

Not that there was much free time! Every day was crammed with classroom lessons, or marching practice. At least once a week, after supper, the entire class was instructed to prepare for a scheduled kit muster, where every item of kit was expected to be laid out on the floor by the side of the bunks, in strict compliance with the kit muster list and photograph posted on the mess notice-board. Everything had to be meticulously clean and pressed, and folded into exactly the right size. Even the tiniest deviation from the photograph was pounced upon by Echo Delta who would kick the individual's kit into a messy pile, and, if by doing so the neighbouring neatly laid out kit was disturbed, then that too was declared unaccept-able. The offending person or persons would lay out their kit repeatedly until either Echo Delta or the Duty PO was satisfied, even to the extent of making the offenders carry their entire kit, involving several trips up those eight flights of steps, down to the dining-hall, if they had not provided satisfaction by lights out.

It was therefore in everyone's interest that each checked the other's layout. Bob and Jock regarded themselves as extremely lucky in that there was no other person in their bunk space and they had only to worry about each other. As is the case in any group of people, there are always a few who find it difficult to conform or comply, and one such occupied the bunk space next to the team. Jibing unmercifully at the nearby unfortunate, Jock had said, after their first kit muster, 'if we had that wazzock over there on our top bunk we would be here all night!' Attempting to sound like a Scottish 'ampshire boy, Jock had quickly adopted some of Bob's country expressions, which usually reduced Bob to a blubbering heap of laughter.

Unscheduled kit musters could be awarded for almost any misdemeanour or misbehaviour, whether real or imagined on the part of their instructor, and not one single evening would pass, in the twelve weeks that they were in the barracks, without at least one person laying out their kit. Two would win the ultimate prize of preparing a kit muster on the day the class left barracks. Lucky devils!

For the most part both Bob and Jock stayed clear of most of the trouble and very quickly learned how to interpret the daily routine, printed each day and posted on each mess's noticeboard. After the first week Echo Delta informed them that he would be selecting a class leader, who would from then on be responsible for the class being in the right place at the right time and, almost as important, in the correct uniform outfit. Over the next couple of days each member of the class was given a trial run at marching the group around the parade ground. Not one single person amongst the 53 in the class wanted the job.

Having discussed the problem of how best to appear completely unsuitable for the job, Jock, who quickly became PJ to the rest of the class when they all discovered what it meant, emphasised his Glaswegian accent to such an extent that Echo Delta threw a wobbly and pushed him angrily back into the squad, screaming in his best parade ground voice, 'Expletive deleted! I can't understand one expletive deleted word you said, you bloody expletive deleted poxy jock!' The class's kind-hearted and softly spoken instructor sometimes, in moments of extreme stress, introduced an additional expletive before expletive deleted!

Adopting a different tactic, Bob's ploy was to be as timid as possible, seemingly making little noise whilst straining manfully with his vocal cords; he was rewarded by a negative shake of the head, and a muttered 'bloody (psst) sparkers,' from Echo Delta, and gratefully took his place back in the squad.

The following morning, after the class had fallen-in (the act of mustering a marching group), Echo Delta called the class to attention. (Unlike the other services the Navy used the term Ho! instead of Attention! when preparing a group to march off.) This signified that any chattering or movement after that command would be rewarded with a 20-lap run around the outskirts of the parade ground, a kit muster, locker inspection, any number of push-ups or whatever other punishment the instructors could dream up. In his usual ear-shattering voice he continued: 'Class leader! Right, were it not for the foreign language the PJ was gibbering he would be class leader, however, none of you would have an expletive deleted clue what he was on about, so Sims, you're it.'

Everyone, except of course Sims, breathed a sigh of relief. Sims was to fail abysmally after only a few days as class leader when he marched the class past the barracks commander without giving the proper salute of eyes right!

In fact he completely ignored the commander, which of course compounded the error. The whole class was awarded an extra kit muster in punishment and when one of their number plucked up enough courage to ask Echo Delta why the whole class was being punished, he said, 'Because one of you expletive deleted assholes should have known what to do, you're not all (psst) sparkers are you?' Joe Sims was one of the other eleven telegraphists in the class, and his early failure as class leader further lowered their instructor's opinion of that elite section of the RN communications branch. Each replacement class leader lasted no longer than a week, all failing in some way to come up to Echo Delta's expectations; but none more spectacularly than poor Joe Sims! Fortunately neither Bob nor Jock were ever offered the job.

Sunday was not a day of rest: up at 0500 as normal, ablutions, breakfast, clean the mess, bathrooms and toilets, inspection by the duty officer, compulsory church services, dinner, wash and iron kit ready for the following week, maybe a quick walk around to the non-beer canteen to gawp at the NAAFI girls, supper, clean the mess again before evening rounds, maybe write a letter or study one of the numerous notebooks containing scribbled notes on any number of subjects, practise a few knots, prepare for forthcoming examinations and tests before lights out at ten o'clock. A nice restful day, at least from the attentions of Echo Delta.

The church services were a complete waste of time as far as Bob was concerned. He was the only one of the class who was not, to some degree, religious. He had no option but to attend the services. However, his basic agnostic belief, and not forgetting his tone deafness, made the whole experience painful to him. Naval clergymen are called padre instead of vicar and *Victory*'s padre seemed a very kindly soul, but Bob and Jock had made a pact from the first day to trust no one but themselves. Throughout the service the venerable old padre, clearly well past retirement age, stood on a raised dais looking down on his flock, his eyes constantly moving across the upturned faces to make sure everyone was responding and singing as loudly as they could. Reverting to his old school ploy, Bob mouthed the words, the veins bulging enormously in his neck, looking every bit as if he was putting everything he had into it. Oddly the two young men had more in common than they both thought, for Jock was tone deaf too and was using the same ploy to disguise the fact.

As their first day of freedom drew nearer, the class began to get more and more excited, and for the last week had spoken of little else. They were coming to the end of their first four weeks of training and, after the coming Saturday, they would be allowed to leave the barracks every Saturday for the remainder of their training period. It was not easy, in the busy training programme, to find time to write letters, but Bob had written to Pat and told her that he would be waiting at Portsmouth station from about 12.30, since he would not be allowed to leave the barracks until midday. He warned Pat not to be too worried if he did not turn up, any number of things could go wrong in the intervening period. He had not put a foot wrong so far, other than being a would-be '(psst) sparker,' but it was best not to tempt fate and be too cocksure.

The Wilsons were not too happy about Pat travelling down to Portsmouth on her own so Pat had arranged for Jimmy and Joy to accompany her. Bob was not at all disappointed about not being alone with Pat, he was looking forward to seeing Jimmy again and showing off his new uniform. Feeling a little guilty at his own selfishness and good fortune, Bob had asked Jock to join them but he had declined. 'I'll be in the pub, rewarding myself for my recent abstinence!' The two friends would be able to spend the evening together because, knowing that Pat would have to leave Portsmouth early, in order to be home by her parents' strict deadline of ten o'clock, Bob had arranged to meet Jock at seven that evening in the fish & chip shop they had seen opposite the railway station.

Everyone was on their best behaviour during the final three days prior to their first day of liberty, for which, of course, the Navy had its very own description – they were going to have a 'run ashore.' Anxious to avoid any of the numerous pitfalls awaiting the careless or unwary, which could potentially cancel their long awaited day's freedom, the class unanimously agreed that it was extremely unfortunate that a visit to the barracks by Admiral of the Fleet, Lord Mountbatten of Burma, the Royal Navy's most prominent member of the communications branch, was scheduled on the day before their run ashore! Of course neither Bob, Jock nor any other member of the class were aware of His Lordship's naval specialisation at that time; it was only later, whilst struggling with their sparker's training that they became aware of the fact.

Throughout the week preceding this famous admiral's visit, the whole barracks had been cleaning up, and the class would receive first-hand experience of the extraordinary preparations that were made for such visiting dignitaries. 'If it moves, salute it, if it doesn't move, expletive deleted paint it,' Echo Delta screamed at them. He seems to be getting louder, the class decided at one of their end-of-day talkabouts in the mess, he's either going to evening classes or has had another part of his anatomy replaced by yet more lungs!

The entire population of the barracks were involved in the preparations, and notwithstanding the fact that the visitor could not possibly see every building, and a detailed itinerary had been published, the *whole* barracks had to be cleaned, just in case the Admiral took a fancy to go off-piste!

Everything was either repainted, cleaned, polished or swept, from top to bottom. Cupboards that had not seen the light of day for months were opened up, the contents either discarded or tidied and the interior washed or polished. Every single nook and cranny in that huge barracks had a spring clean.

There would be a parade, the Navy called it Divisions, from which only essential personnel would be excused, and just to make sure that the trainees knew what to expect, they had a full dress rehearsal the day before. Divisions were nothing new to the class: every morning and every afternoon before lessons they marched from their accommodation blocks on to the spacious parade ground, were inspected by their divisional officers, and marched off again. For the routine daily Divisions they wore ordinary working dress, number eights, the blue denim-like outfit, but once a week, usually on Friday afternoons, either the barracks captain or commander would inspect them and for this they wore their best blue uniforms, number ones.

After the main barracks Divisions, inspected by the Admiral, the trainees would receive a nice bonus, Echo Delta gleefully informed them. They would have their own private Divisions with the 'old man' in the dining-hall of one of the accommodation blocks, cleared especially for the occasion. 'Old man', in Navy speak, is an endearing name for the captain or person in command.

While Echo Delta was imparting this piece of good news, he appeared to be in an especially good mood and went on to inform the class that they had also been awarded the signal honour of sweeping the parade ground. An enormously wicked grin spread across Echo Delta's face as he added that he had gone to great lengths to ensure that his class got this supreme honour, because there were so many expletive deleted sparkers in it!

The whole class believed that he was joking; the parade

ground was probably a little over a hundred yards square; and who in their right mind would ever dream of sweeping it? Immediately after daily morning Divisions on Friday morning, Echo Delta marched the class to the slop room and each was issued with a brand new broom, handle and a nail. Off to the stamping room to borrow the hammers, where they hammered the nail through the bottom of the broom up into the handle. Marched back to the parade ground, they were spread out in a long line and commenced sweeping. It was nearing the end of May and it was a very hot, cloudless day, and at dinner time, apart from a short stand-easy, they had been sweeping for three hours; they were hot, dusty, ached in every conceivable muscle, were thoroughly pissed-off, and, as might be expected, were looking forward immensely to the Admiral's visit!

Following their marathon sweep, the class barely had sufficient time to eat dinner before preparing for the afternoon routine Divisions, immediately after which they were dismissed to get themselves ready for the main Admiral's Divisions at 3 p.m.

For the ship's company of HMS *Victory*, being inspected by an admiral was not the testing experience that they had anticipated. The Admiral simply stood in an open Land Rover as it drove amongst the massed sailors, and the personage was seen only as their group marched past and gave the traditional 'eyes right' salute. For some reason the Royal Marine Band had opted to play a particularly difficult piece of music for the sailors to keep in time with, instead of one of the numerous and better known musical pieces, and marching past the Admiral had been the most trying part of the whole proceedings for everyone taking part. Despite the best efforts of the band to ruin the entire afternoon, the march past went very well for Bob's group, which pleased Echo Delta immensely. 'Perhaps we're getting somewhere,' said Echo Delta after they had completed

233

their march past, his class having kept perfectly in step with the band's soulful dirge. 'Even the bloody sparkers seem to have worked out their right from left.'

With just enough time for a quick cup of tea, before forming up again in the converted dining-hall to await the arrival of the Admiral, the class raced to the canteen, but the queues were long and the NAAFI girls sometimes staged a go slow, and many left disappointed. Admittedly, most of the sailors' comments were below the belt, but the girls sometimes overreacted to the less ribald suggestions.

Extremely tired, fed-up, far from home and impatient for the day to come to a blissful completion, the 'Awkward Squad' stood, waiting as patiently as they could, already formed into classes for their fourth Division of the day, standing at ease and waiting for the Admiral to make his appearance. Nervous instructors double-checked that which they had double-checked two minutes ago, tugging at and adjusting parts of the unfortunate trainees' uniforms. The amassed group waited for what seemed like ages for the Admiral's arrival. Almost 300 of the Navy's most recent recruits fidgeted, frustrated at the long delay and weary of their instructors' incessant screams to 'keep silent, stand still.' The walls in the dining-halls were very high and this particular room had a huge clock array suspended from its elaborately decorated ceiling. The clock array consisted of four clocks so that one of the clock faces could be seen from anywhere in the room. Every minute or so they all glanced up at the clocks; each person had the same thought at one time or another: the clocks must have stopped!

Just before 6 p.m. a chief GI, standing on the dais in front of them, in a magnificent stentorian voice that would have shamed any pongo regimental sergeant major, called the assembled trainees to attention, just as the Admiral walked into the room. The chief GI had previously issued the preparatory 'Divisions' – which warned them of the impending command to come to attention, but all the Admiral heard was the explosive 'Ho!' as he entered the room. The Admiral was in full view to Bob, who saw him start, wince slightly and with his retinue trailing in his wake, continue towards the dais, stopping only occasionally to speak to a trainee.

The retinue consisted of a long line of about 30 officers, all trying to keep as close as possible to the Admiral, which included the captain, commander, padre – keeping up quite well, despite his age, Bob noticed. Their divisional officers were also part of this entourage, bunching in a frenzied group ready to respond to any question the Admiral might have, and other officers with a distinctive sash dangling from their left shoulders, denoting, Bob later discovered, an admiral's aide.

The Admiral stopped in front of Bob, who was standing in his customary place in the front rank of his class. 'What's your name?' he asked. Jolted by this unexpected turn of events, Bob's legs, already trembling from the day's exertions and the hour spent standing waiting, now trembled uncontrollably, and he had to push his kneecaps firmly backwards to stop himself from an impromptu imitation of a wobbly jelly.

'Leonard, sir,' he croaked, forcing himself to look the inspecting officer straight in the eye as he had been taught.

'How are you getting on with your training?' the Admiral asked in a very precise and even voice.

'Fine, thank you, sir,' replied Bob, feeling just a little more relaxed as the vision of Mrs Sandsfoot entered his mind, invoked by the similar voice of the Admiral. 'What branch will you be joining?' asked the Admiral, 'Communications, sir.'

The Admiral nodded approvingly and moved on.

Lord Mountbatten, forever thereafter held in the highest esteem by Bob (not to mention every other communicator he would ever meet), climbed onto the dais, whispered something to the chief GI who screamed, 'gather round the Admiral,' at which the assembly broke formation and pressed in a huge semicircle around the dais. The great man spoke for several minutes, telling them of the honour they should feel at joining the Senior Service, with its fine traditions and history, serving their Queen and Country, making them all feel about 10 foot tall.

He was a fine looking man, tall and handsome, bedecked with medals and gold braid, and with his long ceremonial sword at his side looked every inch the natural born leader that he was.

Apparently the Admiral had been so pleased with his visit that he had ordered 'splice the main brace,' four little words that filled every sailor's heart with joy, since it signalled the issue of an extra tot of rum. It did not, however, bring much joy to the trainees because they were all under 21, not just the country's legal age for the attainment of manhood but the Navy's legal age for a ration of rum.

The class did get a reward. Echo Delta was beside himself, glowing in the praise from the captain and divisional officer for his class's performance during the day. Obviously well pleased with himself, he added that providing the scheduled kit musters went well after supper, he would leave them to do as they pleased for the rest of the evening. 'And I just might,' followed by a slight pause as if reconsidering a rash decision, 'make sure you all get ashore tomorrow.' He made a point of coming over to Bob and whispered, which was probably a painful way of speaking for a GI, 'Well done, young Leonard, good effort for a (psst) sparker,' forgetting that their esteemed visitor was not only the most senior admiral in the Navy but he was also a communicator.

Thus it was that the following day, just after midday, Bob and Jock left the unfortunate member of their class to complete his kit muster rescrub, and walked through the side gate of HMS *Victory*. They stood on the wide pavement, looking around, feeling totally bewildered and not really knowing what to do. Waiting to be told what to do was now so deeply embedded within them, after only four weeks, that they instinctively hesitated, looking for some guidance about where to go and what to do. Each looked at the other; they had an identical, almost guilty feeling of being somewhere that they were not allowed to be.

Just getting outside the barracks had been a trying business. Echo Delta, who was Duty PO that day and therefore responsible for putting the whole trainee division to work, an activity quaintly described in RN speak as 'cleaning ship.' Following the Admiral's visit, it was difficult to find anything to clean, but the Navy's routine continued regardless of the previous day's activities.

In a naval ship or establishment, particularly training establishments, there is always something to clean or polish, but on this Saturday Echo Delta had allocated the usual dirty and heavy jobs to other, more recently joined trainees, and after dismissing the others to their jobs, told the class to skirmish around their accommodation block and then remain in their mess until they heard the pipe for liberty men to fall in. One of their class, clearly simple-minded and destined for the seaman branch, was of the opinion that their instructor had a heart!

The two young sailors, standing stunned and indecisive on the pavement outside the barracks, resplendent in their smart new uniforms, shiny shoes, and brilliantly white caps, looked at one another, shrugged, and set off along the pavement towards the park that they had walked through, in the pouring rain, just four very, very long weeks ago. They felt like different people, not connected with the civilian shoppers strolling along the pavement in front of them. They were no longer merely 'the public,' they were Navy; and they were very proud of that fact. The wide bell-

237

bottoms forced them to swing each leg slightly sideways before stretching forward, producing an easy, rolling gait, which, in all honesty, they did exaggerate just a little!

At the park gates Jock said he would continue straight on; he could see a pub in the distance. It was a beautiful early summer's day, maybe a trifle hot for the heavy serge blue uniforms, but not too uncomfortable. Warning Jock not to get legless too early, Bob bade Jock farewell and walked through the park towards the railway station. A group of young girls passed him and whistled that unmistakable double note of appreciation and invitation. Returning the girls' compliment, Bob gave them a cheeky wink and with a huge grin on his face continued on his way.

Other passers-by must have wondered what the young sailor was so happy about: the huge grin lasted for several minutes! He was sublimely happy, he knew that he had got through the worst part of his initial training, instinctively knowing that the remaining eight weeks would become increasingly more easy; and he was on his way to meet his lovely girlfriend. His pockets were not actually bulging with money, but he did have a few pounds in his pocket, plenty for the day. The remainder of the cash that he had brought with him four weeks ago had been deposited into a Post Office account; money management had been the subject of a lecture from their divisional officer very early in their first week of training. 'Large sums of money left in lockers is a temptation to all.' The officer had waved his index finger to emphasise the point, and a Post Office account had been one of his suggestions.

Arriving at Portsmouth Central station well in advance of Pat's arrival time, Bob checked the arrivals/departures board for any delays, and waited nervously by the metal railings separating the platforms from the main concourse. He toyed with buying a platform ticket and waiting on the platform, but decided that he might miss her and rejected the idea. Eventually the train arrived in clouds of hissing steam. The doors opened and what seemed like hundreds of people descended onto the platform. Fearful of being trampled underfoot, Bob moved away from the heaving mass of humanity trying to exit the platform through the single narrow gateway; eventually a railway worker opened the second, wider gate, and the scene calmed a little. Still a country boy at heart, Bob hated crowds.

At last, Jimmy came through the gate, with Pat on one arm and Joy on the other. 'Hello Bob.' So Pat had told him of his newly adopted diminutive. 'I was hoping you wouldn't turn up,' Jimmy quipped, 'I was quite enjoying having a pretty girl on each arm!' Before Jimmy could finish his jest, Pat dashed forward and leapt into Bob's arms, and the feel of her slim, delicate body crushing against him transported Bob to the borders of paradise. He had never before experienced such joy at seeing another person; it was almost overwhelming and he had to fight back his own tears when he felt the warm dampness of her salty tears on his face.

'Damn,' she sobbed, 'I didn't want to do that,' dabbing at her tears with the back of a faultless, creamy-white hand. Having someone crying with joy at the sight of you is a very nice feeling, Bob decided, with a glow in his heart.

The quartet caught a double-decker bus to Southsea Pier and settled into a small café for a snack. Answering the barrage of questions from the other three kept Bob busy, and also doing most of the talking for a good part of the afternoon. Feeling the warmth of her tiny hand still firmly clasping his, he was surprised when she suddenly turned to look at him and kissed him gently on the mouth. It was just a tiny, magical moment that restated their love. She looked lovely, her hair framing her sweet face in ringlets. She had used a very light application of lipstick and the aroma of her perfume swept over him; he was besotted.

239

There was a moment of confusion and humour when the waitress brought the menu: one of the items on the handwritten menu was *Cajun Chicken*. Immediately underneath on a separate line was added *Breast, chips and peas*. Not having the slightest inkling what constituted Cajun Chicken, Jimmy opted for 'Breast, chips and peas please!' Unable to correct the customer's error, the waitress was in fits of laughter; it was sometime before the group of friends could order a meal.

The conversation eventually got around to Jimmy's impending national service, and Bob was not at all surprised when Jimmy said that he had already received his call-up papers, ordering him to report to Aldershot at the end of October. Basking in his own recent experience, Bob felt able to advise his friend. He told Jimmy to prepare himself, over the next few months, by making sure that he practised the housekeeping and personal skills required to take care of himself and his kit; and told him a little of the hardships he would face. In fear of upsetting Pat and Joy, Bob did not describe the hardships in too much detail, intending to have another chat with Jimmy at some future date.

After their meal the foursome decided to spend an hour or so in the adjacent fairground, Bob's suggestion of going to the cinema, where he could enjoy a kiss and cuddle with Pat, being rejected. Jimmy had a broad, mischievous grin on his face when, looking straight at Bob, he said that he could go to the cinema any time at home, but he did not very often get a chance to visit a fairground. *Twist the knife, you expletive deleted soon to be pongo*, flashed through Bob's mind, smiling inwardly as he realised that, even had he spoken the words, not one of his companions would have understood! There was no animosity in Jimmy's words. Bob knew their relationship was not just that of good friends, and not that of brothers, which, as everyone knows, can be difficult and painful at times, particularly if you happen to be the youngest. It was more like the love a boy feels for his father, relaxed and close in the full knowledge that this person can be relied upon, unconditionally, to provide help and support whenever needed.

Decision taken, they left the café and walked the short distance into the fair.

At 6 p.m., after a wonderful afternoon at the funfair, everyone contributing towards the cost, they all caught a bus back to Portsmouth Central so as to arrive in good time for the visiting trio to catch the 7 p.m. London train, change at Liss and get the last bus back to Alton. Knowing that the Wilsons had already made it clear that they would not allow their 16-year-old daughter to travel to and from Portsmouth on her own, Bob asked Pat to check the timetables and let him know if it might be possible for him to make the return trip to Alton between about 1 p.m. and 10 p.m.; Pat promised to write him a letter in the week.

Since Bob would be permitted to leave the barracks each Saturday from then on, assuming of course that he managed to avoid any punishment, he would make the effort to get home to see both his parents and Pat on a couple of weekends.

Parting was not the harrowing experience it was when he had left to join up. They both knew that they would be seeing each other on a regular basis from then on, at least for the next year or so while he was under training. Holding each other for long minutes until it was time for the trio to pass through the barrier to the train, Pat finally gave him a soft, warm kiss and he watched as she walked to the train; he had not previously noticed her long, slim and very shapely legs.

Waiting until the train pulled away from the platform, Bob waved to Pat as she leaned out of the carriage window, blowing kisses until she was out of sight. It was a good feeling, standing there watching the train disappear out of sight. He had enjoyed a very pleasant afternoon with his best friend and the girl he loved; he was content. He knew he would make sure not to upset anyone in authority, or give any excuse for someone to stop his leave on the forthcoming Saturdays; time spent with Pat was too precious.

As the train disappeared from sight, rocking from side to side on the uneven track, Bob decided it was time to find Jock. Leaving the station and crossing the busy main road, Bob entered the small fish & chip shop. In the main restaurant area every table was occupied with people enjoying an early supper and he could not, at first, see Jock. Eventually he spotted a white cap, pushed jauntily onto the back of a head, in a small alcove at the rear of the restaurant.

Having walked through the crowded restaurant, Bob found Jock sitting at a table sipping gingerly at a cup of hot black coffee. He looked very much the worse for drink and Bob knew he was going to have trouble getting him back into the barracks. The crushers on the main gate would be only too willing to take action against a trainee returning onboard drunk, and there was no way of avoiding the confrontation since they would have to ask for their station cards.

The busy waitress finally came over to their table and Bob asked if they might have two more cups of black coffee before they ordered a meal. He needed to talk to Jock for a while to find out how far he was into his cups. Quickly assessing the situation, Bob knew that he had to do two things: one, keep Jock away from any further alcohol intake; and two, give him as long as possible to sober up before making the attempt to re-enter the barracks. In reply to Bob's question, Jock said that he had been in the pub all afternoon, the same pub that they had seen when

Bob had left him at about midday, until closing time at 3 p.m. 'I managed to talk the landlady into selling me a take-out.' Jock's voice was very Scottish and very slurred and Bob had to ask him to repeat himself twice.

Eventually Bob discovered that Jock had bought four cans of beer and a half bottle of whiskey and had sat in the park, watching the Portsmouth lasses go by. He had consumed all of the drink and had a snooze on the grass, woken up and made his way to the fish & chip shop. Adamant that he was not yet ready to return to the barracks, Jock declared his intention of rounding off his day by 'having a wee drink and seeing if we can find a punch-up.' *Not if I have anything to do with it,* Bob decided. Echo Delta had already lectured them about how the Navy viewed brawling.

A fight between two naval personnel, whether onboard or ashore, was frowned on and would be rewarded with severe punishment, but a punch-up involving civilians was regarded as a heinous crime; usually involving the naval shore patrol or the civilian police to break it up, the consequences could include spending a little time at her Majesty's pleasure in a naval prison. Understandably, Bob was very worried and hoping that with further cups of coffee and a large portion of fish and chips, Jock might think again about continuing his boozy day.

Over their meal, Bob was thinking hard, racking his brains for a solution to his problem. *I wonder how much money he's got left,* he suddenly thought. In response to Bob's order, Jock emptied his pockets noisily onto the table: just a few shillings. 'Where's your paybook, Jock?' Having checked between the pages and in the small slot intended for storing vaccination certificates, Bob found that the paybook was devoid of notes. Jock was virtually broke.

Great, thought Bob, *I'll have to pay for the meal but at least I can pretend that neither of us will have enough money to go boozing!* They remained at their table in the fish & chip shop until the waitress lost patience and, wanting the table for other customers, asked them to leave. Making a display of paying for the meal, Bob said, '*That's me out of money, Jock, nothing for it but to go for a walk and back onboard.*' At first a little unsteady on his feet, Jock leaned heavily on his pal and bemoaned his luck about missing his Saturday night punch-up. The pair set off and walked, or rather staggered, through the park. Emerging from the park, Bob steered his muttering friend away from the barracks and followed the signs that led them, in a roundabout way, to the entrance to the naval dockyard.

The two young sailors stood silently in the darkening gloom of the evening, leaning on the metal stanchions defining The Hard, near Portsmouth Harbour station, watching the ferries busily plying their trade of transporting tourists and commuters to and from the nearby Isle of Wight. Slowly, Jock's bearing and diction improved sufficiently for Bob to make the decision to return to the barracks.

Arriving at the small side entrance that they had used on their first day, Bob asked Jock to remain close behind him and, whatever happened, 'keep your mouth shut!' Following the coffee, meal, and long walk, Jock *appeared* quite sober: he could *walk* in a reasonably straight line; *talking*, however, was out of the question, and doubling across the parade ground might not be a good idea; best to try and keep him quiet and go the long way round! Attempting a confident attitude, Bob cheerily called out 'Leonard and Muir returning from shore leave, sir,' addressing a bored-looking able seaman and mightily relieved to find that there were no crushers or more senior personnel on duty. The able seaman was a bit surprised to be addressed as sir, looked at Jock, and with a knowing smile and a nod, handed over their station cards.

'Don't go across the parade ground,' said the able seaman, 'there's a do on in the pigsty and they'll all be waiting to jump on someone!'

'Thank you, sir,' said Bob, grabbing their station cards, and feeling an enormous weight being lifted from his shoulders. He dragged Jock around the perimeter road to their accommodation block. Fortunately Jock occupied the lower bunk so Bob just undressed him and rolled him into it. Apart from a few muttered *Och Ayes* and numerous evil-smelling farts, he heard nothing more of Jock until the following morning.

Despite having cleaned his teeth three times, Jock's evil-smelling breath – 'I've got a mouth like a gorilla's armpit' – throbbing headache, and blotchy complexion bore witness to his excessive alcohol intake the day before.

No longer the 'Awkward Squad' – for many more classes of new intakes had arrived in the last week or two – training continued for the class. The strict daily routine of early to rise and being fully occupied until late evening remained as for their first four weeks, but Echo Delta seemed to relax his stranglehold on the class; noticeable mainly in his attitude towards the class rather than his harsh treatment of transgressors.

The end of their sixth week saw the departure of the first two casualties from the class, two of the seaman branch candidates were back-classed. For some unknown reason the back-classed pair just could not keep their kit clean; struggling with both washing and ironing, they just could not seem to get it right and they were continually being awarded kit musters and locker inspections.

The whole class had, at one time or another, tried to help the hapless duo, and the additional hours that the back-classed pair spent trying to reach the required standard of kit upkeep, left other studies neglected; one personal inadequacy affecting performance in all other subjects. The overall effect on the back-classed pair, as their

245

performance deteriorated, was quite obvious, not to mention a harsh lesson to the whole class, and everyone knew that the dreaded punishment of being back-classed was the only option.

The class was further reduced the following week when another was badly injured in a road accident; he was crossing the road outside the barracks whilst heading for a run ashore to the hotspots of Portsmouth. Just a few short days after the unfortunate road accident the class approached two hurdles that they were dreading more than others; the gas mask test and the swimming test.

The item in a sailor's kit that is most often neglected, most rarely used, and which attracts the most attention when lost, is a gas mask. In the eyes of those in authority there existed no acceptable excuse, apart from death, for the loss of this piece of kit, and replacement costs were high for both the culprit and the RN. Echo Delta had lectured them consistently and at great length concerning any action that might cause a sailor to render himself, by his own actions, unfit to do his duty. 'If you can't do your job you're no expletive deleted good to man nor beast, and a sparker (sparkers were always used as the subject in this type of example) without a gas mask becomes an early casualty; vital signals could be lost which could endanger the whole expletive deleted ship!' Examples of stupid or dangerous actions, when given by Echo Delta, usually involved the direst of consequences, court martial, captain's punishment, jail, death, the loss of a warship, or the end of the world; exaggeration was the norm for this man!

During the first four weeks of training it was virtually impossible for the loss of an item of kit to go unnoticed, there were just too many daily or weekly inspections for it to happen. Since they had passed the milestone of their first major Divisions, mustering of kit, for the majority of trainees, was discontinued; they would all face a last invitation to lay out their kit, at the barracks, in their final week. However, in the few weeks since that milestone no fewer than five of the class had lost their gas masks, and their loss did not become apparent until the day of the gas mask check. On the day of the dreaded test the class had been told to attend morning Divisions with gas masks, stored in the small khaki satchel, similar to that used by Bob's father as a conveyor of sandwiches.

The five unfortunate young men, who had been scouring the mess decks in search of their missing kit since the small hours, anticipating their punishment and wearing disconsolate expressions but not gas masks, were told to double off the parade ground and wait in their accommodation block. There was to be no mercy: they were back-classed immediately and the thought of having to go through the first few weeks of training again served as a further incentive, for Bob, not to become complacent over the next few weeks.

It was thus that just 45 young sailors turned up for the test that would prove the efficacy of their respirators and, much to Echo Delta's disgust, the group of 13 sparkers was still intact. The class entered a large building, one end of which had been bricked off to provide a smaller room with two doors, marked IN and OUT. There was an expectant silence as Echo Delta explained that the class would enter the room, adding, 'for the benefit of the sparkers, that's through the door marked IN!' Once everyone was inside he would close the door and shout 'gas, gas, gas,' the order to don gas masks; he would then explode two or three tear-gas grenades, the class would remain in the room whilst he checked that each individual respirator was functioning properly, they would then be told to remove their gas masks to give them an opportunity of tasting the gas, after which the OUT door would be opened and they could leave the room in an orderly fashion, in single file.

Keeping close together, Bob and Jock walked into the small, dingily lit room. There were no windows and it smelled horribly of gas. Bob had not been looking forward to this experience, but there was nothing for it, it had to be done. Both he and Jock had spent some time adjusting their masks to ensure a good tight fit around the face and stood awaiting the rest of the class into the room.

All chattering had ceased. Bob nudged Jock and whispered, 'Let's go and stand by the OUT door, we will be first out then.' Trying to remain inconspicuous, Jock followed Bob as the pair edged towards the OUT door. It was obvious that several others intended using the same ploy, because eventually there was a group of about twelve hovering around the door. The crash of the IN door closing signalled the start of their ordeal. Not one of them missed Echo Delta's explosive scream 'gas, gas, gas', nor failed to hear the pop of the tear-gas grenades in the absolute silence of the windowless room. Three pops: their kindly instructor had not failed them and, although he had indicated two *or* three gas grenades, they had all known that they were held in such high esteem that they would be awarded the third.

Both doors to the room were firmly shut and it was an eerie feeling, just standing, watching and waiting for the grey cloud, approaching very slowly, to envelope everyone in the room. As the gas swirled around Bob's ankles he looked down. His knees disappeared from view below the layer of gas and he felt as if the floor had fallen beneath him, a very strange sensation that added to his fear. The masks were very efficient but, despite Bob's meticulous application of the anti-fogging cream onto the lenses of the eyelets, they rapidly misted up and it became very difficult to see. Feeling a few moments of panic, particularly from the feeling of being totally alone when everyone and everything disappeared from sight, Bob awaited the arrival of

Echo Delta to check his mask. Feeling a loss of balance, as the cloud wrapped itself tightly around him and his vision deteriorated further, Bob jumped in surprise when Echo Delta's face appeared, pressed very close to the glass eyelets of the mask. Grasping and bending the tube linking the face unit to the satchel containing the cleansing unit, and thereby stopping the air flow, Echo Delta watched carefully to check that the edges of the face mask pressed into flesh as air stopped flowing.

A cacophony of coughing and choking sounded eerily through the fog of foul gas-filled air, a sure sign that a few of the respirators had not been fitted correctly, and Bob felt instant concern for those of his classmates having more than their fair share of the gas. He was having problems enough with a fully serviceable breathing machine. Both he and Jock knew their gas masks were working perfectly. While they could still see, they had each given the other the thumbs up signal when, shortly after the pops of the grenades, they had not received even a whiff of gas.

Time dragged interminably whilst Echo Delta checked the remaining respirators. Normally the only adjustments required of the masks was tightening the straps around the rubber face pieces. Either Echo Delta was making a lot of adjustments or he was deliberately extending their discomfort. As he tried desperately to retain his composure, Bob was about to move towards the exit, thinking that perhaps he had missed the order to evacuate the room.

Suddenly an ear-shattering blast of sound ricocheted around the small room. Echo Delta had somehow obtained a portable siren and was, he later explained, trying to simulate the panic-induced actions of frightened seamen when a ship is under fire or in danger of capsizing. For Bob, the unexpected event worked perfectly; he needed little prompting to leap into action like a startled rabbit, and, galvanised into instant movement, he turned towards where he remembered the door to be and slammed painfully into the wall, rebounding onto his backside on the floor. He tried to scramble to his feet, but someone, moving much too quickly, trod on his fingers, and groaned as he too slammed into the wall. Amidst the confusion, and all the time aware of bodies dashing in all directions Bob heard Echo Delta howl, in his best parade ground voice, 'Off masks!' The initial taste of the gas was shocking, seeming to burn the inside of the nostrils and the back of the throat, and Bob felt an urgent impulse to run for the OUT door. There was no point in trying for the IN door, Bob had already noted that there were no internal handles. Eyes firmly closed, Bob decided to remain on the floor and await the order to leave the room.

A whiff of fresher air followed the opening of the OUT door and encouraged Bob to open his eyes. Vision improving slightly, he desperately wanted to wipe the streaming tears from his eyes but remembered something he had read warning against this natural response; at the last second he lowered his hands and let the tears flow. Through itching and watery eyes, Bob could not see Jock but he did spot Echo Delta, who had removed his own respirator, guarding the OUT door, barring any early attempt to exit the room, and the class stood, heaving and retching, their eyes streaming as they breathed in the gas. Most had not known of the exacerbating consequences of rubbing eyes during a tear-gas attack, and these would suffer greatly over the following days.

Glaring at the class, Echo Delta waited a few minutes more, stepped through the door himself into the clean air and, laughing and yelling at the same time, screeched at the top of his voice, 'If you all breathe deeply you'll soon get rid of that gas,' leaving the rest of the class to follow as best they could. As he left the room, Bob noticed the instructor step through the door, raising his leg high above a metal coaming, which surrounded the door, simulating the hatches found in a warship. Not everyone had noticed, however. There was a wild mêlée at the door, and Bob saw a few attempting to find some way of opening the IN door, but, of course, to no avail. A group had become wedged in the doorway in their haste to get into the fresh air and the raised coaming was creating an additional stumbling block. Reunited with Jock, Bob yelled at everyone to push as hard as they could and the group shot out into the fresh air like a cork from a bottle, several nursing severe bruising to their buttocks!

It was a wonderfully satisfying day for Echo Delta. He was laughing like a mad thing at their antics but he was also watching very carefully. After Echo Delta had left the gas-filled room, Bob had considered replacing his gas mask but had instantly thought better of it. No such order had been given and Echo Delta would undoubtedly find some reward for a 'clever dick sparker!' Most of the group had suffered some form of minor injury. Bob sported an impressive purple bruise above his right eye that would, over the next few days, develop into a black eye, scraped knuckles, having been trod upon, and a whole-body itching reaction from the gas. The metal coaming had caused most of the injuries, the most common of which were badly scraped shin bones. It had been a most unpleasant experience and they had an uncomfortable wait until they could return to the mess for a shower and a much needed change of clothing.

The class agreed that the course planners must have been in a particularly vindictive mood when deciding the syllabus for the Initial Training Course, because it was only a few short days later that Echo Delta informed them that they would undergo the Navy's version of a swimming test the following day. Two stressful events in the same week might well see the departure of a few more of the class.

The initial instructions from Echo Delta were brief: take

251

a towel and overalls with them. Like most of the kit with which they were issued, their overalls were much too big. Bob had to roll both legs and sleeves up and tie a lanyard around his waist to get a reasonable fit. No trainee would be allowed to go to sea on a warship without having the ability to swim, and the Navy had its own way of making it as difficult, as the recruits saw it, or as realistic, as the Navy saw it, as possible by expecting them to swim two lengths of the pool, fully clothed.

The whole class knew that the test was scheduled for this week. It was clearly shown in the programme of weekly activities promulgated on their mess deck noticeboard. They also knew that it was another potential back-classing event but some people were still totally unprepared, having made no effort to use the pool or learn to swim during the preceding weeks.

Both at ease in the water, if not both strong swimmers, Bob and Jock had confidence in their ability to stay afloat and complete the two lengths of the pool. By no means an elegant swimmer, Bob's only means of propulsion was by employing the 'doggy paddle,' but it had served him well in the rivers and lakes of the estate when he was a boy. In contrast to most, Jock was brimming with confidence in his known strength and natant ability and could not wait to get started.

At some point in his life, Jock must have had some experience of surviving in the sea whilst fully clothed, because he saw fit to warn Bob that the swim would be extremely tiring. 'Pace yourself, don't turn it into a race, laddy, save your stamina and concentrate on completing the two laps, there's no prizes for winners!'

Only two swimmers were permitted in the pool at any one time, each to swim along opposite sides of the pool so that they could be pulled out, if necessary, by the remainder of the class lined up along the edges. An important aspect of the test was to jump rather than lower the body into the water, obviously, everyone realised, to simulate jumping overboard.

Fortunately Bob was not selected as one of the first into the water and he watched carefully as two of his classmates leapt from the lowest diving board. He noticed how the voluminous overalls hampered the swimmers as they struggled up the sides of the pool; all knew that reaching for the safety of the sides was an instant failure. Again no mercy was shown; it was back to the end of the line, soaking wet, to await a second attempt. A second attempt was usually doomed to failure; those that failed on the first attempt were just too weary for any hope of success on the second.

For once, however, the Navy demonstrated a softer side. Failure at the swimming test would not mean immediate back-classing; there would be two more attempts permitted, at a time chosen by the trainee, up to and including the last week of training. To be back-classed in the final week of training would be purgatory and Bob flexed his muscles and jumped up and down to keep himself warm and supple before his attempt.

At the order to 'abandon ship,' Bob inhaled deeply and, lifting his knees up to his chest, jumped into the water. He barely made it. The sodden overalls seemed to weigh a ton, and after just a few yards he was breathing heavily. 'Tread water,' Jock yelled from the side, pushing others to one side as he monitored his pal's progress up the pool. 'Don't touch the sides, don't touch the bottom, tread water, go on!' Soaking wet from his own successful, almost effortless swim, Jock urged Bob forward, ignoring Echo Delta's close scrutiny. Unable to speak, Bob worried that Jock might be disciplined for his careless brushing aside of his colleagues, but nothing was said.

It took all Bob's remaining strength to drag himself from

the pool – success was acknowledged only when standing clear of the water. It was at the end of the swimming test, whilst they were standing around the pool, dripping wet and feeling cold, that they were suddenly ordered back into the water by a voice that no one recognised. The whole class immediately leapt from the sides of the pool and either stood on the bottom, hung on the sides or trod water, all looking expectantly at Echo Delta.

Standing at one end of the pool, Echo Delta was looking very pleased indeed. His class had instantly obeyed an order and all realised that it was another of the hidden tests, sneakily thrown into the proceedings to see how the group reacted to various unscheduled events.

The man who had shouted the order could now be seen standing at the far end of the pool. He was a very slim man, skinny almost, with spindly arms and a completely bald head. He appeared to be very young to be sporting the crossed hooks of a petty officer on his left arm, and as he turned to one side Bob realised that he also wore the wings denoting a sparker. When he spoke, the voice of the PO Telegraphist (abbreviated to PO Tel or POTS) was very precise, well-educated, and very effeminate. His voice mimicked that of the tall, burly WRNS officer, from whom the class had received a lecture on nuclear warfare and the effects of radiation sickness; the class had nicknamed her Maid Mountain! *I bet Echo Delta has a field day with that sparker,* thought Bob. During the class's final week at the barracks, Bob plucked up sufficient courage to ask Echo Delta what a PO Tel was doing teaching rope tricks to trainees.

'Like all bloody sparkers, he's a bloody poofter,' replied Echo Delta. 'Been caught with his finger in the rum fanny and is being discharged, services no longer required in a week or so.' Being discharged *'services no longer required'* is the Navy's version of a dishonourable discharge.

The baby-faced young PO Tel said that his aim today was to teach the class something that may, one day, save their lives, and Bob was to witness the cleverest example of instructional technique that he would ever see. The young PO stood above them trailing a long piece of inch thick rope from his left hand and proceeded to demonstrate how to tie a knot that would not tighten under strain, allowing a body to be pulled from the sea without restricting breathing.

'Pass the rope around your body so that it extends past your outstretched hands by about 2 foot, make a loop with the rope in your left hand, pass the end of the rope up through the hole, and,' he added, 'it might help here if you imagine the end of the rope is a rabbit, coming up from its hole [indicating the loop], going around the back of the tree [the other end of the long rope], having a pee and going back down its hole again.'

It was called a bowline and it was the one knot that Bob never forgot how to tie, but, as is the case in so many such things, was also never to find a use for.

Having successfully negotiated both the respirator and swimming tests, both Bob and Jock knew that, short of any major misbehaviour or medical problem, there was nothing that stood in the way of their completing their basic training, and they started looking forward to two weeks leave before joining HMS *Mercury* for their communications training.

After lights out one night during their penultimate week at *Victory*, Bob was lying in his bunk, having one of those nights when it is impossible to switch off, and the more effort you put into going to sleep the more impossible sleep becomes. Bob considered what a real stroke of good fortune had come his way when he had met Jock. They had managed to stay out of any real trouble. True, they had joined in the semi-serious inter-mess rivalries, pillow fights, water fights, pranks, practical jokes etc., not to mention the disgusting ritual, quite early into their training period, of disrobing and scrubbing the 'great unwashed,' as the poor unfortunates who needed a bath were treated. One of these was a young black boy, one of the seaman candidates with the outrageous name of Aloysius Prudence. When undressed and standing under the scalding shower, it was immediately evident that this man was overly endowed with manhood, and it was lifted, on a broom handle, by one of his peers. Remaining perfectly calm and controlled, Aloysius looked down and said, 'Whatever you do, don't drop that, you'll break my expletive deleted leg!'

The course had not been easy for them, they had not been paragons of good behaviour, but they had a common incentive: they wanted to be in the Navy; they wanted to succeed and they each needed a new, more rewarding way of life. They had each won their fair share of kit musters, doubling around the parade ground, etc. But they were still a team, and Bob hoped, would so remain for their forthcoming training at *Mercury*.

The final week was as hectic as their first few days. Each individual had to complete a draft routine, which involved visiting the management offices of each naval department, from administration office to naval tailors, all of which needed to know when anyone was leaving the barracks on a permanent basis and where they were going. The barracks covered a large area, no extra time was allocated to complete this leaving ritual, and it was a question of giving up a few tea breaks and lunch hours, or not get it done and risk further punishment.

Friday was to be a day of preparing for their final Divisions, packing their kit into kitbags and suitcases and placing these, together with the almost obsolete hammock that no one had yet used and most had not even unrolled, into the lorry waiting to transport them to *Mercury* to await their owners' arrival. Needing only sufficient kit to get home and to report to *Mercury*, Bob packed all his kit except his best uniform, which he intended wearing when he left the barracks.

The class had a whip-round to buy a parting gift for Echo Delta, who, they all knew, had probably gone through his own sort of hell to get the majority of them to this final day. After Divisions they were all sitting around in their mess, left exactly as they had found it twelve weeks previously, ready for the next incumbents. They all felt sad yet elated, full of confidence but fearful of leaving what had become a place of refuge, if not always happiness, unsure of their future yet dreaming of getting started on the next phase of their training. In his own inimitable tick-tock fashion, Echo Delta came into the mess. Jock had been elected to hand over the gift, a wristwatch engraved with a simple E.D. and the year 1957. Echo Delta looked at it, turned it over, and read the inscription, nodded, turned on his heel and left; speechless for the only time in twelve weeks!

Just after the midday meal, Echo Delta was standing in his usual place, attempting to remain out of sight but still observing his class's performance, when the class mustered in response to the pipe 'liberty men fall-in,' and as Bob and Jock went through the gates to the park he was still standing, watching until the last of his latest batch of 'real sailors' went out of sight. As far as Bob or Jock ever knew, not one of the class ever saw or heard of Echo Delta again.

A celebratory drink had been planned at the pub where Jock had spent his first run ashore, and the whole class piled into the public bar. The landlord must have made a healthy profit that day; when Bob and Jock left at about 1.30 the party was still going strong. Before separating at Portsmouth Central station the two firm friends shook hands. They both understood how their teamwork had

257

provided each other with unfailing support and words were unnecessary. They had left the party a little early because Jock had a marathon trip to Scotland whilst Bob had a mere 30 odd miles to go. They would next meet in two weeks time, the middle of July, 1957, at *Mercury*.

7

Mercury

The next two weeks were nothing short of glorious for Bob. He had hoped that Pat might take a week, or maybe two, off from work, but she had already agreed to go on holiday to Bournemouth with her parents late in August. He had not been very keen to resume the uncomfortable nights on his aunt's settee; unlike Jock who could sleep on a clothes line, Bob suffered badly if he was not in a proper bed. By some stroke of extreme good fortune, Pat's sister Ann and her husband George had now moved out of the Wilson home and were living in rented accommodation in a nearby village. Mrs Wilson, on hearing of Bob's uncomfortable living arrangements at his aunt's offered to let him occupy the recently vacated spare room. Naturally Bob was delighted and for the next two weeks spent his days with his parents, out with his father looking for permanent work, but always returning to Alton in time to meet Pat from work. At the weekends they went to the cinema either on their own or with Jimmy and Joy.

The time passed far too quickly and almost before they knew it the last weekend of leave was upon them. Before leaving Portsmouth Bob had been ordered to report to *Mercury* by midday on Monday 22 July, 1957 so they decided to have a full day out on the preceding Sunday. Sitting on the top deck of the bus to Winchester, the foursome intended walking up St Catherine's Hill for a picnic followed by a visit to the cathedral. In the warmth of the summer sun they enjoyed a most relaxing day and returned to Alton in plenty of time to spend the evening watching a film. There was little to organise on his last day of leave, having prepared his uniform ready to report to *Mercury* days before. Hopefully the rest of his kit would be waiting at *Mercury* when he arrived the following day, and the two young lovers spent the rest of the evening comfortably ensconced in the cinema.

After a wonderful English fry-up provided by Mrs Wilson, Bob left Alton early on the Monday morning, wanting to get to *Mercury* as early as possible. Arriving late on your first day at a new establishment or ship was pretty much frowned upon and would, no doubt, earn him some sort of punishment. It was to be his lucky day for when he arrived at Petersfield at about 9.40 there was a *Mercury* RN minibus already waiting. He checked with the driver that it was indeed destined for *Mercury* and climbed aboard.

The bus started up immediately and started off towards its destination. Bob was the only passenger and settled back to enjoy his own private transport.

Not knowing exactly where *Mercury* was located – he knew it was somewhere quite close to West Meon – Bob sat concentrating on the route taken by the driver, trying to commit the various twists and turns to memory. From the village of West Meon the bus climbed to the top of a large hill; the radio masts and aerials could be seen long before the buildings came into view, and turned into HMS *Mercury*, Bob's home for the next year or so.

Entry into the establishment was much more simple than had been the case at *Victory*, The sentry at the main gate saw the naval minibus approaching and raised the barrier immediately, allowing the bus to sail straight through. A short distance into the establishment, off to the left, Bob saw a huge country house, even bigger than the Sandsfoot house on the estate. It was an extremely imposing building called, Bob later discovered, Leydene House, and it was home to Mercury's officers, the Wardroom. Inside this imposing house, according to the literature that Bob found in *Mercury*'s library some months later, was a rare staircase, one of only a handful throughout the world. Use of this staircase was restricted to commanders and above, and Bob felt quite privileged a few days later when he was allowed to walk up the hallowed stairway – to polish the handrails!

The bus pulled up outside a small building marked Officer of the Watch at which Bob alighted. *Mercury*, otherwise known as the Signal School, looked to be quite large. Roads disappeared in all directions, and the numerous Nissen huts reminded Bob of the pigsties back on the estate. *Nice*, he mused, *life in a pigsty!*

The establishment was strangely deserted, just the odd sailor wandering around, a world apart from the hustle, bustle, double everywhere of *Victory*. He went up to the small sliding window of the OOW hut, as he came to know it, which was immediately raised by a young man with the flags of a signalman on his right arm.

Yet to win his specialisation badge for the sleeve of his own right arm, Bob felt a little naked and self-conscious. The cap-tally, tied around his white cap, still indicated that he was part of HMS *Victory*. He would change the tally this very day to HMS *Mercury*. The young signalman was very polite, although he must have known that Bob was the lowest of the low – a trainee, or new entry in *Mercury*'s terminology.

Although an explanation was hardly necessary, nonetheless Bob went through his prepared speech, giving his name, which ship he had been drafted from, and adding somewhat lamely and pompously, that he was joining for his first day and 'any help or assistance would be most appreciated.' The young signalman gave him a curious glance, pointed to one of the Nissen huts, and told him to report to the regulating office, the home of the crushers. Bob pushed open the door and got his usual friendly greeting from the Navy's crushers: 'You're in the wrong building, go next door to the New Entry Divisional Office!'

As soon as Bob entered the next Nissen hut, he saw that there were at least half a dozen of his *Victory* shipmates already standing around, waiting in line to be dealt with by a very large regulating petty officer (RPO), with sparse hair and huge horn-rimmed spectacles. As each new entry reached the head of the queue he was given a card on which the various departments of *Mercury* would rubber stamp the fact that they knew of one's existence.

As Bob approached the front of the queue he repeatedly looked around to see if Jock had arrived. None of his shipmates had seen him so Bob moved to the end of the line to await Jock's arrival. Reasonably sure that Jock would have waited for him, Bob returned to the end of the queue on two more occasions. He was beginning to attract some attention from the crushers in the office but he was more concerned with repeating the team strategy employed at *Victory*.

Eventually at about ten minutes before their stipulated leave expiry time of midday, Jock burst through the door, sweating profusely and looking hot, bothered, and uncomfortable. 'Bob, thank Christ you're here,' he said in his broad Scottish accent. 'I need two quid for a taxi, explain later!' Without a moment's hesitation, Bob gave him the money and Jock dashed back out of the door to pay off the waiting driver.

Later Jock explained that he had fallen asleep on the train from London and had gone straight past Petersfield, missing the RN transport to *Mercury*. Lacking the necessary funds, he had no other option than to take a taxi and hope to borrow from Bob when he arrived at the camp. With only a few minutes to spare, they collected their joining routine cards, had the first office pointed out to them, then were told to ask for directions at each office and report to Anson Block on completion.

The first place for them to call at was the pay office. A large handwritten sign proclaimed *gone to lunch, back at 1300*. Recalling their first day at barracks, the two lads thought lunch a good idea and set off to find a dining-hall and, after some considerable explanation about their having just arrived and not yet having station cards, were allowed to eat.

Later they returned to finish their joining routines and eventually managed to arrive at Anson Block, at a little after 3 p.m., laden down with kitbag, suitcases and hammock. Anson Block was a connecting series of single-storey buildings, with black, highly polished floors, providing mess decks, bathrooms, toilets, and games areas for the whole New Entry Division consisting of about 15 classes, each of about 15 to 20 trainee signallers or telegraphists.

The reunited team of two eventually spotted the remainder of their class through a partially open door marked LS12, obviously their class number. Politeness being their normal demeanour when commencing a new activity, Bob knocked on the door and as they pushed it inwards heard a voice say, 'Ah, here's the last two.' They were the last to arrive yet again and Bob hoped that their late arrival would not trigger the same abusive reaction they received at *Victory*.

There were 17 young men in the room together with a young petty officer, their course instructor, sitting at a table in the centre of the room. As they noisily dragged all their belongings into the room, Bob nodded a greeting and said, 'Good afternoon, sir,' keeping his voice polite in the hope of mollifying the petty officer, just in case they were *really* late. 'Good afternoon,' the PO Tel replied politely 'I think that's everyone now so we can begin getting settled in.'

263

Their instructor's name was William Bailey and his attitude towards the class was a refreshing change after the near brutality of *Victory*. As the PO Tel stood up to commence his initial briefing, the exertion forced a noisy, watery fart to erupt from his rear end, winning him his nickname for the next several months – Willie-the-Poo! 'I beg your pardon, curry for supper last night,' he said, totally unconcerned and continued with his briefing.

The newly dubbed Willie-the-Poo told the 13 trainees from *Victory* that their number would be increased by four. He indicated their presence by a backward thumbed signal over his shoulder. 'Back-classees,' he added somewhat disdainfully, extending the last syllable of 'classees' in an exaggerated way. 'Don't think too badly of them. I am sure they did their best,' he added haughtily. 'The very first thing to tell you is that you do not call me sir, my rating is PO Tel and we PO Tels, being the elite of the communications branch and, indeed, of the Royal Navy, are known, quite affectionately as POTs.'

The PO Tel seemed to be acting not a little unnaturally, almost as an actor would read his lines in a film and the class later discovered that POTs was an officer candidate; guiding the class through their communications training was a time-filler for him while he waited to join his sub lieutenants qualifying course the following year. Within the next few days it also became apparent that their instructor was also a grammatical phenomenon, being both a master of hyperbole and having been blessed with the tautological tongue of an Irish tinker.

The young POTs told them that he had not had any formal instructional training and LS12 was to be his first experience of teaching; and he was to prove easily distracted as demonstrated by one of the four back-classed individuals, Tam Torrance, when he directed a lazy, almost insolent 'how does a rating become an officer?' at POTs.

The red herring was accepted immediately by Willie-the-Poo, who launched himself into a lengthy explanation of the educational, seagoing, and other qualifications required. Thoroughly enjoying demonstrating his knowledge of his subject, he was eventually cut off, in mid sentence, when the tannoy system announced 'Secure,' which signalled the end of the working day at 4.20. Without further comment the young PO left them, without any indication of what was to happen that evening or the following morning, presumably assuming that the four back-classed individuals would make sure that LS12 got to where it was supposed to be.

Whilst POTs was busily demonstrating his knowledge of the officer's promotion system, Jock had unobtrusively edged himself to the end of the mess and had already bagged a tier of three bunks in the far corner, away from the door. Probably expecting bunks to be allocated, the rest of the class had not made any selections and, by the time they finally realised that it was to be a free for all on a first come first served basis, Jock was already sitting on his and guarding Bob's. The ex-*Victory* class members knew better than to argue with Jock, and the back-classees took one look at Jock's fierce grimace and backed off, accepting that relinquishing ownership of the best two bunks in the mess was better than risking a few 'Glaswegian kisses.'

The tiers of bunks were three high, just as in the mess at Victory, and there were ten tiers in the large mess deck, far too many bunks for the class. Eventually Tam Torrance, who seemed to have elected himself as their guiding light, suggested that the mess would look much less crowded if they removed the top bunk from each tier and stacked them in one of the corners, so the class noisily rearranged the bunks. Shortly afterwards chaos returned as the class unpacked their kit into the metal lockers and changed into night clothing before supper. The Navy's ultra-clean routine required everyone to bathe and change out of the normal daily working dress, before sitting down to the evening meal. Every member of the class was quite happy for Tam to assume a leadership role and willingly followed him to the new entry dining-hall.

Every evening, 365 days a year, the new entry accommodation blocks were inspected by the duty new entry officer, so after supper the whole class combined in the effort to clean up their living space. As the inspecting officer entered their mess it was Tam again who called them all to attention and reported the mess 'ready for inspection, sir.' On subsequent days only those class members in the duty watch would be required to clean up for 'rounds,' as this evening inspection was known.

The 13 ex-*Victory* members of LS12 dragged as much information out of the four back-classed young men as they could, and before they climbed into their bunks, had unanimously elected Tam as their temporary class leader; a post which he readily accepted. Most were very tired; everyone had travelled much further than Bob and lights out were at 10 p.m. The duty instructor would call into each mess at random times throughout the night to suppress any misbehaviour so there was little point in doing anything other than turning in.

Early next morning Tam led LS12 through their first enactment of what was to become their normal daily routine: up at 0630, breakfast at 0700, muster for cleaning stations 0730, Divisions at 0830, stand-easy at 1000, lunch at 1200, Divisions at 1300, stand-easy 1415, secure at 1620. The Navy used the 24 hour clock and the class decided that they had better get used to it, particularly since it was a fundamental system of recording time in communications procedures.

Occupying approximately 100 acres of Hampshire countryside, HMS *Mercury* was the Navy's main centre for

266

communications training for both UK and other foreign navies. Almost completely unfenced, the only secure area was that section called North Camp situated to the north of the public road, which bisected the establishment. In addition to Leydene House, the officers' quarters and Anson Block for new entries, there were approximately eight other blocks accommodating more senior communicators returning for advancement courses; and those other specialists required for the day-to-day running of the signals school. Being readily accessible to the public from the bisecting road, it was a nightmare in terms of physical security and required almost continuous patrolling.

Many of the ship's company, including officers, instructors and other establishment personnel lived with their families in the surrounding towns and villages, commuting daily to the top of the hill. These were known as RAs, Rationed Ashore; those living in *Mercury* were known as VMs, Victualled Members. Whilst at *Victory* the would-be communicators had been told that *Mercury* had a poor communications system, but in fact a very good transport system existed with frequent busses operating between Petersfield and Portsmouth.

In 1957 *Mercury* was the only RN establishment involved in trialling a proposed new pay system whereby payment was made on a weekly basis, in cash, rather than fortnightly. Most sailors preferred the weekly pay system because it made budgeting much easier, however it was a heavy workload for the Pay Section and was discontinued after about a couple of years. Most young sailors, having been paid each Thursday, tended to spend their money over the weekend on essential items like beer, cigarettes, and girls. Ending up broke on Monday morning, at least they had only to wait until Thursday for their next pay-day.

Unlike *Victory*, bathroom facilities were quite adequate in Anson Block and this, together with the spacious individual mess areas, gave the building a more relaxed and homely feel. There was also a laundry service within *Mercury*, a very welcome, reasonably priced, and frequently used facility for every single member of the class. Anson was a lively, noisy, and generally happy block in which to live, and, notwithstanding numerous occurrences of inter-mess battles and rivalries, there was very little physical abuse or victimisation.

Dining facilities, presently located in two large Nissen huts, were spacious, with one of the Nissen huts reserved for new entries; however, a new block, to be called Mountbatten Block was in the process of construction and would provide new dining-halls, messes, and recreation facilities for both senior and junior ratings.

Classrooms consisted of old-style Nissen huts in the southern half of the camp and newer brick buildings in the northern half. Many of the classrooms were school-like, simply furnished with desks and chairs with A-frame easels and chalkboards.

Cleaning these classrooms was a very dirty business. The floors were black and required daily polishing and each was fitted with an old iron stove that had to be lit on winter mornings. These buildings had no insulation whatsoever; they got stiflingly hot in the summer and freezing cold, despite the stove, in the winter.

Other classrooms, in the more secure area of the camp north of the public road, housed expensive communications equipment and specialist rooms for morse and automatic telegraphy training.

Well used to hard physical labour, Bob had little difficulty with cleaning the classrooms, and polishing, dusting, cleaning windows, and lighting fires was second nature to him. Some of LS12 had not previously been required to do the sort of cleaning required at both barracks and *Mercury*; they found it very hard going and difficult to meet the standards of the duty officers who inspected the classrooms each morning. Returning always to his own philosophy, Bob strove to *get it right first time*, for the officers had a penchant for requiring the work redone in one's own time!

Morning and afternoon Divisions were very quick affairs, in essence a head count and a quick check on the appearance of individuals. Unkempt, unshaven or scruffy appearance, long hair, dirty boots or a dirty cap, all were indications that an individual was skimping on his kit; the instructors at *Mercury* were no less eager to award a minor punishment of kit muster or locker inspection to those who were obviously in need. Keeping people at their cleaning stations until the very last minute, because of poor standards, was an easy way to ensure that an individual was either late on parade or had insufficient time to prepare and turned up looking scruffy; giving everyone an opportunity to dish out the punishments! A few of Bob's classmates seemed incapable of understanding that what they saw as a menial cleaning task, if hurried and poorly done, almost always led the shirkers onto an ever downward spiral of failure; the minor punishments for shoddy work infringed on other important course activities resulting in an overall poor performance and back-classing.

Each Monday and Thursday morning required a clean set of working clothes – the blue denim outfit, with boots, anklets and blue belts; and woe betide anyone who did not concur. Availability of the establishment laundry meant that no one could be forgiven for appearing at any duty or activity in dirty clothing. Some, but not much, latitude was granted between the changeover days.

Morning and afternoon New Entry Divisions at *Mercury* were somewhat different to those at *Victory*. At *Mercury* the commands were given in flag signals! LS12, or at least those members of LS12 who had, as yet, had no experience of these commands, had a very interesting first couple of weeks until they all managed to memorise them. Foxtrot November – attention, turn 9 – right turn, 9 turn – left turn, turn 18 – about turn, corpen 9 and 9 corpen – wheel instead of turn, speed 10 – quick march, speed 15 – double march were the basics. Having issued the order, or orders, the class indicated their receipt (but not necessarily the correct interpretation) by raising their right arms in the air; the imperative being *down*, i.e., drop arms and move. Many was the time that LS12 had to march back onto the parade ground and have another go during the first few weeks. On the first day, having been briefed by Tam, when Willie-the-Poo gave the order 'Foxtrot November, 9 turn, speed 10' everyone put their hands in the air, and at the order *down* Bob turned left, Jock turned right and three did a smart about turn and walked into the wall behind them! If it had not been so embarrassing – the parade ground was right underneath the captain's office window – it would have been hilarious.

The primary aim of the course was, of course, to improve their morse and typing skills, and in addition to this the course work involved a variety of subjects. Each method of message transmission, whether it be by morse, automatic telegraphy, voice, flags, semaphore, or carrier pigeon, required the message to be formatted in a special way. Those of LS12 who survived the next ten months would emerge fully proficient in these basic message formats, together with their associated minutiae. In addition, the students would have to know which of the hundreds of communications publications included any given subject. Many of these publications were highly classified, as were the individual students' notebooks. Most lessons started with three or four of the class queuing up at the classified book store to collect the books ordered by POTs, and all had to be returned at the end of the lesson. Keeping up with the course syllabus involved considerable homework, completed under the supervision of a duty new entry instructor each evening; during which the classified book office was reopened. Most of LS12 were destined to become very familiar with putting in extra evening effort to keep up, none more than Bob and Jock, who, still working as a team, devised their own test papers during these evening sessions.

After secure at 1620 trainees were allowed to do as they pleased, go ashore, maintain their kit, swat up for forthcoming exams, play a variety of sports or just sit around chatting, unless of course you were part of the duty watch. The whole establishment of junior ratings, except for a fortunate few who had special jobs, was divided into four watches, Red, Green, Blue and Yellow.

Every fourth day, and every fourth weekend each individual did extra work involving cleaning up the dining-halls, keeping sentry duties, being part of the fire and emergency party (which involved sleeping, fully clothed, in a special room at the main gate), or, if no specific additional task was available, being part of the supernumerary group that could be called upon by almost anyone in authority for unforeseen activities or emergencies. Leave, of course, was cancelled when on duty.

Normal leave, for new entries, was evenings up to 2300, short weekend from midday Saturday (if duty on Friday), otherwise long weekend from 1620 Friday to 0730 Monday.

In order to make his journeys home both a little more convenient and a lot more frequent, Bob was hoping to buy a small motorcycle and had allocated some of the money in his Post Office account to make the purchase. Since leaving the Army, his brother Ronald, with his mechanical engineering skills, had managed to obtain a job at a Post Office garage in Portsmouth and was living, with his new wife Marjorie, in a nearby flat. The brothers had not corresponded frequently but Bob had written to

271

his eldest sibling asking if he might visit towards the end of August, whilst Pat was on holiday with her parents, adding that he was looking for a motorcycle and hoping that Ronald might be able to help him choose a reliable machine.

It was thus that Bob and Jock, not being required for weekend duties, left *Mercury* in full uniform, on one of their free Saturdays.

They caught the RN transport from *Mercury* to Petersfield and the train down to Portsmouth. Finding Ronald's home, a few rooms in a semi-detached house quite near Portsmouth prison and St Mary's Hospital, involved a considerable amount of walking and asking directions, but they eventually knocked on Ronald's door mid afternoon. The brothers had changed considerably. They had not seen each other for some time and Bob looked totally different in his uniform. Marjorie was a tall, slim, pretty woman, and she made both her visitors very welcome, laying out a tea of sandwiches and cakes. Conversation was, to say the least, stilted, since all four were virtually strangers and had very little in common. In normal conversation, Bob and Jock unknowingly included a lot of Navy speak, and Ronald told him, on his next visit, that neither he nor his wife had much of a clue what the two sailors were talking about.

Ron, the diminutive chosen by his wife and therefore from then on how Bob thought of his brother, said that he might be able to get an ex-GPO despatch motorcycle for him, a BSA Bantam. With his engineering skills, Ron would make sure that it was in good working order.

Later that evening Ron drove the two friends to Southsea pier, but not for the funfair, Jock was more interested in the pub. Whilst not a total repeat of his last boozy run ashore, Jock was still well-oiled and displaying a lack of ballast by the time they returned to *Mercury*. However, he was sufficiently sober not to attract too much attention.

It was only a week or so later that Bob, having obtained

272

all the necessary paperwork and kit, picked up the bike from Ron's house in Portsmouth. Whilst listening to Ron's explanation of the various controls, Bob tied on the L plates. A couple of wobbly practice trips up and down the side street and, waving his thanks to his brother, he disappeared in a cloud of smoke from the two-stroke engine heading for *Mercury*.

Bob had already asked permission to keep the bike at *Mercury*, wishing to observe all formalities, and after numerous U-turns, arrived at *Mercury* with the means to a new freedom. The trip home to Alton took about 30 minutes. After his first weekend in Alton using his new bike, Bob left Pat at about 0630, giving him plenty of time to get to *Mercury* and be on time for cleaning stations at 0730.

He decided to take a short cut that he had recently discovered on the Hampshire road map in *Mercury*'s library. The road was very narrow and passed through the tiny hamlet of Privett, the twisty road descending quite steeply. Conscious that there was very little room for a car in the narrow road, he was being ultra careful, keeping close to the side of the road in case he should meet one. As he descended the hill he noticed a road sign for an S bend and an open-topped sports car appeared at what seemed excessive speed. The car made no attempt to slow down or move over to make room for Bob's bike, forcing him to move dangerously close to the steep bank on his left.

Bob thought *ignorant sod* and turned to wave a fist at the departing car, completely forgetting about the S bend. He managed to negotiate the first part of the sharp bend but was going too fast for the second. The bike hit the soft roadside bank, stopping instantly and catapulted Bob over the hedge into the field. To add insult to injury he landed in a very sloppy cow-pat. Fortunately, apart from a few scratches from the hedge, he was not badly injured, except of course for a severe bruising to his pride. He could not

273

get back through the hedge, it was too dense, and he had to walk down the field to a nearby gate and walk back up the road to his bike.

By the time he got back to the point of impact, the sports car was parked on the side of the road, the driver standing, nonchalantly smoking a cigarette, wondering, no doubt, where the motorcyclist was. He started speaking before Bob got too close. *Probably expecting a smack in the mouth*, thought Bob.

'Sorry, old chap, didn't see you until the last minute and couldn't do anything about it.' His voice was clipped and precise and very old school tie, as the trainees described the officers' mode of speech. He was looking down at Bob's bike, which appeared to have suffered not too badly from its contact with the soft roadside bank. 'You're Navy,' he said, noticing Bob's small brown attaché case strapped to the rear mudguard. 'What a stroke of luck,' the clipped voice continued, 'I'm Navy too and,' he hesitated for a second or two looking thoughtfully away into the distance, 'I'm just a tiny bit lost! Looking for Leydene House and I seem to be a tad off course. I'm Lieutenant Griffiths.'

With thunder in his heart and an overpowering stench of cow-dung, Bob thought belligerently, *Well you're not getting a salute, wazzock*, and explained that he was a new entry telegraphist and had only recently joined *Mercury*.

'How's the bike?' the officer asked. Bob picked it up, wiping the grass and dirt from the machine. It didn't look too bad apart from a slight wobble from the front wheel and a bent front mudguard. 'Better not ride it,' said the officer, 'we'll chuck it in the back of the car and I'll get it fixed for you during the week. Stroke of luck really,' the officer continued, 'you can navigate!'

After removing his crash helmet Bob climbed into the seat next to the officer and the car shot off at tremendous

274

speed towards West Meon, Bob shouting instructions at the top of his voice, hanging on grimly as the car screamed around the hidden bends. As they passed through the village, the speed limit completely ignored, the driver spotted a motorcycle garage, did a U-turn and pulled up outside. He drove over a small bridge, crossing the stream that flowed through the village, into a small courtyard at the rear of the garage. They unloaded the bike just as the garage proprietor appeared from his workshop. 'Bit of a problem, old man,' the officer said to the proprietor, 'think you can fix it up?'

The mechanic had a quick look at the bike; he couldn't see any major problems. 'Maybe have to get some spare parts, but it should be ready by the end of the coming week.' The lieutenant handed over a richly embossed card.

'Send the bill up to *Mercury* for my attention if you please,' he said, ignoring the garage proprietor as he climbed into his car. Bob had to engage brain and leap in as well, as they drove off through the village to complete their journey.

By the time the car pulled up at the OOW hut it was 0745 and Bob was officially *adrift*, absent without leave, a serious offence punishable usually by several days extra work and stoppage of leave.

The lieutenant removed his full-length sheepskin coat, revealing his naval uniform with the two gold braids on each arm, donned his cap and breezed into the officer of the watch's own private office, leaving his car parked in the middle of the road.

The young telegraphist whose duty watch job was that of assisting at the OOW hut, known as the bosun's mate, was carefully examining Bob's station card, obviously with a view to handing it to the regulating department, commencing the charging procedures that would eventually produce some form of punishment. Almost immediately the OOW appeared and ordered the bosun's mate to hand over Bob's station card, Lieutenant Griffiths having explained the circumstances of Bob's tardiness.

The following Friday Bob picked his bike up from the garage, it was immaculate, the front wheel had been respoked, a new headlamp had been fitted, all the scratches and scrapes removed, and there was nothing to pay. The headlamp had been flickering since he had got the bike so he had got something out of his unplanned flight over the hedge. He was not to see Lt Griffiths again until the very last week at *Mercury*.

Despite the frugal consumption of fuel by the BSA, Bob could not afford to travel home each evening; he had to keep up his course work, and a certain amount of evening study was essential and expected of him. Most evenings were spent in Anson Block's recreational areas, or in the mess. Associating with the many female sailors under training at *Mercury*, WRNS, was not possible since the girls were accommodated at the nearby village of Soberton. Some contact with the Wrens was possible during the day and many attachments were made, especially by Jock who seemed to make a new conquest each week.

One of the facilities regularly used by *Mercury*'s ship's company was the cinema, one of the few places where new entries mixed with the more senior sailors. A large auditorium with a sloping floor fronted a large stage, used infrequently for amateur productions, backed by a large cinema screen. The seats were ordinary metal-framed, straight-backed, flimsily padded dining-chairs that were very uncomfortable to sit on for a couple of hours, but could be easily stacked ready for the enormous weekly effort of polishing the large building.

Shortly after they joined *Mercury*, Bob and Jock decided to attend an evening screening and took their seats in the front row. The cinema could hold about 500 and was always full. Before the film started, the noise and general hum of a large number of people gathered together was of jet engine proportions. The evening's entertainment usually included a news report, a cartoon or two, and the main film. As the cartoon credits rolled, Bob and Jock were completely unprepared for the roar of 'Good old Fred' that was shouted by the 498 others in the cinema. The noise was deafening and Bob clearly saw Jock's backside leave the seat of his chair.

The reason for this extraordinary, coordinated vocal outburst was because some of the Disney cartoons were produced by a person called Fred Quimby and it was to him that the Navy gave their salute. Without exception, the men loved the Mickey Mouse cartoons and 'Good old Fred' became a traditional part of a naval film show. Many was the time, in the years to come, that Bob would find himself in a civilian cinema and have to stifle his salute to Fred Quimby when the name appeared on screen! When Bob first heard it, on that first visit to the *Mercury* cinema, he felt a real sense of belonging, being part of a huge family; he felt, quite simply, at home.

In the first few weeks, their training concentrated on learning to read morse code and typing. Their passing out target, in about ten months' time, was morse at 25 words per minute (wpm) recorded by typewriter. To this end every day involved reading morse and typing practice. Both Bob and Jock, and no doubt many of the other would-be telegraphists, had been learning the morse code since before joining. Bob would translate everything he saw, car registration numbers, notices on the busses and trains, and everything else he saw. However, he, like all the others, made one big mistake: they learned the code thinking of the words 'dot' and 'dash' as the two symbols. It is very difficult to think of the morse code at any speed using these two words, but by using 'dits' and 'dahs' (di da) it was much easier and Bob often wished, while he struggled to make the conversion in his mind, that someone, preferably at his first induction interview, had told him about it.

Over the next few weeks LS12 strived to increase their speeds, the first target being 6 wpm, which most reached with relative ease. Normally, POTs sat in front of the class and transmitted the morse code exercise by hand, which the students received through their earphones, but on a few occasions a member of the class would be instructed to transmit the exercise. At the beginning of each morse session there was always a certain amount of chaos and lost time whilst the class searched for earphones that worked; and again at the beginning of each typing session, trying to find an old-fashioned Imperial or Olivetti on which there was a complete spool of ribbon and on which the keys did not jam.

At the end of each day, POTs diligently marked each exercise and expressed the result in percentage terms, posting the results on their mess noticeboard. A pass mark of above 80 per cent was required to avoid backward exercises. Additional sessions were programmed during the evenings, compulsory for those who did not achieve the required standard.

For the first few weeks Willie-the-Poo decided that the four back-classees would take it in turns to carry out the duties of class leader, Tam taking the first turn. POTs added that he would appoint a permanent leader as their individual telegraphist skills were assessed.

The weeks passed quickly and it was towards the end of September before POTs finally decided on who would win the doubtful honour of being the permanent class leader for LS12. Friday afternoons were the longest hours of the week, especially when waiting to dash off on a long weekend. The custom of LS12 was to sidetrack POTs from whatever the planned lesson was and get him talking about

278

something completely different; his mind would wander far and wide during these red herring sessions. He just loved talking about himself and almost any comment sent him off at a tangent, only returning to the present at some outside influence.

During one of the many red herring sessions, the class's divisional officer walked into their classroom, unannounced, with the intention of listening in to POTs, probably assessing his IT skills or just observing how the class behaved. Willie-the-Poo was reminiscing about some long ago run ashore in Mombasa and came back to earth with a jolt when the lieutenant walked into the room, almost but not quite catching POTs unawares; without the smallest hint of hesitation he changed step in the blink of an eye: '. . . the girls in Mombasa are the most willing . . . the importance of not guessing words when reading morse is paramount,' and continued with the lesson.

Just before secure, he announced the class leader, selected on course results to date – Bob! Flabbergasted is an excellent description of Bob's initial reaction. He knew his marks were consistently higher than the rest of the class, even Jock had to undergo the dreaded backward exercises, but he had never considered himself a strong candidate. The role could not be refused. Any attempt to do so would mark him down as a person with no ambition, frowned on by the RN, or alternatively, one without leadership qualities, another dubious quality in the eyes of divisional officers who had to write an assessment of each sailor in their division every quarter and were forever watching their flock for clues to new, innovative expressions that they could use in these reports. One of the back-classees had proudly announced that he had been assessed as being 'out of his depth in a car-park puddle.'

Having come prepared to make the appointment, POTs handed Bob the small badge of rank to sew onto his left arm, a small embroidered crown; Pat did the sewing over the weekend. Class leaders also wore white, instead of khaki, anklets. *Great,* thought Bob, *something else to keep clean.* There were, however, a few perks that came with the job, the most important of which from Bob's point of view was extended leave to midnight, which would give him longer to spend with Pat on the few weekdays that he travelled home.

At first he was a little hesitant, but as his confidence grew so did his ability to control the class. LS12 was now quite fluent in the flag commands used for manoeuvring, and they all knew how to behave in any given circumstance. They had all experienced several class leaders and were quite willing to give Bob a fair chance. Bob quickly developed a style, based loosely on his own father, changing the tone in his voice when the time came to 'stop messing around and do as you're told!' The class soon recognised this technique: they knew when they could relax and when to tighten up and take notice. The only drawback was that the class leader took responsibility for the actions of the class, whether good or bad. The fact that class leaders stood at the front of the class at Divisions, with their backs to the class, and any misbehaviour or fidgeting out of sight, did not absolve the leader of any blame.

Towards the end of October Bob reached that wonderful milestone in life: his eighteenth birthday. Not only did RN service time commence at this point but legal access to the pubs was finally granted. Another week must elapse before Jock reached his eighteenth and the pair had decided to delay their celebrations until then.

LS12 had reached a crucial point in their training, a morse reading test at 12 wpm, after which, if successful, they would be issued with their branch badges; another sewing task for Pat. Failure at this speed would have a serious consequence: back-classing. The original 13 from

Victory passed without any real problems, but all four of the back-classees failed and were back-classed yet again. Their next attempt would be their third and final effort to become telegraphists; failure would mean months of uncertainty whilst recategorization to another branch was considered. If all else failed, they would then be returned to civilian life as unfit for naval service. But not presumably unfit for national service. (All four did eventually pass out as Telegraphists, but Bob did not learn this until long after he had left *Mercury*.)

For their birthday celebrations, Bob and Jock, together with three others from LS12, went down to the Rising Sun pub at Clanfield, a dingy pub at the crossroads in a small village. It was a popular pub with *Mercury*'s ship's company and was usually packed full every evening. The group managed to get a small table in one of the corners and spent a pleasant evening drinking, playing darts, and generally relaxing.

Bob was watching very carefully for any skylarking with drinks; he had a low tolerance to alcohol and some of the lads liked to spike the party person's tipple with a 'little extra'! Jock was in his element, sinking pint after pint and eventually moving on to whiskey chasers. By about 2215 they were preparing to return to *Mercury*. A taxi had been ordered and all would pile into it somehow; the taxi drivers in the area knew *Mercury* well and were accustomed to overloading their taxis. Bob was thinking about Jimmy; he would by now be enjoying his induction into the Army for his national service. *Good luck, Jimmy, enjoy*, thought Bob, knowing full well that Jimmy would be going through hell!

It was then that the trouble started. An older signalman, sporting the two stripes signifying that at least eight years had been completed, jostled his way through the crowd to their table. He was obviously quite drunk and seemed to fall from person to person rather than swagger, which Bob thought was his intention. He was well known at *Mercury*, name of Bloom, and nicknamed Thumper because of his predilection for punch-ups. Otherwise known as a knuckle bosun, he was also what the Navy called a 'scrumpy rat.' Scrumpy, of course, is rough cider, it has a high alcoholic content and if consumed in sufficient quantity can be very addictive; a scrumpy rat is a cider alcoholic. LS12 had all seen Thumper sitting outside *Mercury*'s main canteen early each evening, waiting for opening time and access to the rough cider that the canteen sold vast quantities of. Years later scrumpy was banned from all *Mercury*'s bars, there were just too many people addicted to it.

The knuckle bosun's words were slurred, almost beyond comprehension, but the group got the gist of it. 'Time you babies got back onboard,' he sneered.

It was quite evident to everyone within earshot that Thumper was looking for trouble and Jock, who could hardly stand upright himself, said politely 'Leave us alone, Thumper.' A smile of triumph spread across Thumper's bright red face; starting an argument was his first milestone in the journey to a punch-up. He glared menacingly at Jock. 'Who you calling Thumper, whippersnapper?' Familiar with Jock's volatile temper, Bob watched as the red mist descended over Jock's eyes. He had been close to a punch-up on several occasions and Bob could recognise the signs. No doubt both hopeful pugilists would get their wishes granted this night.

Heaving himself to his feet, Jock stood, several sheets to the wind, unsteadily in front of Thumper who immediately took an enormous swing with his fist, aimed at Jock's head. It was all over in the blink of an eye. Jock parried the blow, sidestepped to the right by a half step and buried his right fist into Thumper's bulging stomach, knocking him senseless with a follow up left fist to the head before Thumper hit the deck. No one moved for several seconds. The whole pub was waiting to see if the conflict would escalate, but no one came to Thumper's aid; whoever had put their hero on the deck was probably best left alone!

At that precise moment the taxi driver entered the pub. He didn't need to shout since there was already total silence. 'Taxi for *Mercury*!' With the aid of two other classmates, Bob dragged Jock out of the pub and bundled him into the taxi before he could get them into any more trouble. Once again Jock was almost incapable of walking when they arrived at the OOW hut to collect their station cards and the bosun's mate gave him a close look.

'Birthday boy,' said Bob, and they were handed their cards.

It did not take long for the story of Thumper's defeat to spread throughout *Mercury*. Drunk or not it was no mean feat to put the knuckle bosun on the deck, and Jock was recruited into the new entry boxing team, easily winning his weight division later that year.

In the run-up to the Christmas leave period, the class were all feeling quite drained; the continual stress of total concentration was beginning to tell on everyone. Duty watches did not help, not so bad if the duty did not involve night-time activities such as sentry or patrol duties or moving down to the main gate as fire and emergency party. *Mercury* was run on a 24-7-365 basis, the duty watch being responsible for all aspects of the safety and security of the establishment. The absolute pits, as far as Bob was concerned, was the duty watch task of North Camp sentry. The part of *Mercury* to the north of the public road, called North Camp, was completely sealed off with high wire fencing with two access gates, one of which would be locked at night, the other with a sentry box to be manned at all times.

The hours between midnight and 0800 were divided into two distinct periods: the middle watch between midnight and 0400 and the morning watch for the remainder. Issued with a torch and a whistle with which to defend himself, Bob would have preferred a machine-gun. The small unlit sentry box was just large enough to hold a chair. It was very spooky, sitting in the chair during the middle watch, trying desperately not to nod off. The duty chief or any of the duty officers were likely to make a surprise visit at any time. Regular patrols around the perimeter fence were part of the job and Bob felt very uncomfortable walking around the gloomy place, gripping the torch tightly, ready to switch it on at the slightest noise.

To add to the mystical atmosphere it was rumoured that the raised earthworks that ran through the length of the site were ancient burial grounds. Bob's mind occasionally flitted back to his childhood, to the end of the garden in the lav, and he would jump at the slightest noise.

Once each term the establishment underwent a mock attack, with sailors from other establishments in the Portsmouth area acting as the opposition. The aim of the attacking force was to gain entry to *Mercury* undiscovered, highlighting in the process any weaknesses in *Mercury*'s defences. Towards the end of November, Bob again had the dreaded middle watch as North Camp sentry. At about 0330, it was pouring with rain and Bob, fairly confident in his assumption that no one would be about in the awful conditions, was having a quiet doze. He was not actually asleep, *off, bum on broomstick* really.

He returned to full wakefulness at a slight noise. The hairs on the back of his neck were immediately highly sensitive and, as he looked out of the sentry box, he saw a hooded figure fiddling with the chain of the gate, just a few feet in front of him. The figure appeared to be dressed completely in black, the hat with a high peak and wide brim much like a witch's hat, and a long ankle-length coat, glistening in the rain. For a few seconds Bob was bewildered. He could not understand how the figure could be inside the locked area. Bob had not admitted anyone since he came on watch. His mind whirled. He was very spooked. Was this apparition spectre or human? *Give it a whack with the torch – ask questions later!*

Gathering his legs under him, Bob sprang from the sentry box, smashing the torch down onto the hooded head. The figure cried out and fell to the ground. 'OK, I give up, I'm rumbled,' the prostrate figure said as Bob blew furiously on his whistle. The whistle proved utterly useless; no one heard the repeated blasts and no one arrived to give him any assistance.

The fallen sailor said that he was from *Victory* and was taking part in the scheduled intrusion exercise. He was dressed in foul weather clothing, rubberised hat and long coat with sea boots. They agreed that they would wait until the morning watch sentry arrived at 0400 and Bob would then escort the man to the OOW. Fortunately, he was not badly injured. He said that the shock of Bob jumping on him had felled him, rather than the blow itself, and Bob mused, *You might be OK, pal, but I will have to change my expletive deleted underwear in the morning!*

The intruder had gained entry over the high fence at the far end of North Camp and, thinking the sentry box unmanned, was going to attempt to climb over the gate when Bob clobbered him. The OOW congratulated Bob on capturing the intruder. Bob made a bit of a song and dance about the failure of his whistle to attract attention, and the intruder was taken away for questioning. Whether the intruder ever made any complaint about being struck over the head, Bob never did discover. He heard nothing more about the incident; but the very next week a telephone and lighting was installed in the sentry box.

*

In December the class went on two weeks' Christmas leave. Although the stress of training had largely diminished, at least for Bob, who had no difficulty in keeping up with the many new subjects introduced, it was another welcome break. He had been training now for almost eight months and still had another six months to complete, assuming, that is, that he did not get back-classed. He had discovered that communications procedures, methods, and equipment changed rapidly and the constant introduction of new subjects together with revising those already learned, shaped his mind to accept such changes as a routine. POTs' own explanation for these constant changes was that the structure of the Navy was very fluid: no one stayed in post for more than two or three years; everyone was striving to move upwards around the promotion cone, hoping to reach the pinnacle; and each new incumbent tried to make his name by dreaming up new ways of doing things, new brooms . . .

During Christmas leave Bob's parents moved into a tied cottage at a farm about ten miles from Alton. Fortunately father had recovered his health sufficiently to obtain a full-time job and Bob was pleased to help them move into their own home again. Despite there being plenty of room at his parent's cottage, and much to their disgust, Bob had decided to spend his leave at the Wilsons. On the day before leaving *Mercury* for Christmas leave it had snowed heavily and the snow still lay about 6 inches deep. Riding the bike home was a very tricky affair, the deep ruts left by the passage of larger vehicles had frozen and progress was limited to less than 10 mph, sometimes even to walking pace.

As he passed through the village of Farringdon, a couple of miles short of Alton, Bob's bike ran out of fuel. He did not want to leave it by the roadside and spent an extremely uncomfortable, back-breaking hour or so pushing the bike for the rest of the journey. He arrived at the Wilsons very wet, very cold, very weary, and very hungry, and, for once, was most grateful for the snack that Mrs Wilson provided.

Feeling Pat in his arms when he met her outside the egg-packing station, warming him with her body, was, after his uncomfortable trip home, especially wonderful. They intended becoming engaged the week before Christmas, committing one to the other for ever. The Wilsons had insisted that George formally ask the head of the household for Ann's hand in marriage when they had got engaged, and Pat had already told Bob what was expected. For several weeks Bob had been previewing the event in his mind, constantly changing his little speech and trying to build up his confidence. In the event, asking Mr Wilson for his permission to marry his youngest daughter was not the excruciating experience that Bob had foreseen, and he had passed through this barrier just a few days previously. A very understanding man, Mr Wilson had recognised Bob's agitation and discomfort, no doubt remembering having to do the same thing himself years before. He had simply asked, 'Is this what Pat wants?' and, when Bob nodded yes, gave his permission.

As the packing station closed down a few days before Christmas, the two young lovers went off to Aldershot on the train to search for an engagement ring. Naturally Pat had already given the matter a great deal of thought and knew exactly what she wanted, but still insisted on visiting every single jeweller's shop in the town, naturally returning to the very first shop that they had called into. The ring of her eventual choice had two small hearts, inlaid with very small diamonds, set diagonally across a gold band. They were deliriously happy, relaxed and content in each other's company and looking forward to the day when they could afford to get married. Happiness did not begin to describe their feelings as they travelled back to Alton that evening, entering into what was to be quite a long engagement.

Old school pal Jimmy came home for Christmas leave and the familiar foursome teamed up again for various outings and visits to the cinema. The young national serviceman, dapper in his khaki army uniform had also gone through the engagement ritual with Joy's father; the couple were officially engaged and were planning to marry in a couple of years.

There had already been much discussion between Bob, Pat, and the Wilson family about setting a date for their wedding. Setting a date was actually a tad premature; setting a year was more appropriate as Bob wanted to wait until he was earning a decent wage and could afford to look after his wife. The Wilsons supported the young couple's stance on the subject of a wedding, appreciating their determination not to rush into marriage without sufficient funds to support themselves.

It snowed heavily again over Christmas and it was not possible to get out to Bob's parents to tell them of the engagement until almost new year. Both parents, rather disappointingly, seemed uninterested in Bob's news, launching themselves instead into how well Ron was doing and how Albert's family was increasing. The only possible excuse for his parents' somewhat reserved reception was that they probably assumed that there was a lot of water to run under the bridge before Pat, who was still only 17, would be allowed to marry by her own parents.

Bob having finally passed his motorcycle driving test early in December, at the second attempt, Pat perched herself on the rear seat as they slowly chugged back into Alton. There was little danger of hurting themselves even if they did fall off; the bike could hardly muster more than 30 mph, and that was downhill with a following wind! However, the bike enabled them to get around a little more easily and Bob even managed to take Pat to meet his brothers, where they received much the same reception as they had at Bob's parents.

New year was celebrated at the Wilson home. George and Ann, with their six-month-old bouncing baby boy Richard returned for the evening party. The whole family seemed to get on extremely well, and Bob now included himself as part of the Wilson clan. Mrs Wilson had provided her usual mountain of food, despite everyone having over indulged throughout the festive season.

It had been a very pleasant, relaxing break from training, ending early in January 1958 when Bob was required to report back to *Mercury*.

The journeys that Bob made by motorcycle did not take very long, but it was very cold during the early part of 1958 and, despite Bob's efforts to wrap up and keep warm, he always arrived at *Mercury* with frozen knees. He did not want to invest in expensive bike clothing so Pat suggested he wrap newspapers around his legs, held in place by large elastic bands, to provide an extra layer of insulation.

It was a good idea and it did help, but it was his usual routine to park his bike outside the OOW hut and remove his waterproof outer trousers whilst the bosun's mate retrieved his station card. On the very first morning that he had adopted Pat's suggestion, he had completely forgotten about the additional insulation. It was very windy and the elastic bands had slipped! Sheets of the Sunday editions blew in all directions and Bob spent a frantic ten minutes collecting and disposing of it all, watched very carefully by the master-at-arms who had witnessed the entire episode!

The spring term was filled with a continuation of LS12's usual routine of morse and typing, followed by yet more morse and typing. The class was now quite proficient at reading morse both manually and on keyboard. Whilst regularly managing to scrape above 80 per cent, a pass mark, Bob always looked for 100 per cent and had been regularly achieving that accuracy for several months.

As the speeds increased there was very little thinking time and the secret was, generally, to skip the letter or symbol that you were not sure about and continue with the text. The lost symbol usually stuck in his mind and he could complete it at the end of the transmission. As the speeds increased above 23 wpm Bob became what he termed 'dit happy,' and sorting them out at the increased speeds became, for a short while, a nightmare. However, he was not the only one suffering from this effect, most of the class were having similar problems, but from then on Bob became known amongst his classmates as 'Dit Happy.'

Other lectures were squeezed into the already crammed curriculum, much more ABCD (Atomic, Biological and Chemical Defence), firefighting, and a lecture by the medical officer on the dangers of venereal disease, at which most of the class suddenly became very much more attentive; the subject provided dozens of superb red herrings for Willie-the-Poo over the next few months.

The lecture given by the medical officer was much enjoyed by the whole class, if a little worrying. Venereal disease was easily contracted in various parts of the world, and an unsuspecting young sailor could easily become infected without proper precautions. One of the most important precautions was *knowledge*, and the detailed descriptions and film show, given by the MO, was, if nothing else, graphically informative. What the MO did not tell the class was that the old-style treatments, demonstrated in his gory movie, had been largely superseded by 1957; more modern treatments were available in the form of powerful drugs.

As they left the classroom, the MO handed out a condom to each member of the class. 'Keep this in your paybook,' he said. 'You never know when you might need it!' Later that evening when one of LS12 decided to open up the condom, it was to be used as a water bomb to play a practical joke on the latest raw recruits to join *Mercury*. They were all surprised at how robust the equipment was and, in common with every other item of naval kit that they had been issued with, how large it was! The rubber looked thick enough to make a good repair on a car tyre inner tube.

'Not much will get through that,' Jock drawled in his Hampshire-ised Scottish accent.

Firefighting lessons were carried out at a small, specialised establishment at Portsmouth, and the whole class piled into one of the large RN coaches for a *day out*. Dragging the heavy hoses in and out of very tiny spaces with no one quite sure whether or when to turn the water on or off, they all ended up soaking wet or covered in foam. There were no messing facilities at the firefighting school so everyone was issued with a packed lunch prepared by *Mercury*.

On arrival at the firefighting school the whole class was issued with special waterproof clothing for use during the various exercises. Like every other item of kit that Bob had so far experienced, these were large. Everyone had to roll up the arms and legs of the enormous hooded tops and trousers, and the wellington boots ('sea boots' in Navy speak) seemed to be all size 11. They looked a sorry bunch, any movement at all requiring a huge effort in the over-sized clothing, and the sight of the class trying to drag the heavy hoses and equipment around must have appeared hilarious to the staff.

Part of the firefighting training was to exit a smoke-filled room, much like the gas exercise at *Victory*, but this time without respirator and in the dark. The 13 were taken into a very dingy room, built in metal to represent the bulkheads of a ship. The lights were extinguished and the room slowly filled with smoke. After just a few minutes they were told to turn around three times and leave the room. The room provided a single exit, and the obvious solution was to walk slowly forward until a wall was encountered and feel around the wall in a clockwise or anticlockwise direction; it should not take more than a few seconds to find the door.

All but one made it without incident. To his undying shame, Jock later explained to Bob that he had decided to drop to the floor, staying beneath the rising smoke, and crawl towards a bulkhead. The problem was that he panicked a little and shot forward, on his hands and knees, head first into the metal wall! He was temporarily stunned, and once the firefighting staff had dragged him from the room, they found him unhurt except for a badly bruised forehead. The incident was to be a source of fear and foreboding for Jock, who told Bob that he had felt claustrophobic in the enclosed space and he was worried how he would react to being at sea in a warship, which is nothing but small enclosed spaces.

There firefighting training came in handy a few weeks later when one of the newest trainees, just arrived from *Victory*, was detailed to light a fire in one of the Nissen hut classrooms. He could not get the fire started – he claimed later that the wood was too damp – and he had been told by Bob to use some floor polish to help get it going. For Bob it became a salutary lesson in the art of issuing clear and precise orders. What he should have said was use a very *small amount* of floor polish instead of *some*.

The poor lad put half the tin onto the fire and it lit with a spectacular bang, blowing the chimney off the top of the stove and blasting the small metal lid through the Nissen roof. Hot liquid floor polish was blasted across the room and soon desks and chairs were burning as were the many flags and photographs on display. Fortunately Jock was working nearby and he collected the fire hose, coiled onto a stake from where it could extend to cover all the classrooms in the section, and doused the fire. The young lad, newly arrived from *Victory*, his face covered in soot marks and polish, apologised to Bob. 'Sorry, sir, but I got the fire going.' It is very difficult, Bob realised at the time, to be angry in the face of such innocence, and he did not have the heart to tell the young lad not to call him sir, and that he did not want the whole building alight.

The weeks and months passed quickly and as their skills improved, the class became involved in live training. *Mercury* had its own radio room, set up to look exactly like a ship's radio room (W/T Office). Called the XWO (Exercise Wireless Office), the interior was a mass of radio transmitters and receivers, set up to communicate with ships at sea specifically for operator training. These were Bob's favourite periods. Marching in the spring sunshine, across the wide expanse of lawn, through the woods to the remote XWO, anticipating exchanging messages with a ship at sea, Bob felt ready for the job, fully trained and looking forward to his first sea job.

Before going on Easter leave, the class had to complete their annual musketry course. These courses were usually carried out on *Mercury*'s own firing range, situated on the way to the XWO. There was a large chalk pit, which reminded Bob of the enormous fun such places had afforded himself and his brothers on the way to their school. The pit had a high back at its rear and it was into this that the weapons were fired using blank ammunition. The maximum possible range was only about 100 yards, just sufficient to blast away with pistol, 303 rifle and Bren gun.

Pistols are generally regarded as officers' weapons and most naval ratings do not receive training in their use. Sparkers, however, received regular training with this weapon. When involved in boarding other ships or taking part in other naval attacks and events, a communicator was always detailed as part of the activity group. This communicator, normally a sparker, usually had to carry a heavy portable radio, including large and weighty batteries. The additional size and weight of a rifle would be far too heavy and cumbersome, particularly when trying to negotiate scrambling nets and other precarious methods of obtaining access to a vessel.

However, on this occasion LS12 were to fire live ammunition and had to bus to the Army's firing ranges at Longmoor, near Bordon. Facilities for firing over greater distances, up to 400 yards, were available there and the class took it in turns to man the targets, hoisting them into the air to be shot at, lowering them for pasting up the holes, if any, and reporting the shot with a long pole. It was a strange feeling standing in the pits waiting for the bullets to whiz overhead. There was no danger of being hit, except for a ricochet, but Bob was very pleased to get back behind the weapons. By no means *under fire*, the experience nonetheless was sufficiently real to give a good indication of the feeling that troops on active service must have had during the war, and Bob was mightily pleased that he was not a pongo.

At distances of up to about 300 yards, Bob's aim was quite true, certainly true enough to hit the target with each shot, but not necessarily in a scoring part of the target, but when the targets were moved back even further he could not make a single hit. One of their number, Joel Harvey, proved to be a remarkable shot, effortlessly hitting the bull from almost any distance.

Any prowess at sporting excellence was pounced upon by the Navy and those with such special abilities were usually incorporated into inter-ship or inter-service sporting events. *Mercury* used these annual musketry courses to identify any possible recruits for the establishment shooting team, and the instructors kept a sharp eye on each person's efforts. Having displayed such skill, about which he had previously been totally unaware, Joel Harvey was immediately attached to *Mercury*'s shooting team and would eventually do well at the tri-service shooting matches at Bisley. Needless to say, neither Bob nor Jock were extended an invitation to join the team!

LS12 were not the only service personnel using Longmoor that day. The RAF had sent a bus load of their own recruits for some target practice. It made for a much more pleasant day for everyone, sitting around a fire at lunchtime, eating the stodgy packed lunches and chatting about life under training in the two services. It also introduced an element of competition into the whole event. An army sergeant was in charge of the range and at the end of the day he instructed everyone to scour the area ('skirmishing' in Navy speak), to pick up all the rubbish and spent cartridges that they could find and throw everything on the fire. One of the RAF lads picked up what he thought was a handful of spent cartridges and, as instructed, threw them casually on to the fire! It didn't take long for them to explode, and bullets fizzed around in all directions. Fortunately there was no one standing around the fire at the time of the explosions and there were no injuries, but everyone knew just how lucky they had been. The sergeant went ballistic and insisted on inspecting all further rubbish before it was thrown on the fire. *Bit late*, thought Bob and learned another lesson to fall back on when, a few years later, he had to supervise another live firing at Longmoor.

Easter leave, once again, was blissful. The spare room at the Wilson home was again made available to Bob for the entire two weeks and, although Pat was at work every weekday, the engaged couple spent some wonderful weekends meandering around the country lanes on the bike.

The fickle nature of April's weather did not allow too many chances to take the bike out, and pretty country scenes and colourful backroads are not limitless, even in Hampshire, and Bob decided to take Pat to see the Sandsfoot estate, passing through the familiar villages to Church Wallop, via Winchester. The bike may not have been very powerful but it was very reliable; except for the odd oiling up of the spark-plug, he had very little trouble with it.

Throughout the journey to the estate, Bob was considering whether or not to call in to see Mr Sandsfoot and some of the estate workers in the cottages. Conversation on a motorbike is virtually impossible so he had plenty of time to decide and, as he drove up the now deeply rutted drive to the estate, wobbling on the bike with Pat hanging on for dear life, he suddenly bottled out and decided, instead, to risk confrontation and just stroll through the fields.

Familiar sights invoked memories of his childhood and Bob was quiet as the couple wandered across the fields and along the river banks. It was clear from the many ducks' eggs on the bottom of the river that no one bothered to collect them, and Pat found his description of retrieving them most amusing. When the couple arrived at the ruined house, Bob showed his sweetheart the entrance to the cellar and explained how he and his brother had gained access.

Life had been less stressful for Bob over the last few months and he had not had to call upon the support of his vision of Mrs Sandsfoot for some time, but the memory was as clear as if it had all happened just yesterday. The inscription on Bosun's grave was fading but could still be read. Pointing it out, he told Pat of his experience and of his attachment to Mrs Sandsfoot.

Sitting near the dog's grave, Pat sat with her long legs crossed beneath her, and listened to his story; eventually tears glistened in her beautiful dark-brown eyes as Bob relived the past. The promise that he had made to himself not to share his experience with another living soul was not forgotten; Bob had decided that Pat was different, there would not be ridicule or disbelief, she would understand. They did not go down into the cellar since there was nothing to use to facilitate climbing back out.

The wood was carpeted in bluebells and they lay together, hugging and kissing passionately. Eventually, quite naturally, they made love, Bob searching for the RN condom that the MO had given him. The memory of that wonderful day, in the peace of the Hampshire countryside and amongst the splash of spring flowers, would remain with him, tucked away in a special corner of his heart, always. This was his first experience of physical passion and post-coital peace, and he thought what a wonderful place for it to have happened, in his own special place. They both knew that their lovemaking had to happen and they both knew that in a matter of a few short weeks Bob would finish his training and be sent off to join the fleet.

The final two weeks of their ten month course, towards the end of May 1958, were extremely hectic for the whole class. Every day was filled with tests and exams, which left them all feeling totally drained at the end of each day. On the last day POTs assembled them in one of the Nissen huts, awaiting the arrival of the captain, who would present his prize to the student achieving the best results. After each exam they had all expressed doom and gloom at their possible results, but the whole class knew that old 'Dit Happy' was in with the best chance. Later when the captain called out his name to collect the prize, a copy of *Horatio Hornblower*, inscribed and dated by the captain, Bob feigned surprise but he also knew that he had done well and would have been more surprised if another name had been called.

He had worked very hard over the past year and he was

now ready and willing to put all his training into practice. After the captain had left, POTs said he would read out their next postings (a 'draft chit' in Navy speak). Everyone was expecting and hoping to be drafted to sea, since sea service was part of advancement requirements, and they all wanted to achieve the next small step up the ladder as quickly as possible.

Being an Ordinary Tel, or OD, meant that literally everyone could order you around and you ended up with all the dirty jobs that no one else wanted to do. The next step would see them as fully trained able seaman equivalents, with a star above their sparkers badges and finally free from the worst of the worst jobs. But that would not be for several months and certainly not before they had completed some time at sea.

To the consternation of the class, before reading out their draft chits, Willie-the-Poo went off on a self-induced distraction, explaining in detail how he had won the captain's prize, had gone off to sea etc., right up to the present day and his hopes for his forthcoming officers course. The class was fidgeting. They had all heard POTs' life story many times before, and having had enough waiting, Bob boldly interjected, 'Can I remove this class leader's badge now, POTs?'

Constant in his slow fuse to anger, POTs took the hint, 'Yes you can, Leonard,' he said, and added that none of the class would be going to sea just yet, ruining in those few short words, the hopes of everyone else in the room. The Navy had a different task for LS12. In less than ten days' time they would all be flown out to Singapore to join the pool of spare sparkers for the Far East Fleet, which left them with just two weekends before departure. Just as at *Victory*, the class had clubbed together to buy a thank you gift for their instructor, and POTs, despite his faults, had been a good course instructor and had gotten them through all the trials and tribulations of the last nine months. They had considered purchasing an officer's ceremonial sword but decided that such a gift might be a bit presumptuous, and when they discovered the likely cost, they were pleased that they were forced to rethink. Their final choice was a silver beer tankard engraved with POTs, LS12, 1958, a choice of words not favoured by the whole class; some wanted POTs replaced with Willie-the-Poo!

It felt quite strange walking out of the classroom on that final results day. No longer a class leader, Bob had already removed the hated white gaiters, which had been so difficult to keep clean since black boot polish does not cohabit too well with white blanco, and he would never again be responsible for the behaviour of the class. The new group of individuals did not quite know what to do when, dismissed by POTs, they emerged onto the road outside. Should they fall in and march around as a class or just make their own way back to Anson Block? Their final task that Friday afternoon was to pack their kit and equipment and move into a ship's company accommodation block; from now on they were RN proper, no longer trainees, and they all felt 10 foot tall. Seeing their confusion, Bob gave his last command as class leader of LS12. 'Make your own way to the mess and pack up to move'.

Thankfully, their last two weekends would both be long weekends, and Bob couldn't wait to get home and tell Pat his good news, although quite how she would accept the news of his absence for probably the next two years he did not know. POTs had not been able to give them any indication of the exact duration of their next draft. Apart from the fact that they would be based at Singapore he had, for once, very little additional information to give them.

That evening whilst waiting for Pat in his customary

position outside the egg-packing station, Bob became nervous about telling Pat the news of his draft. Yes, they were engaged to be married, but could a young girl of just 18 cope with anything up to two years' separation before seeing her fiancé next? At a few minutes past five she came out of the station, saw him, and ran into his arms. As they walked to her home Bob was unusually quiet and Pat eventually asked what was wrong. She knew him so well already. Well rehearsed words completely forgotten, Bob blurted out the details of his draft, words falling over one another in his rush to get it said. In her usual calm and reassuring way, Pat immediately put his mind at rest. She knew that separation was part of the lot of a sailor's wife and she was quite ready to accept it when necessary. Resigned to her role, she would wait for him, of that he could be absolutely sure.

The Wilsons were ambivalent about Bob's news. On the one hand they were happy that Bob had completed his training and, on the other hand, they were concerned about their daughter's happiness during his absence. They knew that their youngest child cared deeply for the young sailor, who seemed already to have become part of the family, and spent so much of his free time at their home, but they also knew that parting does not always make the heart grow fonder. For himself, Bob was able to forget about the Navy for the weekend and concentrated on enjoying his last few days with his sweetheart.

Most of the following week was spent in sorting out which kit would go by sea mail and making sure that necessary tropical kit was packed to take with him; and the dreaded inoculations. The class had been receiving various jabs for several months. The Navy liked to keep its personnel ready to go anywhere at almost a moment's notice. They already had international medical forms for cholera and typhoid and would now be given a yellow fever inoculation. The injection was administered into the upper thigh, and Bob was shocked at the size of the needle, fully 4 inches long; he tightened his thigh muscle in anticipation of the needle and received a heavy smack on the leg to make him relax! The anticipated pain was nothing in comparison to the actual pain and all 13 limped, maybe just a tad excessively, away from the sickbay.

Just as with their previous inoculations, each person suffered a variety of after-effects, some severe, some fairly moderate and some no reaction whatsoever. Turning a handsome shade of yellow, Bob's leg swelled enormously. It was also very painful and he spent a few uncomfortable days hobbling around *Mercury*. The nights were also very uncomfortable since any weight on the swollen leg caused instant pain. Sleep was almost impossible; the leg seemed to ache continuously and when the aching finally stopped the swollen area around the needle's point of entry developed an irritating itch. Strangely the symptoms disappeared, almost miraculously, during the fourth night following the injection, much to everyone's relief.

On the Friday before they were due to depart for Singapore, Bob had a very worrying experience, which was to threaten his last few nights of liberty with Pat. The class, as they all still thought of themselves, had very little to do. Fully packed and ready to go both Bob and Jock decided to get in the front of the queue for a stand-easy cup of tea. In an establishment the size of *Mercury* there were hundreds of people vying at the same time for a quick cup of tea at tea breaks. Whilst they were under training it had not always been possible even to attempt to obtain a cup of tea, because they had to be at their next classroom, sometimes on the opposite side of *Mercury*, in good time for their next lesson.

With so many hoping to get a mid-morning drink, the NAAFI girls made up huge urns of pussers' tea, dark brown and very thick, and had them carried down from the galley to the lower floor of the newly opened Mountbatten Block, by willing volunteers. As many as six girls were usually employed during these rest periods, dishing out tea, three pouring the steaming brew into sturdy ceramic mugs, two more handing it out, and a highly efficient older lady taking the money. Stand-easy had not yet been sounded on *Mercury*'s tannoy system, but Bob and Jock were happily sitting, backs to the wall, at the front of a queue of about 30 others, about 5 minutes before the start of stand-easy.

The *Victory* team, as the two friends often thought of themselves, had compiled their own check-off list, containing the many tiny items that, when completed, should produce a successful draft to Singapore, together with the kit that they might need. The pair were deep in thought when suddenly the double doors of the main entrance burst open and three crushers appeared. 'Everyone stay where you are,' the senior PO shouted, glaring around the room and daring anyone to move, while his minions collected the station cards of all those present. Both lads knew they were in trouble, and what a time to do it, their last weekend in the UK before being drafted abroad. They both very much doubted that any leniency would be afforded them because of that fact. It was probably nothing more than bad luck that the crushers chose that particular day to make a point to the entire ship's company that knocking off early was to be frowned upon, and they could be relied upon to press their case for a severe punishment.

When charged with any misdemeanour contravening good order and naval discipline, the naval punishment system called for the offenders to be brought before the OOW, who, if he felt he did not have the powers to deal with the severity of the crime, might forward the case to

302

the commander, who had the option of forwarding it to the captain. Each increment of authority, up through the naval chain of command, was limited in terms of the severity of punishment that it could award. For example the OOW had power to award punishments involving loss of leave, pay, or extra work, whilst the captain had power to reduce rank and award prison sentences. The captain's decision, under normal circumstances, was final. In exceptional circumstances, if a sailor felt unfairly treated, it was possible to ask for a decision from the local commander-in-chief, or Admiralty.

Every dog has its day and there comes a time when everyone is due a portion of extreme good luck. By such a stroke of exceptional good fortune, the OOW, on that fateful Friday, was none other than Lieutenant Griffiths, the officer involved in Bob's motorcycle accident. As he walked by the long line of offenders waiting to appear before him, he stopped next to Bob and whispered, 'When I ask for those people who helped the NAAFI staff to carry the tea down from the galley, step forward.' A slight nudge from Jock indicated that he had heard the whispered advice, and when the order was given both lads stepped smartly forward with a group of other young men. 'The NAAFI helpers are dismissed,' Lieutenant Griffiths declared in a loud voice, and Bob and Jock left the OOW hut feeling very relieved indeed, not to mention extremely lucky. As would become apparent so many times in the future, it was one of those times in life when *who you know* is so much more important than *what you know*. It was not possible to thank Lieutenant Griffiths, he was too busy dealing with the remaining defaulters, but the incident did convince Bob that not all officers were necessarily vindictively cruel tyrants whose sole reason for existence was to make his life a misery.

That last weekend with Pat was a sombre affair. On Sunday afternoon they rode the little BSA, which had served Bob so well, to his parents' home. Once again Pat got a less than warm reception. His parents did not actually give Bob any reason for their coolness towards her and Bob would not ask them in front of Pat. They did not stay long, for Bob could already see the tears welling in his mother's eyes. If I stay much longer I will be blubbing myself, thought Bob, so he said his farewells and departed with a cheerful '*see you in about two years.*'

Jimmy was in Germany serving with the Army, so Bob and Pat had a quiet night in the Wilsons' front room, watching the television until the white blob appeared, signifying the end of that day's transmissions, about midnight. He would be leaving in the morning at about ten o'clock. His orders were to report to RAF Hendon by 3 p.m. and he did not want to be late. *Trouble comes in threes* – his mother's words came into his head, and after his recent lucky escape, he made a mental note to watch himself very carefully over the next few weeks or so.

The young lovers had agreed to say a quick farewell the following morning and, to this end, Bob walked Pat to work shortly after eight o'clock. A quick kiss and he was gone, he could not turn around to see if she had watched him out of sight. He was afraid of duplicating the tears he had seen in her lovely eyes.

8

Kranji

Due to meet Jock at Waterloo station at 1130, from where they would make their way together to Hendon. Bob, dressed in civilian clothes, arrived at Waterloo and waited under the station clock, sitting on his weighty Pusser's green, with the small Pusser's brown – his cabin baggage – on his lap. The voyage to Singapore was scheduled to take 72 hours by Handley Page Hermes aircraft recently acquired from BOAC for troop movements.

A little after 1130 Jock arrived. He had been in the station bar for about an hour and smelled of drink, and Bob was hoping that he was not too far gone. They had about nine hours before the flight was due for take-off from Hendon, and if Bob could keep him off the booze until then he should be OK. Quite how he had managed it, Bob could not guess, but Jock was overburdened with kit. He had the same Pusser's brown and green suitcases as Bob, but in addition, his hammock. As Jock staggered across the station concourse under the weight of his kit, Bob watched dumbfounded. What on earth was he doing with his hammock? The large sausage-shaped hammock was not in sight when they mustered for leave inspection on Friday, he must have gone back to the mess and got it! 'You'll never get that on to the flight, Jock,' Bob exclaimed, 'did you not read the flight instructions: one suitcase in the hold and one piece of overnight hand baggage!' After Jock admitted in a slightly slurred Scottish accent that he had not both-ered to read the stapled pages of instructions, the pair sat for a few minutes wondering what to do with the hammock. After some contemplation Jock finally decided to leave the hammock in left luggage. 'What? For two years' said Bob.

'Well, if it's not there when I come back I'll buy a new one,' Jock replied. Whether Jock ever did return for his left luggage, Bob never knew.

The pair made their way to Hendon, struggling through the London underground system and other trains and busses with their luggage, on a blisteringly hot June day. When they arrived at the main gate of RAF Hendon they were directed to a reception area, an old wartime hanger on the other side of the base. 'Bloody crabfats,' whispered Jock, 'they didn't even offer us a lift.' Forty minutes later, they staggered into the staging area.

There were about 80 others, a mixture of RAF, Army and Navy personnel with wives and families, sitting around or queuing up to have passports and medical documents checked; and filling in next of kin forms. It was a relief to complete the check-in procedures and hand over their weighty hold baggage. Their mood lightened even further by the announcement that busses would take them to a nearby RAF dining-hall for a meal.

There remained little more than three hours before boarding and both Bob and Jock, neither of whom had flown before, were distinctly nervous, fidgeting and glanc-ing fearfully about them. They suddenly did not feel too much like eating, but not knowing when the next meal might appear, decided to eat as much as they could. They sat at a table with a lone airman, already tucking into his supper. All three started chatting quite naturally and the airman asked where they were going. It felt really good to be able to say Singapore, a real adventure, and at the same time trying to give the impression that they were old hands.

'Watch out for those Hermes aircraft,' said the airman, 'there have been loads of crashes, near misses, and other incidents over the last few years.' The two intrepid mariners gulped, pushing their food away. 'Don't you want that?' asked the airman as he emptied the remains of their suppers on to his plate.

The older hands at *Mercury* had told them of the chequered history of the Hermes aircraft, but both Bob and Jock had discounted the stories, considering them to be a wind-up. The doubts concerning the aircraft's reliability seemed to be confirmed by the airman, and the two lads left the table quickly, not wanting to hear any more details.

Three hours later the two friends were now severely rattled and sat, immersed in their own thoughts, waiting to board the plane. Seats were not allocated, the lads just joined the queue and walked up the boarding ladder into the waiting Hermes, staying glued together as they had so many times before, and occupying adjacent seats. There was a bit of a tussle about who sat by the window: neither wanted to look down once they were airborne! Eventually Jock made so much of a fuss that Bob agreed to take the window seat, glaring at Jock and calling him a 'Bloody PJ wuss.'

Oddly the seats were arranged so that the passengers faced the rear of the aircraft. It felt very strange to Bob, and he suddenly realised that each time he had travelled on a train he had subconsciously sat facing the direction of travel.

Glancing out of the window, Bob could see the long port-side wing with the two huge piston engines and giant propellers, which were belching clouds of grey smoke as they roared into life. The noise was deafening, and the smell of aviation fuel almost overpowering. As soon as they had taken their seats they had buckled up their seat-belts and, at the roar of the engines, both nervously tugged them a little tighter.

As the aircraft taxied around the perimeter of the base towards the runway, Bob tried to relax a little and looked around for something to occupy his mind. The lovely, tartan-clad stewardesses had brought round a tray of hard-boiled sweets, and Bob had received a glare from Jock when, in an attempt to lighten the sense of foreboding, he had said 'You'll be alright, Jock, stewardesses are PJs.'

Eyes bulging, Jock was sweating profusely from the heat inside the confined space of the cabin and his knuckles were a line of white lumps as he grimly gripped his seat-belt. With these small distractions Bob managed a chuckle as he thought, *Now I know what they mean by a white-knuckle ride!*

The take-off was a noisy affair; numerous bumps, bangs, and squeaks played havoc with their imaginations. It was some minutes after the aircraft had levelled off, at a comfortable cruising altitude, before they relaxed; the stewardesses brought round drinks and said that a meal would be served in about an hour's time. The seat-belt lamp was extinguished but neither unsnapped, they were not *that* confident and they remained firmly attached to their seats until the aircraft next returned to earth.

The first leg of their journey was to Basra, Iraq's second largest city, and it was here that the aircraft was scheduled for its first refuelling. The landing, a much quieter and more gentle experience, left Bob completely unconcerned; the fact that he could feel the aircraft getting closer and closer to the ground reassured him immensely. Both lads, having remained in their seats, were now desperate for a toilet and queued impatiently to disembark after landing. As their turn came to exit the plane, Bob felt a blast of very hot air strike him in the face and his first thought was that someone had turned on a hot-air fan. Of course it was no such thing, just the normal daytime temperature and steady breeze in that part of the Middle East.

The heat was incredible; Bob had not before known such temperatures were possible. Even while they sat in the airport terminal for the hour or so it took to refuel, the temperature did not abate, and both lads, who were so pleased to get out of the aircraft, could now not wait to get back onboard and out of the fearsome heat.

Throughout the long hours in the air, Bob gazed down at the dull brown surface of the earth: perpetual desert with no sign of life in any direction. Conjuring up visions of an aircraft going down into the hostile terrain did nothing to improve Bob's confidence in flying, and he had to force his mind away from further thoughts on the subject.

Their next scheduled stop would be a night's stopover at Karachi, in Pakistan. A meal had just been served and Bob was feeling much more relaxed about the whole business of flying. He had been a little edgy during the take-off from Basra but he found that once the aircraft stopped climbing and levelled out, he could relax, up to a point of course! Away with the fairies, Jock did not move. Steadfastly refusing to remove his seat-belt, he once again refrained from visiting the toilet. 'I'll wait until we land,' he said.

Bob had relaxed his stranglehold on his fear of flying too soon. Suddenly the aircraft dropped into an air pocket. His body went rigid in fearsome anticipation of the aircraft dropping to the ground below. A strangled scream from Jock told Bob that his friend had experienced the same reaction. The rippling vibrations and loud bangs, as the aircraft hit the bottom of the air pocket, created worrying groans from its frame; and both lads were extremely worried about their safety.

On disembarking at Karachi they did not enter the terminal building. Instead, they reclaimed their hold baggage from below the aircraft, where it had been dumped unceremoniously by some very bored-looking bearded

Sikhs, and boarded busses, which slowly dawdled through the suburbs of the city to a dingy military establishment.

The naval contingent were all billeted together. In addition to the 13 from LS12 there were 6 others. None were senior ratings. Soon after they arrived, an RAF sergeant appeared to explain where the various eating, washing, and sleeping facilities were. He added that Karachi was currently suffering from a water shortage and suggested that they all be frugal when taking showers, leaving the room giggling hysterically at his own version of a short shower – *armpits, asshole, testicles and toes!* Overnight stopovers are of little use, especially when accommodated in a run-down military establishment. No doubt the families and crew, comfortably ensconced in an air-conditioned hotel, would disagree, but for the troops on the flight, the wait to re-embark was almost intolerable. Mosquitoes, like a plague of locusts, were everywhere, and when not enclosed within the nets over their bunks, the thin-blooded Europeans were attacked incessantly. A great deal of squirming, scratching, and cussing accompanied the next leg of the journey.

Once again everyone regained their good humour as they walked up the boarding steps into the aircraft the following evening, ready for the last leg of the flight, this time from Karachi to Singapore.

The air pockets recommenced shortly after take-off and continued, intermittently, until the aircraft started to descend into Singapore. Bob hoped that he would eventually get used to the sensation of dropping through the bottom of his trousers, but it was not to be. He found himself permanently on edge, sitting in his seat just waiting for the next drop, some of which would be just small dips and others heart-stopping swoops; every single time the aircraft moved Bob anticipated the worst, expecting the plane to drop straight down into the mountains, jungle, or sea below.

A meal had been served on each of the two previous legs of the journey. Both previous offerings had been acceptable, if not *haute cuisine*. Bob's head shot backwards in revulsion when he peeled the lid from the container laid before him. The smell was dreadful. A dark brown, almost black, mixture of lumps of goat meat floating in a runny sauce was revealed beneath the lid. Most of the class would most probably have tasted the vile-looking concoction, for it resembled their breakfast favourite – shit on a raft. But the smell was atrocious, summed up nicely by Jock's caustic comment, 'Christ mon! What the hell was that?'

The Hermes aircraft, miraculously still in one piece, touched down at Paya Lebar airport in the early hours of the morning. Bob was just too thankful to have arrived safely to even notice the time. As soon as he passed by the smiling stewardesses, who by some miracle of feminine *je ne sais quoi* still looked fresh and immaculate, out into the fresh air of Singapore, he noticed an overwhelming stench of decaying vegetation. He assumed that it was the smell of some nearby refuse dump, not realising that Singapore is a relatively small island surrounded by swamp areas and other smaller swampy islands; the smell was to be part of life in this otherwise tropical paradise. As time passed he would grow accustomed to the aroma and recognised a strong underlying smell of mangoes; eventually it ceased to bother him.

The trip out from the UK had been the first journey by air for both Bob and Jock, and both fervently hoped that, in future, they would be able to stick to sea travel – *at least you have a chance if the ship goes down* – but in this wish for limited air travel, Bob was to be deeply disappointed.

After the interminable wait for luggage, the very weary naval contingent were loaded into open-backed lorries to be transported to HMS *Terror*, Singapore's main naval base,

311

located next to the RN dockyard. Very little could be seen in the total tropical darkness. It seemed to be a much blacker darkness than anything he had seen before, the blackness impenetrable and somehow mystic in its density.

It was still very hot, despite being the middle of the night, and they were all soon sweating heavily even though they were doing nothing other than sitting in the back of a lorry. The chefs at HMS *Terror* had laid on an early breakfast for the new arrivals. The duty crusher met them at *Terror*'s bus terminus to give the new arrivals their welcome to Singapore speech, part of which was a warning not to walk across the parade ground. Obviously *Terror* was another barracks Bob decided ruefully, hoping to spend as little time as possible there.

LS12 left their kit in the lorry and went into the high-ceilinged dining-hall with its rows of twirling fans cooling the air. It felt glorious sitting in the breeze eating the wonderful English breakfast prepared by the naval chefs. The class of LS12 would not be remaining at *Terror*, they would have to complete a joining routine since *Terror* would be their administrative centre, after which they transferred their kit into a waiting RN bus and were driven to the Navy's radio station.

Kranji Wireless, as it was known to the RN communications branch, or more formally RNWT Station Kranji, was located between the causeway, the border passage to Malaya, and Singapore city. Having left the naval base area, the bus travelled along the Bukit Timah road for a few miles, and turned off the main road, traversing a level crossing as the huge array of radio aerials came into view. Weariness from their journey temporarily forgotten, the whole class was gawping out of the windows of the bus, trying to get a first glimpse of Kranji. The road followed the railway for a few hundred yards, turned a sharp bend to the right and disappeared into tall jungle up the slope of a hill.

The main gate came into view, manned by a smartly uniformed Singapore policeman, a Sikh with his high turban immaculately woven around his head. As the bus approached the gate, the Sikh slammed his feet to attention, saluted and waved the bus into Kranji's interior. The bus was waved straight through and after negotiating sharp left and right turns, drove past a swimming pool and tennis courts, finally coming to a halt in front of the regulating office.

At the sight of the pool, glistening in the wonderful hot sunshine, Bob thought *this looks good.* The whole class whooped and shouted; the place looked like a holiday camp! A leading patrolman (crusher) came onto the bus and told them to fall-in outside. 'Don't unload your kit yet,' he added, 'some of you are not staying.' Every young sailor's heart soared at this announcement, obviously some of them were being sent straight off to ships, which, for one reason or another, needed replacement sparkers. Of course, Bob was bound to be one of the lucky ship-bound sparkers. Assuming the allocation of ships had been done Navy fashion, in alphabetical order of surnames, he was certain to be called; there were not many surnames alphabetically in the class before that of Leonard.

Dreams of finally going to sea were shattered, just a few minutes later, when Bob found himself just one of three to remain in Kranji. The other ten were dispersed around the Far East Fleet in various ships from frigates to cruisers. The first name to be called, Jock was going to HMS *Cavalier*, a destroyer; the two friends who had supported each other through thick and thin for so many months were, at last, to be separated. They did not have time to say their farewells. As a name was called that person was ordered back on to the bus; when Jock disappeared onto the bus, Bob was not too concerned because he still assumed that he would be given a sea job and would soon be climbing back on to the bus himself.

313

By the time he realised that he was to remain in Kranji, it was too late; Jock was on the bus, and he could only turn and wave as the bus disappeared from view. It had not occurred to any of the class that sea drafts would be waiting for them as soon as they arrived, and Bob wondered why they had brought all 13 from *Terror*, only to send 10 back to the dockyard. He later discovered that Singapore's pool of sparkers was administered by Kranji and only they knew of the fleet's requirements.

Devastated and depressed by this unforeseen turn of events, Bob felt, for the very first time since he had joined, very much alone. Both he and Jock knew that the Navy's requirements would, in time, separate them, but the sudden and unexpected nature of their separation had badly shaken Bob. The other two destined to remain ashore were, of course, well known to him so he would not be completely alone, but they were not friends. Fate was destined to conspire against the mutually supportive duo and it would be many years before the friends would meet again.

The forlorn looking trio, still dressed in their wrinkled and sweaty civilian clothing, in which they had been travelling for almost four days, stood outside the regulating office in the hot sunshine, surrounded by their kit. They were careless of the heat and mindless of their surroundings; they felt deserted; LS12 was no more. It had all happened, in the end, so quickly and so unexpectedly that they were shocked and temporarily disbelieving of it having happened at all. After today even these remaining three would see little of each other, for each would be allocated to a watch, keeping hours that did not coincide with the others.

Given the now familiar joining routine, they did the usual tramp around the establishment, getting their piece of card stamped by all and sundry. Curiously, there was not a recognised naval tailor outlet in Kranji, instead just a little sentry-like hut, or 'caboose' in Navy speak, next to the regulating office, in which a wizened old Malayan woman provided whatever was needed in terms of civilian clothing and sewing. She was called Sew-Sew and Bob later learned that she would take it as a form of insult if any purchase was made without the customary ten minutes of bargaining! Her more expensive items, all made to measure, could be obtained on the never-never if required, which was the reason that this lady was included on both joining and drafting routines.

As the trio appeared at the door of her tiny shop, she piped in her sing-song voice '*Lo-la*,' her way of saying hello, an expression that was recognisable the world over by anyone having served at Kranji. It had become the traditional Kranji greeting and was used by everyone from the officer-in-charge, Kranji's commanding officer, downwards. Sew-Sew's caboose never seemed to close and this well-loved old lady sat in the doorway of her tiny shop calling her greeting to every passer-by.

The remaining three were accommodated in A Block, right opposite and within about 25 yards of the swimming pool. The familiar metal-framed naval bunks had been de-tiered and were arranged around the outsides of the large mess area with ample room around each. Over each bunk was a large mosquito net, that ubiquitous netting that was so invaluable in the tropics. Over the next few weeks, Bob was to find that once inside the netting, it felt as if he were in a world of his very own; and the knowledge that most of the tiny insects, with the potential to cause so much pain and suffering could not get to him, was a very reassuring feeling. It was impossible to escape the bites completely and Bob found that in his sleep he might move an arm or a leg close to the netting, and be rewarded in the morning with an itchy lump for a few days.

A virtually autonomous outpost, Kranji covered a large area of about 500 acres, surrounded by a high wire fence. By virtue of its naval role, that of providing the Far East link in the Navy's worldwide communications network, the place was a virtual sleepy hollow since almost all of its ship's company were shift workers.

There were four accommodation blocks: B and C Blocks were accessed via a long walk around a perimeter road, or by using a short cut across the football pitches and through a jungle path; with D Block next to a large cinema adjacent to a small parade ground. The canteen adjoined the block in which Bob was accommodated, separated from the large Comcen building by a small, homely dining-room. The senior ratings' accommodation was next to the swimming pool and their mess area was immediately opposite the regulating office.

In the valley below the senior ratings' mess there was also a small communications training section, a mini *Mercury* to cater for the advancement requirements of the Far East Fleet. At the edge of the football pitch was a gnarled tree, much revered by the indigenous population and which they referred to as the hanging tree, where reputedly, the Japanese had hung British and local prisoners during the last war.

Kranji's Comcen, manned 24 hours a day, used the '48 about' watch-keeping system, which was employed in almost all naval Comcens. On day one, eight hours were completed from 1200 to 2000, the afternoon watch. Day two included the hours from 0800 to 1200, the forenoon watch, and again that same evening from 2000 to 0800, the dreaded all-night-on. This was followed by two and a half days of free time until the cycle was started all over again.

Sometimes extra work or routine basic skills exercises of morse and typing, required monthly to ensure that communicators kept their skills honed, were scheduled before the afternoon watch. Assigned to C Watch, Bob was pleased that he was due to commence his duties the following morning at 0800, which meant that he would do the all-night-on that same night; at least he had something to concentrate on, he was already missing both Pat and Jock considerably.

The following morning at about 0745, Bob, having got up especially early to shower and breakfast, pushed through the swing doors into the Comcen. He was feeling a little self-conscious in his white shorts and white-front top; his lily-white legs sticking out of his overly large shorts made him feel inferior to the bronzed sparkers walking ahead of him. He made an instant decision: that very afternoon he would commission some tailor-made shorts from Sew-Sew and he would make a start on obtaining a tan, have a 'bronzy-bronzy' session in Navy speak. The sooner he looked the part the sooner he would feel a part of this, his new home for the foreseeable future.

As the swing doors closed behind him, Bob walked along the long, highly polished corridor feeling the welcoming coolness of the powerful air-conditioning; and waited until the POTs in charge of the watch could find time to settle him into a job. Everyone had a job to do, and most ignored him as he waited. Some glanced at him and smiled, probably remembering their own first day or finding humour in his appearance. While he waited, Bob looked around his new workplace; this place was nothing like the XWO at *Mercury*, which had been set up to duplicate a ship's radio room. It was remarkably spacious, all meaningful activity, hustle and bustle. Comms ratings could be seen carrying around messages, each message with its associated Murray Code tape version rolled up neatly and attached. Most, but not yet all, long distance, high frequency, point to point communications channels used automatic telegraphy and its associated Murray Code, rather than hand speed morse. Gazing around, trying to commit everything to memory,

317

Bob could see other rooms marked 'Taping', 'Crypto', 'Traffic' and 'Ship-Shore'.

The leader of the watch returned to his desk and sat down. 'You must be Leonard,' he said and asked, 'straight out of training?'

Nodding an affirmative, Bob replied politely, 'Yes, POTs.' Phones seemed to be ringing all around the building and POTs answered a call before leading Bob into the ship-shore room, otherwise known as the morse room, manned by local Singaporean operators with just a single Leading Telegraphist in charge.

'Report to the killick,' POTs told him, pointing to the Leading Tel, and said over his shoulder, as he left Bob standing in the middle of the large room, 'Over to you, Mac!'

The Leading Tel was called McElfinney, a stick insect of a man, so thin that you could almost hear his bones rattle. 'Lo-la, Bob,' he said in a very friendly manner – he must also have done his homework to know Bob's Christian name – 'we don't stand on ceremony in here, make sure you call POTs POTs but it's first names for everyone else. Everyone calls me McElskinney, can't think why!'

McElskinney was one of the most intelligent people that Bob was ever to meet, and his current claim to fame was that he was the reigning and undisputed hang-em-high champion of Kranji. This intelligent man was also to be the only person he would meet able to read morse at 32 wpm, a remarkable feat, particularly in Bob's eyes, who knew exactly how difficult that feat must be. He was even whiter than Bob, despite the fact that he had been at Kranji for at least half of his expected two and half year posting, so white that it was difficult to tell where his immaculately starched and pressed shorts joined his legs.

The warm reception from the Leading Tel, and by the highly skilled local operators who each stood up to shake his hand in welcome, made Bob feel immediately at home.

318

'Go make a brew and we will get you settled into a job, oh and that's a brew for the whole watch by the way,' McElskinney ordered. It was, of course, a clever way of introducing Bob to the rest of the watch and he traipsed from operator to operator, asking their preference for a brew and about an hour later served it around the watch. He feared that he was to be used as the tea-boy, but it was not to be the case, everyone except POTs took a turn brewing up in strict rotation.

Brewing up was not a problem to Bob. Though not for 20 people, he had done it plenty of times both at home and back on the estate in the fields with his father. There were no complaints about the tea and coffee and McElskinney gave him a quick thumbs up and 'well done!' *Obviously some sort of initiation ceremony* was Bob's conclusion.

There were a few tea and coffee splashes on his white uniform, which POTs glared disapprovingly at. 'Next time put the pinny on,' he said. Whilst finding his way around in the kitchen, Bob had seen the plastic pinafore hanging behind the door but thought that he would look like a bit of a wuss wearing it and even considered the possibility of it being a wind-up. 'It'll save you replacing your whites,' added POTs.

McElskinney sat at his desk, continuing with his work of dealing with all the messages coming in from ships, both commercial and military, received on the morse ship-to-shore frequencies, which Kranji would relay to all parts of the world. He seemed quite able to question Bob on his new entry course results and brightened considerably when Bob produced his most recent 100 per cent accuracy at 25 wpm. 'OK' chirped McElskinney in his cheerful voice, 'we will start you off doubling up on MCCN,' (the Malayan Coastal Command Net). For the final couple of hours of this, his first operational job as a sparker, Bob watched and listened as the highly skilled Indian operator exchanged

319

signals with ships at sea as they entered or left the naval dockyard, or operated in local waters. He had no difficulty in keeping up with the rapid exchange of signals and felt confident that he would be able to do the job himself.

The afternoon watchmen had relieved C Watch just before 1200. The comms branch prided itself on being five minutes early for every duty and Bob, due to return on watch that same evening at 2000 for a twelve-hour shift, was looking forward to it immensely. He had one major misgiving, however. He remembered the night watches at *Mercury* and the difficulty in staying awake, and worried about being able to remain alert *all* night.

Most tried the obvious solution of sleeping during the afternoon hours but, try as he might, Bob found it impossible to nod off, his mind constantly reviewing the events of the morning. At lunchtime Bob had sat in the almost empty dining-hall; most of his watch lived ashore with their wives and families. Having failed to get to sleep, a course of action strongly advised by McElskinney, Bob had changed into swimming trunks and gone for a swim, calling on a very attentive Sew-Sew to order some new white shorts on his way.

Aware of the dangers of sunbathing for too long, which was part of the medical officer's lecture at *Victory*, Bob remained in the water for most of the hour he spent at the pool. Unfortunately he had not realised that, although his body felt as if it were totally submerged, in reality the tops of his shoulders were exposed to the vicious sun for most of the time. By about 1800 he was in agony, the large blisters that had mushroomed frighteningly quickly along the ridge of his shoulders testifying to the power of the sun.

Night watches required a slightly warmer mode of dress, most people opting for the blue denim style action working dress with long trousers or shorts since the powerful air-conditioning lowered the temperature to such an extent that it could get quite chilly through the night. Completely unaware of this fact, Bob turned up in his white uniform. As soon as Bob walked into the morse room, McElskinney took one look at his reddened face and shoulders, visible under the low neckline of his white-front, tutted and sent him off to change into something warmer.

Wearing anything that rubbed against his sore skin was extremely painful and Bob was feeling very sorry for himself when he returned to the Comcen, until one of the Asian operators produced some soothing balm and gently rubbed it into the burned skin. The application of the potion stung the sunburned skin like mother's iodine for a few seconds and then, thankfully, the pain subdued and eventually faded away.

The night dragged slowly on. Bob was kept quite busy manning his morse circuit up until about 0100 when, apart from routine 'are you still there' type calls, all signals ceased. With very little message activity, Bob was beginning to feel very drowsy. Everyone else appeared to be fully awake and busy with their work, or sitting around having a quiet chat when an opportunity arose.

At about 0200 the watch prepared a meal, partially funded from naval sources, involving three or four people at a time going into the galley area to prepare a fry-up, curry, or whatever. Unbeknownst to Bob, McElfinney had been watching him and called for Bob to accompany him when he went for his meal.

The actions of preparing the food that Mrs McElfinney had semi-prepared for her husband, revived Bob, and he willingly did what he could to help with the meal. Mrs McElfinney had been an army cook, McElskinney told Bob, and she could 'cook for England.' At the time it seemed a strange remark to Bob, coming from the beanpole in front of him, but the food was excellent, some sort of Asian dish called *nasi goren*. Later, one of the more senior sparkers told Bob, in a hushed voice and glancing around in fear of discovery, that in McElskinney's house the grey mare is the better horse, and she wore the trousers with a rod of iron!

By 0400 Bob was in trouble, head lolling from side to side as he strived to maintain wakefulness. He knew he was going to fail miserably and being caught asleep on watch was anathema to any sparker worth his salt. No matter how he tried, he could not drag his mind away from thinking about his tiredness; he seemed totally focused on that single item and could not force himself even to think of his sweetheart. The same Asian operator who had rubbed the soothing balm into his sunburned shoulders came, once again, to Bob's rescue. 'You will get used to it,' he said, dropping his hand onto Bob's shoulder and giving him a frightful start, 'but for the first few nights when the tiredness gets too bad, get up every fifteen minutes or so and go for a walk outside the Comcen for a few minutes; the fresh air will revive you. Put your receiver on loudspeaker and we will listen out for any calls whilst you are away.'

The kindness, understanding and extreme politeness of these Asian operators never faltered over the months that Bob was to serve alongside them as he departed and returned to Kranji. They even offered to share their night rations, wrapped up in tightly folded palm leaves, prepared for them by their wives, and, after a few night watches, there always seemed to be enough for Bob.

The first time that he went outside the Comcen to revive himself, Bob noticed an adjacent derelict building. He had not noticed it before but he now walked up to the door and read the plaque declaring that this was the site of the first Kranji Comcen, captured and used by the Japanese during their occupation of the island. Inside was total devastation, almost nothing identifiable as communications equipment left in the building. The interior, in the beam of Bob's torch, was gloomy and seemed heavy with a deathly atmosphere. Dilapidated and abandoned, the building left Bob feeling somehow saddened by his visit and he never went into the building again.

Before he left the Comcen, just before 0800, when relieved by the oncoming watch, POTs told him to report to the sickbay and get his sunburn treated, adding that he would have a word with the sick berth attendant (naval male nurse) to try to avert the SBA from reporting Bob's self-inflicted injuries. The Navy did not take a kindly view of personnel rendering themselves unfit for duty through their own, stupid actions, of which getting severely sun-burned was the most common.

Presenting himself at the sick bay, with two full days of rest in front of him to do with as he pleased, Bob assured the SBA that he would be quite able to do his job when his watch was next on duty. 'Actually it doesn't look too bad,' said the SBA, making his mind up not to report the incident and handing Bob a large bottle of calamine lotion. 'Did one of those Asian chaps treat it for you?' The best that Bob could manage was a nod, he was bone tired and went off to breakfast.

No meal tastes better than a full English after a long night's work, and the chefs at Kranji prepared each break-fast individually, a rare occurrence in naval catering. The galley and dining-hall was manned by Asian personnel, providing consistently excellent meals together with table service. It was just as Bob had imagined it would be staying in a plush hotel and, once again, the Asian personnel were politeness personified. They seemed to take an immense pleasure in whatever work they were assigned; the dining-hall and galley were spotless, except for the hordes of cockroaches that engulfed almost every nook and cranny in almost plague proportions. Despite regular fumigation, nothing seemed to deter this creature and the only remedy was to splat them with a heavy fly-swat, or tread them underfoot.

After his brimming breakfast, Bob flopped onto his bunk and slept the sleep of the fully satisfied, in both mind and body, waking at about 1300. The mess had been empty when he came off watch and was still deserted. Had it not been for the other made-up beds and personal gear lying around, Bob might have thought he was the only occupant of the mess. Waking in the peace and quiet of the large mess deck, the only sound the swishing of the overhead fans, Bob was convinced that he had been transported to another dimension. In that mind-bending period between sleep and full consciousness, his senses disorientated by time and weariness, drifting between fantasy and reality, Bob fought to pinpoint his location in the universe; smiling contentedly when truth dawned.

After a leisurely shower and a light lunch – the Asian chefs were willing to prepare a meal at any time for Kranji's watchkeepers – Bob sat down and wrote a letter to Pat, giving her his correct postal address. It was strange to be alone in such a cavern of a mess deck. He had not yet begun to feel the real pangs of homesickness and, more used to a well organised, regimented routine, he just did not know what to do with himself. Returning to the pool was out of the equation, at least until his sunburn healed completely. Without a companion to talk to, Bob sat silently in the straight-backed chair, the gentle susurration of the fans whispering to him, inducing sleep. He woke suddenly in mid-air having fallen off his chair! By 1700 he was feeling completely bored with his own company; he badly missed Jock, his sounding board for any new ideas, and he really wanted to do two things: walk around Kranji to get the lie of the land and go into Singapore city. Neither of which looked very possible; he certainly did not want to venture into Singapore city on his own. Yes, the locals had been extremely friendly in the Comcen, but in every barrel of apples there were a few bad ones! He could not, under any circumstances, go into the city centre on his own.

Supper was served from 1800 and Bob went down to the dining-hall alone. Kranji's dining facilities really were most civilised. A delicious well-done steak and chips, followed by duff and custard, boosted his flagging spirits and Bob returned to his bunk in a much happier mood.

Approaching the mess, he heard voices and, as he walked through the door, he was pleased to see several people relaxing on their bunks or going about their own business. A very short, stocky man, about a year or so older than Bob, occupied the bunk next to Bob's. The diminutive young man was still dressed in white daytime working uniform, and Bob could see a signalman's badge on the short sleeve of his white-front. 'Lo-la,' he gave the Kranji greeting, 'you must be new?'

For the next few minutes Bob gabbled an explanation about having just left *Mercury* training, pouring out his problems of being left at Kranji instead of going to sea, his sunburn, and his desire to visit the city. Joe Sims, Shorty to his friends, was the signalman's name, and he must have thought Bob a madman, ranting on about his problems, without so much as an introduction. In answer to Bob's question, Shorty said he worked in the main signal office in the dockyard on a nine to five basis. 'Why don't you live in Terror?' asked Bob, 'which is right next to the dockyard.'

'Don't know,' replied Shorty, 'I suppose all comms have to live in Kranji.'

Stripping off his outer clothing, Shorty said that he would grab a quick shower and supper and they could catch the RN leave bus into the city for a run ashore. *Great,* thought Bob, *just what I needed.* When Shorty stripped off in preparation for his shower, Bob could not fail to notice that he was literally covered in tattoos, his back was covered in a mismatch of animals, ships, names, skull and cross bones, pirate flags, and a treasure map annotated *'ere there be dragons!*

Much later, Shorty explained that he wanted to have the whole of his body – at least the bits that could not be seen when wearing his tropical working rig – tattooed; he even had an artist's impression of his plans for upper arms, thighs, calves, chest, and stomach, not to mention two staring eyes – one on each buttock! 'When I do a moonie they'll get something extra!' Shorty couldn't stop himself from chuckling at his own humour.

Having been at Kranji for about two months, Shorty was searching for somewhere to live for his family who were still in the UK awaiting approval to travel; the Navy would not allow families to fly until proof of accommodation was provided. 'Married quarters in Singapore are rarer than rocking horse shit,' was Shorty's disdainful opinion of the Navy's limited efforts in providing accommodation for its personnel. Waiting for one of these rarest of commodities might take anything up to 18 months. Married accompanied drafts were also pretty rare and, not wishing to spend too much time unaccompanied, most took the only other available alternative, that of finding a civilian flat or house to rent. Consequently, Kranji's living-out members were spread all over the island.

It had quite suddenly got dark at about 1830 and had started to rain. Though to describe it as merely rain was understating what was actually happening: it was tipping it down, huge droplets of water falling vertically like stair-rods. Almost unable to believe the intensity of this precipitation, Bob looked across the road and saw the tennis courts, in the glow of the street lights, awash with huge puddles; and the globules of water jumping off the surface of the swimming pool as each plump drop of rain fell into it.

The dark blue RN bus was waiting outside the regulating

office to take passengers into the city, but they would have got soaked just walking the few yards from the covered walkway to the bus. The taps in the sky were turned on at about the same time each day. Most people were prepared for this heavy rainfall, and Shorty grabbed a strange looking umbrella from under his bed; it was made of what looked like bamboo and some sort of covering identical to glossy brown paper. 'You should see Sew-Sew and buy one of these,' Shorty told him, 'it rains a lot here!'

Of course, the Navy had its own name for this piece of equipment. Shorty called it his *Wanchai Burberry*. As the bus travelled into Singapore city, Bob noticed that the huge drains on each side of the road, 'mossie ditches' in Navy speak, were filled to the brim with rain water. 'Stay away from those,' Shorty advised, 'a favourite place for snakes,' and Bob filed the information in the *do not forget* part of his brain.

The RN bus dropped them off outside the Britannia Club, a purpose built, tri-service recreational facility adjacent to a palm-filled park and directly opposite the world famous Raffles Hotel. It had most, but not by any means all, of the amenities that a serviceman could wish for: bars, restaurant, snooker rooms, swimming pool, and a very large Scalextric car circuit that always had a long waiting list of young servicemen only too willing to pay for its use.

Having already eaten at Kranji, Shorty led the way to the first-floor bar, overlooking the swimming pool, and bought the first round of drinks. The local beer was the Navy's favourite, Tiger beer, served in draught and ice cold, but on this occasion Shorty had chosen bottles of Anchor beer, determined no doubt to introduce Bob to both.

The taste took a little getting used to, particularly for a virtual non-drinker like Bob, but he persevered and after only a couple of bottles was feeling quite merry! Shorty was drinking two pints for each of Bob's (why did everyone he

327

meet seem to drink so heavily?), and the beer did not seem to affect him at all. They had a few races on the Scalextric track, enormous fun for both participants and spectators, and sat around watching the world pass them by.

Over a pint of delicious, cool Tiger beer, Bob told Shorty about Jock, and Shorty, whose eyes were beginning to roll and whose speech was getting more and more slurred, told Bob all about his wife and his newly born son. At about 2100 Shorty stood up and twigged his index finger at Bob. 'Come on, we're off to Boogis Street!'

'What's that?' asked Bob.

'You'll see,' was all that Shorty would say.

Stepping into the busy traffic, Shorty flagged down a passing taxi – there was certainly no shortage of them – and told the driver to take them to Boogis Street. In Singapore, taxis were inexpensive and everywhere, much like cockroaches. Servicemen were paid special overseas allowances, which increased their income dramatically; that, together with the current rate of exchange set at eight Singapore dollars to the pound gave Bob a much larger surplus income than he had been used to in the UK.

Soon after the pair had settled into the cab, Shorty yelled at the driver, '*La cas,* John!' Apparently *la cas* was the local lingo for *get a move on* and every single taxi driver was called John! Whatever the truth of the matter, this particular driver obviously knew the expression and answered to John because the car suddenly shot forward, which seemed to please Shorty immensely because he started to rub his hands together and chuckle to himself. Their taxi came to a halt at the end of a fairly wide street with tables and chairs along each side, much like the pictures of pavement cafés Bob had seen of Paris. The tables were jam-packed solid with men, mostly European, and women, mostly Oriental.

The two new pals walked slowly up the street and sat at a table occupied by two young Asian girls. Bob considered

Shorty's behaviour rather rude, since he did not ask permission to sit with the girls; however, they did not seem to take exception at his forwardness. No sooner had bums met seats than one of the girls said, 'You want good time? You want drinks, sailor?'

A sure sign of his intense enjoyment, Shorty was again rubbing his hands with glee. 'This is the life eh, Bob!' and ordered drinks for them both, but not for the girls. 'Don't let them con you into buying them drinks all night,' he added in a loud voice, with the obvious intention of allowing anyone within earshot to hear and, no doubt, understand that he knew the ropes.

Not much chance of that! Bob was beginning to regret his rash decision to accompany Shorty on a run ashore. *The last bus goes back to Kranji at midnight and I'm going to be on it,* he said to himself. He already had a sneaking suspicion about how the rest of the night would pan out for Shorty.

As suspected, when Bob mentioned at about 2330 that it was time they returned to the Britannia Club to catch the bus, Shorty guffawed loudly, dripping spittle down his shirt. He was now very drunk. 'I'm taking this one home,' Shorty slurred. Bob could not remember any such decision being made in the somewhat one-sided conversation during the evening; the girls had done most of the talking. He had been surreptitiously scrutinizing the girls for sometime. Something was not quite right. Yes, they were very slim, curvaceous, pretty, and had girlish voices and mannerisms, but something was still not right. Then, at last, Bob twigged: the Adam's apple in the neck was the giveaway really; it was masculine, there was no doubt about it, these were boys; and Shorty intended spending the night with one of them!

'Do you know that these two are boys?' Bob whispered into Shorty's ear.

'I don't care if they're donkeys,' slurred Shorty and he stood up and wobbled away with his prize! The remaining girl/boy eyed Bob hopefully, but there wasn't a dog's chance in hell of Bob going to bed with anyone except himself, and he left the table immediately, walking back to the end of the street, hailing a taxi for the Britannia Club, and returned to Kranji on the midnight bus.

The following morning Shorty had still not returned onboard by the time Bob went down for breakfast. When he returned to the mess, however, he could see signs of a hurried arrival and departure on the bunk next to his. So Shorty must have returned and left immediately for his day job at the dockyard.

Spending his second full day off watch, Bob allocated a few hours towards sorting out his kit, dhobying his underwear and socks himself and sending the other items to the excellent local laundry. In the afternoon Bob went over to the swimming pool and sat under one of the large sun umbrellas, watching two of the officers' wives playing tennis and thinking how fortunate he was to be serving in such an idyllic location. As the afternoon wore on, Bob borrowed Shorty's Wanchai Burberry and walked around Kranji, getting the feel of the place.

Shortly before 1730, Shorty returned to the mess, had his usual shower, and changed into civilian clothes, and they went to supper together. 'See you got some new tattoos.' Bob pointed to the swollen, angry looking lettering on the backs of Shorty's hands; on the right hand the word *death* was written and on the left *maimed for life.* Both avoided the question about his liaison with the girl/boy the previous evening. Bob did not know his new acquaintance well enough to discuss such intimate subjects and Shorty did not mention the matter.

Eventually Shorty apologised for leaving Bob on his own the previous night. 'It can get a bit iffy down Boogis Street,' he added thoughtfully, 'and I shouldn't have left you, the rule is always to stay together.' He went on to say that he did not often behave like that, but he was very worried about not being able to find accommodation in preparation for bringing his family out. He was depressed and too much drink had got the better of him.

Over the next week, Bob settled into the routine of watchkeeping. The long night watch became easier to contend with and he was getting to know more of the people in C Watch. Each of the four watches were, of necessity, quite insular, only occasionally meeting when changing over watches or for inter-watch sporting events. Group activities, involving the whole watch, were sometimes organised to provide entertainment, and McElskinney had told Bob that he sometimes organised such outings. He called it a *banyan*, adding that a trip to nearby Coney Island had been arranged for two weeks' time. That suited Bob fine because Shorty had just picked up a small car that he had purchased, and wanted Bob to accompany him on a flat or house seeking expedition over the coming weekend.

When Bob first saw Shorty's car, his first impression was that it was a bit of a banger, an old Austin A30, which, to Bob, resembled an upside down bathtub! Despite Bob's initial impression, the car went well, and Shorty must have had some Italian ancestry, Bob decided, as the little car hurtled down the hill from Kranji, negotiated the sharp left-hand bend by the aerial field on two wheels, struggling for grip on the wet roads.

Intent on finding some accommodation for his family, Shorty was heading for two residential areas, about 15 miles from Kranji, much favoured by the comms staff, at Seletar and Serangoon. The trip along the infamous Mandai Road, built by British prisoners of war who deliberately set the cambers incorrectly on the sharp bends, was another white knuckle ride for Bob. How the little car remained on the road was a mystery. 'How long have you been driving?' Bob tried to distract Shorty in an attempt to slow him down.

'Years,' Shorty briefly replied.

'Where did you take your driving test?' Bob tried again, somewhat breathlessly this time for the car had just had a bottom squeezing loss of traction on a particularly sharp bend.

'Oh, I haven't bothered with a licence,' Shorty answered, 'I'll worry about the details later!'

The road narrowed as they passed through the small village of Sembawang and Bob spotted an old Malayan man carrying two buckets dangling from the ends of a yoke around his neck; Shorty misjudged his passing manoeuvre quite badly and the car just nicked one of the dangling buckets. After the clang of impact, Bob turned to see if the man was all right, just managing to get a glimpse of the poor chap pirouetting in the road as the car shot around a bend and the man was lost from view.

The two traipsed around the shops and bars at Serangoon asking for details of any vacant accommodation. Their search was fruitless and they jumped back into the car and sped off to Seletar village, just outside RAF Seletar. In a row of newly built terraced units, a mixture of shops and flats, they found two units that had not been fitted out. Outside the building, on the wide pavement, was a long line of tables and chairs, occupied by older locals sitting in the sun, drinking tea and playing mah-jong and Bob asked the nearest group how they might find the owner of the two vacant units.

In their usual helpful way, the mah-jong players interrupted their game and, after a great deal of Chinese shouting, waving of arms, and gabbling, an address was produced. The address was only a few hundred yards away, and Shorty drove his scruffy little car up the drive of a very imposing and expensive looking villa. The wealthy Malayan was a most generous host, his amah producing cold beers and delicious titbits before the serious business commenced. After a great deal of discussion and bargaining, Shorty made a deal to have one of the units converted into a flat and furnished, the Malayan owner promising to have it ready within a month. Deliriously happy because he had finally managed to fulfil the requirements to have his family flown out to join him, Shorty headed back towards Kranji, calling at Changi beach *en route* for a beer in the small seaside servicemen's leave centre.

After their beer, the two young men walked along the soft sand of the beach, enjoying the sound and smell of the sea. Their feet sank quite deeply into the sand, and, looking down, Bob's keen eyesight saw the circular shape of what looked like a coin. Popping the object into his pocket, Bob continued his walk and, as the afternoon wore on, the two returned to Kranji. A few days later Bob cleaned the coin, using brick dust scraped from one of Kranji's buildings. The coin was marked *1 cent, Straits Settlements, 1861*, and Bob had found an excellent keepsake to remind him of his time spent in Singapore.

Destined not to see very much more of Shorty nor to sample the delights of a watch *banyan*, Bob was summoned a few days later to the Chief Tel's office and told to pack his kit for deployment. *At last, a ship*, the assumption leapt instantly into Bob's mind, but he was to be disappointed once again. 'You're flying to Aden tomorrow,' said the Chief, 'be ready to leave at 1300.' *Where the devil is Aden?* Bob's mind was whirling as he went to find an atlas. Someone thought it was in the Middle East, one of the Arab countries – the Navy referred to Middle Eastern natives as A-rabs!

Eventually locating Aden on the map of the world hanging in the OIC's office, Bob discovered that it was in a country called the Yemen, which bordered the Red Sea and the Gulf of Aden. *Half way home*, thought Bob *and by air, how wonderful!*

Looking forward to another long flight so soon after his first mind-blowing trip, Bob sorted out his kit. Packing did not take long, having little choice of kit to take with him. His kitbag had not yet arrived from the UK and he was living on what he had brought out with him in his Pusser's green. There was not much to do in the way of bidding farewell either; he had not been in Kranji long enough to get to know anyone very well.

Shortly after breakfast the following morning, having packed everything he possessed into his green suitcase, he did the rounds with his draft routine. Greeting Bob with a loud 'Lo-la,' Sew-Sew checked in her impressively large and neat, not to mention unintelligible, ledger, written in Chinese, to confirm that Bob did not have any outstanding debts, stamped his form with an elaborate rubber stamp bearing the head of a roaring male lion, and asked him if he would return to Kranji.

9

Middle East

The posting to Aden had come as such a surprise that Bob had not thought to ask his chief the duration of the deployment, and all he could tell the old lady was that he did not know if or when he would return. 'You come back,' she replied with a very knowing smile, obviously possessing more information than Bob did.

Standing outside the regulating office, just before 1300, once again surrounded by his kit and looking around at the now familiar sights, he knew that he would miss Kranji and he hoped that, one day, he might bring his own wife and family to this beautiful island.

On arrival at Paya Lebar airport he discovered, on check-in, that he was booked into a first class seat on an Indian Airways Super Constellation aircraft. *They must be desperate for me in Aden,* he thought. First class seats were notoriously expensive and rarely used for transporting lowly sparkers.

Sitting in Paya Lebar terminal building, idly watching the Indian pilots walking out to the aircraft, Bob resolved his severe doubts about the piloting capabilities of any other race than the British, when he remembered the slick skills of the Asian operators at Kranji. Inside the aircraft the interior of the 'plebs' section (Navy speak for non-business or first class sections) looked small and cramped, but the first class cabin was spacious. The lovely Indian stewardesses in their colourful saris were kind and considerate despite the difficulty in communicating, Bob resorting to cumbersome hand signals to make his requirements clear.

The aircraft was extremely noisy and any sort of conversation was almost impossible, not that there was any possibility of exchanging the time of day with his neighbours, they were all Indian; as far as he could tell he was the only European on the flight. He would make the journey to Aden in two hops, the first to Calcutta in the comparative luxury of the Indian Airways flight; the second by RAF transport aircraft into Aden.

The food, served shortly after the Super Constellation left Singapore was ghastly, similar to that served on his flight out from the UK, and Bob felt very guilty about leaving it. In truth, it was most probably *caviar to the general* but he just could not force himself to put it into his mouth. He would wait until the second flight in the hope of something more to his taste. The flight to Calcutta was uneventful, except for the usual air pockets and general turbulence and, as the aircraft started its descent into Calcutta, Bob thought that the bottom had fallen out of the plane. Loud banging and a squealing of tortured metal accompanied the lowering of the landing gear, very disconcerting to a nervous flyer!

Inside the Calcutta terminal building, Bob felt completely lost. There was not a white face in sight and no one, apparently, spoke English. He had not been given any instructions about who or where to report to; he did not have a ticket, only his passport, medical certificates, and a vaguely remembered verbal instruction to 'catch the crab flight to Aden!'

At a loss as to his next move, Bob, decided to have a pint in the bar, or whatever served as a pint in this God-forsaken place, and was just about to belly up to the bar, wondering if the bar-keep might accept Singapore dollars and thinking of which hand signals might serve him best, when a voice behind him, in a very strong Scots accent said, 'Ah, Sassen-ach, you must be the sandscratcher we're looking for.' The well-remembered accent caused Bob to turn quickly, hop-ing against hope that it was Jock, but no, instead it was a very short, very fat RAF sergeant with a shock of ginger hair and a bright-red face.

The sergeant, offering no assistance with Bob's kit, led the way to a waiting aircraft that looked similar to the Hermes aircraft that had carried him to the Far East. There were four other people in the cabin area, sitting on the pull-down seats flanking the sides of the aircraft. After the first class seats on the first leg of his journey, this was very much roughing it! Given no time to speak to anyone, which was just as well since, once again, the noise of the engines was so loud that any conversation was out of the question, Bob was pressed down into one of the many vacant seats. The meal, served shortly after take-off by the ginger-haired sergeant, doubling as steward, consisted of a bundle of sandwiches tossed carelessly into his lap, washed down by a plastic beaker of lukewarm tea from a flask. The RAF, wishing to spare no expense for members of their Senior Service, provided the very best in in-flight entertainment, the choice between listening to the deafening roar of the engines or spending the entire flight with fingers jammed firmly into each ear.

I wish I was at sea, Bob prayed to anyone who might be listening, as the aircraft slammed onto the ground with a sickening thud at RAF Khormaksar. As he left the aircraft, Bob jokingly mentioned to the sergeant that the landing had been a bit heavy. 'Ach no,' the sergeant replied, grin-ning all over his face, 'gotta fly these things into the ground, and anything you can walk away from is a safe landing!'

Once again Bob was left to his own devices. No one was waiting for him, no one seemed to know anything about him. He wandered around the RAF station, looking for some form of inspiration or someone who might be able to help him. He was dripping with sweat in the intense heat and his suitcase seemed to get heavier by the minute. Eventually, after several unsuccessful attempts to obtain information, Bob decided to walk into the next building, no matter what it turned out to be, to see if he could find a way of getting to his final destination.

The decision was a good one. He got lucky, and he stumbled into the officers' mess, which was guarded by someone called the hall porter. Dripping with sweat, tired, hungry, and thirsty, Bob must have appeared a sorry state and explained his predicament to the hall porter, a young RAF corporal. *Not all crabfats are witless wonders, Brylcreem boys, or sport motorbike handlebars as moustaches,* Bob decided, after his clean-shaven saviour had made several telephone calls and discovered that transport would arrive shortly to take him to HMS *Sheba,* his home for the next heaven knows how long!

The corporal also provided Bob with a huge plate of pie and chips and a mug of tea whilst he waited for the transport and even helped to throw his kit into the back of the small twelve-seater minibus ('tilly' in Navy speak) when it arrived. Feeling much chirpier, Bob thanked the corporal profusely as he took his leave.

By the time he got to *Sheba,* which was a small walled enclosure close to the sea, containing little more than a Comcen and a few utility buildings, it was pitch dark. The Arab driver had not spoken during the trip, which took about 45 minutes, and there was no one about, again! A lowly sparker does not, of course, expect a naval guard and marching band to welcome him at each new posting, but Bob was getting just a tad peeved at being totally ignored! The apparent lack of organisation and the lackadaisical arrangements for his trip to this sea of sand made him

338

wonder if he was actually in the right place; it wouldn't be so bad if he did not have to drag his kit everywhere!

Looking around the dimly lit interior of the enclosure, he saw a door marked *Comcen No Admittance. That'll do me!* He welcomed the familiar sign and dragged his Pusser's green noisily through the door. Pusser's greens were, fortunately, very strongly built, each corner strengthened with thick leather patches; a good thing from Bob's point of view. His had certainly already been through the wars and was beginning to look a bit travel worn.

The familiar buzz of a busy Comcen filled his ears, the clipped tones of morse code, the chatter of the teleprinters, and the smell of freshly brewed coffee revived his flagging mood. The PO Tel in charge of the watch looked up at Bob, surrounded by his kit and said, 'Who the bloody hell are you?' The warm welcome returned Bob to his previous peeved mood. *And welcome to bloody Aden to you too, pal!* Bob had expected a slightly warmer reception, and feeling not a little discombobulated, explained as best he could, all the while thinking that he wasn't even *expected* here.

Following Bob's brief explanation for his unwelcome intrusion into the usual smoothly operating Comcen, POTs made a telephone call and finally confirmed that Bob was in the right place by saying, *Welcome to Comcen Aden, Leonard.'* A few minutes later Bob was mortified to learn that he was not to be accommodated in *Sheba*, there just wasn't a spare bunk as the base had recently had to accommodate an additional squad of Royal Marines; he was told to go across the town square to the Hotel Manama, who would be expecting him.

Immediately suspecting a wind-up – there is nothing the Navy likes better to further confuse a tired and weary young sailor than a good wild goose chase – Bob fully expected to be called back as he picked up his kit and prepared to leave the Comcen; but it was not to be. As Bob struggled back through the Comcen door, once more launched alone into the unknown and his request for assistance with his kit flatly refused, his usual sweet nature deepened into a thoroughly evil mood. Aching feet squelching with sweat inside his shoes, smelling pretty badly, and desperately in need of a shower, Bob staggered to the hotel.

Ready to give someone a piece of his mind in no uncertain terms, Bob had just about had a bellyful of planes, crabfats, foreigners, inedible food, total disorganisation, sweat, sand, A-rabs, the Navy, and the whole expletive deleted bloody universe. What had he, a mere ordinary telegraphist and a genuine sweet-natured Hampshire boy done to deserve this? *I must have knocked an old lady over with my bike when I was a boy.* One of his father's quaint expressions sprang into his mind. *And if no-one here can speak English I'll lie down in the middle of the expletive deleted foyer and throw a bloody wobbly!*

By the time he reached the hotel reception Bob had whipped his temper to a level seldom reached, ready to dish out a serious tongue lashing, and perhaps other bodily damage, to the next person who gave the slightest inkling of not knowing exactly who he was and why he was there. It is not surprising, therefore, that he was immediately deflated to find that at last he was expected, a room had been prepared for him, a late supper had been reserved for him, and the porter would take his suitcase to his room, all conveyed to him in an obviously well-educated English voice, despite the fact that the little, wizened old man in front of him was obviously an Arab, dressed in his off-white *djellabah.*

Only four additional mild disappointments were left for our intrepid traveller for that day. The room was stiflingly hot and without a fan, the shower was little more than a dribble, the hot supper was some dreadful stew, and the toilet was a hole in the floor. Although not a disappointment, Bob suddenly realised just how his pristine white uniforms were going to look in a few weeks' time. The bed linen was the same off-white as the old Arab's *djellabah!* Might be better to give the hotel laundry a miss!

The next morning, after a thoroughly uncomfortable night in the lumpy, squeaky bed and a breakfast of fruit and diabolical black coffee that had the consistency of treacle, Bob sauntered over to the Comcen. The previous evening no one had given him any instructions and Bob decided that perhaps a little arrogance on his part would not go amiss and deliberately took his time in reporting for duty.

In this he was, of course, sadly mistaken, and received a full-blooded bawling out from the resident Chief Tel. Returning the chief's verbal lambasting in full measure, Bob gave as good as he got, under his breath and after he had left the room of course! Obeying his chief's last command to 'piss off and get out of my sight,' Bob, not feeling the urge to urinate, presented himself at the Comcen to start his watchkeeping duties.

He was set to manning a morse channel from Whitehall and began the now familiar routine of getting to know a new Comcen fraternity and settling into his new watch. The work on this channel was completely different than it had been working with the ships off Singapore. Not many such morse direct links, or fixed services as they were known, remained throughout the world, and this was the direct link with the Admiralty. And it was hectic. The messages were never ending, always very long, and required total concentration. Since it was a morse channel and since most of the messages were highly classified, they were always encoded into five letter groups and sometimes the number of groups in a single message might exceed one thousand. At the end of a twelve hour night shift Bob departed the

Comcen, his head ringing from the constant morse reception and transmission. Searching for sleep in the sticky heat of his hotel room, Bob found that sleep almost never came easily, despite his total weariness. The morse rang in his head for hours after he had left the Comcen.

Aden Comcen was a tiny affair, in comparison to Kranji, with just four sparkers in each watch, overseen by a PO Tel. But the establishment did have real Navy chefs and Bob took to eating his meals in *Sheba*, with his other watch members; he had tried asking the English-speaking old chap if the hotel kitchens could rustle up something more to his taste, and had failed miserably. The old chap had tried his best by bringing out the hotel chef to speak to Bob, an elderly old lady, obviously destined to *lead the apes in hell*, who badly need a shave; all to no avail for she could no more speak English than Bob could speak Arabic.

A few days after his arrival at *Sheba*, Bob was invited for an evening out with a couple of the lads from his watch. A short walk out of the town was billeted the resident British Army presence, the Third Royal Regiment of Fusiliers (3RRF). The poor devils lived in tented accommodation. *Conditions must be abominable*, thought Bob, but they did, according to his two new run-ashore oppos, have a reasonable canteen, which sold English beer. 3RRF was a Scottish regiment which seemed to take great delight in wrecking its own canteen on a regular basis. Fights broke out for no apparent reason and what might start off as a disagreement between two soldiers, quickly escalated into all-out war involving everyone in the canteen. Tables, chairs, bottles, fists – they used any weapon available; but they never involved the few Navy visitors, clearly recognisable in their white uniforms, to whom the Army displayed a remarkably friendly air. Many times, over the next few weeks, Bob found himself sitting in the middle of a battle zone, bodies hurtling all around and over his small group, but never

342

once was he attacked or molested in any way. The Scots seemed to love their punch-ups and must have spent hours each week making good the damage to the canteen; it was always repaired, clean, and tidy each time Bob arrived. *Good job Jock isn't here!* Bob inwardly smiled at his thought. *He would be joining in!*

Occasionally Bob would take a lonesome stroll around the small town of Aden. He found it to be a dusty, depressing place; there was so much inactivity and the place had a kind of empty, derelict, seedy feel about it. An air of indolence pervaded the people who seemed happiest sitting around smoking some evil-looking hookah pipes or sitting in the shaded pavement cafés drinking the liquid molasses, which served as the local version of coffee. Considering that it was generally accepted that coffee originated from the Yemen, Bob was surprised how disgusting the local brew tasted, at least to a highly educated naval palate.

On 1st August,1958 the Navy decided to restructure the communications branch. Telegraphists became radio operators and signalmen became tactical operators. As radio operators, ordinary ratings became RO3s; able ratings (Bob's next level) became RO2s; leading ratings became LROs; petty officers became radio supervisors; and chiefs became CRSs. It was a major change and it would take months before Bob was able to actually think of any POTs as an RS.

The weeks passed slowly. It was decidedly uncomfortable being billeted in the minus one star hotel and also lonely. Bob missed the mess deck banter and the general skylarking found in any group of young people. Using the hole in the floor toilet was impossible, it felt disgusting and unnatural and many was the time that he sprinted across the town square in Aden, heading for a proper toilet in *Sheba*.

After only five weeks in Aden, Bob was relieved to be told that his world tour was to be extended; he was moving on yet again. Not back to Kranji as he had hoped, but on to the Persian Gulf, Bahrain. 'Be ready to join the transport at 0330 tomorrow morning,' the Chief RS, who had never really warmed to Bob, told him towards the end of September, 1958.

Suspecting that the chief had deliberately scheduled the early morning transport from *Sheba*, instead of directly from the Manama Hotel, Bob decided that it was the unfriendly chief's method of forcing him to drag his kit across the town square again! In fact, Bob fully expected to see the vindictive old chief waiting for him when he arrived at *Sheba*, just to watch him struggle.

However, Chiefy wasn't there, neither was anyone else, no tilly, no driver; it was just as deserted as the day he had arrived. *Not again!* thought Bob. Once again he had no ticket, just an instruction to take the tilly transport to RAF Khormaksar and get the RAF flight to Bahrain. Standing idly in the darkness, Bob waited until 0345 for any sign of life before going into the Comcen to see if they could roust out the driver of the tilly. Despite several attempts they achieved nothing. Desperate measures were now required. Options included taking a taxi, walking, hitching a ride, all these options discarded almost as soon as they arose. It was far too late at night to get a taxi, and walking and hitching were out of the question, it was far too great a distance especially with all his kit.

It was then that Bob remembered the Comcen van, kept in Sheba for urgent hand-message distribution. 'How about running me to Khormaksar in the van, POTs? – sorry, RS,' Bob asked.

The RS considered for just a moment. 'OK', he said, 'it's

344

about the only way you will get there at this time of night,' gambling that a really urgent message would not require distribution for the next hour and a half, or so. After loading up his gear, the van sped out of the town. There was very little traffic around and the journey was totally uneventful.

At the gate to Khormaksar Bob asked the sentry where he should report for a flight to Bahrain and was directed to a nearby hangar. As the van sped away on its return trip to *Sheba*, Bob watched it depart until it was out of sight, he was hoping that Bahrain would be a little more friendly than Sheba had been and also that the journey there would not be so uncertain. His stay in Aden had lasted little longer than a working holiday; his work had consisted of long hours of gruelling concentration, bombarded by morse code, and he was glad to be going; with a bit of luck he might never see the place again.

Opening the door to the hangar, the blast of noise set him back on his heels. There were several hundred Army personnel milling around, much shouting of orders, piles of kit and ammunition boxes, and vehicles of all shapes and sizes being driven in through the large sliding doors at the front of the hangar. Dressed in his lightweight civilian clothes, Bob was temporarily stunned by the commotion, and for a few minutes he just stood inside the door, mesmerised by the intense activity.

Creating little interest from the beehive of soldiers, Bob stood quietly watching. In time his senses returned to normality and he approached the nearest officer, explaining that he had been told to report to Khormaksar for a flight to Bahrain. 'You've come to the right place,' the officer told him, 'go see the warrant officer over there, he'll fix you up.' The warrant officer led Bob over to a waiting squad of soldiers. 'Stay with this group,' he was told, 'when they get on the aircraft you go with them.'

The corporal in charge of the squad gave him a package of sandwiches and a bottle of water, and Bob was grateful that the Army did not serve the Arab stew. It was 0530 and he had already had a trying start to this journey. He quietly ate the sandwiches and was just about to start asking some of the Army lads what was happening when their group was ordered onto the waiting aircraft. It was another aircraft similar to the one that had borne him from Calcutta. The RAF does not mess around with departure slots and ground clearance, as far as Bob was aware, and immediately after the main aircraft doors closed, the noisy engines choked reluctantly into life and the aircraft was taxiing away to the end of the runway.

The journey took longer than Bob expected. He had checked the map at *Sheba* and it did not look very far across the Yemen, over Saudi Arabia and into the Persian Gulf for Bahrain. However, after what seemed hours of uneventful boredom, in a most uncomfortable bucket seat, the aircraft touched down safely in Bahrain. It was a relief to get out of the noisy aircraft and the noise was intensified even further when about six of the Army personnel left the aircraft before it had landed. Staring in disbelief, Bob had watched as the RAF sergeant, in charge of the flight, had opened the aircraft's door shortly before they landed. The six jumpers had stood close behind one another and at a simple thumbs up from the sergeant, leapt out of the door.

Some of the options open to RN sparkers were the opportunities to qualify for working in submarines, parachuting, flying duties, and naval gunfire spotting. He had been seriously considering volunteering for parachute duties; being dropped behind enemy lines to zero the naval gunfire onto its target seemed a worthwhile job. However, since he had seen the Army personnel leap from the aircraft, he had decided to reconsider his options! He had enough problems just sitting in the aircraft; looking down

346

was difficult enough without having to deal with jumping out of it, particularly with a heavy portable radio strapped to his back!

Parked on the Tarmac at Bahrain airport was a most welcome sight, a naval tilly sent to collect him and take him to the naval base, HMS *Jufair*. At least he was expected. The heat was almost overpowering and the inside of the tilly was even hotter. The Arab driver would have given Stirling Moss a run for his money; forcing the engine of the tilly to maximum revs between each gear change, it literally screamed away from the airport.

Apart from the odd palm tree, the island looked quite barren, another sea of sand. They passed through a town called Manama and Bob thought, *What a coincidence, the same name as the hotel in Aden.* As the tilly approached *Jufair*, Bob could see the sea; there were many more palm trees and he spotted the glint of the sun on the surface of a swimming pool as they passed through the main gate. They passed the accommodation blocks, built within 50 yards of the beach. All the windows were wide open and the curtains were billowing in the strong on-shore breeze. It all looked extremely comfortable, so different from the inhospitable first impression of *Sheba*.

HMS *Jufair* covered the same sort of area as had Kranji, spacious, clean and ship-shape. He completed his joining routine and, of course, was assigned to Comcen duties. When he first entered the Comcen, Bob was surprised how small it was, even smaller than *Sheba*'s Comcen, but the chief was a friendly chap, only about 5 foot tall and almost as wide around the middle.

Chief wore the biggest pair of shorts that Bob had ever seen, hanging huge and long, reaching well below the knee-line. His name was Nick Bamber, known to all and sundry as *dung-hamper Bamber*, because most people thought that he had room for a portable toilet down his shorts. He

347

also sported the two stars below his sparker's badge, denoting a highly specialised communications expert, the elite of the elite. He asked Bob if he had yet gained any sea experience, to which Bob replied with some embarrassment, 'No, Chief, but I must get some in soon because I want to start getting ready for advancement to my next rate,' hoping that there might be a possibility of getting to sea whilst in the Persian Gulf. Disappointed once again, Chief made it quite clear that Bob was in *Jufair* to help out in the Comcen, at least for the next few months. Unlike both Kranji and *Sheba*, Bob was given a day's rest before starting his watchkeeping duties. *Jufair* used the 48 about system that he had, by now, become accustomed to.

Joining new watches was becoming quite routine, and Bob quickly settled into his new watch. The work required was similar to that which he had been involved with in Kranji, manning a morse circuit with ships in the local area.

Included in Bob's watch were three other sparkers who lived in the same comfortable and airy accommodation block. There was little to do once off-watch; the town of Manama was a few miles away but there was very little of interest there. Leisure time was usually spent playing sport, lounging around the swimming pool, on the beach, or in the canteen. Hockey was the preferred sport at *Jufair*, played on the rock-hard, compacted playing surface that doubled as a parade ground. Bob learned that hockey was not a girly game, particularly when 22 young sailors are involved, each armed with a long stick!

As with civilian professions, the Navy is made up of all sorts of personalities, some good, some bad and some downright evil. One of the sparkers in Bob's watch was a big, ginger-haired bully of a Welshman called Michael Palmer, nicknamed, of course, Ginger, who was fond of using his physical advantages over smaller men. He delighted in tripping people up, or throwing them into the swimming pool, and on one occasion he picked Bob up and hurled him into the deep end of the pool. Usually too nimble to be caught by the lumbering giant, Bob had been taken unawares whilst sunbathing. The incident caused little injury, other than to his pride, but he often wondered what circumstances might surround Ginger being brought to task for his bullish behaviour.

The inevitable happened one day, late in the afternoon, as people were packing up their towels and effects in readiness for returning to their blocks for showers and changing for supper. Ginger grabbed another young sparker, as he had manhandled Bob, lifting him effortlessly high above his head and hurling him into the pool. Unfortunately, on this occasion, Ginger had misjudged the depth of water into which he threw his victim and the lad crashed headlong into the shallow end of the pool, cracking his head on the bottom.

The unconscious body floated back to the surface of the pool, a circle of blood blossoming around his head, and Ginger, who had been laughing hilariously at his prank, suddenly fell to his knees in total shock, unable to move or assist his victim in any way. Having watched the entire incident, Bob and a couple of his pals jumped into the pool and dragged the body to the side, keeping the injured boy's head well clear of the water, always careful not to bend or twist the torso in any way. 'Go and ring the sick bay,' Bob yelled at one of the onlookers, and the young lad dashed away to find a phone. 'Best to keep him in the water,' Bob expressed his thoughts out loud, 'we will let the doc decide how to move him!'

Some minutes later the sound of the Navy ambulance could be heard, siren howling, as it sped along the perimeter road to the pool. The medical staff attached neck supports to the motionless body and lifted him out of the water and onto a waiting stretcher. 'Well done,' said the doc as he strode away after his patient, 'keeping him floating in the water was the best thing to do.' As they left the pool area they could see Ginger, still on his knees and gazing into the pool.

'What shall we do about him?' asked one of the onlookers.

'Leave the bastard where he is,' replied Bob, 'he'll get no help or sympathy from me.' The hostility felt by Bob was clearly shared by everyone else at the pool; not one person moved to help the fallen giant in any way, leaving him to stew in his own self-induced recriminations.

The injured lad was flown home within a week; he had suffered severe spinal and head injuries and there was little hope of him ever walking again. The personality of the perpetrator changed overnight. Instead of the bullish extrovert he became intensely introverted. He spoke very little and lost several stones in weight. In truth, Ginger was given very few opportunities to express his regret; he was shunned by all. Eventually he was sent back to the UK for psychiatric treatment. Bloody good riddance was the consensus at *Jufair*.

One might expect that greater use of the beach would have been made by Jufairians; its proximity to the accommodation blocks and soft warm sand should have seen it packed with relaxing sailors on a regular basis. This was not the case, however, mainly because the water was too shallow for swimming. It was possible to walk out to about 200 yards, the water never exceeding a depth of about 18 inches, before reaching the deep water channel, clearly marked by gigantic concrete pillars sunk into the seabed, to guide the oil tankers in and out of port. These concrete pillars reached about 3 feet out of the water and it was a favourite pastime to walk out to the deep water channel, which was wonderfully cool in comparison to the lukewarm water of the swimming pool, and use the pillars as a resting place.

Apparently all new arrivals at *Jufair* were exposed to an initiation prank, whereby they were invited to accompany a group out to the deep water channel for a swim. When Bob was invited along he thought it a great idea and splashed happily through the shallow water, which was crystal clear, and he enjoyed poking around amongst the scattered rocks for signs of life. Swimming the last 50 yards or so to one of the concrete pillars, it was a gloriously sunny, hot day, perfect for a cooling swim in the deep water. Bob had been happily swimming around the pillar and was about to attempt the climb onto a pillar when he heard a scream: 'Shark, shark!'

Total panic was Bob's instant reaction; he twirled around in the deep water, searching for the direction of attack, and saw the unmistakable tell-tale fins of several sharks circling a short distance away, their fins slicing menacingly through the surface of the water. Quickly assessing the situation, he realised he was shore-side of the pillar and decided to make a dash for the shallow water rather than the pillar. Actually climbing onto the pillar did not look too easy. A few powerful strokes took him to the shallow water and he flew the couple of hundred yards to the safety of the beach. It was later estimated, by the delighted group of onlookers, forewarned of Bob's initiation, that he probably broke the world 200 yard sprint record, and everyone agreed that his feet barely touched the surface of the water!

Throughout his mad dash to safety, Bob had not bothered, or even considered for that matter, to look around to see how his companions were coping with the sharks. Had he done so he would have seen that they were happily playing with the beasts in the deep water. They were, of course, porpoises. The following day's daily orders, detailing

351

the planned events for *Jufair* and including any other useful information to its ship's company, described graphically Bob's escape from the sharks, and included a postscript awarding him *freedom of the pillars* during his remaining stay at *Jufair*. Unanimously voted the best reaction to the establishment's initiation test so far, it also became widely accepted that Bob was capable of walking on water!

It was a wonderful part of the world, perhaps not quite as exotic as Singapore, and there certainly wasn't much in the way of nightlife, except for the canteen. This organisation was manned and managed by locally employed civilians and, at *Jufair*, was used by all three services. It was situated on the second floor of a large two-storey building with the naval stores section occupying the ground floor.

All around the building were flower beds, full of colourful blooms and tended by locally employed Arab gardeners. Large boulders defined the borders of these gardens as they defined every other area: parade ground, car-parks, footpaths, etc. Some were painted white and glared in the sun; there was no shortage of boulders. About a month after his arrival at *Jufair*, somewhere towards the end of October, 1958, Bob was in the canteen with several other Comcen staff, enjoying a pint and a singsong.

The Navy has its own, very special, lyrics to several popular tunes. These lyrics are learned by joining in the singsongs in canteens all over the world, usually beer induced but enjoyed by all. 'There were three crows up in a tree, they were as black as black could be.' The opening lines of one of the better known naval 'hymns' had just been completed, and, before anyone could continue, a young Royal Marine stood up, obviously well canned, and declared his intention to 'do a turn.'

The bootneck's friends were sitting at a small, round table, near the large windows at the rear of the canteen, open to catch the sea breezes. The young booty stood on the table and started the routine for 'This Old Hat of Mine,' a routine whereby the performer slowly undresses to the words 'this old hat of mine, has seen some stormy weather, I don't want it, you can have it, this old hat of mine,' tossing the hat across the room. The same words and action completed for each item of clothing, until the performer stands, bare assed, in front of the audience; the final act being to turn his back to the assembly and do a moonie, whereupon the onlookers toss their beer over the bare backside! In this case, the young bootneck's friends were overly enthusiastic in their beer tossing, some going as far as to push the glass into the bare skin. One particular idiot decided to smash his glass first and rammed the jagged edges into the young lad's bottom. The young bootneck screamed and jumped off the table onto the window-sill, lost his balance and fell to his death on the rocks below.

About the middle of November, Bob was involved in one of his favourite pastimes, picking the dates from the palm trees growing next to the swimming pool. He had been amazed to discover that the dates grew, in small bunches, exactly as they appear in the boxes purchased at Christmas in the UK. They were delicious and he never tired of climbing over the high fence to get at them. On this particular day he was enjoying a mouthful of juicy dates when he heard his name being called from the pool area. He poked his head over the high wooden fence to see who was calling him and was surprised to see that it was the chief. 'Come out here and sit down, Bob.' Chief called everyone by their first name. Bob did as he was told. 'Bob,' said Chief, 'there's no easy way to tell you this, your father is very ill and it has been decided to send you home to see him.'

Questions tumbled out of Bob's mouth but the Chief did not have any answers. The signal had been very brief, simply authorising Bob's return to the UK. The Navy does not return people to the UK for compassionate leave unless it is really necessary and Bob knew that his father must be very ill indeed. There was a flight to the UK the following morning and Chief told him to take whatever kit he might require for home use, the rest would be packed up for him and forwarded to his next posting; there was little likelihood that he would be returning to *Jufair*.

10

Compassionate Leave

It would be cold in the UK, the only civilian clothing Bob had with him was a couple of pairs of lightweight cotton trousers and a few cotton, short-sleeved shirts. Arriving in UK temperatures with so little protection against the cold would be ill-advised. Bob tried to think of some way to obtain a Pusser's Burberry without paying out for a new one; at least that would help to keep him warm. There was very little chance of a Burberry having found its way into the scran-bag, but he went along to the Regulating Office to ask; he was correct in his assumption, in fact there was nothing at all in the scran-bag. Doing the rounds of all the accommodation blocks, Bob asked everyone if they had a Burberry that he might borrow, but of those that were offered none fitted Bob. He had just about resigned himself to spending a fairly large amount of money on a new Burberry – his own was still in his main kit transitting from the UK – and had returned to his mess to pick up some money. There on his bunk was a neatly folded brand new Burberry; there was no indication of the donor and, despite his asking everyone in the mess, he failed to discover who had helped him out.

The scheduled BOAC flight to Heathrow departed on time and for the first few hours the journey was uneventful. The aircraft, a Britannia, nicknamed the whispering giant, provided its passengers with a smooth and comfortable trip, a far cry from his previous experiences of air travel.

Throughout most of the flight, Bob sat worrying about his father and wondering how he was going to get from Heathrow to Alton. He wasn't sure whether he would have to go into central London to catch a train, or whether he could go across country to Woking or Aldershot. He was deep in thought when the announcement was made that, due to fog at all UK airports, the flight would be diverting to Rome for an overnight stay. *One of these days*, thought Bob ruefully, *I will have a trouble-free flight*, as the aircraft lightly kissed the ground on landing at Rome airport.

Frenzied activity of collecting baggage completed, all passengers were bussed to an elegant hotel in the heart of Rome, and Bob was escorted to a room on the top floor with a magnificent view across the city. The bed was gigantic; Bob had not seen a king-size bed before and he had a nasty suspicion that he might be expected to share the room.

It was freezing cold, far too cold to go sightseeing dressed as he was, so he remained in his room, reading a Dennis Wheatley novel. He had taken to reading a great deal of late. He found it helped him to wind down after a long shift, and at the moment he wanted to divert his thoughts away from his father. No one else was assigned to his room, thankfully, and he went down to the swish hotel restaurant for supper, feeling a complete twit dressed in his light-weight trousers and shirt; all the other guests were smartly dressed in suits and ties.

For some inexplicable reason, the interior of the hotel was cold, or so it felt to Bob. Covered in goose-bumps and enormously self-conscious, Bob sat shivering throughout the meal. Forgoing pudding from a heavily laden sweet trolley, he returned to his room to curl up under the blankets. After reading a few chapters of his book, Bob drifted off to sleep at about 2130 and spent a restless night tossing and turning, repeatedly getting up for water from the bathroom taps; he wasn't sure whether the water was completely potable, he didn't really care, he was thirsty.

The various notices in both English and Italian indicated that breakfast was served from 0730 and Bob was sitting at a small two-seater table at 0725. *Be five minutes early for everything, the communicator's motto*, thought Bob. Fully awake since about 0400, Bob had remained under the bed covers, previewing the coming day and his arrival at home. Waiting for the arrival of the restaurant staff, Bob felt that, if anything, it was even colder than the previous evening, but he was feeling quite comfortable; he was wearing his Burberry! He might look an odd-ball in his navy-blue Burberry, but he wanted to enjoy his full-English in comfort, so *sod 'em all*, thought Bob and turned the collar up to highlight his disdain in return for meaningful glances from the waiters.

'Would sir like to hang up his coat?' asked one of the tuxedo-clad waiters.

'No thanks,' Bob replied as haughtily as he could, 'and I'll have a full-English breakfast please with a pot of tea.' To Bob's disgust it was a continental breakfast and he had to mingle with the milling throng of chattering guests around the buffet-style food tables, feeling distinctly uncomfortable in his Burberry. Croissants and jam, with a couple of hard-boiled eggs and some cheese provided a less than fulfilling breakfast for Bob. 'Bloody foreigners,' he mumbled under his breath. The Navy, of course, has a special name for hard-boiled eggs, 'cackle-berries,' obviously referring to the loud flatulence they produce, especially when mixed with a few pints of beer! *Ah*, thought Bob, *if they work through my system quickly enough I might be able to give these wazzocks something to remember me by!*

Just before midday the bus returned to take passengers back to Rome airport, to continue their journey to Heathrow. The fog had now cleared and all UK airports had reopened. The flight into London was uneventful. Without the awful air pockets, flying was really not too bad, and they landed at Heathrow at about 1600.

As Bob walked down the steps from the Britannia he saw a naval staff car waiting on the Tarmac, with a lieutenant and a chief standing by its side. They recognised Bob immediately, not too difficult really since he was the only passenger wearing a Pusser's Burberry. The lieutenant said that he had no further news of his father other than he was still very ill and had been taken into hospital at Alton, awaiting an operation. The naval welfare system, to which both the lieutenant and the chief were seconded, was a very efficient organisation and Bob, miraculously bypassed the usual airport formalities of customs and immigration. He was driven to Waterloo station, where the two naval personnel gave him a railway warrant, an advance on his pay, and told him that he should ring *Mercury* in two weeks' time for further instructions.

After the heat, dust, and sand of the Middle East, Bob was shocked by the intense cold as he waited at Waterloo for the first available train to Alton, and as luck would have it, it was a slow train, stopping at every station between Waterloo and Woking where he had to change to the Alton train. There was still just enough daylight left to look out at the surrounding countryside and, although the year was late into autumn, Bob realised, when gazing impatiently out of the train window, how lucky the population of this beautiful island was, such a colourful aspect in all directions, and not a grain of sand in sight.

Hugely frustrated by the frequent and lengthy stops, Bob finally arrived at Alton at about 1900. It was pitch dark and he could not decide what to do first. He hesitated outside the station, assessing his situation. He knew that he should go to see his mother first, but the chances

358

of getting a bus or train to the remote village of Privett were pretty poor.

After some moments of indecision, Bob finally decided to call at Pat's house. Perhaps she might have some additional information about which hospital his father was in, and hopefully, his mother might be at the hospital. His knock on the Wilson front door was answered by Pat, who flew into his arms. Bob felt the salty tears running down her face as he kissed her. She wouldn't let go of his hand as she led him into the living-room where the Wilsons were waiting to welcome him home.

They told Bob that his mother was staying in Alton with his aunt, while his father was in hospital. A bed had been provided in Alton General Hospital and father was scheduled for an operation the following morning.

Still hand in hand, the two reunited young lovers left the Wilson home, just a few minutes later, to see if the nursing staff would allow him to visit his father. The nursing staff could not have been more helpful. They knew that Bob had been flown home on compassionate leave to see his father, and ushered him straight to his bedside. The nursing staff informed him that his mother had just left, Ronald and Albert had been in earlier that evening and Bob, with Pat still holding his hand, found his father asleep.

The pair sat by the bedside. Father looked very ill, he was painfully thin and the flesh seemed to have dropped from his face. The deep eye-sockets were so darkly rimmed that it appeared as if he had two black eyes. Sitting silently by the sickbed, it must have been about 20 minutes before his father stirred and opened his eyes. He looked at Bob with those blue-grey eyes that resembled Bob's own so closely. He smiled at them both and took a hand from each of them.

Struggling with the effort to speak, father managed to croak just two words, 'be happy,' before returning to sleep. They were allowed to remain at father's bedside for a couple of hours before the nurse told them that they must leave.

The next morning father underwent his operation. He never regained consciousness and died just before midday. Looking back over his short 19 years of life, Bob found comfort in the knowledge that his father had lived a life that he had wanted, a happy marriage and a close relationship with his three sons. However, dying at the relatively young age of 53, without a single day's retirement was little reward for working so hard.

Having seen his father awake for those few brief, but oh so precious seconds, Bob felt an overwhelming loss at his father's death. The staff nurse firmly believed that father had hung on to life long enough to see his youngest son and had then paid nature's tab.

The egg-packing station had generously allowed Pat to take some unscheduled time off work and she accompanied him everywhere, visiting and comforting his mother and helping out with all the funeral arrangements.

Without the support of insurance policies, the funeral costs were shared between Ron and Bob, both agreeing not to burden their mother or Albert, who was out of work and had no means of contributing. A double burial plot was purchased so that, one day, their mother would be reunited with father. Just a few short days later it was all over; mother had moved in with Bob's aunt, at least until she could find some accommodation of her own, and Ron had returned to his wife and new council house on Hayling Island.

The BSA Bantam, left at Pat's house under an old tarpaulin, finally burst into life after several hours of fiddling with plugs and carburettor. It was unlikely that Bob would have much use for the bike, everything he needed was within walking distance at the moment since he had been invited to stay at the Wilson home again. However, he just might need it to commute to *Mercury* when his two weeks' compassionate leave had expired.

As instructed, Bob rang *Mercury* about the middle of December. He was told to remain on leave until a return flight to Singapore could be found. About a week before Christmas Bob told Pat that he thought it unlikely that he would be leaving before the new year; he didn't expect trooping flights to continue over the festive season. He was thus doubly disappointed to be told that a flight was scheduled for 24th December, Christmas Eve, 1958, and that he would be on it, destroying the couple's Christmas plans.

The Wilsons agreed with Pat's wish to accompany him up to Waterloo. Bob had been told to report to RAF Hendon, just as he had done the first time. They sat closely together on the crowded train. Bob wondered where so many people could be going on Christmas Eve; he had expected the train to be virtually deserted. He had decided to return to Singapore wearing the clothes in which he had arrived, with the addition of a smart new sweater that Pat had painstakingly knitted for him whilst he had been abroad.

As the train sang its clickety-click song and lurched its way towards London, the young lovers held hands, as they had been doing for the past several weeks, and spoke of their hopes for their future, marriage, children, their own house and mortgage; they fully intended to be the first from either family to purchase their own home.

At Waterloo, Pat said a tearful farewell. She had only to change platforms for the return trip to Alton, and Bob passed through the metal barriers and disappeared into the crowded station concourse. Hesitating under the con-

361

course clock, remembering his meeting with Jock on his first journey to Singapore, Bob, feeling very alone and disheartened, looked around for a familiar face. At that moment in time he would have given anything to see his old friend come sauntering along the concourse, dragging his kit; with a faint smile Bob wondered if Jock's hammock was still locked away in the left luggage locker. Hoping for a last glimpse of his sweetheart, Bob went across to the metal barriers admitting passengers onto the Alton train. He watched Pat as she opened the carriage door and jumped aboard. She did not know he was watching and did not look back. He could see that she was dabbing at her eyes with a handkerchief, and he felt angry at himself for bringing his love so much unhappiness. He waited until the train pulled away from the station, turned and continued his journey to Hendon.

11

Return to Kranji

The flight back to Singapore was exactly the same as the first, except that Bob did not have his friend with him, but this time Bob was more prepared with his own sandwiches, crisps, pork pies, and biscuits stowed in his trusty Pusser's brown. For a great deal of the flight, Bob's thoughts turned to his old classmates. He had received a few brief letters from Jock, who was enjoying his time on HMS *Cavalier*, but had heard nothing of the rest of the group.

In Jock's most recent letter *Cavalier* had been to Hong Kong, Australia, New Zealand and was scheduled to visit the Philippines early in 1959. One of a fortunate few, Jock had been told that he would complete *Cavalier's* current commission and return to the UK with her. Never before in competition with each other, Bob was envious of Jock. He had not yet managed to get to sea and, as he sat on the Hermes aircraft, bouncing around in the air pockets and turbulence, which for once did not bother him, he decided to take the bull by the horns and ask for a ship as soon as he arrived at Kranji.

The flight refuelled at Basra and spent the night at Karachi, just as before, and at the same hotel. Opposite Bob sat a young mother with three small children, the youngest of which was a babe in arms. The other two children were about five and three and an obvious handful for the young mother travelling on her own. As the Hermes struggled through the turbulent air the baby became quite fractious. The young mother was desperately trying to calm the two older children, obviously upset by the violent and frightening movements of the aircraft. Despite there being several other young women in close proximity, travelling alone to join their husbands in Singapore, none offered to help the obviously stressed young mother.

Unsure of how his suggestion might be received, Bob offered to take the baby for a while and the young mother handed the tiny girl over with a very grateful nod and 'yes please.' At such a young age, Bob had not had much experience in handling tiny babies, except for the occasional cuddle with the young son of Pat's sister; but he had read somewhere that a tiny baby will react to the heartbeat of whoever is holding it and he concentrated hard on keeping himself very calm, breathing very slowly and very deeply. The continuing violent movement of the aircraft prevented Bob from doing what he really intended, that of getting out of his seat and walking with the baby up and down the aisle, but the seat-belt sign glowed continuously, warning of further turbulence.

It was a wonderful experience, feeling the little bundle of warmth in his arms. She calmed down and fell asleep a few minutes after he held her, her head on his shoulder and his hand gently rubbing her back.

The other two children had also fallen asleep almost as soon as their baby sister had calmed down and as Bob glanced over to the mother he could see that she too had drifted off. For several weeks Bob had been grieving for his father, whose death had affected him deeply, and he knew he would never really get over the loss. But holding the sleeping child, Bob realised that there was always the hope that people actually returned from that special place, to which we all go after death, possibly awaiting another chance of mortal life. Who knows? And he brightened

364

considerably at the realisation, that perhaps father would return as one of his own children.

Two hours later the little mite was still sleeping contentedly, and Bob realised, with a start when he felt the fingers of the mother picking up her child, that he had also dozed off. She thanked Bob and asked him if he would mind helping with the family at Karachi and disembarking at Singapore. Agreeing readily, Bob spent the rest of the trip with one or the other of the three children on his lap. It gave him something else to think about and took his mind off father and Pat.

There was nothing festive about Karachi on Christmas Day. Most of the passengers wished one another a Merry Christmas, but it was all pretty meaningless. Christmas could not possibly be Christmas unless you were at home, in the UK, with your family and friends around you and every single passenger really wanted to push on to Singapore. All were to be bitterly disappointed when a delay of about six hours was announced, because of engine problems, which did nothing for Bob's confidence in the Hermes aircraft. During the last leg to Singapore, the baby girl's two elder siblings helped Bob demolish his supply of food; unable to attempt the odd-looking mixture, they too decided to give the stew a miss.

The aircraft touched down at Paya Lebar on 27 December, 1958, precisely at its rescheduled time. The familiar, and now strangely welcoming, aroma of the island wafted over Bob as he carried the baby girl out into the large hangar space, where expectant husbands were awaiting their wives and families. The young mother ran up to a tall, heavily built, curly-haired man, wearing the badges of a radio supervisor, the other two children wrapping their little arms around their father's legs. Standing to one side of the embracing couple, Bob waited patiently while the family was reunited. As they parted he handed over the baby to its father and left them to continue their reunion in private.

Sitting on the *Terror* bus, which had been waiting at Paya Lebar, Bob looked at the passing familiar sights and looked around at the 25 or so other single men on the bus. Answering the questions of the waiting regulating staff, Bob realised he was the only communicator, and was told to wait for the Kranji transport.

During his enforced wait in *Terror*, Bob took the opportunity of walking around the base and was impressed at how large and how immaculately it was maintained. The broad-leafed Singapore grass grew at a surprising rate and gangs of coolies, wielding long-handled machetes, were employed to keep it under control. The wait at *Terror* lasted for a couple of hours before the scheduled tilly arrived from Kranji, and Bob sat in the rear seat with the bags of mail from the UK.

During his joining routine almost everyone gave the impression that they remembered him from his previous brief stay. Sew-Sew seemed particularly pleased to see him again. *Perhaps she knows I don't have much kit,* Bob guessed. One pleasant surprise awaited him: he was pleased to find that his sea mail kit from the UK had arrived, at last, and he set about getting it all sorted out. The outstanding kit from *Jufair* had not yet arrived but a signal had been received saying that it had been forwarded by RAF airfreight so it should not be much longer before he was, once again, reunited with his full kit.

As expected, Bob was assigned to watchkeeping duties in the Comcen, B Watch this time, which was not due to commence its next 48 hours of duty until the afternoon of the 29th December. Regarded as an 'old hand' and billeted in one of the remote accommodation blocks, B Block, Bob made his way across the football pitch to his new temporary home.

366

There were eight bunks in the mess to which he was assigned, of which only one was vacant, so he had no choice of where he slept. The peace and solitude of these remote accommodation blocks was almost tangible, accommodating shift workers who were either working, sleeping, or ashore. Entering his allotted mess, Bob saw that there were just three of the eight occupants present, all in the watch that he would be joining.

One of the off-watch sparkers was lying flat on his bed, engaged in what became a competition over the following weeks: attempting to spear one of the eagle-eyed chit-chats by throwing darts at them. These nimble little lizards shared the accommodation blocks and devoured the swarms of mosquitoes and flies, and although the competition might seem cruel, Bob was never to witness one of the animals actually hit. The new member of the mess exchanged identities and life stories in the few hours before supper and all agreed to have a run ashore in Singapore the following day.

One of Bob's new acquaintances, Brassy Brassington, was very effeminate, and when he got himself ready to go ashore he was immaculate, beautifully fitted trousers with an open-necked shirt complete with a pale-pink cravat, smart civilian sandals with no socks, golden bracelets on each wrist, and smelling evocatively of what Bob suspected was an exotic female perfume. A single earring and a heavy golden medallion around his neck completed the ensemble.

Brassy made no attempt whatsoever to hide his sexual preference, openly flaunting it at every given opportunity, which made Bob quite nervous about living in the same mess and also about the forthcoming run ashore. As the foursome walked along the footpaths to the dining-hall for supper, Bob dragged behind the leading pair with little Pete Deadman. 'Does Brassy bother anyone in the mess?'

he asked and was mightily relieved to learn that Brassy restricted his proclivities to visits ashore.

'At least to my knowledge,' added Pete ominously.

After supper they had a few pints in the canteen, played some snooker, and walked back to B Block. It was now pitch dark, the short cut would take them across the football pitch and through the narrow jungle path and, despite his bravado, Bob was feeling very uncomfortable about the possibility of treading on a snake. He noticed that somehow the other three had dropped behind him. He had been manoeuvred into the lead position and was later told that it was an old trick, getting the newly joined to break the trail; the long grass on either side of the path was alive with snakes. Throughout his stay at Kranji, Bob was not to come to terms with using the short cut; even during full daylight he was constantly scouring the ground in front of him, just in case! Their usual mode of footwear when off-watch, flip-flops, afforded no protection at all, but strangely, and despite the numerous stories of people treading on a snake, no one actually got bitten.

The following morning they caught the RN bus into the city centre and called into the Britannia Club for a swim. The afternoon drifted by and after they had completed their sun-tanning session they showered, Bob keeping a healthy distance between himself and Brassy and making a mental note to check who was in the showers at Kranji before he used them. Their plan was to sit in the bar for an hour or so, awaiting their turn on the Scalextric, have a meal, and then attend one of the large air-conditioned cinemas.

Nearby, on the balcony overlooking the pool, sat a crowd of very young Royal Marines, obviously having already sunk several pints since they were extremely noisy and boisterous. Two of the bootnecks were heatedly arguing about something. Bob heard 'pool' mentioned several times, when suddenly one of the young Marines climbed onto the ornate metal-framed fence surrounding the balcony and launched himself towards the pool. There was no way that anyone could reach the pool from the balcony, and no one in their right mind would ever attempt it; it was at least 15 foot away.

The sickening crack, as the bootneck hit the deck below, told its own story and they all crowded over the balcony to see if he had survived. The injured young man could be seen quite clearly. No one had yet reached him to assist and he didn't look too good, one arm was twisted under his torso and blood was pouring from one ear. But he was still conscious and started screaming loudly when two off-duty Army Medical Corps sergeants tended him. Callous wit overwhelmed sympathy for the fallen bootneck; the vote for the quality of his dive achieved no more than 5 on a scale of 1 to 100.

A couple of weeks later Bob noticed that a new rule had been invoked, published around the Britannia Club by means of large red notices: *No diving from the balcony*. This he thought a little unfair; it should have said *No bootnecks diving from the balcony*, since only they would be thick enough to attempt it!

A few beers after the foursome had watched the ambulance take the young Marine off to hospital, it was time to walk the half a mile or so to the cinema. As they took their seats Bob could see several New Zealand Navy ratings, in uniform, sitting in the same row. Brassy brushed past Bob to take the seat next to them and Bob made an excuse of going to the toilet to avoid sitting next to Brassy.

The film was the usual lone, but always successful, attempt by John Wayne to win the Second World War single-handedly, and as they left the cinema, Pete asked Bob where Brassy was. Searching amongst the throng of people exiting the cinema, there was no sign of Brassy. Bob had not seen him leave the cinema; they waited for about ten minutes before realising that Brassy must have gone off with the New Zealanders. Brassy was not on the bus as they returned to Kranji but no one was very worried about it, since he was not required for duty until midday the following day.

The next morning at breakfast there was a buzz going around that someone had been killed taking the short cut across the railway line from the Bukit Timah road to Kranji. They all feared the worst: Brassy had not yet returned and they were all feeling very worried for his safety. The relief they all felt at about 1130 when Brassy came breezing into the mess, just in time to get changed and go on watch, was expressed in typical naval manner, with aggression – they turned the hose on him and gave him a good wash down. In a later explanation, Brassy revealed, quite naturally, that he had spent the night with his new Kiwi boyfriend and had made arrangements to see him again when the Watch was next 48 off. They learned later that afternoon that the person killed on the railway line was one of the locally employed kitchen staff, a distant relation to Sew-Sew.

The foursome walked into the Comcen together just before midday, ready for the afternoon watch until 2000. Having been through it all before, Bob went straight through to the desk occupied by the watch supervisor, previously POTs, now renamed RSOW, Radio Supervisor of the Watch. The RS was giving some instructions to one of his LROs and Bob could not, at first, see his face.

Recognising him immediately when he turned around, Bob saw that it was the husband of the young mother he had assisted on his recent flight from the UK. 'Just the man I've been looking for,' said the RS, 'I didn't get a chance to thank you for helping my wife with the children on the flight out.'

For the next 15 minutes or so Bob, in response to

370

numerous questions, outlined his activities since joining up, ending with his usual complaint that he had not as yet managed to get to sea. The RS had an easygoing manner, casually delegating control of the watch to an LRO whilst he chatted with Bob. He seemed to ooze leadership and was instantly obeyed. Later that evening, Pete Deadman told Bob that the RS, Dave Kale was a member of the Navy's rugby squad. He also had a nickname attributed to his short curly hair and slightly negroid facial features – the white wog! 'But,' and Pete had waved his index finger under Bob's nose, 'don't ever call him that to his face!' Not that physical size was the RS's only attribute, he also possessed a wicked wit that he used freely, but only when absolutely necessary. He possessed that remarkable ability to conjure up an instant withering response to any verbal confrontation that he might become involved in. Naturally, Bob had the same ability, but his responses came 20 minutes too late!

The very next day, during the forenoon watch, Bob was told to report to the executive officer's (XO) office. This was a newly arrived officer, a large-framed Cornishman who had retained his natural mode of speech, that quaint, countrified and easygoing lilt of the West Country man. He cared not for rank but treated everyone he met with the same degree of cordiality and politeness and was to become, to Bob, the finest naval officer he would ever have the privilege of serving with.

Immediately invited to sit when he entered the XO's office, unusual in itself since ratings usually remained standing when summoned before a naval officer, Jan Froud, Lieutenant Commander, Royal Navy, chatted casually with Bob for a few minutes.

'I have the reports from *Sheba* and *Jufair* here,' said the XO, 'and very impressive they are, young man. *Sheba* were particularly pleased with you and have given you a glowing report.'

Blimey, thought Bob, *that miserable chief in Aden certainly hid his opinion from me – mother always said you should never judge a book by its cover!*

'POT,' and here the XO used his own unique, but perfectly accurate, version of the recently defunct POTs, 'tells me that you want to get to sea, and quite rightly so.' The XO, like Bob, was to take some time before coming to terms with the new comms branch terminology. Lt Commander Froud promised to make it his business to find a ship for Bob, and sent him back to continue his forenoon watch.

At Kranji most off-watch activities involved a great deal more social interaction between senior and junior ratings than would have been the case under normal circumstances. Senior ratings had their mess areas and junior ratings, theirs, and never the twain shall meet! However at that time, the cancerous, ever growing social killer called television, had not yet arrived in Singapore. Consequently, parties, barbeques, and *banyans* were commonplace, usually held at a watch member's home and attended by the whole watch. At parties and barbeques everyone was expected to take a bottle of something, whether it be spirits or wine, with the host providing the food, or if it were to be a *banyan* to the beach there might be a whip-round for funds. Shortly after he joined B Watch, the RS invited the watch around to his house for a house-warming party.

The family lived at Serangoon, in a three bedroom bungalow just off the main circle in Brockhampton Drive. Most of B Watch lived ashore with their families so there were always plenty of cars available to pick up the 'Victualled Members,' as those living in Kranji were known. When Bob arrived, the bungalow was packed solid with people, those that could not get inside overflowing onto the front lawn. The ceiling fan in the living-room was rotating at maximum speed in an attempt to cool the still

372

high, evening temperature and blast the cigarette smoke out of the gaping windows.

Helped by a certain amount of pushing and shoving, Bob managed to force his way into the tiny kitchen and grab a beer. The air was thick with tobacco smoke and Bob's eyes immediately started to water and he hurriedly greeted Mrs Kale, 'call me Dawn,' and went back out to the lawn to chat around the barbeque. Quite happy amongst his newly found compatriots, Bob chatted away to some of the watch members that he had not, as yet, had a chance to get to know. After an hour or so, the heat from the fire, the several beers that he had consumed, and the effects of the previous night's twelve hour shift, began to make him feel quite drowsy.

Drifting over to the side of the bungalow, Bob sat down with his back leaning against the wall. Pete Deadman was sitting there as well and he asked Bob if he had heard of the tragic death of a young sparker who had come out to join the fleet pool.

The sudden news rammed a spear of fear into Bob's heart. Pete could only be talking about a member of LS12. Bob had not mentioned to his new messmates that his whole *Mercury* class had arrived together. 'Who was it? asked Bob, fearing the reply.

After a heart-stopping moment of thought, Pete told him it was Johnny Bevin. Bob felt enormously relieved that it was not Jock but immensely saddened that it was John. The dead man had not been a special friend to Bob, but he had been a member of the class and Bob knew that fate could well have drafted him to the ship that had killed John. The circumstances surrounding John's death were equally tragic. He had, apparently, been on watch in the wireless office of the frigate HMS *Hogue* when the Indian cruiser *Mysore* had sliced through the smaller vessel, killing John instantly.

In the silence following this news, Bob remembered John, one of the most handsome of men, and the furore over his impregnating the daughter of a local garage proprietor whilst at *Mercury*, not to mention his other numerous conquests. The extraordinarily handsome, almost pretty young man, had, Bob reminisced quietly, come very close to being inaugurated into the 'mile high club' on the flight from the UK, when he was interrupted in one of the toilets by a member of the female cabin staff looking for her very pretty supervisor!

The party eventually came to a noisy end, well after midnight, by which time Bob was asleep on the lawn, oblivious to the commotion and noise. After everyone else had left, Dawn Kale shook him gently awake. 'Come on, Bob, we've made a bed up for you in the lounge.'

Up early the next morning, the Kale children were early risers. Bob stayed at the Kales' the whole of that day, playing with the children and cleaning up Dave's old Citroen car that he had recently purchased. Shortly after eight o'clock, a middle-aged Malayan woman turned up at the bungalow and started on the family washing, ironing, and other household tasks, leaving Dawn free to care for her children. This was the amah, and every serviceman serving in Singapore, regardless of rank, was entitled to the services of such a servant. For naval personnel these servants were funded from naval budgets, and Dave assumed that it was a clever way for the British Government to provide jobs for the local women.

Neither Bob nor Dave would consider themselves to be mechanics, but between them they knew how to clean the spark plugs, set the timing, change the oil and adjust the brakes; and throughout that very pleasant day the pair managed to give the car a reasonable service. That evening, after a gargantuan meal – Dawn resembled Pat's mother in her attitude towards feeding her guests – the whole family piled into the fine old car and escorted Bob back to Kranji.

The whole episode gave Bob a wonderful insight into married life and that night he dreamed of himself and Pat, with two lovely children, living happily in Singapore. When he awoke in the morning he wondered if the dream would ever materialise.

About a week later Bob was again sent to see the XO. 'Got a ship for you, Leonard,' he said in a self-satisfied way, 'you will be joining *Chichester* at the beginning of February.' *At last!* Bob sighed with relief, and left the XO's office on cloud nine, dashing off to find out what sort of ship. What he did not know at that time was that he would have to fly to Calcutta to join his ship!

The night before he took the flight to Calcutta, Bob was again invited to the Kales' for an evening meal. Almost the entire evening was spent listening to Dave as he prepared Bob, as best he could, for his role at sea, explaining how things were done, how to react to various circumstances and generally, what to expect. The lengthy, one-sided conversation was to prove invaluable to Bob over the next few months.

12

Chichester

The flight to Calcutta was fairly uneventful, if typical in terms of the jolting and bouncing around. He was pleased to find a crusher waiting for him at the airport, clearly identifiable with his cap band proudly proclaiming HMS *Chichester*. After his evening with Dave, Bob was well prepared. He stepped out of the taxi about an hour later, after a tortured, twisting journey through the narrow streets packed with humanity. At least he was not expected to pay for the taxi, the funding for which was unknown to him.

The sleek grey shape of *Chichester* was anchored in midstream, in the middle of the dark, brown waters of the river Hooghly, which Bob knew, from the brochures on the Air India flight, was part of the Ganges; to Bob, the ship looked magnificent with her pennant number F59 emblazoned amidships. The pair waited for a boat to come out from the ship and jumped aboard; the crusher made no effort to assist Bob with his kit. The crusher obviously considered his duty done and saw no reason to manhandle suitcases around for the very junior sparker, and Bob questioned the man's parenthood and muttered a suitable curse under his breath!

Lugging his kit behind him, he walked up the gangway to board HMS *Chichester*. He may well have forgotten to stop at the top of the gangway and salute the white ensign, had he not been reminded of this custom by Dave the previous evening. After he had saluted, Bob looked down at the steel deck of the ship; he had not yet stepped aboard, wanting to implant this first experience firmly into his memory banks. The deck had been painted dark green and the finish was patchy and worn around the gangway area and, as he looked up at the ship, he could see that the battleship grey of her superstructure was tarnished with rust streaks, evidence of long weeks at sea. The ship was obviously overdue for some tender loving care.

It was uncanny: the moment his feet touched the metal deck, Bob felt queasy! The ship was anchored in a river; fast flowing though it was there were no waves, and it was virtually motionless, tied firmly to a buoy by huge ropes. Surely he was not going to be seasick! Swallowing hard, Bob forced his mind to concentrate on the immediate future. He strode up to the officer of the day and identified himself. The OOD said 'very good,' and dashed away to shout at a young sailor who was ditching the gash into the river. Something else Dave had told him, never ditch the gash in harbour, but it was a small sign that he was not the only greenhorn on the ship.

The crusher led Bob below deck and pointed out the door to the regulating office; there was one on every ship and establishment and he remembered to doff his hat as he knocked and walked through the door. Much of the paperwork involved in joining a ship had been preprepared, and a short time later Bob was heading for the comms mess deck, to be handed over into the care of the leading hand of the mess, usually, but not always, the senior rating in the mess. In *Chichester*'s case it was LTO (Leading Tactical Operator) White, Knocker to his messmates.

Dragging his kit, Bob followed his guide along the Burma Road, the name given to the main passageway in a warship, and struggled down a steep ladder into the mess; he did not know it at the time but the mess was immediately below the quarterdeck at the stern of the ship. One piece of useful information that Dave had failed to impart to him was the correct way to descend a ship's ladder. Turning automatically, to face the ladder, Bob had descended slowly, hanging on to the sturdy metal rails. It did not take him long to discover, as others virtually slid down the ladder supported almost entirely by their hands on the rails, facing away from the ladder, that his own chosen method was both cumbersome and slow.

The mess was tiny, only about 6 foot wide but about 20 foot long, just room enough for about 18 bunks, in banks of 3. At first sight the mess did not look too crowded, there were only four people awake in the mess, with another two asleep when Bob arrived, and most of the bunks had been folded to their non-use positions, the bunks doubling as seating when folded down. Not surprised to find people asleep in the mess, Bob knew that, unlike most other branches of the Navy, the comms branch maintains its watchkeeping duties on a continuous basis, even whilst in harbour.

Sitting in the mess, tired and sweaty, chatting to the occupants, Bob noticed, on closer inspection, that one of the bulkheads was not a metal one, but a line of tightly packed steel kit lockers, mounted so as to separate what was in fact a larger space, into two separate areas. The other area was occupied by the ships' stokers who, much to Knocker's obvious disgust, shared the ladder.

Escorted around the ship by one of the RO2s, detailed off by Knocker for the job, Bob completed his joining routine. By the time he had completed the routine he was totally disorientated; he could not have found his way to the gangway in a month of Sundays.

The RO2 leading Bob around was to be his watch leader; the radio staff of a small warship consisted of an RS, two

378

LROs and about seven operators, four of which would normally be RO2s and the rest RO3s or JROs who were still regarded as under training. Due for advancement to RO2, Bob lacked the required six months sea time. However, he felt fully competent to carry out the duties of his next higher rate; he had continued reading the various manuals on procedures and technicalities since he had left *Mercury*.

The young RO2 who had helped Bob with his joining routine had an unforgettable name, one which Bob committed to memory – Skrzypczak, Tim, pronounced skripjack, Skip to his friends! He was a chunky, cheerful, and extremely likeable chap, with a shaven head and a large half-moon shaped scar by his left eye, and the pair felt a mutual liking, one for the other.

Chichester was not due to sail for a few days. She had recently arrived from Singapore and Bob wondered why he could not have joined the ship earlier, saving him yet another trip by air. Nothing mattered now, of course, he was onboard his first ship and very keen to get on with his career. The ship was an air defence frigate, one of a group known as the Salisbury Class. She was a new ship on her first commission, commanded by Commander R.D. Butt RN and, to Bob's delight, she was fitted with the latest communications equipment. Jan Froud had done him proud, a brand new ship for his first taste of life at sea, he would be forever grateful to the kindly Cornishman.

Moving around the ship, chatting to various members of the ship's company, Bob forgot about his queasy stomach and the sensation abated very quickly. Allocated a top bunk of three, he quickly mastered the agile technique required to swing himself into the bunk without disturbing those sleeping below him. Once in his bunk there was very little headroom, not quite sufficient to sit upright; space on a warship is always at a premium. Nightmares took on a whole new aspect in the high top bunks; waking in the middle of a deep sleep and sitting bolt upright rewarded the occupant of the bunk with a nasty crack on the head.

Part of his joining routine took him to the bridge wireless office, to report to his new divisional leader. The bridge wireless office (BWO) on *Chichester* was quite small, smaller than Bob had expected, and the RS, a Scotsman called McClane, who liked to be referred to as POTs, was obviously *old school!* Like so many other comms senior ratings that Bob had so far met, POTs was an easygoing, relaxed, highly competent and very intelligent man. He was extremely fair in his dealings with his staff, never favouring one person above another, and delegated the unpopular jobs even-handedly; and he had made it abundantly clear that he would not tolerate any mistreatment of the JRO who would form part of Bob's watch.

The JRO referred to was the other member of Bob's watch, whom he had yet to meet, a very young junior RO called Tony Fenton. Tony had come through the Boys Training Establishment, HMS *Ganges*; the route that Bob would have taken had he been able to talk his father into consenting. The trio would eventually and quite naturally form an alliance, doing most things as a group, with Skip very much the leader.

Skip, Bob, and Tony did manage one run ashore in Calcutta, it was Skip's twentieth birthday and luckily they had the evening off. Already a hardened drinker, just as Jock had been, Skip was determined to enjoy himself on his special day. The trio managed to find a bar, crowded with other members of *Chichester's* crew and proceeded to help in drinking the place dry!

Sinking pint after pint, Skip certainly did his share, but Bob was still unable to stomach more than three or four pints. Fortunately neither could Tony because it required both of them to support Skip as they struggled under his weight back to the bank of the river where the ship's boats landed.

They were dressed in their full-white number 6 uniforms, because *Chichester* was making a courtesy visit to a foreign port, which required all liberty men to wear full uniform whilst ashore. Standing each side of Skip, supporting his chunky weight as best they could, Bob was already thinking ahead, trying to work out how to get the wobbly sailor up *Chichester*'s gangway, preferably without attracting the attention of the OOD. They had not yet walked out to the end of the jetty, which reached over a smelly mud bank into deeper water, where the ship's boats came alongside; Bob was keeping Skip out of sight as much as possible.

Suddenly Skip burst out of their restraining arms and threw himself off the river bank, landed in what looked like a foot of oozing, thick mud, fell flat on his face, managed to stand erect and splashed through the mud to the water's edge. The suddenness of Skip's move left his two friends rooted to the spot; it had all happened too quickly but now that Skip had reached the water the watching pair expected him to turn back. Pressing on, having to lift each leg high into the air, like an exaggerated goose step, Skip pressed on towards the ship and dived into the swirling current of the river and started swimming towards the ship, Bob and Tony jumping up and down trying to attract the attention of the ship in midstream.

In a turmoil of indecision, Bob did not know whether to risk following Skip into the water or attempt, in some as yet undecided way, to signal a warning to the ship. Any decision was taken out of his hands when Bob spotted a motor boat leave *Chichester* and head towards the bobbing head in the water. Whether they were spotted making a commotion, whether a sharp-eyed QM had witnessed Skip's early bath, or whether an already out-going boat's crew had seen the event, Bob never discovered. Only a couple of

381

minutes had elapsed since Skip had started his swim, but it was clear for all to see that he was now in difficulties, struggling to stay afloat in his uniform. The boat's crew pulled the birthday boy unceremoniously from the water and even took the time to race down stream to retrieve Skip's cap!

On the day that *Chichester* sailed from Calcutta for Bob's first day at sea, he was on watch in the BWO. POTs was in the office, as was his custom every time the ship left or entered harbour. Currently a very worried man, Bob was not at all sure how his stomach would react when the ship started to move. He felt the quivering vibrations as the propeller started to turn and his stomach lurched. It was 0730, he had been on watch since 0400, and until the vibrations started he had been looking forward to a hot breakfast.

Tony had made a cup of hot kai (Navy cocoa) just before 0700 when POTs had arrived in the office and Bob could feel the cocoa slurping alarmingly around in the pit of his gut as the ship started to move. Rapidly losing all control of his stomach, Bob burped loudly, which attracted POTs' attention. 'You all right, Leonard?' he asked. Fearing an eruption, Bob dared not open his mouth to reply. POTs was quite close to him and would not have appreciated being sprayed with the bilious, chocolate flavoured contents of his stomach!

Chichester, now vibrating violently as she turned in midstream using one engine thrusting forward and the other thrusting astern, rolled to starboard as the strong current caught her. Not much of a roll really, probably not even noticed by the rest of the crew, but quite sufficient to send Bob hurtling for the upper deck and the ship's side, whereupon he made the classic mistake of failing to check the direction of the wind before vacating stomach, and received his just reward; as did the First Lieutenant who was having a last minute inspection of the nearby seaboats' stowage.

Behind Bob sounded a loud cheer. He had been so intent on reaching the ship's side that he had not noticed the squad of white uniformed sailors, in their ceremonial leaving harbour positions. Both mortified and acutely embarrassed, what he did not know at that time was that the whole ship's company knew that he had not been to sea before and his reaction was the subject of many a small wager. The cheering was obviously from those who had predicted Bob's reaction to the movement of the ship correctly, happy in the knowledge that they would receive a small part of someone's tot; the currency for wagers was usually rum.

Much later, upon reflection, Bob suspected that the cheering was also sheer glee at the sight of the First Lieutenant's brilliantly white uniform flecked with chocolate spew! Never to be physically seasick again, Bob nevertheless remained close to the ship's side, in the fresh air, while *Chichester* completed its long, slow river passage and moved into the deeper waters of the Bay of Bengal. The move into deeper water produced a slight change in the ship's movement, the side to side rolling was further modified by a fore and aft pitching movement, which added to Bob's discomfort.

The advice from Dave, on the night before he left Singapore, helped him once again. 'Do not stop eating, no matter how difficult to swallow, eat!' And that is what Bob did. The general unsettled feeling of queasiness continued for some days and nights. Lying down appeared to make the symptoms more pronounced, but he was never actually sick again. Oranges were almost his undoing later that first day. Thinking that fruit might settle his queasy stomach,

Bob had relished the juicy orange, but the acidic content seemed to make matters distinctly worse, but he did manage to hang on to his supper!

The three worked well together and Bob settled in well with his watch partners Skip and Tony. Both Bob and Skip were skilled operators, but Skip was the watch leader and made all necessary decisions at their level. The three shared all the jobs in the BWO. Apart from actually tuning the radio equipment and sending and receiving messages, there were other tasks to be completed. Callsign encryption changed on a regular basis, as did the settings for various crypto machines; radio equipment required setting up for other users in the ship, and the frequencies required changing on a daily basis.

Unlike most other parts of a warship, the BWO was visited regularly by the ship's senior officers, either to collect or deliver signals or to discuss communications requirements with the RS. The office was therefore routinely cleaned during the morning watch, from 0400 to 0800: desks were dusted and polished; floor scrubbed and polished; many fittings were finished in brass or heavily chromium plated, and these, known collectively as the 'bright-work,' required a daily polish.

There could be no excuse for failing to clean the office, nor to keep it neat and tidy; POTs might walk in at any time of the day or night and, despite his mostly friendly demeanour, would not hesitate to 'tear a strip off' anyone who did not toe the line.

Another regular visit to the BWO was the captain. Messages to ships at sea, within a geographical command area such as the Far East Fleet, were broadcast on predesignated frequencies. It was the responsibility of each ship to extract its own messages from these broadcasts and, to give each ship a better chance of identifying which messages it really needed, the address part of the message was transmitted twice. In theory this procedure meant that ships need not read the whole of each message. As soon as they could definitely identify that they were not the intended recipient, they could disregard the rest of the message, some of which could take up to 15 or 20 minutes to complete, usually by morse at 22 wpm.

In practice, however, most commanding officers liked to see the bigger picture and expected their comms staff to maintain a complete log of messages on the broadcast; and this was the reason for Commander Budd's frequent visits to the BWO. The visits were always informal, usually just before midnight, and the captain, usually not wearing his cap, which reinforced the informality of the visit, was always immaculate, beautifully starched white shirt, trousers and cummerbund with the three gold rings denoting his rank on each shoulder. He seemed to know everyone's name and even pronounced Skip's surname correctly, which most frequently did not.

Chichester, heading south towards Western Australia, entered the Indian Ocean and crossed the line (latitude 0) on 26th February, 1959. Crossing the line, Bob received his certificate, after formally making the required obeisance to King Neptune. The certificate was signed by the captain, acting for and in the name of the King. Several others of the ship's company had to undergo this traditional right of passage, for which Bob was most grateful; he might have been the last to join *Chichester,* but at least he did not have to endure King Neptune's warped sense of humour alone!

A few days later the ship stopped at sea, on a hot and humid, cloudless day, and the ship's company were invited to take a swim. Sea boats were sent out to circle the ship, with rifle bearing marksmen embarked in each; 'to deter the sharks' the pipe on the ship's tannoy system had said, quite casually!

Extremely dubious about leaping off the side of the ship,

Bob looked down at the slightly choppy surface of the sea, undecided about risking a swim; but it was very hot and sticky and the water looked so refreshing. The off-duty watchkeepers, which included Bob and Skip, who had been rewarded with seven days' number nine punishment for his attempt to swallow the river Hooghly, still hesitated at the ship's rail; it looked a long way down to the surface of the sea.

However, after about 10 minutes, there were upwards of 30 people bobbing up and down, some just treading water, others demonstrating their powerful swimming strokes and striking boldly away from the ship, and Bob decided to give it a try. They both climbed over the ship's railings, balanced on the side of the ship, finally leaping outwards in their best swallow dives and belly-flopped painfully into the sea.

It was a very strange, unworldly and totally unnatural feeling, out there in the middle of the ocean, with thousands of feet of water under his toes and who-knew-what swimming around in it! Instantly Bob's mind flipped back to Bahrain, to a memory of being tricked into believing that a school of porpoises were killer sharks; and he had already seen the enormous stingrays, wider than *Chichester*, swimming near the surface of the sea. For several minutes Bob tried to obliterate these unsettling thoughts, but his mind would not let go and the memories persisted, diminishing his confidence with every second. For several minutes he trod water, looking around at the boats circling the ship, feeling very insignificant, and the sea, which had looked so warm and inviting, had started to chill. His mind was beginning to play tricks on him again, and every small wave, highlighted against the horizon was instantly assumed to be the fin of a predatory shark.

Shocked at how quickly his body temperature dropped, Bob had suddenly become very cold. He started to shiver violently and headed back to the ship's side to climb the rope ladder back onto the warm deck. The whole experience had been very unnerving; he would never again swim from the ship's side in deep water. That night his oil drum nightmare recommenced and continued for several nights to follow, which, he reflected ruefully, was most unfortunate. He had only just got used to the perpetual drone of machinery throughout the ship, which had, at first, prevented him from sleeping.

Time passes very quickly indeed in a watchkeeping environment and the days at sea, regulated by a strict routine, seemed to pass almost without notice. Early in March, *Chichester* called at Albany, Western Australia. The small town looked much like the towns portrayed in the western films Bob had seen as a boy, with raised walkways and pubs with swing doors. Women were banned from the pubs, for some unknown reason. Bob hazarded a guess that it was probably because the Australian men drank so much they couldn't afford to treat their women!

Beer was purchased by the jug and Skip spilled most of the contents, late in the evening of their first run ashore, staggering back to their table from the bar with a jug in each hand. The pubs became very raucous as the evenings progressed. There was much good natured back-slapping and storytelling, and each evening the happy-go-lucky Australians seemed bent on consuming as much of the bar's stock as they could, aided and abetted in no short measure, by *Chichester*. The Australian male had a completely different attitude towards boozing than Europeans; they liked to get it done early in the evenings. The pubs were filled to capacity from about 1500, with deeply tanned, dusty Aussies wearing their strange headwear, consuming beer like there was no tomorrow, until about 2000 when most returned to their homes.

The naval and civilian communities mixed well. The average Australian was very fond of the Royal Navy, and numerous hospitality invitations were received by the ship. As always the Navy had its own word to cover these invitations – 'grippos' – and the ship's noticeboard was covered in them.

The three watchkeepers, after perusing the invitations on offer, added their names to an invitation to a barbeque and were collected from *Chichester* by a local butcher at the stipulated time. They were driven a few miles out of town to a lovely two-storey dwelling, with a wide veranda around both ground and first floors. The house occupied the centre of the 30-acre site, with a stream flowing through the lower levels filling three large ponds as it made its way through the grounds, presumably, to the sea.

Their host provided them with civilian shorts and T-shirts and threw a crate of chilled beer in the middle of the cool veranda. 'Get stuck in, blue,' he drawled, effortlessly de-capping a bottle on the edge of the veranda as he spoke. The butcher and the sailors enjoyed a very pleasant evening and the biggest steaks Bob had ever seen. The butcher's wife, who did everything from lighting the barbeque to cooking the food and clearing away afterwards, was absolutely enormous, as were her two daughters aged about eleven and thirteen whilst the butcher, in comparison, was as thin as a rake. The females of the family resembled a set of Michelin women, their rings of wobbly fat started just below the chin and continued in ever increasing girths to the hips, decreasing down to the ankles. Despite their obvious weight, all three of the large female members of the family possessed a remarkably fluid walking action; they appeared to float gently over the ground, much akin to ripples crossing a pond.

In the midst of his wife's feverish activities, the butcher yelled for another crate of beer and she dutifully carried it out to them, opening a bottle for each before returning to her cooking. *What a wife!* thought Bob, already feeling the effects of the strong Australian beer, *bit big for my taste but does she know how to look after a man!*

As the evening progressed, the conversation ranged far and wide, sometimes neither quite knowing what the other was gabbling on about, properties, creeks, dams, paddocks, and trucks were confused with houses, rivers, ponds, fields, and lorries; and the naval vocabulary left the butcher scratching his head on many an occasion! It was an idyllic spot, not another house in sight, eight horses, four dogs, two budgies, and three cats – the cats gave Bob a wide berth; they must have had a sixth sense warning them of his antipathy, they just knew! Not one of them attempted to sit on his lap.

As they had approached the house, up the 400-yard twisting driveway, Bob had noticed the bodies of several snakes, in various stages of decomposition, hanging over the wire fence. 'Many snakes around here?' Bob asked casually which launched the butcher into a lengthy lecture on the various species on the property.

'Browns and Tigers to name two; so fast and so poisonous that they could kill a man!' At this point he gave a graphic and extremely comical demonstration of how to tackle a deadly killer snake with a long-handled shovel. The butcher pranced around, jumping up and down, swearing profusely at his imagined foe; all he needed was a few dabs of white and black paint and he could have been a bushman *away in dreamtime!*

Mr Butcher was out cold by midnight and the mammoth Mrs Butcher had to drive them back to the ship. They had seen little of her during the evening but it was now her turn to speak; and could she speak!

Mrs Wilson, Pat's mother, could talk the hind leg off a donkey, at a rate of decibels sufficient to deafen half of

Alton, but she was a mere babe in arms in comparison to the butcher's wife. Tony got the brunt of it. Bob and Skip had jumped into the back seat of the car before Tony realised what was happening, leaving him to occupy the seat next to the driver, not that either doubted the ability of womankind to drive a car, of course!

The car was a big 5-litre Ford, with huge bull-bars on the front – 'Just in case we hit a roo,' Bob heard her bellow. She did not seem to need more than an occasional glance at the road ahead, turning her head towards Tony and ranting on about life in the bush, her good-for-nothing drunken husband and anything else she could think of, spittle bursting from her gaping mouth as she shouted at the top of her, not inconsiderable, voice. Beer induced relaxation removed all fear from Bob's mind, he was feeling quite unconcerned, the car was travelling at a tremendous speed and even the imagined vision of a dismembered kangaroo flying over the top of the car did not cause him any anxiety.

Sliding to a screeching halt alongside *Chichester*, all three remembered their manners and thanked the butcher's wife for the family's generous hospitality, promising to send photographs of both themselves and *Chichester* as soon as possible. It really had been a most wonderful, relaxing evening and, all things considered, and despite the butcher's quirky personality, they were very agreeable and pleasant people. A few weeks later they posted the promised photographs and some time later received a short letter and a photo of Mrs Butcher and her two daughters. Out of sheer generosity, Bob and Skip insisted on Tony having the photo for his memoirs.

About ten days later *Chichester* docked in Fremantle, gateway to Perth. Again the comms branch had to continue their watchkeeping duties and again the grippos came in thick and fast. One of the Navy's preferred invitations is that of visiting a brewery and actually getting added to the list of takers was no mean feat. Having a friend in the captain's office, into which all grippos were first delivered, was every sailor's dream.

Unfortunately neither of the three had such a contact. It was just lucky that Bob, passing the noticeboard on his way to the BWO, noticed an invitation to visit a nearby vineyard. The notice must have been very recently placed on the board because there were only about 20 of the 30 vacancies already taken. He hastily added his, Skip's and Tony's names to the list. Luckily the visit was scheduled for two days hence when they would be off-watch.

At the appointed time, the group of 30 to visit the vineyard were mustered on the quarterdeck by the OOD, all in uniform, a few senior ratings but mainly junior rates. Embarking noisily onto the waiting coach, the group set off out of the town, turning off the main highway after about ten miles onto a dirt track.

The vineyard owners were waiting for the bus and an informative and very detailed tour of the vineyard commenced as soon as the bus arrived. Standing to one side of the semicircle of sailors gathered around the owner, Bob glanced at his shipmates and surmised that there is no more sorrowful, pitiful, and pathetic sight than a crowd of thirsty matelots trying desperately to take an intelligent interest in the machinations of producing a fine wine!

However, the group was rewarded for its polite forbearance when they were later escorted into the sampling room. Long picnic tables, laden with cartons of the several different labels produced at the vineyard and a delicious, meaty buffet lunch, awaited them. It was nothing short of superb, once again demonstrating the generosity of the Australian people.

By no means could Bob be considered a connoisseur of the fruits of the vine, he had of course imbibed the odd glass during special family occasions, but apart from that, his experience of this heady liquid was very limited. Also unschooled in the finer points of wine tasting, he watched carefully as his compatriots filled a fairly large stemmed glass, twirled the wine inside the glass, sniffed briefly at it in an appreciative, knowing way, and downed it in one gulp. Gasps of appreciation and small comments could be heard: 'an interesting bouquet, just a hint of the dark side of the hill, earthy texture, maybe a dash of rosebuds,' and just the odd 'shit, where's the beer!'

Sailors are recognised as the world's finest judges of all things alcoholic, and Bob accepted without any doubt that the 29 aficionados were demonstrating the correct way to sample a fine wine. Not wishing to be singled out as lacking in the finer social graces, Bob copied and was once again the butt of a *Chichester* bet. The whole room burst into laughter at his imitation, pointing their fingers at him and laughing uncontrollably. The jest did not bother Bob one tiny bit, he was quite familiar with naval humour and simply refilled his glass and repeated the entire process! Such jokes and pranks were mercifully ephemeral; he knew that it would not be long before someone else took his place as the *ship's idiot!*

Without any preference about the colour of his wine, Bob was tucking into the white. Slightly chilled, it tasted both bitter and sweet at the same time; it was delightful. Feeling hungry, the two large glasses of wine heightened his awareness of his hunger, and Bob filled his plate with cold ham, beef, and chicken breast, topped it off with a selection from the salad tray and a crusty bread roll. This was his first visit to a brewery – to Jack Tar all establishments producing alcohol were breweries – and Bob was enjoying the experience immensely.

Two more large glasses of the delicious potion washed down Bob's meal and he was beginning to feel just a tad light-headed. Long periods of continuous watchkeeping can have strange effects upon the participants; one such effect was known as the battery effect, whereby short periods of rest produced only sufficient energy for short periods of concentration or activity. Having stood the morning watch Bob's energy levels were falling rapidly; he was beginning to feel quite weary and he occasionally leaned against the wall for support, whilst enjoying yet more wine.

The afternoon wore on, the boxes of wine were replenished, and, for Bob, the plentiful wine and the hot room combined to produce an hallucinatory effect. His mind drifting and playing tricks upon him, he sometimes could not quite grasp where he was in the world, and he may well have dropped off to sleep for a while.

Slowly, he returned to full wakefulness and watched the proceedings descend into a shameful mélée of over-imbibed sailors, grabbing bottles of the bubbly wine, shaking them vigorously, removing the restraining wire over the cork and yelling with glee when the cork-missiles, expelled from the bottles with incredible force, ricocheted from the ceiling onto their shipmates below.

The remains of the buffet was used as ammunition in a disgusting food-fight; jellies, sausage rolls, salad, bread rolls all flew around the room in the madness of the drunken moment. By this time Bob could hardly stand; he had consumed a further three glasses of wine and had slumped to the ground, leaning against a wall. He looked down at his white uniform and saw that there was a large blob of custard dripping into his lap. He felt a moment of intense sadness at the discovery; he had not noticed custard on the pudding table and it was one of his favourites. How the custard got there he had no recollection.

Eventually their hosts returned. They seemed unconcerned about the state of the room or of their guests, simply announcing that the bus was ready to return to the ship. Needing the assistance of Skip and Tony to move, Bob felt fine until he walked out into the heat of the Australian sun. One whiff of the fresh air and the wine hit him hard and fast. For some inexplicable reason, Bob felt compelled to look down at his feet, and his befuddled brain could not comprehend why his right foot did not seem able to move in front of his left. Flanked by his two pals, Bob looked down at the bottom step of the bus as he made the initial move to board – and that is the last thing he remembered until the following morning.

Apparently he collapsed into the red dust and was bundled onboard the bus by some of his shipmates. Both Skip and Tony were no longer able to assist; they had suffered the same reaction shortly after Bob had passed out and were *feeling no pain!*

However, the following day a very strong buzz was doing the rounds of the ship that one of their party, a senior rating and President of the Chief's Mess, floated on half a dozen bottles of wine down to the front of the bus. He asked the Aussie driver if he could be dropped off in the centre of the town to continue his run ashore, a request that was denied, apparently in no uncertain terms, by the driver. Chief, feeling that the driver was being completely unreasonable, cuffed him around the ear and returned to his seat. Unfortunately the driver reported the incident to *Chichester*, the chief was banned from cocktail parties and brewery runs for the remainder of the ship's commission!

The OOD had seen the bus stop at the end of the jetty, and the state of 30 of *Chichester's* finest staggering up the gangway, many requiring the assistance of their shipmates, including Bob. Their white uniforms, now a gentle shade of pink, were covered in wine stains, red dust and particles of food; most had also lost their caps.

The OOD, the navigating officer, deciding it was time he checked that the Union Jack was flying correctly in the bows of *Chichester*, turned his back on the chaos coming up the gangway and marched smartly out of sight. The two stokers carrying Bob tried to manhandle him down the ladder to his mess, but for some unknown reason, and Bob had no memory of the event, he grabbed the handrail and would not let go. The two stokers left him hanging there, completely unconscious; they had done their best and just wanted to curl up and sleep it off.

An experienced sailor, soon to be promoted to PO, Knocker White took charge. He and one of the LROs pulled with all their strength but could not loosen Bob's grip. The sick berth attendant was sent for, no joy! Finally the doctor appeared; they tried everything, pouring olive oil over his hands, prizing his fingers loose one at a time, nothing worked. Eventually they had no other option than to smash his knuckles with a length of wood to force him to release his grip. Having dealt with drunken sailors on many occasions, Knocker knew that the greatest danger was that the unconscious man might drown in his own vomit during the night; and he didn't want Bob, Skip or Tony vomiting all over the mess.

The drunken trio were carried on deck and laid to sleep, using camp-beds on the signal deck and some of their messmates were detailed to keep watch over them through-out the night. Many of his messmates had their own leave stopped to watch over Bob, so he was not very popular the following morning.

Returning to the land of the living, Bob awoke about 0530. It was pitch dark and, still confused, he could not for the life of him work out where he was. Feeling very cold, Bob was still dressed in his ruined white uniform, he smelled abominably, and he had a mouth like the insides of a jockey's underpants, an expression he had recently overheard from the stoker's mess.

The effects of the alcohol and the manhandling he had

received returning to *Chichester*, left him with numerous aches and pains. His stomach was heaving and his head felt like he had been kicked by one of father's cart-horses. A body moved back alongside him and a torch was shone into his face. It was Skip. He had sobered up about midnight and had been awarded the pleasure of the morning watch caring for Bob.

Remarkably, Bob had not been sick. He wanted a cup of tea, a shower, and some clean clothes; he wasn't sure whether breakfast would be possible or not; he would worry about that later. After his shower, during which he noticed that his hands were badly skinned and bruised, he disposed of his white uniform; it would cost him a few hard-earned pounds to replace it and, feeling much better, decided to try for breakfast.

The lads in his mess did not ostracize him, as he half expected; as he descended from the ladder into the mess, Knocker said, 'Good run ashore then, Bob?' They all curled up with laughter as Knocker described the antics involved in making Bob release his hold on the ladder guard rail; and Bob knew that he had been accepted. However, such behaviour could not remain unpunished, and Bob, ever the lucky one, received two punishments for his crime of returning onboard drunk.

Firstly, Knocker decided that because Bob had involved his messmates in extra watchkeeping duties he should do extra work in the mess. He was therefore to be cook of the mess for the next week, assisted ably by Skip and Tony. This involved bringing the trays of food from the galley to the mess deck – *Chichester* did not have a dining-hall – clearing away the used crockery and utensils, scrubbing the deck, and generally keeping their living space clean and tidy. He was also *in the rattle*, paraded later that day before the OOD and charged with returning to the ship in a drunken state. Both Skip and Tony escaped this

396

additional punishment – they had not caused as much rumpus as Bob.

Standing before the OOD, Bob removed his cap when the crusher ordered 'off caps' and waited at attention while the charge was read out. When asked, Bob had nothing to say for himself in mitigation. He could not remember anything until he had awoken earlier that morning. 'Captain's report,' said the OOD. Bob knew he was in trouble, the OOD obviously felt that the severity of Bob's crime demanded a punishment in excess of the powers invested in him to award.

Three days later, with *Chichester* again at sea heading for major international exercises *en route* to the Philippines, Bob appeared before the captain. Catching Bob completely off-guard, the captain asked as soon as he had doffed his cap, 'How are your hands, Leonard?' The captain's voice had been conversational, not in the least bit severe and threatening.

'Fine, thank you, sir,' Bob replied, looking the captain straight in the eye and standing straight and proud, just as he had been briefed by the master-at-arms.

'What do we know about this man?' asked the captain. Bob was about to say 'pardon, sir,' thinking the captain was addressing him, when POTs stepped forward next to Bob and delivered a superb eulogy, describing some paragon of sober virtue, who rarely drank, was an exceptional young sparker with a great future in the RN ahead of him, and who had been lead astray by more senior members of the crew. The captain gave Bob the obligatory mini-lecture on the dangers of drinking heavily and pronounced his punishment 'fourteen days stoppage of leave, dismissed.' *Chichester* was scheduled to remain at sea for the next three weeks and the captain had chosen not to award the more severe penalty of stopping pay; Bob knew that the captain had been very lenient with him.

The captain of a warship takes a huge risk in dealing leniently with cases brought before him. Bob, inexperienced as he was, knew this. The punishment awarded, stoppage of leave, was not as straightforward as it might sound and involved mustering at fixed times for inspection and extra work, avoided only when actually on watch in the wireless office. These extra musters and work periods, added to the additional work in his mess, left Bob facing an extremely tiring two weeks.

Expecting to be used as an example and punished so heavily that the crew would be wary of duplicating his crime, Bob was not surprised when, shortly after he had received his punishment from the captain, the ship's daily orders contained a warning from the first lieutenant. Clearly with Bob in mind, the warning stated that the *disgusting behaviour of the 30 ratings, who had besmirched the name of Chichester at the recent visit to an Australian vineyard, would not be tolerated in future, in particular any member of the ship's company returning onboard drunk would be dealt with most severely.*

It was later discovered, by someone who did have a contact in the captain's office, that it was the coach driver, not the vineyard owners, that had complained; and 30 more names were added to the *banned from brewery visits* list held by the master-at-arms.

Chichester's messing arrangements involved a duty cook of the mess, detailed each day from each mess, to collect large dishes of cooked food from the ship's galley to carry down into the mess decks for consumption. Part of Knocker's punishment meant that Bob, Skip, and Tony were cooks of the mess each day for the week after the trio's drunken return from the brewery visit. Sometimes unfortunate incidents conspire against the unwary and, shortly after leaving Fremantle, the three cooks of the mess had collected the trays of hot food from the galley and were descending the ladder down to their mess. They could not know that on the bridge of *Chichester* an incident was developing and a passing ship, having failed to correctly obey the rules of the road, was standing *Chichester* into danger. As is routine in these situations the captain had been called to the bridge; his instant reaction of hard a-starboard, repeated by the quartermaster in the wheel-house below caused the ship to heel over sharply, just as Tony was half way down the ladder with an armful of hot dishes. Naturally, Tony dropped the trays and grabbed the ladder railings to save himself from a nasty fall, but it was Tony's pure bad luck that one of the heavy trays landed on the mess deck table and knocked over the rum fanny. The cries of lament from his mess mates, waiting for their grog, although not heard in heaven since a replacement issue of rum was not allowed, must have been heard by the rest of *Chichester*'s ship's company!

Looking forward to the ship's next visit to Manila, Bob, having completed his punishment, gratefully settled back into his normal watchkeeping routine. In his last letter, Jock had mentioned that *Cavalier* would be calling at the Philippines early in 1959, he did not say to which port, but Bob was hoping it would be Manila.

The international exercise, involving British, American, Australian and New Zealand warships was a busy time for *Chichester*'s comms branch. Any exercise, particularly those involving large numbers of ships, increases the amount of signal traffic immensely, and identifying which messages were intended for *Chichester* was a minefield.

Chichester had her own international callsign, MTXB; whilst on exercise she would also be part of a task force, a task group and a task unit, each of which had its own unique callsign. All of these callsigns might also have coded versions, which changed on a routine basis and POTs took to checking the broadcast log every hour or so to ensure that *Chichester* did not miss any messages. The current exercise was called Sea Demon, and *Chichester* was part of a task force of about 30 odd ships. Her immediate operating task group included US ships *Yorktown* and *Ozbourn* together with the Australian ships *Quiberon* and *Queenborough.*

As the exercise drew to a close and the ships headed towards Manila on 25th April, 1959, the whole task force formed up in line astern (one behind the other) and *Chichester* was somewhere in the middle of a line of ships 32 miles long. Once again there was to be no rest for the comms branch whilst in Manila; watchkeeping continued as normal throughout their stay. Each day Bob scanned the list of ships in harbour but could not see *Cavalier.* Fate had somehow transpired against him once again; he had therefore missed a reunion with Jock.

All sorts of entertainments were arranged during their stay, including a brewery run, but Bob made no attempt to be included amongst the lucky 30 selected to attend. *Chichester*'s programme was well known to every member of the crew, and Bob knew that in 15 days' time she would return to Singapore and he would have to leave the ship and return to Kranji, and he was not feeling too happy about it.

The recent punishment endured by Bob convinced him to restrict his alcoholic intake to those beverages he was accustomed to, namely tea, coffee, and beer. Both his friends, Skip and Tony had also learned a lesson and the trio ventured ashore on just a couple of occasions.

The city was crawling with sailors, from the multinational warships in the harbour. Bottles of spirits, rum, whiskey, gin – whatever – could be purchased in almost any café at ridiculously low prices. The spirits were of dubious quality and known as *hooch*. The ship's company had been warned of the dire consequences and frightening side-effects produced by consuming large quantities of this very cheap, alcoholic beverage. Blindness, deafness, muscular spasms, diarrhoea – every conceivable ailment was possible, even the loss of the family jewels!

The ship's company was also warned about the possible side-effects of cavorting with the ubiquitous ladies of the night, and the trio of Bob, Skip, and Tony were accosted on numerous occasions, both in the street and in the cafés and bars.

Nature will have its way, however, and Tony could not resist. He was still a virgin and begged his pals to go with him to ensure his safety.

'Have you got a Pusser's sock [condom] in your paybook?' Skip made sure that Tony had the necessary protection against the various sexually contracted diseases so prevalent in the seedier, red-light districts of many Far Eastern ports.

Tony made his selection from the huge variety available. The girl – and Bob made sure it was a girl by insisting on her dropping her drawers – was not in the least perturbed when all three lads jumped into the rickshaw with her! They did not go far. After about ten minutes, the rickshaw pulled up outside a high-rise block of flats, and the foursome climbed a few flights of stairs to a flat on the fourth floor. The girl was chattering away gaily, expecting all three to partake of her wares. She got quite stroppy when Bob told Tony to go into the bedroom and 'do his best!' About 90 seconds later Tony was out again, looking more sheepish than elated. It was over so fast that Bob and Skip had not had enough time to flip the top off a bottle of Coke and they stared in amazement at their pal as he stumbled from the bedroom.

Both Bob and Skip declined the girl's pleas to finish the job and the lads left her in the room. Looking extremely pleased with himself later that evening, Tony was bragging about his conquest to anyone willing to listen. Strangely, Tony's detailed account of the actual sexual act stretched the duration to 15 minutes, rather than the actual 90 seconds. Neither of his two friends had the heart to contradict him!

Ten days later Tony was not quite so boastful when Knocker, having heard of the lad's symptoms, told him 'you've caught the boat up, lad' and sent him down to see the doctor. In the heat of the moment Tony had forgotten to 'cloak his toggle and two,' and he would spend the next two weeks under medical supervision and soaking up the ribald comments of his messmates, not to mention the graphic descriptions of the medical treatments yet to come! One of the stokers told Tony to check his toenails every evening; if they started turning black they, and every other body appendage, would eventually drop off! Every day, from then on, Tony could be seen carefully inspecting his feet.

Before returning to Singapore, *Chichester* was involved in another exercise, Showboat, with the aircraft carrier HMS *Albion*, following which she entered the RN dockyard next to HMS *Terror* on 10th May, 1959. Bob was still hoping for a last minute reprieve allowing him to remain onboard. He required three more months' sea time to fulfil the requirements for his advancement to RO2. He had been enormously happy on *Chichester* and his pain at having to return to Kranji was plain for all to see.

Not many non-naval people will ever understand the attachment a sailor forms with his ship; she is his home, and her company is his family. The attachment is deep and permanent, especially for a sailor's first ship; once a *Chichester* forever a *Chichester*.

A sure sign of his acceptance, particularly by *Chichester*'s comms team, was displayed as he took his leave: the whole comms mess were on the flag deck to see him depart; Skip and Tony helped him down the gangway with his kit and hefted it into the waiting Kranji tilly, specially diverted into the dockyard to pick him up. With their whistles, shouts, and comments breaching the peace of the naval dockyard, Bob twisted in his seat to catch a last glimpse of his first real naval family. The memories of the last few months would remain with him, warming his heart on many an occasion, for the rest of his life.

Over the next week or so, after Bob returned to Kranji, he scanned the ship's movements in the reports, looking for *Chichester*'s departure for the UK. On the day she sailed, he sat in the morse room at Kranji, reading *Chichester*'s signals on the local command net. He had made an arrangement with Skip to identify himself on the morse circuit; he would commence his transmission with a sign reserved for commercial shipping and Skip would do the same, strictly against naval procedures, but providing no one else was listening too carefully, they should get away with it. This was their final farewell.

At Kranji, Bob was once again assigned to B Block and told to report to the XO in the morning. He was to receive two surprises. The consistently cheerful XO was sitting behind his large desk when Bob knocked and entered the following morning. He was invited to sit, and listened as Jan Froud read him his report from *Chichester*. 'Good work, Leonard,' he said, grinning broadly, 'this is what we like to see!' The first surprise was almost beyond belief as the officer handed Bob the badges of an RO2, the Mercury wings with a single star above them. 'We have decided that you are fully qualified for this advancement immediately. You will not be required to wait for further sea time.' Jan went on to explain this extraordinary generosity on the part of the Navy. Apparently Bob's recent period of deployment to the Middle East was acceptable as sea time, a fact recently unearthed by the canny lieutenant commander.

Flabbergasted only partially describes Bob's reaction. He had been worrying about achieving the remaining three months' sea time. The second surprise was almost as good. Jan went on to inform him that he had been awarded nine months' seniority in the higher rate. This meant that he would receive nine months' back pay and would have a basic date (the date from which further advancement is calculated) of August, 1958.

A third surprise awaited the newly promoted sparker when he reported to the chief for watch allocation. 'I'll put you into B Watch,' the chief told Bob, 'RS Kale seems keen to have you back. It won't be for long though,' the chief added, 'you will be returning to the UK in a month's time.'

That evening, in the quiet of the mess, a very happy Bob lay contentedly on his bunk and wrote a long letter to Pat, telling her the good news about his impending return home. What he did not know was that he was not going to fly home, which he would have gladly tolerated, accepting the discomfort in exchange for the relative speed. Instead he would depart on the Troop Ship *Oxfordshire* on 7th June, 1959. She would take four weeks to reach Southampton, delaying his homecoming until about the middle of July.

During his last few weeks at Kranji, Bob accepted invitations from both Shorty Joe Sims and RS Dave Kale to dinner, or 'up-homers' in Navy speak. The visit to Shorty's residence, in the converted shop, was a harrowing experience; the atmosphere was fraught with an underlying aura of resentment on the part of Mrs Sims towards her husband. She made Bob very welcome, provided an excellent meal and clearly delighted in her baby son; but her frosty attitude towards Shorty made Bob feel most uncomfortable. Shorty gave him a lift back to Kranji, in itself another unwelcome event, speeding along the narrow, twisting roads with Shorty under the influence of several beers. Neither mentioned the behaviour of Julia, Shorty's wife, and Bob was much too polite to enquire into his friend's personal circumstances. He did suspect, however, that Shorty might well have preferred the attentions of the boy/girls in Boogis Street rather than those of his wife.

An evening with the Kale family was, for Bob, always a happy event. The familiar old Citroen, with Dave at the wheel, picked him up from Kranji just after 1900 and they set off towards Serangoon, the old car coughing and spluttering, steam wafting from around the engine cowling and producing the most horrendous grinding and banging from the many gear changes. Unlike most other men, Dave was a person who, when he looked at his car, saw just a machine, something to get him from A to B and, providing the machine achieved its purpose with the minimum of maintenance, it warranted no further attention other than a routine annual service. If the day ever came when the Citroen did not manage to fulfil its role in Dave's life, then Bob knew it would be discarded without hesitation or regret.

They arrived at the family home in time to kiss the baby good-night; the other two children were already fast asleep. Leaving the two men alone, Dawn Kale took a leisurely shower whilst Bob and Dave chatted casually over a beer. The aroma from the passing hawkers, selling their ethnic dishes from a kitchen on the back of a bicycle, was very strong throughout the bungalow. The evening was warm and a gentle breeze sighed through the open windows and doors. Throughout the course of the dinner and the remainder of the evening, Dave outlined his own method of achieving accelerated advancement in the RN. 'Make it known that you wish to become an officer,' Dave managed to say through a mouthful of very rare steak. He ate with gusto, great speed, and with obvious enjoyment, washing down each mouthful with a fresh nip from his beer glass. The evening passed quickly and by the time Bob had expressed his thanks to Dawn and returned to Kranji in the old Citroen, Bob knew precisely what he had to do over the next few years.

The family life that he had been invited to share had both appealed to him and pleased him enormously. He must achieve his next advancement to LRO quickly; he could not afford to look after Pat on his present income. Once again Dave's advice would help him achieve that goal and, although it was too soon to ask to be considered as an officer candidate, Bob filed his friend's advice away for future reference.

13

Oxfordshire

The last few weeks at Kranji passed in normal watchkeeping duties and Bob's feelings were deeply divided when, on 7th June, 1959, the same day that Singapore, previously a Crown colony, became a self-governed State, he stood on the deck of the troopship *Oxfordshire* as it nosed gently out of Singapore harbour heading for the Indian Ocean via the Straits of Singapore and Malacca. On the one hand he was deeply disappointed at leaving Kranji; it was a most delightful part of the world; he had grown accustomed to the heat and the smell of the island; its inhabitants, although multiracial and multi-religious, were a most kind, polite, and gentle people. He fervently hoped that he would return one day.

On the other hand, he was excited at his return home, to Pat and his family and to his old pal Jimmy, who Pat had told him, was due to leave the Army in about four months. It struck Bob as very odd that the two friends, who in previous years had been inseparable, had not exchanged a single letter, communicating only through their respective sweethearts.

Oxfordshire, loaded down with a little over 2,000 passengers and crew, including some 1,000 servicemen, 500 family members, and 500 crew, was a modern liner launched in 1955, specifically for troopship duties throughout the British Empire, and weighing about 8,000 tons. Of those

1,000 servicemen there were only six sailors onboard, all from Kranji. In charge of the naval contingent was an LRO, Ivan (Taff) Jones with the upper body and huge bull-neck of a weightlifter. They were accommodated in the bowels of the ship, squeezing into a small mess with about 40 Army personnel. There was very little space and the tiers of bunks were stacked four high; even a warship, where any space not allocated to a weapon is regarded as wasted, did not stack its bunks that high.

A very officious Army corporal attempted to include the six sailors in his squad, issuing orders to jump here and clean this. The five young lads looked to their 'killick' for guidance. Taff smiled that tiny half-smile that was almost a smirk, which they would all come to know so well, indicating that Taff was getting just a little annoyed, walked over to the corporal, lifted him clear off his feet by his lapels, and whispered something in his ear. Whatever the whispered message, it must have been clearly and concisely stated, true to naval communications principles, because the corporal left the six Navy personnel well alone for the remainder of the trip.

As the troopship made its majestic way across the Indian Ocean, the days dragged. Being at sea, Bob thought, was not nearly as good when you didn't actually have a job to do. Apart from meal times the daily routine for the six sailors involved the cleaning of the stepladder down to the ship's canteen, the rest of the day being their own. Sunbathing and the occasional session of voluntary physical jerks occupied most days, with frequent visits to the ship's cinema in the evenings, whether or not the film had previously been seen. Quite how Taff managed to secure the plum job of cleaning the canteen ladder, none of the five younger ratings knew. The cleaning task took all of 30 minutes, following which they were allowed into the otherwise locked canteen to join the crew for an early pint or two, free of charge, of course.

Through the Red Sea and into the Mediterranean via the Suez Canal, the ship plodded on, one monotonous day followed by another with very little to speed the passage of time. Endless games of cards – patience, cribbage, three-card brag, for which the currency was matches – and the Navy's own special game of ludo, called 'uckers.'

The Army lads crowded around the mess deck table whenever the Navy played uckers, always ready to issue a challenge whenever they considered that they had mastered the rules of the game. The cries of 'suck-back, blow-back, blobs, and mixy-blobs' echoed around the mess, enticing the Army lads to risk their half-crowns on a game. The Navy won, without exception, and the beer kitty, which Taff had set up amongst his crew, was bolstered enormously throughout the voyage.

Just before the ship passed through the Straits of Gibraltar into the Atlantic Ocean, *Oxfordshire* organised a rifle-shooting competition. The prize was £5, an amount of money that would inflate the Navy contingent's beer kitty enormously, especially with beer at 8 pence a pint! The beer kitty funded the Navy's entrance fee and Bob was elected to do the shooting. *I hope they know what they're doing,* Bob chuckled to himself, *I'm as bad as father was with a rifle!*

After the event, he need not have worried. By some mysterious shenanigans the Navy was elected to blow up the balloons that were dropped over the stern as targets. Each competitor had ten balloons, released one at a time, with a single shot, at the competitor's convenience, allowed for each. The list of competitors filled an A4 sheet of paper, and the best of the Army and RAF sharpshooters managed to hit six; Bob exploded eight of his and won the day.

Pretty impressive story for me to tell my grandchildren, thought Bob, *providing I don't tell them how big my balloons were!* The ship's daily programme for the following day had the following headline: *Navy humiliates Army and RAF in shooting competition.* Even stranger than the Navy being elected to blow up the balloons was the fact that not a single competitor complained about the size of Bob's balloons! Making a futile attempt to retain some of the £5 prize, Bob reasoned that he had done all the shooting, but a glimpse of the tiny half-smile, flitting across Taff's face, convinced Bob to hand over the lot; and they enjoyed free beer for the rest of the trip.

In hindsight, it was extremely lucky that the Navy team had won the shooting prize, because as soon as the ship turned north, with the coast of Portugal on her starboard side, the uckers challenges from the Army and RAF ceased, and with the departure of challenges went their source of income.

Oxfordshire was equipped with the very latest design of stabilizers, but these could not completely dampen the movement of the ship in the huge seas that she ploughed through. The Bay of Biscay reserved a special welcome to the homebound ship, Storm Force 8 winds and seas buffeted her, causing her to roll and pitch alarmingly. Crockery smashed onto the decks in the galleys and dining-halls, not that there were many takers for meals. Apart from the crew who ate separately, only the Navy contingent had mastered that unique skill of eating with one hand gripping the edge of the table, thumb anchoring the plate, the other hand manipulating fork or spoon, with one leg firmly wrapped around a leg of the table.

To the ship and the seafarers onboard the liner, the Force 8 storm was nothing more than a gentle blow, little inconveniencing their daily activities, but to the less experienced marine travellers it was hell. No respite was to be given from the elements, the Force 8 continued as the ship passed through the Channel. Not until she turned to port, entering the Solent, followed by another turn to port into Southampton Water, did the storm abate and the various dining-halls filled to capacity once again.

Arriving at low tide, late in the evening of 6th July, 1959, Bob could see the Isle of Wight off the starboard side, absolute heaven to a Hampshire boy with the south Hampshire coast to port. He was not unduly disconcerted when the ship slowed, but his heart missed a beat when she stopped in the water and he heard the unmistakable sounds of the anchor chains clattering through the hawse pipes.

Oxfordshire would not enter Southampton until early the following morning. Reception and customs personnel were not available so late in the evening to deal with the ship's arrival. Spending what was left of that summer evening gazing out over Southampton Water, Bob eschewed the warmth and revelry in the canteen. The Navy team had decided to hold an impromptu 'up channel night.' It might not be his part of Hampshire, but any part of Hampshire was home.

About 2230 he went down to the canteen, officially closed but quietly accessible to a chosen few. He was permitted entrance after giving the correct password.

The party continued until the early hours. Bob deliberately refrained from drinking too much; he wanted to be fully fit and alert for his homecoming. Their rowdy joke-telling and singsongs failed to create any interest from the rest of the ship or from anyone in authority. By some devious method, Taff managed to *obtain* a few crates of beer to take back to the mess and distribute amongst the pongos, the six of them waking their khaki compatriots by rattling a bucket full of empty beer cans whilst giving a rousing rendition of 'Three German Officers crossed the

411

line, parlez vous, etc.' The song has many verses and is well known to both Navy and Army. Once their messmates saw the crates of beer, they enthusiastically joined in, ending up clasping each other, slapping each other on the back and swearing life-long friendship, finally united as *Oxfordshire*'s ship's company.

After breakfast the following morning, the six Navy men took their places in the long queues to pass through customs. Most of Bob's kit was being returned to the UK by separate sea mail, he had brought only his faithful Pusser's green, now covered in stickers from exotic destinations and airline trivia, containing only essential pieces of kit and a few presents for Pat and family.

The leader of the RN contingent had been through customs on many previous occasions and he insisted that they all wear uniform for this formality. He wanted the customs officers to know that they were Navy. A special affinity existed between the two organisations, Taff had pointed out, built up over many years and, if you followed the rules of the game, which Taff painstakingly explained to them, it was possible to take one's foreign purchases through customs at minimal cost.

There was not much of any real value amongst Bob's possessions; he had bought a cheongsam for Pat (which she subsequently refused to wear, because of the slit 'right up to my bum'), a few odd Chinese trinkets for other family members; but he had bought a new watch for himself, for which he had paid the princely price of £12. As Bob presented himself in front of the customs officer he said a polite good morning, to which the officer replied, 'Hello, sparks, good trip? Anything to declare?'

Knowing that he should declare the watch, he expected that he would pass through customs many times in the future and needed the slip of paper declaring that duty had already been paid. Unbuckling the watch from his wrist, Bob handed it to the customs official. 'How much did you pay for this?' asked the customs officer. Bob remained silent. *Let them suggest a price,* Taff had told them. 'About £4' continued the customs officer after a brief pause, to which Bob nodded. 'Nothing to pay' Bob heard him say and watched as he wrote the details of the watch on the official customs form.

Several hours elapsed before the six sailors finally managed to disembark from the ship. When they did so they filed down the gangway in line astern, Taff in the lead, immaculate in their navy-blue uniforms, every inch the representatives of the Senior Service. The *Oxfordshire* naval contingent started to disperse at Winchester station when Bob alighted from the London train to catch his connection to Alton.

The trip home by troopship had not diminished Bob's fear of flying but it had been sufficiently time consuming, tedious and uncomfortable to convince him to more readily accept the chances of disaster whilst in the air.

Sitting on the Alton train, which made several stops on its journey to Alton, Bob reflected upon his first year of post training active service. It had been a year of feverish activity and continuous new experiences, never really given an opportunity to settle down, moving on every few months. He thought that he should be feeling drained of energy, confused, and unsettled, having passed through the world's time zones on so many occasions. His actual physical well-being was completely the opposite. He felt totally at ease with himself, fulfilled in some special way by the people and places he had met and seen, and he knew, without a shadow of a doubt, that his chosen path would be a true and happy journey. Chuckling to himself, as the train lumbered into Alton station, Bob thought, *and I joined the Navy for stability!*

413

Epilogue

The handsome, dark-haired young man alighted from the train, handed his ticket to the station master and passed through the booking hall into the street. It was a beautiful summer day, the sunshine strong but not overpoweringly hot.

He was deeply tanned and wore the uniform of a Royal Navy radio operator; he wore the uniform proudly and in the correct regulation fashion, sleeves rolled down and buttoned at the cuff, his pristine white cap set exactly one inch above his eye-line. The seven horizontal creases in his bell-bottom trousers were razor edged, as was the 'T' on the back of his jacket. The Navy collar, pale blue from many visits to Chinese laundries all over the Middle and Far East, was banded by the three white bands around the edges. He walked with a natural rolling gait, the bell-bottoms swinging each time he thrust a highly polished shoe forward.

As he walked through the small market town he oozed confidence and worldly knowledge and many a male passer-by had sudden visions of exotic places and dusky maidens. Every female that saw him allowed their eyes to sweep over his slim, muscular body; some eyes lingered on his face in open invitation but were deterred by the grey-blue eyes that returned their gaze as if they were invisible.

The sailor, having reached his destination, stood in the

market square, standing tall, awaiting someone who had waited for him and who was destined to make his life complete, fulfilling all his hopes, dreams, and desires.

From the building between the two public houses in the market square emerged a group of laughing girls, all dressed in jeans and summery blouses, mostly with their hair in pigtails. One pretty girl stopped and raised her hand to her mouth in the quintessential female gesture of uncertainty, reminiscent of a young doe preparing for flight. She sensed the presence of someone for whom she had been waiting for several long months and searched the throngs of people in the market square. Then she saw the unmistakable white cap across the square and, ignoring her friends, she sprinted across the intervening space and threw herself into his waiting arms.

Naval Terminology

A (alfa time)	British summer time
Bootnecks	The Navy's derogatory term for the Royal Marines
Bootneck band	Royal Marines Band
Brylcreem boys	The Navy's derogatory term for the RAF
Bunting tossers	Visual or Tactical Operators, Comms Branch/Dept
Burberry	Naval raincoat
Burma road	The main passageway, linking all parts of a warship
Cackle berries	Hard-boiled eggs
Commander	Second in command of a large naval ship, or establishment
CPO	Chief Petty Officer
Crushers	Naval policemen, Regulating Branch/ Dept, patrolmen
Dab-toes	Seaman Branch/Dept
Dhobying	Washing clothes
Ditching the gash	Emptying waste bins
Divisions	Naval parade and inspection
First Lieutenant	Second in command of a small naval ship, or establishment
GI	Gunnery Instructor, Drill Instructor

Greenies	Electrical, or Radio Electrical Branch/Dept
Grippo	Hospitality invitation
IT	Instructional Technique
Jack (Tar)	A sailor
JRO	Junior Radio Operator, trained at HMS *Ganges*
Junior ratings	All ratings below PO
Kai	Cocoa
Killick	Leading Hand, one rank below Petty Officer
Lower Deck	Ratings quarters
Master-at-Arms	CPO in charge of the Regulating Branch/Dept
Mess deck	Accommodation areas of junior/senior ratings, usually abbreviated to Mess
Old man	Captain or Commanding Officer
OOD	Officer of the Day (usually of a ship in harbour)
OOW	Officer of the Watch (usually of a ship at sea)
Oppo	Friend
Paybook	Forerunner to the naval identity card; means of identity
Pigs	Officers
Pigsty	Wardroom, officers' mess
PJs	Poxy Jocks
PO	Petty Officer
Pongos	The Navy's derogatory term for the Army
Pusser(s)	Anything naval and Supply Branch/Department
Pusser's brown	Small naval issue attaché case
Pusser's green	Large naval issue suitcase

QM	Quartermaster
Sandscratchers	The Army and RAF derogatory term for the Royal Navy
Scran-bag	Depository for lost or confiscated kit
Senior ratings	CPOs and POs
Ship's company	The whole crew of a ship or establishment
Ship's fund	Cost centre or amount of money used to purchase almost anything that benefited the whole ship's company
Shit on a raft	Devilled kidney served in a thick brown sauce, served on fried bread
Slops	Naval stores
Sparker	Radio Operators, Communications Branch/Dept
Stand-easy	Short rest period, or the relax command whilst on parade
Stokers	Engine Rooms Branch/Dept
Tilly	Naval minibus
Upper deck	Officers' quarters, or any deck open to the elements
W/T	Wireless Telegraphy
Wheaties	Breakfast cereals
XO	Executive Officer, second in command